The Old Enchantment

Young Vane took my hand in his grimy one and led me to see the piglets scrambling round their vast pink mother. Venetia, looking so grown-up and graceful in her dotted muslin dresses that I could hardly bring myself to address her, took me to find white raspberries in a cool forest of leaves and showed me how to look upward for them from the depths of green. Theodore instigated a boating-party on the little river that marked the boundary of my uncle's farm, and showed me how to climb trees, choosing one with specially low branches and hauling me up with his strong hand, his laughing face turned to follow my progress, wreathed with leaves. He showed me how to cut out my very own flag from an old cushion-cover he had found in the attic, and we ran it up the flagpole in the stackyard to tell the world that I was in residence. It was pale blue with roses on it, and I had never felt so important in my life.

About the author

Sarah Neilan was brought up in Northumberland and Durham, educated in Harrogate and at Oxford University, and was a publisher's editor for several years before retiring to raise four children. She lives with her lawyer husband in London and Sussex. She loves travelling, especially in France and Canada.

The Old Enchantment

SARAH NEILAN

CORONET BOOKS
Hodder and Stoughton

First published in Great Britain in
1990 by Hodder and Stoughton Ltd

Coronet edition 1991

British Library C.I.P.
Neilan, Sarah
 The old enchantment.
 I. Title
 823'.914[F]

ISBN 0-340-55101-1

Printed and bound in Great Britain for
Hodder and Stoughton Paperbacks, a
division of Hodder and Stoughton Ltd.,
Mill Road, Dunton Green, Sevenoaks,
Kent TN13 2YA (Editorial Office: 47
Bedford Square, London, WC1B 3DP)
by Clays Ltd, St Ives plc. Typeset
by Hewer Text Composition Services,
Edinburgh.

I am very grateful to Marian Fowler, Brenda Gwyn-Williams, John Brooke-Little, Carolyn Caughey, Anna Powell, and the members of the Historical Society of Truro, Nova Scotia, for their kindness and the help they have given in connection with this book.

This book is dedicated
to Rosalind Steel,
with much love and gratitude for such kindness
and so many happy days.

Contents

Ontario	1
Northumberland	9
Ontario	153
Northumberland	161
Nova Scotia	261
Ontario	333
England	347
Ontario	367
New York, Florence	373
London	395
Riverlaw	407
Durham	423
Riverlaw	431

ONTARIO

1

Once or twice in a lifetime one has the sense of worlds meeting, of time telescoping, of lives crossing in a way that suggests a huge and significant pattern.

One windy afternoon in August 1970, on one of the great terraces between the twin towers of Toronto City Hall, I began to glimpse this grand design.

I was waiting there for a man. To be precise, for my cousin's son, whom I had never met. He had told me in his letter that he would be carrying a blue window-pane check jacket and a copy of the *Toronto Star*. I was early because I could hardly wait to see what he was like.

I smoothed down my pleated silk skirt as the wind caught it, picturing myself, the woman he would see; a tall, elderly – no, old – Englishwoman, at a distant view slim and elegant, in a well-cut red jacket; hair softly swept back, grey streaked with white; the face plain, apparently innocent of make-up, weatherbeaten but healthy; the small nose and round cheeks less obvious than the strong eyebrows; the blue-grey eyes, I hoped, kind. I had known sad years but also marvellous ones. I had been lucky.

But these things are transient. I turned my face out of the wind and looked down to the terraces below and the endless stream of tourists, schoolchildren dancing away from lecturing teachers, giggling girls in sloganed T-shirts, young men shouldering toddlers, tired women with babies in slings on their backs, elderly couples drooping in the heat. *Tout lasse, tout passe, tout casse*. In a few decades all these people would be forgotten, and so would all the marvellous people I had loved in my life. Perhaps, too, there would one day be no heroes left.

But there was just one thing I could possibly do for posterity. Perhaps all we can really hope to achieve in life is to pass on one pleasure, one wonderful thing, to future generations. And this is what I was in Toronto to attempt.

All the happiness of my whole long life stemmed, ultimately, from Riverlaw; and its survival was now in danger.

It has occurred to me since that every life is to some extent propped upon myths, and when the myths of a lifetime collapse, the personality collapses with it. I had seen one battle of this kind; I did not want to be at the centre of another.

And there was just one person in the world who might be able to help. If I could make him want to.

I was about to meet – if he was who he said he was – the rightful heir to Riverlaw.

I looked around again for blue window-pane checks.

There were not many people on the top terrace where I stood. It had a stunning view over the lower levels and the glass and concrete forest that was the city, but the towers made a chill downdraught that even in the Toronto heat was disconcerting. I held my skirt down with my ugly, freckled hands. At the far side of the terrace, beyond the gap between the towers, another woman was doing the same.

There was something about her. Age indefinite – not young; slim figure, pretty legs, high heels, one hand on a good leather shoulder-bag. Her face was in deep shade under an elegant, wide-brimmed coolie hat. From the shadow beneath, eyes glowed. She was staring at me. And something about her reminded me of someone.

"I like the red jacket," said a Canadian voice behind me.

"I imagined all types of red jackets after your letter came, but that one's real elegant!"

I swung round.

Knowing his parents, I had expected to see someone with something that was familiar about him. Indeed, I had hoped and longed for our meeting. But here was a complete stranger of fifty-odd, tall (where I had assumed that he would be short), with longish mousy-grey hair, a rich tan, a moustache, heavy-rimmed dark glasses, wearing a dark-checked cowboy shirt that hung over his trousers. I thought in sudden panic, Who is this? What have I done?

He stuck out his hand.

"I'm Kitchener. Well, Cousin Elizabeth," he said, "that your case? Here, I'll take it. Come on down and we'll get a cab to the parking lot where I left the station-wagon. I guess if you've seen enough of Toronto we'll go straight back home. We're out at the farm this weekend – it's on Highway 89, around eighty minutes' drive. My wife had to stay with our grandchildren, but she'll be there."

I thought of the woman in the coolie hat. "You didn't bring any of the family with you?"

"Nope, we thought this would be private." (Why did he think that, I wondered?) "But you'll meet the grandchildren back home. Oddly enough," he added, perhaps by way of filling an awkward silence as we left the terrace, "we did meet up with someone else a while ago who knew you, years back. Maybe – "

I looked back, suddenly, urgently, hoping against hope.

But the woman had gone.

From downtown we headed north under big, shady maples, their branches sometimes almost meeting across the street, the windows of large brick houses glinting behind them at the end of manicured gardens. As we approached the suburbs the trees were smaller, with behind them the brownish lawns of bungalows; further on there were streets of almost identical houses with, increasingly, open stretches between that gradually revealed glimpses of fields and trees. The sky looked as if there were never any kind of weather but sunshine.

My cousin twiddled the knobs on the radio and a seductive, confidential voice urged me to get my muffler tested, any time, by the Speedy Muffler King on Lake Shore Drive. The radio broke into soft hillbilly music.

We drove on past villages, each with three or four churches, a post office and a collection of houses; past forests of maple, and fields of wheat and tall tightly-packed corn.

"I'm so glad you came," said the strange man beside me at last. "I've got so much to ask you. You know, I don't even have a photo. Isn't that something? When I was a kid I really minded about that. Still do."

"I've brought lots of photos."

"You have?" That eager voice – did I recognise the timbre? It was a light baritone, slow and attractive – but overlaid with that Canadian accent, and the slight roughness of middle age, it was impossible to tell. "I can't wait to see them. You've brought photos of the rest of the family too?"

"All of them. And of the house."

"The Old Hall at Riverlaw, eh? . . . Yeah, we've had that in mind quite a lot recently. The place is pretty tumbledown now, I guess."

"It does need a lot of repairs," I said cautiously.

"But I heard it described so often. It seemed like it was a Disneyland castle and Brideshead and heaven, all rolled into one. The unattainable paradise."

"Yes." Yes, it would be. I saw it in my mind's eye, the long façade punctuated with square-paned Queen Anne windows, the old pinkish-golden stone clothed in Aunt Emily's heavy-scented François Juranville roses. I smelt the sweet warm scent of evening there, the lavender and mignonette; stood in the shade of the dark yew-tree on the lawn, heard the distant screech of the white peacocks, and the gentle moan of the white fantail doves on the thatched garden-house roof.

The villages were now farther apart and smaller. Past the station-wagon at a smooth speed the open country of Ontario unrolled along Highway 50, punctuated by silver-grey barns of unpainted, weathered timber, often with a family name in white paint along the side above a row of giant sunflowers; past silos and red-brick farmhouses shimmering in the late-afternoon heat, each with sheltering firs or maples on the north side of the drive and an overgrown lilac at the door, hollyhocks straggling by the fence, and beside the pond, maybe, a bright clump of orange and pink zinnias. Could they, I thought desperately, be a good omen?

"Venetia, Zinnia, Theodore, Vane, Louisa," murmured Kitchener suddenly, like an incantation or a line from a poem. "That was the order they were born in?"

"Yes. In 1910, when I first consciously remember them, Venetia would be fifteen, and Louisa about eight."

"And you knew them real well?"

I couldn't help smiling. "I spent more time there than I did in my own home."

"I guess what I know about them all is perhaps something of a . . . biased account," he said suddenly. "Maybe there's another side to it."

"I'll tell you about them."

"I wonder," he mused, "if it'll change my life."

I thought, but did not say, Maybe more than you know.

"You been in Ontario before?"

"No, never. I lived in Nova Scotia once, but we never got this far."

"We're not a long way from Niagara and Stratford. Maybe we could take you."

"I'd love that. That's really kind of you."

I felt my words, the awkward thanks of an unknown guest, put a little more distance between us. I'm here for

7

a purpose, I told myself. I might have only one chance – just one, and if that fails, all will be lost. I mustn't make a single mistake.

It seemed as if my whole life had been a series of journeys, endless travel that would one day culminate in a destination still unknown; and this unfamiliar station-wagon, with country-'n'-western music humming from the radio and a strange man in the driving-seat on the wrong side, was taking me on to the next stage, in a direction I had never suspected I would have to go . . . but one that was crucial both for me and for the people I loved.

There was no denying it; I was afraid.

And there was something else.

"That woman you mentioned," I said, "what was her name?"

"Woman? What woman?"

"Someone you met, who knew me."

"Oh – no, that was a man."

A pit of disappointment yawned at my feet.

Nevertheless, "What was his name?" I asked.

"Aw, shucks, I forgot. My wife might remember."

"I'd like to contact him," I said. "Do you have his phone number? Could we meet him?"

"I'll see if we have it."

O, call back yesterday, bid time return . . .

"I just can't wait to see those photos," he murmured.

And – as the station-wagon purred northward along the straight road towards the distant mirages of heat-haze, past woods and fields and tree-shaded stretches of creaking corn-plants as tall as a man – from beneath random deposits and vast geological strata of memory, from under fugitive and fleeting impressions of cars of different makes and sizes and vintages, of trains in long-forgotten countries and planes in exotic airports, there came into my mind an earlier journey, in another continent, another era, almost another life . . .

8

NORTHUMBERLAND

2

. . . And I heard the rumble of wheels and the clip-clop of our black horse Bess as we drove past the time-hazed fields and dry stone walls in Northumberland, and the slight sharpening of these sounds as we passed the first stone cottages of the village of Riverlaw and dipped past a tree-shaded village green, and I saw my father in his tweed hat with the reins relaxed between his leather-gloved fingers, my mother opposite me in her Sunday brown silk with her hat-feathers trembling in the breeze, and myself in my best cream serge coat with the caped shoulders of which I was so proud, the pink silk bonnet-ribbons snug under my chin, my white-socked ankles sticking out in front of me and my stubby, round-toed boots buttoned to the very top. My father with a smooth movement of the hand turned Bess and the carriage between the tall gateposts crowned with stone pineapples, and there, as always, was the long front of the Old Hall stretching away on our left, and on our right the lawn and my five cousins waving and running to greet us.

It was August, it must have been August because Louie came rushing with a basket of fresh raspberries on her arm from between the twin urns on pedestals that marked the entrance to the kitchen garden, and her eldest sister Venetia appeared in a pale blue muslin dress and holding a croquet mallet, with behind her a stocky young man with a shock of sandy hair and a square, snub-nosed face, and Zinnia rushed out of the front door in her pinny, her black curls flying, shouting "*There* you are! What *have* you been doing, you're dreadfully late!" And Cousin Theodore in his stiff Sunday collar, with the quiff of black hair flapping on his forehead and his cheeks rosy as befitted a farmer's son, opened the carriage door and lifted me out and carried me, with my arms round his warm neck and his arms strong around me, up the drive, giving me a smacking kiss as he went. "And how's my favourite cousin today?" he said. "How old did you say you were?"

I laughed, because I hadn't said it and he knew I hadn't. "Nearly six!"

"My goodness, you're getting on, quite long in the tooth," and when I felt my teeth to see, he laughed and put his cheek against mine.

Young Vane tumbled out of the garden house in his kilt and velvet jacket, which he wore on state occasions because he went to prep school in Scotland. "Can I take Lizzie to see the piglets?" he demanded.

"May I, not can I," said his mother, emerging behind him. "You can but you mayn't, at least not until after tea." She held out her arms and Theodore handed me over to be hugged. She smelt of lavender and violets and her skin was white, and soft like her dress. Aunt Emily, who was my mother's cousin-in-law, always wore silk, with in winter a rose-coloured cardigan. She had dozens of dresses, all the colour of roses – deep rose, peach-rose, lavender-rose, or (as today) pale pink with a little white flower pattern. They always had a V-neck which was filled in with a tucked or embroidered or lace-trimmed front. Her eyes were bright blue and her hair was dark brown and drawn up in a soft bun at the back of her head. She was quite stout, with a comforting bosom, and she loved me. Everyone loved me. Well, perhaps not Zinnia, but she didn't love anyone, as far as I knew.

"Well, if it isn't my dearest Lizzie," said Aunt Emily into the side of my silk bonnet. "Your mother and father are going on holiday, dearest. Will you come and stay with us?"

The very idea of staying in the dear, dearest Old Hall, with my aunt and uncle and my delightful cousins, was happiness beyond my wildest dreams.

"Oh, yes, yes," I said, "please!"

I slept in Louie's room, in a brass bed with a squashy feather mattress and a fat, rose-silk eiderdown, and a pillow with a lace-edged linen cover threaded with pink satin ribbon. Everyone came to kiss me good night, even Henry Grey, the young man with a snub nose and sandy hair, who was not a cousin at all but a friend of Cousin Venetia's who lived with his aunt in the next village. Beside the family, who had fine skins and oval faces and long noses, he looked ordinary; but he had bright eyes and a nice smile.

Another boy, a school-friend of Theodore's, arrived the same evening to stay, and was brought in to say good night to me. His name was Peregrine Fenwick and he must have been almost thirteen. He was tall for his age, slim and dark-haired, with level dark eyebrows, a quizzical look and a husky voice. He looked at me doubtfully, and did not kiss me like the others. I resented that. But I sank into the bed like a small bird into its feathers, and fell instantly asleep.

Staying at the Old Hall was the great happiness of my childhood. The house was full of laughter. All summer the square-paned sash windows were kept open, and from the croquet-lawn, as I heaved at the mallet between my buttoned boots and sent the ball flying towards the lupins, I could hear the voices rising and falling and the laughter floating out.

At meals there were great bowls of raspberries and jugs of velvety cream. At breakfast I sat next to my white-whiskered uncle who smelt of Harris tweed. "Here, Mary-Jane, you can have the cob of my egg. Do you know what a cob is?" And when I shook my head, tongue-tied, he cut off the top of his egg with one stroke of his knife. Try as I might I couldn't do the same with mine, so he did it for me. I never minded when he called me Mary-Jane; he was famous for his bad memory, and there were always so many visitors at the Old Hall that he had given up trying to remember people's names. He usually called girls Mary-Jane and boys George, but with a twinkle in his brown eyes under his bushy white eyebrows, so that nobody was offended; it was just Uncle Vane's little joke.

Young Vane took my hand in his grimy one and led me to see the piglets scrambling round their vast pink mother. Venetia, looking so grown-up and graceful in her dotted muslin dresses that I could hardly bring myself to address her, took me to find white raspberries in a cool forest of leaves and showed me how to look upward for them from the depths of green. Theodore instigated a boating-party on the little river that marked the boundary of my uncle's farm, and showed me how to climb trees, choosing one with specially low branches and hauling me up with his strong hand, his laughing face turned to follow my progress, wreathed with leaves. He showed me how to cut out my very own flag from an old cushion-cover he had found in the attic, and we ran it up the flagpole in the stackyard to tell the world that I was in residence. It was pale blue with roses on it, and I had never felt so important in my life.

Before I went to sleep at night, Louie told me stories and poems. Louie was not beautiful like her older sisters; her nose and chin were too long for beauty and her dark hair, parted in the middle, was scraped back close to her head and twisted into a pigtail which even I knew was unbecoming. But she was droll and brave and determined. She was only eight, but even then she had brains and good sense beyond her years.

"Now go to sleep like a good little girl," she would command, when her nightly story of fairies or giants or gallant knights and beauteous maidens was finished, with

14

villains dispatched and everyone else living happily ever after.

"Kiss me good night," I would beg.

"I already have. Everyone has," she pointed out on the second night of my stay.

"Just once more. Please, Louie."

"Very well. Just once," and she jumped out of her own bed, pattered across the Turkey carpet in her smocked white nightgown, and gave me a soft peck on the cheek. "I'll just tuck you in. Hands inside."

"Louie. There aren't any witches here, are there?"

" 'Course not, silly." She pattered back and clambered into the high bed.

"Are you sure there aren't any ghosts, Louie?"

"Positively sure and certain. Only in stories."

"I'm a bit afraid of the dark."

"It isn't dark outside yet. We could draw the curtains back, but it might be too light to sleep. Anyway, you needn't be afraid of anything with me. Theodore said I was as brave as a lion."

"Heroes are as brave as lions, aren't they?"

"Yes."

"Well, p'raps I'm not afraid when you're here. 'Night, Louie."

" 'Night. Sleep well."

"Louie?"

Sigh. "Yes?"

"We forgot our prayers."

Louie clicked her tongue. "I say mine to myself in bed."

Shocked, I said, "We should kneel down by our bedsides."

"I don't do that. It's too cold in winter – I'd freeze to death," declared Louie, ever practical.

From the depths of the feather mattress, with Aunt Emily's cool, monogrammed linen sheets and the eiderdown nestling over me, prayers in bed seemed a good idea. "What shall I say? Help me say them, Louie."

"Very well. God bless Mother and Father . . ."

"God bless my mother and father, and Uncle Vane and Aunt Emily . . ."

"And Venetia and Zinnia and Theodore and Young Vane – "

"Venetia and Zinnia and dearest Theodore and Young Vane."

"And Cook and Hannah and poor Mary Broughty who cleans the lamps, and Mrs Hothersall, and Fred the gardener, and Will Broughty and Bob – "

"Who are Will Broughty and Bob?"

Louie laughed. "Bob's the groom and Will's the cowman. And God bless Peregrine and Henry – "

"They're not in the family, are they?"

"I always include anyone who's staying in the house. Henry's mad on Venetia, p'raps he might marry her when he's old enough, though I don't 'spect she'll have him," added Louie in a very grown-up voice. "And God bless the Admiral and Aunt Letitia and Cousin Giles and Cousin Cedric."

"I'm not praying for *Cedric*," I sat up indignantly. "And I don't think Aunt Letitia likes children. They don't live here, anyway," I pointed out.

"We should pray for people even if we don't care for them," reproved Louie, a touch sanctimoniously. "They are family and they do live very near, at Riverpark."

Riverpark was a large and pompous mansion; I dimly remembered going there for tea when I was about four.

"The Admiral is Father's elder brother, so we really ought to pray for him, at least."

I sank among the feathers, satisfied.

"And God bless Prince and Duchess, and all the other horses, and Buttercup and Bluebell and all the other cows, and Rover and the hound pup, and Snowflake and Blackie and Blackie's kittens, especially the littlest one, and Lottie the sow and her new litter, and Mr Oughtred at the nursery garden, and Vic and Daisy and . . ." And Louie's sweet, firm voice went on and on. I was too tired to listen any longer.

"God bless Louie, and God bless me, and thank You for letting me stay here," I added, and I snuggled down and went straight off to sleep.

Why did the Old Hall inspire such love in everyone who knew it well? It was not, after all, architecturally distinguished, apart from the elegant string-course between the ground-floor and first-floor windows and the neat but unremarkable pillared porch. Nor was it in prime condition; woodworm lurked in some of the beams, and the nursery roof leaked in wet weather so regularly that old pans and a bucket were kept there permanently. True, its site was charming; the house and farm-buildings (hidden behind a high, ivy-covered wall) took up the whole of the narrow side of the triangular village of Riverlaw, a village as pretty and unadulteratedly rural as one could wish for; the house itself was at right angles to the road so that all the main rooms faced south over the garden. Beyond, assorted trees and a gnarled orchard screened the site from the farmland, which descended gently to a small and sluggish river.

Nor was it a very big house. It only seemed so because when one swept through the pineapple-topped entrance pillars the south façade stretched away, seemingly into the distance. Because most of the house was only one room thick, it was far longer than one might reasonably expect. Most of these rooms opened out of each other, which made it interesting when people came to stay. Unless the family knew them extremely well, rising in the morning (and retiring at night) had to be done in strict order, otherwise one had to rush through people's bedrooms politely averting one's eyes from the beds and tactfully gazing out of the windows in order to reach the bathroom. The alternative was to trot down the main staircase, through the ground-floor rooms and up the steep back stairs (though even this was less inconvenient than the plight of a distant cousin in Oxfordshire, whose house, as Aunt Emily was fond of telling us, had one bathroom for thirty-nine bedrooms).

The main staircase rose in wide, shallow steps near one end of the house, so that at least Uncle Vane and Aunt Emily had privacy in their large bedroom to its left. Above them was the attic room shared by twelve-year-old Theodore and nine-year-old Young Vane, who were away at school much of the time. Across the attic landing was a chain of low-ceilinged rooms under the eaves, occupied by Louie, Zinnia and Venetia, with beyond them a dusty, mysterious cavern of a room, too low for an adult to stand up in, with secret cupboards and spider-haunted nooks among the rafters. This was the day-nursery, where Theodore spent hours with his train-set which occupied much of the floor. The curves and figures-of-eight of the rails, the tunnels and signals and cottage-like stations, fascinated me greatly, and Theodore kindly allowed me to do the hooting.

Below these rooms were the big best guest-room with the oak four-poster that Uncle Vane said had been there since the house was built, where doubtless Henry Grey (who was almost grown-up) was now sleeping, and the smaller one that must at the moment be Peregrine's. Beyond the back stairs, which descended from a dark lobby, was the bathroom with a bath, washbasin and lavatory of majestic proportions, made of blue-and-white willow-patterned china. I believe they had been chosen by Aunt Emily, who had extravagant tastes.

The lobby also led – up a couple of steps, along a passage over the stable arch, and down two more steep steps – to the dear little panelled schoolroom, where a log fire was lit on most days of the year, behind the safety of a brass-and-leather club fender. The room was used both for homework by my female cousins during termtime (they attended a day-school in a market town two stations down the railway-line); and, in the holidays, for endless games of Snap, Happy Families and Patience.

Outside its window was a big pear-tree. Theodore used its branches as an entrance and exit, much to his mother's fear and wrath. Even now I can see his rosy grin outside the glass, framed by leaves, like the Cheshire Cat's.

Down the back stairs were the bootroom, stacked with hunting-gear and shooting-sticks and binoculars and fishing-rods, tennis-rackets, motoring-goggles, hockey-sticks and enough assorted boots to fit the entire membership of the Riverpark Hunt; and the pantry (tall, ginger-coloured crocks full of eggs preserved in isinglass, beside marble slabs and a huge wire-mesh meat-safe), behind the kitchen, where Cook dozed or knitted in a rocking-chair beside the big black range, with Uncle Vane's old black dog at her feet, and Hannah chopped vegetables at the stone sink under the hams and bunches of herbs that hung from hooks on the beams. There was usually other company in the kitchen, too; the farm-hands (hinds, we called them in the Northumbrian way) drinking their eleven-o'clock ale round the big scrubbed table, or a party of Irish threshers tucking into a huge dinner of stew and raspberry pudding and whisky, or Mrs Scratcher, smelling of suds, taking a break from her weekly marathon in the wash-house to warm her pinkly wrinkled hands and sample the latest batch of ginger biscuits, or Bob conferring with Uncle Vane about the next trip to the blacksmith's; or Fred asking Aunt Emily where she wanted the marigold seedlings, or Bert the postman bringing the latest gossip from the village, or Janey the bondwoman, in her apron and matted shawl and battered straw hat held down by a spotted kerchief, excitedly stuttering some news about a badger in the bottom covert or a fox skulking near the henhouse.

If one wanted quiet, it could often be found next door in the oak-panelled dining-room where silver candlesticks were reflected in the big oval oak table. Quietest of all was the big drawing-room across the front hall; it was forbidden to children unless they were expressly invited in, because the gilt furniture was upholstered in porcelain-blue watered silk. To sit on one of these chairs, among the bowls of roses and shelves of Meissen and Bloor Derby, listening to Venetia play her big golden harp, was as near heaven as I ever expected to reach. I never noticed the worn carpet or the tears in the silk; I loved it the way it was.

There were other rooms, in a dark, low-ceilinged wing of great age and decrepitude (it was rumoured to have been built in the Middle Ages, but the Delmaynes were vague about dates) beyond the deep arch that led to the stables, the trap-house and the farm-buildings. Here was Uncle Vane's office, with a many-pigeonholed desk where he puzzled over his accounts, and a leather-topped table behind which he sat on Fridays while the hinds, caps in hand, filed past to collect their wages and a kind word. Here, too, were the still-room, where we sometimes gathered to help Hannah to turn the heavy handle of the bread-making machine, or to admire longingly the rubies and amber of the jams and preserves shining in their locked glass-fronted cupboard; and a little hole-in-the-wall room where poor Mary, Will Broughty's halfwit sister, cleaned and trimmed every lamp in the house every morning and polished the boots every night. Upstairs were the maids' rooms, with black iron bedsteads and white cotton counterpanes and a bare, spare elegance. At the end of this wing, with a separate entrance, was the cold, sparkling-clean dairy where Daisy the dairymaid heaved at the butter-churn and cleaned the dozens of parts of the separator and swilled the flagstones, every day of her life. And right at the end, up a tiny secret stair that curved out of sight behind a little door that looked like a cupboard, was the apple-room, smelling of dust and autumn and of the rows of wrinkling fruit on the rotting floorboards under the tiny, cobwebbed window.

It wasn't a very large house like the Admiral's Riverpark, but big enough to have many unexpected cupboards, secret nooks, hidden steps and irrational corners where the country builders, centuries ago, had miscalculated. The sun shone through the sheaves of roses round the windows, through the square panes and over sills wide enough to sit on, into rooms fragrant with pot-pourri and lavender polish and big silver bowls of flowers. And from the front door, which was never locked (indeed, the key had been lost many years before), to the dusty little cranny on top of a rafter in the day-nursery where Theodore kept a secret store of striped humbugs, I loved it with all my soul.

3

The morning after Louie and I said our prayers together, the older girls were marshalled by Aunt Emily into picking peas in the kitchen garden, and I found myself inspecting the duck pond with Theodore. To my great enjoyment I fell in, with a loud splash accompanied by much startled quacking.

When he hauled me out, "Now you've done it," said Theodore. It was a measure of his sunny and equable nature that this statement, which coming from (say) Zinnia would have been shrieked with alarmed rage, exuded his usual benevolent calm. I followed his gaze down my pink cambric dress. It was hanging lankly, dark with pond water and draped with green slime. I could feel my frilly petticoat clinging wetly to my legs. I bent over to confirm that my white socks were no longer white. My boots squelched.

"Oh, jiminy," I said. "Aunt Emily will be cross."

Theodore took my hand again in his warm, dusty fist. "Don't worry. She doesn't bite."

With my sleeves dripping and my sodden petticoat slapping at the backs of my knees, I was rather cold and uncomfortable, but the very idea of Aunt Emily gnashing her rosebud chops was so irresistibly funny that I cheered up immediately and giggled all the way back to the house.

We crept in at the back door, Theodore scouting forward to the boot-room to make sure that the coast was clear before beckoning me in. He whisked me in among the tennis-rackets and stooped to wrestle with my still-wet bootlaces. His bent head was level with my chest, the black hair glossy and gently curling. Tentatively, I patted it.

"Theodore," I whispered. "I do l – "

"Sh." He put up his face, finger to smiling lips, cowlick flapping on his broad, well-scrubbed forehead. Through the half-closed kitchen door came Hannah's grating voice, raised in reply to an inaudible comment from Cook. Cook always mumbled; she was old and rheumaticky. But Hannah's voice was as harsh as her big red hands. She was forthright and capable, and in another life might have made an excellent engineer or factory manager; but her father was old Fred the gardener, and she had left school at twelve – the age Theodore was now – to go into service. Her face was pink and shiny, with wrinkles across the forehead and around the eyes and mouth, and she seemed to me to be fearsomely old, though I suppose she can't have been older than forty. She had a strapping figure, strong, beefy arms, and (as I saw when she tucked up her skirts to scrub or polish the floors) thick ankles. Her one physical attraction was her blonde hair, which grew in tight curls all over her head; but even that was hidden for most of the day under a turban made from an old red-checked duster.

"She's only storing up trouble," she rasped in her broad Northumbrian accent, as Theodore bent silently again to my bootlaces, one of which was by now a wet granny-knot. "She married above her, that's the truth of it. Them's allus the wust."

"Don't 'ee talk like yon," said Cook. "Ee, me feet's killing me."

"It's the children my heart aches for. You mark my words, she'll no' be content until they all marries lords and ladies. There's that nice young Grey lad eating 'is 'eart out already, but *she* thinks 'e's rubbish."

"There's plenty of time," protested Cook. "Miss Venetia's nobbut fifteen, and sae bonny she'll have the pick o' the county."

"I reckon if the Duke 'imself warn't wed, the mistress

would settle for nothing less for wor little treasures. But would they be happy, I axe meself? 'Tain't right to be too ambitious." Poor, dear Hannah.

I understood nothing of all this, but when Theodore's head came up again I saw that his mouth was shut in a tight line. I wriggled my feet and discovered that he had freed the knots. He steadied me with one hand as I stepped out of my boots, and with comically exaggerated stealth led me into the back hall on tiptoe, and up the back stairs. At the top we looked at each other conspiratorially – and burst simultaneously into gales of laughter.

"They *nearly* saw us!" I gasped, clinging to him.

"You'll have to change all your clothes, Lizzie," he said. "Can you dress yourself?" He led me through the empty guest bedrooms to the main staircase. The carpets felt silky beneath my bare feet.

"Oh, yes," I said importantly – dressing was one of my most recent accomplishments.

"You must be sure to put on lots of warm clothes so as not to catch a chill. Are you sure I can't help you?" Suddenly his face brightened. "What about your back buttons?"

I hadn't thought of that. However, a mental riffle through my extensive wardrobe reminded me that although most of my dresses fastened down the back, I possessed a coat-dress.

"I can manage perfectly, thank you," I said with dignity.

Something was overcoming Theodore. "Oh, Lizzie," he beamed, "I do love your funny little fat cheeks," and to my ecstatic pleasure he gave me a big hug, and as suddenly leapt away and clattered down the stairs, blushing.

My fingers seemed too small and plump for the button-holes. But once I had tussled my buttons undone, I made short work of hauling my sopping clothes off and stepping out of my drawers, leaving everything in a wet heap on Louie's rag rug. By this time I was quite chilly; my teeth were chattering and my toes, once free of the clammy socks, were icy. Clever Theodore had been right, of course; I must put on a *lot* of clothes.

There was a towel on the wooden towel-horse beside the wash-stand. I dabbed at my round, pale-pink body. Why didn't I have an hourglass waist like Venetia and Zinnia?

Outside, the sun shone and the doves cooed. Far in the distance, in the fields behind the stackyard, a cow mooed. From outside the gateposts came, faintly, the voices of children at play. Through the gates clopped and creaked a light carriage. It came to rest on the drive below Louie's window. A moment later I heard the front door open and Hannah's harsh voice floating up.

"Mrs Delmayne is down in the kitchen garden. I'll just go and seek her out."

I was deeply curious to know who the visitor could be, but I couldn't descend the stairs naked. I hauled at the big drawer in the dressing-table, one knob at a time, and fished out my combinations and a liberty-bodice. I put the liberty-bodice on back to front, which meant that I couldn't fasten it; but reversing it seemed too hard. Putting my black wool stockings on, and getting the feet pointing in the right direction, took ages, and the legs were in concertinas of wrinkles. But at last I found the tabs at the top and managed to get them over the side-buttons of my bodice. Next I thought I'd better wear a vest and my best, lace-edged drawers. On top of all this, my tucked coat-dress felt rather tight; the buttons were fiddly and strained, and after one of them flew off and a strand of my long hair caught round another, I had to abandon any idea of fastening them, and tied myself together somehow with my pale-blue satin sash. I added, for warmth, a knitted spencer and my cream caped coat. My best boots came last; I couldn't yet tie bows, so the laces would just have to drag.

As I went out to the landing I caught sight of myself in Louie's pier-glass. My hair was all over the place; I tried to smooth it down. My frilly, caped muffling of clothes looked completely spherical. Still, I felt warmer, and looked like a large, pink-cheeked, bright-eyed china doll. I felt rather pleased with myself at having acted so sensibly, just as Theodore had recommended.

I went downstairs. The drawing-room door was open.

Inside, Aunt Letitia, the Admiral's wife, was sitting bolt upright (as she always did) on the watered-silk sofa. Opposite her, bolt upright also and with his hands primly folded in his lap, was her son Cedric.

"Why, if it isn't Elizabeth!" said Aunt Letitia, the mauve ostrich-plume trembling on her hat-brim. Her large, curiously blank eyes opened wide in astonishment. "Goodness gracious, child, you look like a haystack. Who dressed you?"

I beamed with pride. "I did."

Aunt Letitia did not smile. She never did. Zinnia always said it was because she was afraid of getting wrinkles (and I sometimes wondered whether this was why Zinnia herself smiled so seldom). "You'll have to learn to do it better than that," she said reprovingly. I felt squashed.

"It's not good enough," chimed in Cedric. He would.

"You remember Cedric, I expect," said Aunt Letitia. "I'm very sorry Giles isn't here. He's at Dartmouth, learning to be a naval officer."

Cedric looked sour.

I had once overheard Uncle Vane describe Cedric as a poor specimen. He had, in fact, some good features – straight nose, square jaw, grey eyes with long lashes – but his face was marred by thick, excessively moist and red lips that habitually turned down at the corners. His skin was pasty and spotty and his body flabby and round-shouldered, and he was much too short for a fourteen-year-old. He had flat feet and clumsy hands. None of this would have mattered if Cedric had been as bright and lively as his Old Hall cousins. Nobody is perfect, after all; Venetia was indecisive and forgetful, Zinnia had an explosive temper and was disconcertingly self-centred; Young Vane would rather spend a whole day doing nothing halfway up a tree than ten minutes learning a couple of Latin declensions. But most of the time they were delightful company. Cedric's mien, however, varied between the self-righteous and the hangdog; and he never seemed to do anything unless he was told to.

To be fair, life had in some ways dealt him a dud hand. He was growing up in the permanent shadow of his elder brother Giles, who was handsome and charming and clever, admired by everyone, and a fitting heir for his father's estate – not that we had any idea in those days how that would affect our lives. Their father the Admiral (Uncle Vane's elder brother) had been a benevolent tyrant in his day; he was now old and frail, and the mantle of tyranny had fallen on Aunt Letitia, who was almost thirty years younger than her husband. Looking back, one can see that the Admiral and his younger brother, Uncle Vane, had married very similar women – both much younger and from a class a little lower than their own; both beautiful, and both strict and strong characters. But where Aunt Emily was emotional, motherly and loving, Aunt Letitia was rigid and cold, her highest mark of affection a polite peck on the cheek. She treated Cedric not as a son to be loved, but as a pupil to be trained. He did his best to please her; and if he seemed to my cousins to be a sneak and a toady, it was not entirely his fault. There was a kind of yearning about Cedric, a sort of wordless desperation behind the politeness, that made me uneasy.

"I expect your Aunt Emily will be here in a moment," Aunt Letitia said to him now. "You'd better take Elizabeth out to play ball with the others. We passed them outside the gate."

Cedric leapt up and led me out. Even to a five-year-old it seemed a bit odd to send a fourteen-year-old boy out to play ball, but he was obviously glad to go. We went out into the sunshine.

"I hope the village children won't be there," he muttered. "I'm not allowed to speak to them."

"We can speak," I said, "because it's polite, but we're not allowed to play with them."

This was Aunt Emily's strict rule. But even so, I knew that the real reason why ball-games were always outside the gates (ostensibly to avoid breaking the Old Hall windows) was because ball-games meant cricket, and a decent, grown-up game of cricket needed as many players as possible, and that meant roping in the village children. If we played outside the gates, Aunt Emily – with luck – would not see them, and she could not shoo them away and tell them it was private land, as she would have done if they had entered the garden.

And sure enough – as we rounded the stone-pineapple-topped gatepost into Riverlaw, and saw before us the triangular village green that sloped up, lined with cottages, past the pump and the elm-trees, to the doctor's house at its apex – a little bunch of ragamuffins was conferring with the Old Hall children on the wide, level extension of the village green that ran up to a row of valerian under the high wall concealing the Old Hall stables. From several directions, eager-eyed and hurrying like the Highlanders of the Forty-Five converging on Bonny Prince Charlie, more small tattered figures were skipping towards them.

"Oh, there you are, Lizzie!" exclaimed Louie. "Goodness me, you must have dressed yourself, what a clever girl! But just look at your bootlaces! Mustn't run about like that, you know, or you'll trip and fall on your little nose," and she bent to fasten them for me.

Henry Grey, who seemed almost a man among the others, raised his voice. "Better pick sides, then. Venetia, and who's eldest?" He looked at Peregrine, who was taller than any of the others.

"Zinnia's older than me," he said briefly.

"What a thing to say about a lady!" sniffed Zinnia.

"Right. Zinnia's the other captain."

"I'll have you," said Venetia hastily. Henry grinned and took his place beside her.

"We should toss for Henry," said Zinnia heatedly. "The side that has him has an unfair advantage."

"Oh, I'm not very good." Henry had a very slight tendency to simper.

"Let's leave him where he is till the sides are picked," suggested Peregrine. "There may be an odd number and we'll sort it out then."

"All right. Peregrine."

"Vin." A lanky village lad, with a brush of red hair that seemed to stand upright on his head, and wearing a torn, collarless shirt and braces tied in a knot, took his place behind clean, white-shirted Henry.

"Dick." Dick was younger, stocky and wiry, with a sharp look.

"Theodore."

"Geordie."

"Bert."

"Rosie."

"Willie."

"Vane." Nothing happened, until Young Vane suddenly looked up from a stone he was kicking, and sheepishly moved across to join Zinnia.

Nobody had chosen Cedric, although he was years older than the last few. He moved nearer to the troop.

"Cedric," said Venetia, with a little sigh.

The bidding proceeded to sort out the tail-end of the village children. I ended up beside Peregrine, behind a nine-year-old girl called Ivy, who was a dirty little urchin with pink cheeks, fair curly hair, and a naughty light in her eye. Nobody said anything more about Venetia's side having an unfair advantage in Henry.

Theodore produced battered cricket-bats, ball and stumps from a hiding-place in the wall, while Henry fished in his trouser pocket for a coin to toss. Zinnia looked round and raised her hand.

"Everyone knows the rules, so this is just to remind you – no shouting, our garden's out of bounds, and if you hear my mother coming down the drive, run!"

"Or my mother," said Cedric. He was ignored. He always was.

It was, strangely I see now, unsurprising that thirteen-year-old Zinnia, rather than Venetia (who at fifteen was the eldest Delmayne), should assume leadership over her elders. She was headstrong by nature, bossy and aloof. I couldn't have contradicted her without actual physical fear of her reaction. And yet her mysterious beauty, obvious even in her early teens, gave her an almost frightening fascination. Her rare, lovely, infectious laugh won you over completely.

Gentle Venetia was obedient and law-abiding, like Louie; but she was also indulgent. I could guess that the cricket match had been urged by Zinnia and her brothers, perhaps egged on by the village boys, and that her more dutiful elder sister Venetia had given in. There seemed, after all, little harm in it, and with luck Aunt Emily would never find out.

"Look at *you*." I found that Peregrine was gazing down at me from, it seemed, a great height. He was tall for his age, and slim. "What a funny little bundle."

Ivy sidled up to me. "Good morning, droopy-drawers."

How rude, I thought. I moved away from her, preserving my dignity. But sure enough, I felt the frilly hems brush my knees.

"Don't talk to her like that," said Peregrine quietly. "She's only a baby."

That, of course, made it worse.

Our team lost the toss and I trudged out towards the valerian, as directed, to be the farthest outfielder.

"A little over to the left, Bundle," called Peregrine's husky voice behind me.

"What do I do?" I reached the flowers, where Snowflake the white cat was lurking, almost hidden by leaves. I turned round gingerly.

"If you see the ball coming, pick it up and throw it to me or Theodore as quickly as you can. Preferably to him, if you can throw that far."

"Not a hope," said Ivy scornfully.

Theodore finished beating down the last stump with the heel of his boot, balanced the bail on top, and took up his position as wicket-keeper, crouching and alert. Henry and Vin made a redoubtable-looking pair of opening batsmen. Zinnia marched purposefully away from the wicket, turned, picked up her long skirt with one hand, galloped back, and bowled underarm at Vin with the other. Vin stepped out and slammed the ball across the green.

" 'Owzat?"

He got two runs before Geordie, a small, thin, spotty boy with a remarkable turn of speed, retrieved the ball from the pansies in front of Mrs Hothersall's cottage and lobbed it back to Zinnia. I seized the opportunity, while the centre of interest was at the far side of the pitch, to heave up my skirts as inconspicuously as possible and try to raise my sinking drawers. Unfortunately I was not unnoticed.

Ivy's eyebrows flew up, her rosebud mouth opened, her pointing finger stabbed the air between us. "Droopy-drawers, droopy-drawers," she jeered.

Everyone looked. The Delmayne children – oh, shame! – broke into giggles. Peregrine laughed, a great hoot of mirth. The village boys sniggered. Only Cedric remained grave-faced.

"Oh, I say," he protested. "Stop that, you vulgar boys."

There was an audible silence, followed by an inaudible comment from Dick and renewed, louder sniggers.

Zinnia bowled again. This time, Vin skied the ball. Everyone's face went up to watch it.

"Good shot, sir," called Theodore.

It was coming down straight for Cedric, but not too fast

– a perfect catch. Vin groaned. Cedric put up a stiff hand in front of him. The ball bounced off it, he staggered, put up his other hand awkwardly to catch it, missed, and fell backwards, sprawling on the grass with his arms and legs waving in the air.

At that moment, out of the corner of my eye I saw Aunt Emily and Aunt Letitia walking out of the drive. As one woman, they looked – stopped – frowned. Nobody noticed them but me and Snowflake, who shot out of the valerian and took shelter in Fred's garden.

"Stop that, you vulgar boy," crowed Dick, in an excellent parody of Cedric's plummy Oxford accent.

"Butterfingers!"

"He bloody dropped it again!"

"Rotten fielding!" – this from Young Vane.

"Stupid sod," shouted Vin.

"Droopy-drawers is losin' 'er drawers," chanted Ivy, to my everlasting mortification.

Aunt Emily marched on to the wicket, her face thunder.

"Give those bats to me!"

Jaws fell.

"I strictly forbade you to play out here," she spat out the words as if they hurt her. "Venetia, Zinnia, Theodore – do you love me so little that you directly disobey me?"

There was a dumbfounded silence. The bats were meekly handed to her. "Go to the house at once!" The Delmayne children, heads hanging, turned towards the gateway.

I felt terrible for about three seconds; then, Theodore raised his head as he passed, and winked at me. Things, apparently, were not so dreadful after all.

Peregrine, probably almost as embarrassed as I was, turned towards me. "Poor little Bundle – here, let me help."

He was almost on me when Aunt Emily turned and saw. "Peregrine – leave her, dear, there's a good boy. Zinnia! Go and help Lizzie!"

Aunt Letitia was bending over Cedric. "Get up at once!" Red in the face and patently terrified, he scrambled up.

Aunt Emily looked round at the village children. "Off you go," she said sharply. "Go off home now." She flapped her hands as if they were straying animals. They scuttled away.

Zinnia, stooping to rescue me from my predicament, pulled such a comical face that I chortled. I was used to strict adults with incomprehensible taboos. But suddenly, everything was all right again. Nobody was cross with me. Playing outside the gates had just been naughtiness.

I didn't wonder why. Not then.

4

The day of the abortive cricket match stuck in my mind for several reasons, not least because it was on that day that I first consciously saw Riverpark.

Perhaps Aunt Letitia had intended to invite all her nephews and nieces back to tea that afternoon, but whether the cricket match decided her that they were unfit company for Cedric, or whether Aunt Emily had as a punishment refused to let them go, I did not know. I would much rather have stayed with my Old Hall cousins than with Cedric, but that same afternoon I found myself sitting – securely knickered, socked and buttoned up the back, with my pink bonnet-ribbons in a large, slithery bow under my chin – beside Cedric in Aunt Letitia's brougham, with opposite me her unsmiling face under the tremulous mauve plume. Behind us was the Riverpark coachman. I didn't like sitting with my back to the horses, and Aunt Letitia and Cedric were scarcely inspiring company. I hadn't done myself any good, either, by whispering to Cedric as we set off, "Wasn't the cricket match funny?" He turned scarlet and said, in his plummy voice, "No, it wasn't."

Admittedly I hadn't seen its comic side at the time, and I had been severely shaken by Aunt Emily's outburst about her children not loving her. That was so awful I tried to forget about it. The other thing that niggled at me was that Cedric, in his inimitably ridiculous way, had been trying to defend me against the lewd mirth of the others. But in retrospect I was on their side, not his. The trouble with

Cedric – one of the troubles with Cedric – was that he could never see the funny side of anything at all.

Silence descended. I suddenly remembered the heap of wet clothes I had abandoned on Louie's bedroom floor. I wondered uneasily if I would get beaten when Hannah found it, as she undoubtedly would when she went up to turn down the beds. Perhaps I was safe. Aunt Emily was not, as far as I knew, a beater.

Aunt Letitia must have heard my whisper; she looked down her long white nose at her grey-gloved hands folded in her grey lap, and said crisply, "It's bad manners to whisper." I knew she would.

The carriage rumbled past the ill-fated cricket-ground, and turned left where the village green proper began. I knew who lived in quite half of the pretty little cottages that edged the triangular green. The one at the nearest corner was Fred the gardener's, and in its own neat little front garden every plant seemed to be in startling bloom, orange, puce, yellow and purple. Ivy was sitting on the garden path with a bright red geranium in her fair hair. She thumbed her nose at me.

Nibbs turned the carriage left again, and a narrow lane took us along by the wall that marked the end of the Old Hall's huge kitchen garden. At the end of this wall there was a tall yew hedge with windows cut in it, and through these windows I caught glimpses, as we rolled past, of the wide lawn punctuated with rose-beds and pear-trees and the white peacocks turning in majesty, with behind them the dear pinkish-golden house, and Peregrine and Theodore hanging out of the spare bedroom window, a coil of rope dangling from their hands. Something exciting was happening, as usual, and I was missing it.

"Do you remember coming to Riverpark last year?" enquired Aunt Letitia as we bowled past the orchard.

"I don't know," I said. "I think I do." I remembered Cedric, that was for sure, and Aunt Letitia, and the Admiral, who spoke to everyone (Zinnia had said) as if he were on the quarter-deck. He looked very much like Uncle Vane, but older and rather grey-faced and doddery. The Vane children liked him in spite of his abrupt manner. Aunt Letitia was not so popular.

"It's not far. We could walk, easily, but your legs are a bit young for the distance."

"Her legs can't be younger than she is," said Cedric, with a pathetic attempt at joviality. His mother ignored him.

The lane curved between dry stone walls. Pincushion tufts of clove-pink thrift clung to the crevices between the stones. Behind the wall were fields with thoughtful cows. There, surely, was the field where last year we had searched for mushrooms among the cowslips, lurking behind bushes in pretended fear that the Admiral would shoot us for trespassing – until Zinnia shouted "A bull! A bull!" and we all hared to the safety of the lane, only to see her collapse with mirth, crowing as she pointed at a large placid cow. Ahead, the road dipped towards trees.

"I'm afraid Giles won't be there," said Aunt Letitia. "He'll be sorry not to have seen you." I doubted whether this could be true. "Do you go to school yet?"

"No. I may go soon, though."

"Can you read?" asked Cedric loftily.

"A bit," I lied. My mother believed that teaching was the business of schools and governesses. I had puzzled away at books and newspapers on my own, without much success. One of the secret reasons why I desperately wanted to stay on for as long as possible at the Old Hall was that Louie, shocked at my ignorance, had promised to teach me.

Nibbs slowed the horses a little for the descent.

Cedric turned and pointed at the house as it came into view below the trees. "That's Riverpark," and he added smugly, "It's rather grand, don't you think?"

"It's very bad manners to point," said Aunt Letitia.

I turned round.

The house was indeed rather grand, grandiose even, and I did now recall having seen it before. It was chiefly remarkable for its setting in a bowl of wooded slopes, with on its far side a little river – the same river that bordered Uncle Vane's land. Here, the water meandered along the edge of a large lawn and was lost in a hidden valley behind the enormous walled kitchen garden that dominated the slope to our left. There seemed to be no flowers, or flowering shrubs, even; the lawn that surrounded the house went right up to the kerb and iron railings that fenced in the basement light-wells, as if the Admiral thought of his mansion as a dreadnought sailing in a sea of grass. The railings gave it a curiously urban look. The house was tall, bulky and forbidding, its width too narrow for its height, its high Victorian windows reminiscent of a railway hotel. On the leaded roof a large Union Jack fluttered on a flagpole. Far to the right, near the extensive compound that housed the stables, coach house and groom's quarters, two gardeners were coaxing an elderly pony with its hooves tied up in sacking as it dragged a garden roller over the grass, altering the tidy pattern of green stripes.

We bowled down to the gravelled carriage sweep and crunched to a halt at the front steps. Nibbs jumped down, opened the door of the brougham for Aunt Letitia, and lifted me out. He smelt of sweat and bacon. Aunt Letitia strode up the steps and through the double front doors, followed by Cedric and myself.

The hall was cavernous, with mahogany panelling and antlered heads above it, and at the far end an entire stuffed tiger in a huge glass case. It had green glass eyes that flashed as one moved past it, and one of its forepaws was resting on a small, brownish creature which I later identified as a stuffed weasel. Not, perhaps, the most realistic possible triumph of taxidermy, but I couldn't approach it without muttering a quick prayer and edging past as far away as I could.

Tea was in the echoing, dun-coloured dining-room, served by an obsequious manservant in a black jacket. We sat at one end of a mahogany table that would have comfortably seated fourteen. A silver tray appeared, laden with enough enormous, ornately-chased pieces to stock the window of a silversmith. There was even a silver kettle on a silver spirit-lamp, in case the grandiose teapot did not satisfy our gargantuan thirst.

"Will you tell the Admiral that we are here?" said Aunt Letitia crisply to the servant as he brought in a cakestand, each tier laden with different goodies.

"Beggin' your pardon, ma'am, but the Admiral's upstairs in his bed. He doesna feel well."

There was a moment's startled silence. "That's impossible," declared Aunt Letitia. "He's never ill."

"I think, if ye'll excuse me, ma'am, it would be well ye'd go up and see him."

Her chair scraped back as she stood up. "Cedric, look after Elizabeth for a minute, please."

Cedric munched in silence, looking worried. The mud-coloured velvet curtains, which must have been at least twelve feet high, framed a static view of lawn, river, and meadow beyond, backed by trees on the rising slope. A solitary moorhen glided into view.

"Where are the flowers?" I asked.

There was a long pause until Cedric finished his mouthful of girdle-scone.

"They grow in rows in the kitchen garden," he said. "And in the conservatory, of course. My father doesn't like flowerbeds. He likes everything shipshape."

"And do you?"

Cedric looked as if nobody had ever asked his opinion before. Perhaps they hadn't. He pondered. "Well, I'm not fussy really." He selected a cream cake. "One should keep the estate in good order for maximum financial return in the long term," he added grandly. He sounded exactly like an elderly man – perhaps the Admiral. I had no idea what he meant, and perhaps he didn't understand it himself.

"I'm sorry your father's poorly."

"Yes. It's a pity Giles isn't here. He would know exactly

what to do." Cedric ate voraciously, taking bites far too big for politeness. It inhibited conversation, because he would not speak with his mouth full. A dab of cream nestled on his glutinous lower lip.

Feet tapped across the hall, and a thin, elderly parlourmaid entered the room, neat in black dress and ecru cap and apron like those Hannah wore in the afternoons when people might call.

"The staff are not allowed to come in without knocking," said Cedric, wiping his mouth on his cuff.

"I'm sorry, Master Cedric, but your mother asked me to tell you that your father's took bad. She's sending Nibbs to get Dr Bond, and she wants you to go back with Miss Lizzie to the Old Hall and spend a night or two there, till he's better in himself."

Cedric looked round him with an offended expression, heaved a sigh, and said "Oh, well, I suppose I'll have to."

"Mary's packing a few clean things for you, toothbrush and that."

"Make sure she puts in my monogrammed hairbrushes."

The maid ignored this. "Nibbs'll be round for you by the time you've finished your tea," she said. "Miss Lizzie, tell me if you want to go to the bathroom before you go."

"Thank you," I said with my most dazzling smile, because I suspected that her opinion of Cedric was no higher than mine. "I ought to kiss Aunt Letitia goodbye and thank her for having me," I added.

Her formal expression melted a little. "I don't think she'd mind this once, Miss Lizzie," she said. "I think she'd be wanting to stay beside the Admiral, until he's a bit mended, like." She went out.

Not kissing Aunt Letitia goodbye was one thing. But Cedric had said nothing and was now stuffing himself with chocolate cake. "Aren't you going to kiss your father and mother goodbye before you go away?" I demanded.

Cedric looked down his nose. There was a strained

silence. "They never kiss me," he said at last. "Why should I? I would shake hands with Father, but I can't if he's in bed, can I? Anyway, they want me out of the way."

This was undeniable. I said nothing. Cedric got up, finished at last, and wandered aimlessly down the room, ending up with his nose to the window-pane. His usually straight back looked hunched and sad.

He was impossible, even I knew that. But I couldn't help feeling sorry for him. I groped unsuccessfully for words of sympathy.

I went out to find the parlourmaid and the bathroom. I had forgotten about the tiger, and went rigid with fright when its green glass eye glistened at me.

On the way back Cedric and I sat side by side facing the horses. We went up the rise easily; Cedric jumped out to lighten the load, but Nibbs told me to stay on for the ride. Being the sole passenger was fun. At the top Cedric hopped in again.

Nibbs was disposed to be chatty.

"Ye'll be glad to be home from boarding-school then, Master Cedric."

"Rather."

"Don't you like school?" I said, astonished. To me, the idea of school was the doorway to all bliss; reading, and writing, and being with dozens of like-minded friends.

"No, I do not." Cedric stared straight at Nibbs's rusty back and almost spat out the words. "Horrible, disgusting, beastly place."

"Theodore likes his school. Peregrine's his best friend, he calls him Birdie. Do you have a best friend?"

He went dark red. "No."

"It would be nice if you could have your friends to stay. Do you?"

"No," said Cedric in a strangled voice.

"Why not?"

I thought for a moment that he was going to hit me.

Finally, "You're too babyish to understand," he said, and looked away.

Nibbs looked over his shoulder. "We're going to Dr Bond's house first," he said, "so he can get to your poor father as quick as he can."

"What's wrong with him?"

Nibbs hesitated for a moment before replying gently, "That's for the doctor to decide."

"Do your children go to school?" I asked Nibbs.

"Aye, they do."

"How many have you?"

"Just the one boy, Albert his name is, and Cora, she's nine years old."

"How old is Albert?"

There was another little hesitation before he said, "Thirteen."

"Do they like school?"

"Aye, they do well at their lessons. But Albert has to leave this summer."

"Why?"

"It's rude to ask personal questions," put in Cedric.

"Well, I want to know."

"Curiosity killed the cat."

I subsided, although Nibbs hadn't answered my question. The afternoon was still warm and golden. As we passed the Old Hall, Theodore and Peregrine were leaning out of adjoining upstairs windows, framed in roses, paying out rope to a system of pulleys attached to the pear-tree.

"We can get out here," I said, desperate to see what was afoot.

"If you don't mind, Miss Lizzie, I'm going to the doctor first," said Nibbs quietly. "It's an emergency. It's better for the Admiral that he gets seen to straight away."

"Oh, yes, of course."

Dr Bond lived in a four-square stone house at the top of the village. It had a central front door, painted green with a shiny brass doorknob and a plate engraved with his name,

Theophilus Bond, M.B., Ch.B., and two chalk-white steps right on the pavement.

Nibbs said "Whoa, me beauties," to the horses, jumped down and heaved at the bellpull. After a moment Dr Bond himself answered the bell. He was bald and stout, with a gold watchchain like Uncle Vane's suspended between his waistcoat pockets in a fat curve.

There was a short, inaudible conversation. Nibbs raised his hand to his flat cap and turned back to the brougham. The doctor called after him, "I'll go straight away. Heart-attacks can't be kept waiting."

Cedric's raspberry-moist lower lip fell. He went pale, and was very quiet and still as Nibbs turned the carriage round the top of the green, turned again when we reached the impromptu cricket-pitch, and steered between the pineapple gateposts.

Nibbs didn't help me down, but banged at the big brass door-knocker. In a moment Hannah, in her parlourmaid's uniform (I always thought the tiara-shaped cap looked ridiculous on her receding forehead) flung open the door and there was a muttered conversation. While he took Cedric's heavy leather case into the hall, Hannah lifted me down, giving me a little hug on the way. Her hands were sandpapery and she smelt of home-made furniture-polish.

"Go round the back," she said to Nibbs, "the kettle's on the hob."

"Oh, blast, look who's here," said Zinnia's voice above our heads.

Hannah looked up at the landing window. "That wasn't very kind, Miss Zinnia," she said, taking my hand.

"Oh, sorry, Lizzie. Didn't mean you."

Cedric studied his shiny boots. He looked very miserable.

"Hey, come and see our aerial railway," came Theodore's voice from high in the tree outside the schoolroom.

The sun shone again.

As soon as Hannah told them about the Admiral, all my cousins – even Zinnia – were very nice to Cedric. They waited patiently while he manoeuvred a tennis-racket on the "railway" from Henry's bedroom window to the tree outside the schoolroom and thence to the ground, and followed it with a secret message to Zinnia, tied to a stick. After she had run downstairs and fielded it she read the message and then ostentatiously tore it in little pieces; but she was rather quiet afterwards.

Before the sky started to fade, Aunt Emily appeared with her big square camera and summoned us to line up on the lawn, in order of height, for a group photograph.

I have it still. It gives me a very strange feeling to look at the line of familiar faces, all smiling except Cedric's, and to see the girls in their long dark skirts (blue they were) and long-sleeved white blouses with a little lace at the high necks, and the boys in their old breeches and baggy jackets with pleated poacher's pockets, Henry Grey rather smarter at the end of the line; Venetia next to him, her hair not yet up; Peregrine Fenwick, one level eyebrow raised in amusement, his slim figure in the negligently graceful attitude of a Hellenic statue; Zinnia's head turned away from him to laugh at some comment from Theodore next to her, her exquisite profile caught for ever with lips parted in mirth; Theodore in mid-speech with that teasing, sideways glance; Louie's eyes creased and shoulders hunched with giggles; Vane, sweet-faced, seeing the joke a fraction later, his big hands hanging out of sleeves too short, one bootlace trailing on the ground; and myself beaming in a frilled pinny beside him. Across the grass to Henry's and Venetia's feet crept a shadow – Aunt Emily's. And behind them (and this I did not notice till long after) the kitchen window with Hannah's homely face topped by her old checked-duster turban, looking out across the stone sink from the dark interior behind the glass, as a zoo animal regards from its cage the laughing children who have come to feed it.

5

After the photograph we all rushed off to practise long-jump in the hay-barn, except for Henry, who couldn't play in the hay because it made him sneeze and his eyes water. I felt very sorry for him, but he didn't seem to mind. His parentless state also aroused my compassion. He had been brought up in a crumbling house in Overriver, the next village to Riverlaw, by an old schoolmistress he called his aunt, though she seemed a great deal older than any aunt I had ever met. Perhaps because of this, he had a touch of the old maid about him; he was clean and tidy, and precise in his speech. But later I realised that his judgement was less sound than one might expect. Though outwardly cautious and conventional, he had a reckless streak; he told us with great seriousness that when he went to Newcastle Races he had put a whole week's pocket-money on a horse called Missel-thrush because he had seen one on the way to the racecourse, and that the horse had come fifth only, he swore, by sheer bad luck. The Delmayne children ragged him dreadfully for being so credulous. When Zinnia told him that Uncle Vane's peaceable old black retriever had caught rabies, he skirted the dog carefully for a whole week and called, "Oh, I say, do be careful," whenever we bent to pat its dear old head as it lay wheezing beside the kitchen range. Venetia, when she heard, was quite cross with Zinnia, who thought (as the rest of us did) that it was a huge joke.

In the hay-barn, early in the evening of the day of the

cricket match, Cedric got into a great state of excitement, tearing bits of hay out of the bales and throwing them up in the air whenever anyone looked like jumping as far as long-legged Peregrine, the reigning champion.

After supper Hannah made up a camp-bed for Cedric in Peregrine's room. I suddenly remembered my little pile of duck-pond-slimed clothes.

"Have you been up to Louie's yet?" I enquired anxiously.

"Yes, bless your heart," she croaked; but her tender look removed any niggling fear of a beating.

Aunt Emily arrived and took me off, rather unwillingly, for my bath while everyone else retired to the schoolroom to play Racing Demon. I could hear the shouts of excitement and howls of dismay while Aunt Emily was patting me dry in her large, soft lap. She powdered me all over with a huge swansdown puff, rinsed my face with the violet oatmeal she used herself, and put a drop of lavender-water behind my ears. I think she enjoyed my bath as much as I did.

"Who's a dear, clean little lady, then?" she cooed, tying the neck ribbons of my nightdress in a beautiful bow.

"Me," I said, beaming. She smiled and gave me an extra hug. Her eyes were very blue and she smelt as nice as I did. "What a canny little pet you are," she murmured. It was strange that when I was alone with her she sometimes spoke, not her usual impeccable King's English like Uncle Vane and the Admiral, but the soft Northumbrian vernacular – never broad and ungrammatical like Hannah and Cook, but nevertheless nearer to their speech than her husband's.

"Poor Cedric, his father's ill, we must be specially kind to him," she said as she tied the sash of my pink silk summer dressing-gown. "Let's go and kiss him good night."

The schoolroom was in happy uproar. The eight of them – five Delmaynes, Cedric, Henry and Peregrine – half-sat or stood round the table, eyes on the cards. They all played at once, hands frenziedly turning over the packs in front of them, or stretching to place cards in the centre of the table; leaping to slam down cards on distant heaps. There were maniacal cackles of triumph as their cards displaced those of others, or groans as they lost to someone quicker.

"Oh, you *viper*, Vane," roared Louie. "Four of clubs . . . Quick, Cedric, your three goes over there!"

"Oh, goodness," gasped Cedric, "thank you," and he slapped it on a two.

"Don't thank me," and Louie's hand shot out to place her four.

"Eights-eights-eights," chanted Henry, who was not as skilled at this game as my cousins. "Hey, Venetia, your king goes out."

"Does it?" enquired Venetia innocently. "*Pst*, Cedric, King of Diamonds," she added in a stage whisper.

"Oh, golly-gosh," Cedric was in a fluster. "So it does," banging it down. He hadn't even noticed that Venetia had the same card. Venetia winked at Henry, who reluctantly removed his glance back to the table, smiling.

The noise of thudding hands was tremendous, when suddenly, "Stop!" cried Zinnia.

The cards were sorted and counted at great speed. Louie had won, but only just.

"I've brought Elizabeth to say good night," said Aunt Emily.

I went round the room, glowing, and everyone kissed me. " 'Night, Bundle," said Peregrine, with a beautiful smile. The others all called me Lizzie. When I got to Venetia I whispered in her ear, "You cheated to help Cedric." She whispered back, "Don't give me away!"

I hated leaving them to go up to bed; but it was almost worth it to hear the affectionate chorus of "Sleep wells" as I went through the spare bedrooms towards the main stairs.

I remembered something.

"I haven't said good night to Hannah and Cook."

"Doesn't matter," said Aunt Emily. "You don't need to. They're servants."

"But Hannah's kind. And Cook has poorly feet."

"I dare say. You'll see them both tomorrow."

I lay awake in bed. The light filtered through the flowered cretonne curtains so that everything in the room was mysteriously visible. The rocking-chair, the mahogany pier-glass, the washstand with its peony-patterned bowl and water-jug, seemed to be waiting in the half-light for something exciting to happen.

I turned over in my mind the events of the day, so different from my only-child existence at home in Newcastle. I quite liked my home and my parents, but my mother was strict and fussy. She was years younger than her cousin Uncle Vane (who, in his turn, was a good many years younger than the Admiral), and she was not at all like him. She was slightly built and quite clever, but very silent. She didn't smile much; perhaps she hadn't much to smile about. Our home, a large, predictable terrace house with a short garden at the front and a long garden at the back, lacked character. Every other house in the terrace had all its rooms in the same places as ours, and the same pattern of plaster mouldings on the dining-room ceiling, and the same brass stair-rods and lincrusta wallpaper in the hall. If only we lived in a house like the Old Hall . . . no, only the Old Hall itself would do. There could be no imitations. I pictured myself living here for ever with my darling cousins, and Uncle Vane and blue-eyed Aunt Emily, and Snowflake and Rover the dog and, of course, Hannah and Cook. And Peregrine. Henry Grey and possibly even Cedric would come sometimes, and my parents would be allowed to visit.

I still hadn't gone to sleep when Louie came to bed.

"The Admiral's not too bad," she announced. "Bob's sister is Dr Bond's cook, and he sent her round to tell us. He has to take things gently, but he's not going to die."

"Oh, good." I had never thought he would; the possibility that any ill person might not get better had never yet occurred to me.

Her voice sank to a dramatic whisper. "There's a plan to creep down and jump on Peregrine when he's asleep." She lay down with her head over the edge of the bed to give her straight black hair the mandatory hundred brush-strokes. "We thought it might take Cedric's mind off thinking about the Admiral."

"I thought you'd rather jump on Cedric." We giggled.

"No, not tonight. Anyway, the camp-bed collapses rather easily. He might get stuck in it. Theodore did once. He put his weight on the join, and the head and the foot sprang up and he *completely disappeared*," and she laughed so much that she dropped the hairbrush and had to turn upside down in order to retrieve it.

"Where did he go?"

This question only produced greater peals of giggles.

"Is Cedric my cousin?"

"Yes. No. Well, I know you call Father Uncle – do you call the Admiral Uncle?"

"I wouldn't dare speak to him."

"Poor little Lizzie, I don't blame you. Well, your mother is their first cousin, so you're our second cousin, and Cedric's too."

I tried to look wise, though I was not much wiser.

"Is Peregrine my cousin?" I asked, wondering whether I could swop Cedric for him.

"No. No relation. He lives in Shoreburgh."

"Where's that?"

"Not terribly far. There's a castle by the sea, he said. His father brought him in a motor-car."

"Oh, I wish I'd seen it! I thought the Admiral would have a motor-car, but we went to Riverpark in a carriage."

"He does have one. It makes an awful noise. Nibbs the coachman is the only person who understands it. I expect it had a puncture today," added Louie knowledgeably. "They often do."

"Nibbs is nice. He has a son called Albert."

"Yes, I know. He goes to the village school. He's really clever. He's going to be a sailor."

"Nibbs didn't want to tell me how old he was."

Louie pulled on her nightdress and began to fasten its mother-of-pearl neck-buttons before she replied. Her smooth brow wrinkled. "How very odd. You could easily have found out, anyway, he's the same age as Cedric."

"Will he be a naval officer like Cedric's brother?"

"Goodness, no. He's not a gentleman. It's a pity, really. I expect if the truth were known he's brainier than Giles." She heaved her white dressing-gown over her shoulders, and began to fasten the couple of dozen silk-covered buttons that marched all the way up the front. "But Giles is very nice, and very handsome. Zinnia's soppy about him."

This was a surprise. It was difficult to imagine Zinnia being soppy about anything.

I was hugely enjoying this girlish heart-to-heart with Louie, of all people, who was three years older than me. But then, my cousins were like that. Unlike most older children – unlike Cedric – they petted me because I was little, but otherwise treated me as a sensible person. They never condescended.

"Zinnia's so pretty," I ventured.

The door flew open as I spoke. "Who is taking my name in vain?" demanded Zinnia grandly. But I could see she was pleased. "Here, I'll brush your hair, Lizzie. Let's try putting it up."

"Like a grown-up?" Oh, happiness!

"D'you think Peregrine's asleep yet?" asked Louie after a sort of bird's nest had been made of my hair, with the help of about fifty hairpins.

"We'll see in a minute," said Zinnia, her mouth full of pins. "There!"

Large eyes looked back at me gravely from the mirror. An untidy bandeau of brown hair surmounted my fringe.

Zinnia peered at me, head on one side. "It needs something . . ." She ran to Louie's wardrobe and rummaged on a high shelf. "Here, try this." It was a pale blue paribuntal straw hat, the cartwheel brim laden with full-blown pink silk roses.

"Oh, lovely!"

"Goodness, be careful," said Louie. "That's Mother's best wedding hat. She keeps it in there because it's so big."

"I know, silly." Zinnia turned to me, tilting the enormous hat so that my eyebrows were hidden and my eyes glowed in the shadow of the brim. "Very becoming, Modom."

"Oh, Lizzie, you do look sweet!"

"They must be asleep by now. Let's creep down."

"We can't go through Henry's room!" said Louie, aghast.

"Oh, yes, we can. He and Venetia are with the parents in the drawing-room, playing Patience till Venetia's bedtime."

"Let's hope they've shut the drawing-room door, then."

"Why is Henry staying here?" I asked.

"His aunt's away visiting her cousin. Now, Lizzie," Zinnia opened the bedroom door and turned to me, eyes sparkling, finger to lips, and her voice sank to a dramatic whisper. "Quiet as a mouse!"

We stole down the shallow, blue-carpeted stairs. Aunt Emily's magnificent hat kept knocking into the wall until I got used to its width. On the landing Zinnia raised a warning hand and stood in an attitude of exaggerated caution, listening. I caught Louie's eye and she clapped a hand to her mouth to stifle her giggles. Zinnia grasped the door-handle of Henry's room, inched it round, and pushed.

We tiptoed through, past the four-poster, and repeated the process at the next door.

In the far corner of this room, Cedric was asleep with his mouth open, snoring gently. In the big mahogany bed Peregrine, too, appeared to be asleep; he lay on his side, almost too beautiful to disturb. His thin mouth was shut, and his feathery eyebrows made a straight line across his face, with a big gap in the middle that helped to give him his open, innocent look. His eyes were closed, the dark lashes brushing his cheeks. As we approached he didn't move, but his mouth twitched in an infinitesimal smile. He wasn't asleep after all.

"Ambush!" shrieked Louie, leaping on to the bed.

Louie and Zinnia yelled like Indians and jumped up and down on the unfortunate Peregrine, who roared in protest and put up his arms and legs under the eiderdown to fend them off. As he was much stronger than they were, he got the best of it. Cedric groaned, sat up, and rushed over to join in.

"I love wrestling," gasped Louie, returning to the fray.

"Let me! Let me!" I shouted, jumping up and down with excitement. Holding Louie back with one arm, Peregrine turned his head to look at me.

"Oh, Bundle, I like your hat." He held out his other hand to me, and I threw myself on to his chest. The hat sailed unheeded to the floor. I thought wrestling meant hugging and kissing – my father had pretended to wrestle with me when I was very small – so I hugged Peregrine's neck and gave him a big kiss. When I stopped he laughed. I can remember that laugh now – husky, delighted, fond – and the delicious feel of him, warm, firm, his mouth smiling under mine, his hair silky under my fingers.

At that moment I felt a painful weight on my back – Cedric, howling with glee.

"Ow, get off," I squeaked. Zinnia had attacked again and I could scarcely wriggle. I was in the middle of a heaving mass of arms and legs. "I'm squashed," I shouted desperately into a mouthful of pillow. "Mind the hat!" I added urgently.

"Let her out," commanded Zinnia, moving away. Just as I was wondering whether I would ever breathe again, I found I could scramble sideways out of the heap. Cedric, in a state of high excitement, put his head down to the other boy's as if he were embracing him. I felt a sudden distaste. So, apparently, did Peregrine.

"Get off me," he said. He hadn't said that to me.

As Peregrine swung his pyjama'd legs over the edge of the bed and, standing up, shook off his attackers, I was so dizzy with delight at the memory of our closeness and our kiss that I nearly forgot to rescue the hat.

I slept well that night, not knowing that in that single day there had appeared the first threads of the grand design.

6

Looking back, it seems to me that the reason why the Delmayne family took me to their collective bosom was not through any intrinsic virtue or wit on my part, because I was a very ordinary child, but because they thought of me for ever after as I had first appeared among them; a large, cuddly doll with big, blue-grey eyes and fat, rosy cheeks, a cheerful and trusting nature, and an unshakeable affection for every one of them. Perhaps my repeated appearances made them feel about me as I felt about them; that we were closer than cousins, that our destinies were in some indefinable way bound together. At any rate, I was accepted, welcomed, included, my presence at even the most private family events taken for granted. I was there not only for the statutory fortnight every summer, but – during 1911, 1912 and 1913 – for many other long periods, once an entire school summer vacation. It wasn't until many years later that I learnt that my mother had had repeated pregnancies, always difficult, that ended in miscarriages and once with a stillbirth. As the years went by she grew more anxious and took greater care of herself than before, but it did no good. She grew a little self-centred and peevish, but perhaps she was worn out by sickness and disappointment.

However, as Louie would say, there's no thorn without a rose somewhere about. My mother's poor health meant that the morning after almost every term ended (for by this time I was at a primary school in Newcastle which, alas, was not the Shangri-La I had expected) my father would take me to Newcastle station, and among the deep-clanking and chuffing metal monsters and the hiss of steam that hung in ghostly shreds under the great arched roof, he would entrust me to the charge of some sober-hatted matron, get the porter to lift her suitcases to the luggage-rack followed by my Gladstone bag, peck me on the cheek and take off his bowler hat to both of us, and leave.

And so the train chugged out from the cavernous station into the sunshine, and gathered speed. My cousins had a chant that reproduced the sound of a train gaining speed over the rails. "*Coffee . . . coffee . . .*" it started; then, with mounting acceleration, "cheese and biscuits, cheese and biscuits," repeated with growing excitement, then faster with "pears-and-custard-pears-and-custard-pears-and-custard" after which you were fairly racketing over the rails with "beef-and-carrots! beef-and-carrots!" until the final triumphant hoot of "SOOOUP!" (Beef and carrots had only to appear on the Old Hall dining-table for all the children to begin chanting it in chorus). In the train I would repeat this formula silently to myself, and by the time I got to the soup we would be in open country, dashing past the flattish pastureland and fawn-coloured stone walls that I knew so well. In time every coppice, every distant church tower, every one-horse station and wayside halt and water-trough, every square stone farmhouse with two sash windows on either side of the front door, every mansion lurking behind its screen of trees, became familiar. And at last the train began to slow, first for Overriver and then Riverlaw station; the woman to whose care I had been entrusted would stir, and someone would take down my Gladstone bag, and I would thank them prettily and see them smile, and the little stone station building would swim into sight (so reminiscent, with its tall sash windows and the ball finials on the steep gable, of a miniature Riverpark), and I would see a familiar caped coat or flower-trimmed straw hat, and arms waving madly in welcome; some unremembered adult would pull down the window and lean out to turn the worn brass door-handle, and other hands would help me down the steps and pass out my bag and, in a whirl of hugs and kisses and exclamations of delight, I had arrived.

The fears and frustrations of school, my dark, hushed home and poor, peevish mother, lying on the sofa with the blinds down, were all forgotten. Life had begun.

The exceptionally cold winter of 1913 came on us suddenly. I had never been away from home for Christmas, but in that year I was dispatched to Riverlaw the day after my school term ended, on the understanding that I would be sent back on Christmas Eve.

On the day I arrived there was a chill nip in the air, and the wind bit my cheek as I clambered down from the train; but the sun was shining, if weakly, and Zinnia and Louie rushed down the platform towards me, shrieking my name.

"Dearest Lizzie!" Louie gave me a big hug. Her long, pointed nose was cold like a dog's. "Goodness, you've grown since last time. Father and Venetia and Theodore are out hunting, so Bob brought us in the trap."

"Afternoon, Bob," I said to the elderly, side-whiskered groom as he came up and took my case. "How are you keeping?"

"Afternoon, Miss Lizzie. Not so bad, thank you."

Zinnia shot me a dazzling smile, which from her was an accolade. "Had a good term?"

"Pretty awful. Miss Bowers did the Stone Age again. I'm so tired of drawing Flint Instruments."

"Oh, poor, poor Lizzie." Zinnia looked ravishing. She had borrowed one of Aunt Emily's feathered hats and her squirrel muff, and looked incredibly grown-up. Her wide, high cheekbones and almond eyes, more noticeable as the years passed, gave her a cat-like quality; and there was something feline, too, in the way she moved.

"You've put your hair up!"

"Don't tell Mother. She says I shouldn't till I'm seventeen, but it seems so silly to wait three whole months. I take it down in the house, such a bore."

"A bit naughty," said Louie, "but it suits her, doesn't it? Cedric thinks it's glorious," and she winked at me behind Zinnia's back as we climbed into the trap.

Zinnia groaned. "Don't talk to me about Cedric."

"Poor old Cedric," I said. "There's nothing really wrong with Cedric. At least, he can't help it."

"There you go," said Zinnia affectionately. "Always defending the indefensible. There's nothing wrong with Cedric, except that he's utterly slimy and impossible."

"I think he's a bit sad," I said. "At bottom he's quite decent really."

"Rather a large bottom," said Louie, and clapped her fur-gloved hand over her mouth in mock-remorse. Zinnia looked warningly first at her, and then at Bob's broad back. But being Zinnia, the dimple twitched at the corner of her mouth.

"What other news?" I asked quickly for fear of an outburst of unseemly mirth.

"Oh . . . Venetia went to a dance at the Bainbridges' last week but she said it was very dull, Henry filled in most of her programme right at the beginning. Young Vane's passed his entrance exam to big school, just. Theodore came back from school last week. He's already been in trouble with Father, for opening the sideboard and drinking a glass of whisky!"

"Goodness. Did he get drunk?"

"Not really," said Louie. "He just slept like a pig. He said it was pretty foul, but having begun it he thought he ought to finish the job properly."

"Just like Theodore. He always does, doesn't he?"

"Does what?"

"Finish the job. Did Uncle beat him?"

"We don't know," said Zinnia. "Neither of them would say."

Louie bent to my ear and whispered, "Shall I tell you a secret?"

Naturally, I nodded.

"Swear not to tell?"

"Cross my heart and hope to die."

"I'm writing a book!"

"It's rude to whisper," said Zinnia, cross at being excluded.

"What's it called?" I whispered back.

"The Passionate Potato-Picker."

"Goodness," I said admiringly.

The trap rattled and squeaked past the doctor's house and down the side of the village green; past the butcher's where one got sawdust on the soles of one's shoes, and Will's father and eldest brother stood in their straw boaters and blue-striped aprons exchanging badinage with the housewives ("He's mutton, I'm lamb," Will's brother had announced when I went in once to obtain information for my holiday homework); past the General Stores, a poky little cave where a stout Gorgon dispensed everything from gobstoppers to blue-bags; past the post office, and the one-up-one-down with a but-and-ben scullery where Mrs Hothersall, the sewing-woman, altered the Delmayne girls' dresses with ancient, knobbly hands.

On a patch of pavement near the pump Dick and Ivy, her skirts pinned up recklessly high to reveal much of her thick black stockings, were playing hopscotch. I waved, and they waved back. Ivy stuck her tongue out at me.

"Is Peregrine here?" I asked, trying to sound casual.

"No, he was coming but he broke his ankle playing rugger."

"Oh dear, I am sorry. What about Henry?"

"Oh, poor old Henry's always turning up like a bad penny," said Louie. "But Venetia's so beastly to him he's started making sheep's eyes at Zinnia."

Zinnia blushed. "Don't be stupid," she said. "Venetia couldn't be beastly if she tried." As we passed the cricket-ground she unpinned Aunt Emily's hat, put it and the muff down carefully on the seat beside her, and started unpinning her dark hair. "You've got the wrong end of the stick as usual, Louie. Mother says he isn't quite out of the top drawer, that's why Venetia shouldn't *encourage* him, and neither shall I." She shook her hair out. It was thick and heavy, and flew up round her creamy-skinned oval face. She smoothed it down quickly with her gloved hands. "But he's quite nice, really, and he's an orphan and still lives with that wretched aunt – he thinks of the Old Hall as his second home – "

"Like me," I said, glad of a subject I understood. All this talk of encouragement was rather over my head. Nobody had said anything about love – and if they had, I had changed since I was six; now, three and a half years later, I would have thought it was soppy.

"Well, it *is* your second home, isn't it?" commented Louie.

Under their smiles I felt like a flower opening in sunlight.

" – So we can't actually drive poor Henry away," finished Zinnia. "Oh, glory, there's Mother. Bob, could you possibly hide her hat and muff in the stables till I get a chance to smuggle them back into the house?"

Louie caught my eye. She was as appalled as I was. She had assumed, as I had, that Zinnia was wearing the hat and muff with her mother's permission.

"Oh, no, Miss Zinnia, it would be as much as me place is worth."

"Oh, hell's bells." By this time we had come to a stop outside the front door, and as Aunt Emily hurried across the lawn, her arms wide to hug me, Zinnia slipped out of the other side of the trap and, shielding hat and muff from her mother's eyes behind her voluminous skirt, she sidled into the house.

During the night before Christmas Eve, it started to snow.

I woke up to a thick silence. Around the edge of the curtains there was a strange bluish light. I felt for the floor with my toes, and pulled the eiderdown around me. In the nightlight's glow I could see my breath making little puffs of cloud in front of me. I tiptoed to the window, pulled the corner of the curtain aside, and caught my breath.

The lawn was pale blue under a dark blue sky, the hedges and trees encircling it were inky black, the rose-bushes like schools of black stick-insects against the snow. The garden-house had a pale blue roof, and round Louie's snow-laden window-ledge the leafless sprays of the François Juranville had grown webs of snow between stem and branch. Fat flakes fell leisurely down, millions of them. It would be a white Christmas, and I would have to spend it here.

My heart sang. I watched the snow fall for a long time until my freezing toes forced me back to bed.

7

"Well, what are we going to do about you, Mary-Jane?" asked Uncle Vane at breakfast next morning as he deftly sliced the cob off his egg. I tried not to grin too hard. The room was bright with unearthly whiteness from the window. "Five inches deep outside, and still snowing."

"Bound to be colossal snowdrifts between here and Newcastle," said Louie, with a wink at me.

"The steam heating on the London and North-Eastern Railway always fails in really cold weather. She'll probably freeze to death," said Theodore cheerfully. "Think of her poor little corpse, completely rigid in a sitting position. They'll have to make a specially-shaped coffin."

"Sort of zigzag," agreed Young Vane enthusiastically. "Might be quite difficult to fit on a hearse."

"They can take it to Newcastle on a coal bogie when the snow melts. What a surprise for your parents, Lizzie, and we will miss you horribly."

"That'll do, that'll do," said Uncle Vane. "I really think, Mary-Jane, that if you can bear the thought of spending Christmas with us, we had better hang on to you until there's a thaw. I'll send Bob down to the station with a telegraph-message for your parents. We're keeping young Lizzie with us for Christmas," he explained to Aunt Emily, who had just appeared in the doorway. "We can't bear to part with her in this weather."

"Just what I thought myself," said Aunt Emily. In her plain rose silk morning-dress and cashmere jacket she looked both prettier and more motherly than ever. I couldn't help contrasting her with my pale, angular mother, who was so often a peculiar shape around the middle.

Venetia was looking out of the window. "It's nearly stopped snowing," she said. "And look – we've got visitors. Charles Dawson and Henry, and Madge Carroun. And goodness, the Seymour twins. I quite forgot – I said if it snowed they must come over for a snow-fight."

"Oh, splendid!" And Young Vane leapt up from his porridge.

"Just wait a minute," Aunt Emily lifted a commanding hand and looked around at her children. "Please remember, no playing outside the gates. Now wrap up well, and don't forget gloves. There's a nice fire in the schoolroom if you want to warm your coats. Come up with me now, Lizzie, and we'll warm yours."

I was impatient to join in the fun, but the lure of a specially-warmed coat was equally strong. Aunt Emily hung it on the brass fender.

"You won't play with the village children, will you, darling?"

Some devil prompted me to say innocently, "Why not?" although I knew this would be taken as heresy. Aunt Emily looked fussed, and moved the coat-sleeves about.

"Well, they're not quite like us, darling. They can't speak the King's English, and some of them can't even read. They'll never be ladies and gentlemen. You're going to be a lady when you grow up."

"But some of them are quite clever. Nibbs's son at Riverpark is joining the Navy."

"Yes, but he can't be an officer, just an A.B."

"What's that?"

"Able-bodied seaman. It would be frightfully awkward, anyway, if he were the same rank as Giles." She lifted the coat and held it out for me to slip my arms in. "It's no good questioning these things, sweetest, that's just how life is, and always has been." She brightened. "Did you know that the Admiral and Aunt Letitia and Cedric are coming here for Christmas dinner tomorrow? And Giles will be here too."

The thought of meeting the legendary Giles, whose beauty I had admired from afar once or twice but whom I had never plucked up courage to speak to, completely distracted me from any unwelcome thoughts about the villagers, as Aunt Emily had known it would.

The snow-fight was a great success. Venetia was at her enchanting best, animated and bright-eyed, in a tight-waisted, fur-collared coat and a big fur hat borrowed, legitimately this time, from her mother. Venetia was an extremely nice person; gentle and kind, good and capable, although lacking in the sparkiness that I loved to see in Zinnia and Louie. Unlike these two she was not at all clever, but it didn't matter. She was very like Uncle Vane, who once told me that all the brains of the Delmayne family had gone to the Admiral, but whose kind heart and peaceable good sense nevertheless contributed greatly to the house's happy atmosphere.

I could see from the way Henry looked at Venetia that he was still severely smitten. Charles Dawson, too, kept his eyes on her. Charles was a new arrival on the Riverlaw scene; he was a friend of Henry's and we had known of him for some time, but had seldom met him because he lived some distance away and had been at boarding-school. Now he had left, and had just begun to work his way up through his father's firm, a big shoe-shop in Newcastle that had branches in several market towns in the north-east. This meant that he was in trade, which would automatically have ruled him out (in Aunt Emily's eyes at least) as a suitor for any of the Delmayne girls. But Henry could now invite whomever he chose to stay at his aunt's, and it would have been impossible to keep Charles away from the Old Hall, where Henry had become almost part of the furniture; Aunt Emily was fond of telling Henry that he and the Delmayne girls were almost like brother and sisters. Besides, Charles was a charmer; bright, well-spoken, presentable, with a long, intelligent face – everyone liked him.

Madge Carroun was a much more welcome visitor as far as Aunt Emily was concerned. Even I knew that Madge, whatever her other disadvantages, was County. She was fifteen years old, and the sister of Sir Rednall Carroun. They lived with their mother in Rednall, an incredibly grand and crumbling Palladian house of immense size, far bigger than Riverpark. It was approached via twin gatehouses and a long avenue of limes, two miles beyond Overriver. Despite some artful angling for an invitation, Aunt Emily had never been inside it. Theodore, much to her excitement, had been asked there to tea twice, but an inquisition after his first visit only produced the laconic comment, "It's falling down." In spite of this, my aunt was always urging Theodore to invite back not only Madge, but also her brother Rednall, whom none of us had ever met.

"He's *years* older than me," protested Theodore. "I've hardly spoken to him."

It didn't take much imagination to guess why Aunt Emily wanted to introduce Sir Rednall Carroun to the Delmayne household. She was almost open about it. She once told me a joke about a professor who had ten daughters. "Oh, Professor," a friend said to him, "you have many resources!" "My difficulty," he answered, "will be in husbanding my resources." Aunt Emily had obviously given the problem much thought.

Madge was short and thin, with straight, straw-coloured hair, a pert little pointed face, a drawling voice and a coy manner.

"What a simply lovely fur scarf," she said to Louie during a lull in the snow-fight. "I couldn't try it on, could I, for a teensie-weensie minute?"

Louie obliged, and didn't like to ask for it back, and Madge kept it on for the rest of the morning. My cold, nine-year-old eye detected a calculating nature.

The Seymour twins, Barbara and Bertram, were also

eligible in Aunt Emily's eyes. Their father was a rich farmer – "a *gentleman* farmer like Father, not a *working* farmer," as Zinnia (who had learnt snobbery at her mother's knee) pointed out. But in their teens, at least, they were fat and seemed excessively placid; lookers-on rather than joiners-in.

The snowfall slowly petered out, and we built a huge snow-woman outside the garden house, with carrot nose and currant eyes.

Just as Venetia was crowning her with a frayed straw hat and a bunch of old pheasant-feathers, to cries of approval, there was a shout from the gate.

It was Cedric with his elder brother Giles.

"We brought a sledge," called Giles. "What about some races?"

Giles took the lead as if by right. If ever there was a golden boy, Giles was his incarnation. He was tall, slim and broad-shouldered, with a fresh, open, handsome face with a Grecian profile, a direct blue gaze, a pleasant and confident manner, and the gift of making people want to do whatever he suggested. Poor, weedy Cedric looked up to him, obeying and adoring.

Giles soon dispatched Theodore and Young Vane to drag the two Old Hall sledges from the coach house, and organised us into teams. We strode out for the sledging-field, which was on the far side of the village beyond the doctor's house. Below it, the fields stretched white, punctuated by the black brush-strokes of hedge-stems and coppice-trunks, to the almost invisible horizon below a thick, whitish sky.

We raced down, shrieking with mirth, the girls' long hair flying, cheeks stinging in the freezing air, and dragged the sledges back up the slope over and over again till we were panting and hot in our thick tweeds and fur gloves.

Some of the village people were there too. Vin Baggs, now as tall as a man, tore down the slope head-first with his lanky legs waving and his ears bright red under his carrot-coloured hair. He had brought a pudding of a girl called Mona; and wiry Dick, still with a wary, sharp look to him, had blonde-curled Ivy in tow. Their rickety, home-made sledges looked rough beside our metal-bound ones, but went just as fast. Ivy screamed with excitement, the boys whooped, Vin stood on his sledge and rode it like a bronco.

"Shouldn't we ask them to join us?" suggested Louie.

"Goodness, no," said Giles. "Wouldn't do at all." And indeed, beside the Old Hall party's tweeds and fur and solid, well-polished footwear, the villagers, in their thin coats and torn gloves and battered boots, looked as if they came from a different planet. They sounded different, too. When they talked among themselves their dialect became even broader, and some of them swore continually and unthinkingly, which we never did except under extreme provocation. Swearing, Uncle Vane always said, was a sign of a slow mind and a poor vocabulary.

On the evening of that day we decorated the house with holly and mistletoe picked from the lane to Riverpark, and we hung a tree with tinsel and apples and bags of home-made toffee. In the corner of the drawing-room behind the grand piano, it looked beautiful. When we had finished, Aunt Emily sat down and accompanied us while we all sang carols.

Because I was the youngest, I was always sent to bed earlier than my cousins. On Christmas Eve I was still awake when Louie came up; but instead of talking to her, as I usually did, I pretended to be asleep in case she was going to put a present in my stocking.

A few minutes later the door opened; Zinnia, on the way to her own room. I kept my eyes shut and practised calm breathing.

"Oh, Louie darling, could you undo my back buttons? My arm's so stiff from chucking snowballs. Hasn't it been a ripping day?"

"Lovely. Don't wake Lizzie."

"Doesn't she look sweet?" murmured Zinnia, a decibel lower. "I say, wasn't the sledging fun?"

"Wonderful, wonderful!"

"We must ask them all to come over again soon. Giles said something about skating – I wonder if it would seem too obvious if we suggested it at dinner tomorrow?"

"You like Giles, don't you?" I could imagine Louie watching her with that shrewd, amused look she had.

"Does it show? Oh, Louie," Zinnia burst out, "if I told you a secret would you promise not to tell?"

"Cross my heart."

"Really, truly promise? You know what a terrible tease Theodore is – I'd die if anybody found out."

"I promise, I really do."

"Well, you know we wondered how one knew when one was in love? Well, I am! I've been just bursting to tell somebody."

"It is Giles, isn't it?"

"Oh, yes, oh, goodness, isn't he *beautiful*!"

And indeed he was.

My ears buzzed with this interesting information. At nine years old I was still rather contemptuous of what my school-fellows called "lovey-doveys"; but even I could see that Giles and Zinnia, equal in beauty, would make a radiant couple. I never doubted that he would return her love and they would get married and live happily ever after. In spite of her shortcomings I was very fond of Zinnia, and I fell asleep full of joy at her good fortune.

I think that was the last whole day on which my childhood was completely happy.

Because on Christmas Day, after Father Christmas had arrived during breakfast (in the unusual absence of Uncle Vane) wearing a red robe and an enormous white beard and driving the bigger of the two sledges drawn by Starlight; and after Uncle Vane had returned to finish his breakfast and drive us (in the wagonette, as there were so many of us) to the little stone church where we all sat squashed together in our best clothes in the oak-walled family pew, where I dreamed of archangels and gazed throughout the sermon at the gracefully grieving stone widow of an eighteenth-century Delmayne; then, we came back with the Admiral and his family to eat Christmas dinner round the big oval table in the Old Hall.

It should have been wonderful.

But in the middle of the meal – to be precise, just after Hannah had carried in an enormous Christmas pudding crowned with holly and wreathed in blue flames – Giles announced to us all what the grown-ups already knew; that this might be our last peaceful Christmas, because Germany was arming, and the Royal Navy, like the rest of England, was preparing for war.

8

At first the war, when it came, made very little difference to the Old Hall and its inhabitants.

The food we ate, for example, was exactly the same; no mere international fight-to-the-death would ever affect the cows' output of velvety yellow cream, or prevent Aunt Emily from having a goose killed to provide a celebration feast whenever the occasion arose. Uncle Vane still rode to hounds three times a week, and so did Theodore in his school holidays. My uncle's cautious counsels of economy to help the War Effort never stopped Aunt Emily from going to the sales in Newcastle, and buying up all the lengths of silk and tweed, cards of lace edging, hooks-and-eyes, fur pieces and hat-feathers she could lay her hands on – *her* daughters would never look like ragbags, war or no war. (Some of these trophies were promptly squirrelled away and forgotten, to be found years later in old pillowcases in the attic.)

Venetia and Zinnia spent much of their spare time knitting khaki mufflers and balaclavas for the troops. Aunt Emily was constantly sending me to look for Venetia to help with some household task or other, and I would track her down eventually via the click of knitting-needles – sitting with her back against a tree in some corner of the garden, perhaps. Often Charles Dawson would be with her, reading aloud or chatting. When I arrived with Aunt Emily's summons, he would scramble up, raise a hand in farewell, and stroll off through the kitchen garden. Half the time I don't think Aunt Emily knew he was there. Zinnia was harder to find; she had become very thick with Madge Carroun, and was always driving or riding over to see her, with her current piece of knitting in a large pink raffia bag. Aunt Emily never stopped her. I am sure she cherished the hope that Zinnia would get off with the mysterious Sir Rednall.

Young Vane went round the house singing, *ad nauseam*,

"We don't want to fight, but by Jingo if we do
We've got the ships, we've got the men, we've
got the money too."

But as Theodore was only sixteen, and Uncle Vane was getting on for sixty and was in any case needed to run the farm, nobody at the Old Hall could fight in 1914 whether they wanted to or not.

Elsewhere it was a different matter. Someone was going to the war from almost every family we knew. From the village, Vin Baggs volunteered as a trooper in the Coldstream Guards. He had been helping on the farm for some time, and one day in the late summer of 1914 he came up to the house in his uniform to say goodbye to Uncle Vane, who had promised to employ him again as soon as the war was over, which we all hoped would be in a matter of months. He still looked like a lanky boy, temporarily smartened up, but with his carroty hair standing on end and a smut on the end of his nose. I met him as he came out of Uncle Vane's office, smiling, on his way to see Hannah and Cook.

"Goodness, Vin," I said. "What a grand uniform."

"What cheer, Miss Lizzie." Cap in hand, he touched an imaginary one on his head. "I'm off to the war, like. Ivy says I look like a dog's breakfast," he added.

"That's not very kind. I think you look very well dressed." I was struck by the expression on his face; he was usually confident and only too ready to bandy insults with the other village boys. "Are you a bit frightened of going?" It was the wrong thing to say; but I was, after all, only nine.

"Why, no. Well," he relaxed a little, and grinned, "maybe jist a little. But dinna tell anyone, mind. I reckon I've got to go. It's for England, like."

"I won't tell. And I do wish you luck."

Several of the older hinds enlisted at the very beginning of the war. So did the butcher's elder son. After he had gone, there was no more badinage in the butcher's shop, and I suddenly realised that the butcher himself was quite an old man.

Among our own circle, Giles Delmayne was now a lieutenant and had been allotted to a ship. Its ultimate destination was very secret, but we heard that he was soon coming home on embarkation leave.

Zinnia's excitement, fear and longing knew no bounds.

"Do you think he *knows* how I feel about him?" she demanded to Louie and myself as we sat one day in the garden-house, shelling a huge mound of peas for Aunt Emily.

The garden-house was quite big and built of cedar. It held a rickety table and chairs and an old sofa piled with faded, rose-printed cretonne cushions, and it faced across the lawn at right angles to the house, from which it was half-hidden by a little thicket of buddleias. The dovecot was behind it, so there was almost always a fantail or two on its roof, cooing softly, and a sweet, musky smell of cedar and of the lavender and mignonette Aunt Emily had planted under its windows.

I had been formally admitted, under oath of secrecy, to the news of Zinnia's grand passion after Louie had pointed out that I was reliable and discreet. I felt rather smug about being so extremely discreet that neither of them ever suspected I had known about it already.

"Why don't you tell him?" suggested practical Louie. "If he loves you, he will be thrilled if you do."

"Oh, I couldn't do that!" Zinnia was appalled. "It wouldn't do at all. It might put him off completely. Anyway, he's so handsome and splendid I expect he has a girl in every port. He may be madly in love with someone else. He probably hasn't even noticed me. No, I must think of some completely original way of attracting his attention. Oh, heavens," she fell on the mothy old garden-house sofa and rolled about, clutching the cushions in agony, "being in love is utterly awful, horrible, ghastly!"

"If you were a man," enquired Louie thoughtfully, "would you enlist?"

She sat up. "Of course. And I shall. As soon as Giles has gone abroad. I wouldn't go while there's the smallest chance of seeing him, but – "

"Girls can't join up," even I knew that.

"D'you mean you would disguise yourself as a *man*?" Louie looked at her half-admiringly, half-doubtfully. I could see her point; Zinnia's narrow waist emphasised her well-developed bust and hips. It was extremely hard to picture how she could possibly conceal her sex at all, let alone maintain the deception for an indefinite period.

"Just you wait. I have a great plan, you'll see."

Louie looked alarmed. "Don't be silly," she said. "Anyway, I expect we'll be needed to help on the farm if any more of the men go. Even Lizzie could milk, and feed the animals." She popped a fat pea into her mouth. "And I suspect Venetia may get married soon, so that'll be one less of us to give a hand."

"Venetia? Married?" I was stunned. I had somehow thought things at the Old Hall would stay as they were for ever, war or no war. I knew she had seen a great deal of Charles, but as far as I knew he had no suitor-like qualities; they were simply friends. I cast my mind back. "To Henry?" It didn't seem credible.

"Don't think so. Poor old Henry."

"He proposed to her last week, right where you're sitting," revealed Zinnia with relish.

"How d'you know?" I demanded.

"You couldn't – Zinnia, even you couldn't eavesdrop on a proposal!" Louie was scandalised.

"I didn't. I was weeding the primulas for Mother, behind the yew tree over there, and it took ages and I noticed it had begun to get dark. So I got up and came out from behind the tree, and then I saw something move inside the open door, here – and it was Henry, going down on his knees to Venetia!"

"Heavens, what did you do?"

"What could I do? I got back quickly behind the tree, and froze. I simply couldn't have him realising anyone had seen him like that. Especially me."

Louie's eyes widened. She surveyed her sister thoughtfully, but said nothing.

"What did he say?"

"I didn't listen. At least, I tried not to."

"H'm, h'm."

"Yes, honestly. But he wouldn't take no for an answer. He kept holding out his arms pleadingly. He got in an awful state. She went into some long, mumbly sort of explanation, but he wouldn't realise she meant it. He couldn't keep his voice down – he kept repeating, 'But I love you, I've always loved you!' It was rather painful, actually," and she bent to the plank floor, ostensibly to gather up some fallen pea-pods, but perhaps to discourage us from drawing her out further.

"Poor old Henry, what happened then?"

"Well, in the end she must have convinced him. By this time it was almost dark, but I daren't come out from behind the tree because I thought they'd be sure to see my white blouse. He didn't kiss her, or anything. He got up and brushed down the knees of his trousers – "

"Typical."

"The floor must have been terribly hard, all that time," I said, feeling for him.

" – And as she sat here with her head drooping, he said

72

in quite a loud voice, rather blustering really, 'But you've all been so good to me always, I really think of the Old Hall as home and the Delmaynes as my family – you know I've got nobody but Auntie – ' but she just looked up very sadly and shook her head. And he gave her a long, last look, and went straight through the stable arch to get his horse and go home."

"Oh, dear."

"But as a matter of fact he came back two days later and was quite ordinary, as if nothing had happened."

"He's quite nice, dear old Henry," said Louie pensively. "But I wouldn't want to marry him myself."

"What sort of husband would you like?" I ventured.

"Oh, a prince, of course," said Louie. "Don't eat that one, Lizzie, it's got a maggot in it."

"Will Henry go to the war?" I enquired.

"Oh, I think so."

"Will Theodore?" I asked, suddenly fearful. How could I do without darling Theodore, who could always cheer us up?

"He's too young. Let's hope the war will be over before he's old enough," added Zinnia soberly.

Louie's brow wrinkled. "I've noticed he's been disappearing a lot lately," she mused.

"Out shooting, I think. He brought back three rabbits this morning, anyway."

"Oh, so he's practising," said Louie darkly.

9

One by one the young men came to say goodbye before they went off to the war. It should have grown easier and easier to say goodbye to them as we got more practice, but it didn't. After a few of them had gone, they began to seem beautiful, rare creatures. One began to see how graceful they had been, how flower-like in their youth, how noble in their innocent patriotism, how supremely, blindingly generous; they were giving themselves.

Not that Henry Grey could ever be described as flower-like. Very soon after his rejection by Venetia he turned up one day, twitching with excitement, as Aunt Emily was sitting down to tea on the lawn. Theodore and I were there at the lace-clothed table, and she had sent Young Vane to fetch the rest of the family.

"I've decided!" exclaimed Henry. "I'm going to learn to fly aeroplanes! I've heard that they're going to form a Royal Flying Corps. That will be just the place for me."

"Getting above yourself, eh?" said Theodore admiringly. "Bully for you."

Aunt Emily's hand, holding the silver teapot, paused for a moment in mid-air. "It's much too dangerous," she said. "Don't go. You mustn't go."

Henry looked surprised, as well he might at her tone; commanding, pleading. "But, Mrs Delmayne, of course I'm going! I'm not intending to be given the white feather."

"Wait for conscription!"

"But that could be years. Men are needed now."

I had never seen Aunt Emily so flustered. "Henry, my dear," she said urgently, and then stopped.

Henry's chest seemed to spread like a fantail's. He appeared to grow. He laughed and exclaimed, "Even you, Mrs Delmayne, couldn't persuade me not to defend my country!" His victory over my aunt seemed to embolden him. "And when I come back," he declared, "I hope perhaps one day I may become one of your family. Perhaps if I distinguish myself enough, a certain young lady will change her mind . . ." His expression changed and he began to colour. He had obviously said more than he meant to.

But that was nothing to the change in Aunt Emily. As she took in his meaning, she became very still. Her face turned white. She looked at the ground as if we must not see her thoughts.

"I'm afraid that's out of the question," she said. She rose and turned towards the house; paused; and turned back to him.

"But you will come and see us before you go, won't you?"

Henry was staring, dumbfounded. And before he could reply she set off, skirt swishing, for the front door.

During this exchange Theodore had noticed a dove preening itself outside the garden-house, and had tiptoed over to attempt to feed it with a cucumber sandwich. It is quite possible that he had noticed nothing. But I had seen how her hands shook.

The realities of war gradually made themselves felt, even in Riverlaw. Uncle Vane reminisced about South Africa. It was hard to imagine him in uniform, shading his eyes to see the distant Boers in their big hats; harder still to believe that he, who was for ever telling Young Vane never to point even an unloaded gun at anyone, had actually shot at men (and probably killed some, for he was a fine shot). War, I realised, made people different; it made them act out of character. I was glad I was not a man.

Henry came to say goodbye the day before he set off for his depot. He bent to kiss me, then hovered in front of Venetia, exactly as if he were about to kiss her too but wasn't sure of his reception. She forestalled him by giving him a peck on the cheek and then briskly shaking his hand and wishing him good luck. Zinnia copied her. Of the girls, only Louie, when he bent down to her, put her arms round his neck and gave him a good hug.

"You'll be up there like an eagle," she said. Henry beamed.

"Will you loop the loop?" asked Young Vane.

"Hold on, I haven't even seen an aeroplane yet," he protested, laughing.

Theodore came up. He put his hand on Henry's shoulder, but said nothing.

Uncle Vane wrung him by the hand. "Good luck, m'boy, and always keep a pair of dry socks in your pocket."

"Goodbye, sir. I can't tell you how grateful I – "

"Not at all, not at all," and Uncle Vane patted him on the back and strolled towards the kitchen garden. The older girls had also retreated. Louie and I stayed beside him in case he felt they were all deserting him. It seemed a little unkind of them at what was obviously, for him, a very emotional moment.

Last of all came Aunt Emily. She gave Henry a long, troubled look and suddenly threw her arms round him and hugged him tight.

"You've been like a mother to me," he muttered.

Her mouth twisted. "Keep safe, my dear boy," she whispered, and disengaged herself. I was surprised to see that, as he walked across the lawn and through the gates while the whole family turned to wave him goodbye, Aunt Emily was crying.

A few days before I was due to go back to school, Giles Delmayne came home on embarkation leave. Charles Dawson, also, was to be at home for a last week before he and Bertram Seymour (now six feet tall, almost slim, and growing rapidly more talkative and self-confident) joined their new regiments. Charles was to be in the Northumberland Fusiliers, and Bertram in the Durham Light Infantry.

"At this rate," said Uncle Vane at luncheon, "by the time conscription comes there will be nobody left to conscript."

"You're not volunteering, are you, Father?" asked Louie anxiously.

"I would, like a shot," he said. "But I'm rather old, you know."

"Will the Admiral have to go?"

"Heaven forbid," broke in Aunt Emily. "If anything happened to him, what would become of *us*?"

Young Vane turned his head to stare at her. But Uncle Vane said quickly, "He's not well enough to go, his heart wouldn't stand it. Besides, he's older than I am." He smiled at his wife. "He's in the best place. He's a tough old bird – he may well see us all out."

"I think," said Aunt Emily thoughtfully, "we should have a party to give these young men a good send-off. Tuesday would do. And I'll write to Peregrine's mother to see if he can join us."

Zinnia scraped back her chair. "I'll take an invitation over to Riverpark straight away for Giles and Cedric," she announced.

"Someone's in a hurry here," observed Theodore. "Giles and Cedric, eh? Cedric's the lucky man, I take it?" He winked enormously at Louie and me.

"Oh, shut up, Theodore!"

"Perhaps you'll get a little time alone with Cedric – that'll be romantic."

Zinnia looked round the table in desperation. Everyone else was grinning. "Lizzie – come with me?"

So after a brief discussion of the time and nature of the party (a luncheon was decided upon because if the weather was fine we could play croquet afterwards) Zinnia and I, suitably washed and brushed, set off on foot for Riverpark.

It was drizzling intermittently, so we shared a big red-and-yellow striped umbrella. I had suggested walking, chiefly because I hoped we might be sent back in the motor-car. I said as much to Zinnia as we walked past the Old Hall orchard.

"What a good idea," she exclaimed. "Clever Lizzie! Now when we get there," her voice dropped to a thrilling, conspiratorial murmur, "you ask Cedric to take you to see the motor – you could say you want to look at the engine. That may well give them the idea of letting you have a ride in it. Meanwhile, I'll have a private word with Giles."

"Oh, but I want to see Giles too!"

"Oh, you will, of course. But you do understand, Lizzie, I simply must have as long as possible alone with him. It may be my last chance." I was so surprised by the intensity with which she said this that I protested no more. Last chance for what? I wondered.

"I have a little plan, you see," she went on earnestly. "I intend to be very direct. Remember that little poem Mother taught us once, 'He either fears his fate too much, or his deserts are small, Who dares not put it to the touch, to win or lose it all'? Well, I realise now that it's perfectly true. I need quite a long time with him, completely undisturbed. Dear, darling Lizzie, do you think you could keep Cedric away from us for as long as you possibly can bear to? Look at the car, the horses – anything. Just don't come back sooner than you absolutely must. And it's our little secret. Swear you won't give me away?"

I was mystified, but it obviously meant a great deal to her.

"I swear," I said obediently.

"Oh, darling Lizzie, you are a brick!" And she hugged me to her side, almost tipping the umbrella over in the process. "Oh, glory, mind my hat. Is it still on straight?"

"Yes, it looks lovely." It was her best summer straw, garlanded with blue flowers, and she had put her hair up. "You look terribly grown-up."

"I feel . . . mature." There was a sort of electric excitement about her. Her eyes shone. I noticed that her dress was Venetia's best white muslin.

I wondered whether Venetia knew.

10

". . . And that's the magneto," said Cedric. "It's always going wrong."

In the dim light of the Riverpark coachhouse, I gazed at it. I decided that machinery was beyond my powers to comprehend. However, I had made my pact with Zinnia.

"What's that pipe there?" I asked, indicating as Aunt Emily had taught me, with a graceful sweep of the whole hand. Ladies do not point.

"Erm . . . Albert Nibbs would know."

"Let's ask him."

"Can't. He's gone to join his ship."

"The headlamps are lovely and shiny. Are they gold?"

Cedric looked at me with contempt. "No, brass."

"Where's Nibbs?"

"He took Mother out calling in the brougham, before you came."

"Why didn't he take the motor-car?"

"He's waiting for a spare part from the makers. Something to do with the carburettor, I think."

"It's always going wrong, isn't it?" I said, sorely disappointed that I was not to be given a ride in it.

Cedric's glistening lower lip bulged defensively. "That's not true. And when the engine does go, it's splendid." He turned away. "We've been here ages. Let's go back and find the others."

"Oh, not quite yet," I said desperately. "Will you show me . . ." I mentally surveyed the Riverpark demesne. What could we look at in the rain? ". . . the conservatory? I haven't seen it for ages. There must be lots of lovely new flowers," I gushed.

"Oh, very well," said Cedric with a bad grace. "Come on."

"Let's walk to it through the garden." I was afraid that if we approached it through the house we might disturb Zinnia executing her Plan, whatever it was. But the conservatory had a door on to the lawn that faced the river.

"What, in the rain?"

"You can share the umbrella. We can look at the river on the way, and see the moorhens."

"Moorhens are boring."

"I think they're so elegant, they look as if they're dressed by Worth."

I was rather pleased with this little piece of sophistication, but Cedric looked blank. Aunt Letitia, I reflected scornfully, had probably never heard of Worth, whose name I had gleaned from a study of Aunt Emily's fashion magazines.

"Oh, come on. I'll carry the umbrella. Do let's get back to Zinnia," he added with a hint of desperation. I remembered guiltily how sweetly she had asked him, as soon as we had entered the hall, to show me the motor-car. He had done it to please her. Nobody, I thought grumpily, would have done it for me alone.

"I want to see the conservatory," I insisted.

So we plodded over the soggy lawn. I noticed that the grass edges were not cut as neatly as usual. I dawdled down to the river in the drizzle, Cedric perforce going with me because of the umbrella. The birds had sensibly stayed at home; none were visible.

I turned back towards the house. The conservatory, an imposing affair with an arched glass roof high enough to cover a small palm-tree, stuck out from the far end of the house. Its white fretted parapet, like the edge of a lacy doily, was surmounted at the corners and the finial of the arch by wooden spearheads. The door was on the side farthest from us. All one could see of the inside from this distance was a mass of greenery, climbing up almost to the mop-head of the palm.

"What does Zinnia like best?" asked Cedric. "I mean . . . If one wanted to give her a lovely surprise, what would give her the most pleasure?"

I stopped; surprised, touched, and (knowing Zinnia's opinion of him) deeply troubled. In that moment I almost liked Cedric, and I felt very sorry for him.

"I don't know. She likes fashion magazines, and sketching. Perhaps some good oil-paints, something like that."

He stood there in the rain, brooding over this. I didn't think it was good for him to brood. No present from Cedric, of all people, would cut any ice with Zinnia. I wondered how I could convey this to him without hurting his feelings, but I couldn't think of a way, so I gave up trying.

I hurried to the conservatory, hoping he would follow. I walked along its side, peering through the wall of leaves. Beyond the steamy glass with its runnels of raindrops, they looked weirdly distorted, as if under the sea. The rain pattered on the roof, and behind the sound of the rain was another sound, an intermittent, strange moaning. I came to a gap in the plants, and saw something move beyond them.

"Come to the door," called Cedric. "You'll get soaked." He was striding over the grass towards the other side, where the door was.

"Cedric," I called. "Don't go in!"

"Don't be stupid!"

I ran back, panting and dripping with rain, and grabbed his hand. "You mustn't go in there." I heard my voice rise. "Please don't."

"Let go of me. What on earth's the matter with you?" And he wrenched his hand away, rounded the corner to the door, and threw it open.

There was a second's dreadful silence. Peering round him, I felt the wave of foetid heat, and saw among the greenery the end of a battered leather chaise-longue, the soles of Giles's shiny shoes, the bunched white muslin, the pearly flesh of a naked hip and thigh twined around him.

"Oh, God," exclaimed Cedric, and slammed the door so violently that the whole wall of glass rattled. "Women, I hate women, horrible, disgusting objects," he howled.

He dropped the umbrella and ran across the lawn to the kitchen garden, the rain darkening his tweed shoulders.

My hair felt wet and my dress damp. The umbrella lolled, obscenely gay. I picked it up. Pursuit and comfort of Cedric was out of the question. I just wanted to get away.

I trotted round the house to the front door, careful not to look back.

The hall was deserted. Looming out of the shadows at its far end, the tiger glowered at me.

"Ugh, you're horrible, I hate you," I said, and burst into tears.

11

On the way home, Zinnia and I avoided each other's eyes.

As we crested the rise out of the Riverpark grounds she turned round, surveyed the house, the garden, the river, and the slopes of the green bowl they nestled in, gave a long and slightly shaky sigh, and breathed, "That's the man for me!"

"I'm going to marry him, Lizzie," she added as we turned back to the lane.

"Has he proposed?" I enquired primly.

"Not yet." Silence. "But he will."

I couldn't refrain from conveying my disapproval. "You certainly put your fate to the touch, didn't you?"

Zinnia gave me a sharp look. Suddenly she broke into giggles, and then threw back her head and laughed and laughed as if she would never stop. I couldn't see anything to laugh about, and there was something about her laughter that frightened me.

Eventually, she must have noticed my silence, because she glanced at me and calmed down.

"Don't tell Mother," she said, and added in an odd, uncertain voice, "We're going to live happy ever after, and I am going to have nothing around me that isn't beautiful, and Giles is the most beautiful of all . . . Oh, Lizzie, life is wonderful, and I am so, so, so in love!"

I trudged on, wishing I were anywhere else. And much later, as we neared the Old Hall:

"Don't tell anyone, Lizzie. Please don't tell."

"All right," I said, as if it were a concession, though I had been so shocked that I don't think I could have brought myself to tell even Louie. I was desolated. I loved Zinnia, but an unbridgeable gulf had opened between us. I felt desperately sorry for Cedric. On the whole, unlikeable though he was, I felt more kinship with his feelings than with hers. I was afraid for her, all the same. Afraid, above all, that Aunt Emily might guess what she had done.

However, when we got back to the Old Hall life seemed to be going on as usual. Venetia was riding with Charles Dawson, Theodore had disappeared on some private mission, Young Vane was feeding the hens. Aunt Emily swooped on Louie and me with instructions to dust the drawing-room.

I said nothing. I felt shaky and apprehensive, as if I had just been caught in an earthquake. For once, the dullness of domestic chores seemed almost welcome.

Almost every day after that, Giles came over to call on Zinnia and take her out. He and Zinnia could scarcely tear their eyes away from each other. I thought it was sickening. I was filled with distaste and apprehension, but Aunt Emily seemed delighted. She made a great fuss of Giles, patting his golden head when she passed behind his chair.

She scarcely seemed to notice – probably she didn't know – that Venetia spent a great deal of time with Charles Dawson. They often met outside the gate, and went off on a walk somewhere; and when we were picking fruit or vegetables for preserving, I would sometimes look up and Charles would be there next to her, picking away, chatting and laughing.

One evening we carried her harp out to the orchard and she played for us under the stars, her white dress glimmering among the leaves, her white hand sweeping the strings, the notes fluttering and drifting like falling petals. I was sent reluctantly in to bed after the first piece, and on the way I saw a man's figure leaning against the orchard wall, his

arms folded. It was Charles. When he saw me he put a
finger to his lips. I didn't split on him. I liked Charles.
He was bright and kind, and I couldn't imagine him doing
anything he shouldn't.

Louie had abandoned *The Passionate Potato-Picker* and
was deep into a new work entitled *Is There Life On Mars?*,
so I spent much of my time grooming the horses with
Young Vane (I was particularly proud of perfecting the
authentic hiss between the teeth as I polished their flanks,
just like Bob). I was also kept busy in the kitchen helping
Hannah with preparations for the party. I cleaned a whole
trunkful of silver, and beat egg-whites with a wire whisk
in a big copper bowl till my arms ached.

"You're more use than them three lazy girls put together,"
said Cook, getting up from her rocking-chair to pop another
home-made toffee in my mouth, by way of reward. I began
to cheer up.

On the day of the party the sun shone, and the older
girls twittered with excitement as they climbed into their
best pale, silk-sashed dresses, fastened the fiddly rows
of hooks-and-eyes down each other's backs, and pinned
flowers into their carefully-coiled hair. Louie and I brushed
each other's hair and tied our hair-ribbons in big bows.
In the deserted dining-room the trifles, hedgehogged with
slivers of blanched almonds and crystallised cherries, looked
as appetising as children's paintings. I ran a proprietorial
finger round each cut-glass rim, and sucked it for the last
drops of cream. Young Vane sidled round the door in
his kilt.

"Don't touch," I said, and he grinned, seized a sugar
biscuit, and dashed out. I was about to pursue when a carriage clopped and rumbled through the gateway, followed
by another. Skirts rustled and feet hurried down the stairs
to the front door.

There were about a dozen of us. The girls fluttered round
the lawn like pastel butterflies. The young men beamed,

running their fingers round the inside of their stiff collars. Cries of triumph or mock-dismay accompanied each hollow click of a croquet-mallet; gales of laughter rose at intervals from the garden-house, where those who were not playing lounged with tall glasses of sarsaparilla at their elbows. Louie sat on the fringe of the group, saying little, gathering material (she told me in confidence) for her next book. Cedric (making his first, obviously unwilling, appearance since the scene in the Riverpark conservatory) hovered silently nearby, looking disapproving; this was so like his normal behaviour that I don't think anyone but me noticed that he was even sourer than usual. He avoided Zinnia, and pointedly did not look at me. I felt both relieved and resentful; had I not tried to save him?

Luckily, perhaps, Young Vane and I were kept busy dashing to the kitchen with messages for Cook, and hither and thither on last-minute missions for Hannah and Aunt Emily. ("Be a darling and count the guest-towels in the bathroom, dear," came at a particularly inopportune moment when Peregrine was reaching the punchline of a riveting account of Theodore's latest triumph on the school rugger-field.)

Peregrine had arrived in one of the first carriages. For a moment I had hardly recognised him, nor he me. Then he leapt out with a joyful shout of "Bundle!" He seized me under the armpits, lifted me off the ground and danced me up and down. I was speechless with happiness, astonished to be remembered and liked by this tall, slim, handsome creature with a sunburnt face and the level, direct, laughing gaze I remembered. He was almost a man. I hadn't thought of Theodore as anything but a large boy, although they were the same age.

As Theodore ran down the drive towards us, cowlick flapping, Peregrine put me down and another distraction arrived in the form of Madge, modish in lettuce green, accompanied by a man of about thirty who was obviously her brother, Sir Rednall, who had never crossed the threshold of the Old Hall before. "Aunt Emily'll be all over him," I thought.

In spite of myself I stared. I had never met anyone with a title before, and quite expected him to bear some distinguishing mark. But I was rather disappointed. He was tall and pale, with small, light blue eyes in a face that looked all right from the front, but seen sideways had a receding chin. He had straight, straw-coloured hair like Madge's, and long thin arms and legs and a rather awkward, rolling walk. He peeled off his driving-gloves to reveal huge, pale hands with thick fingers – so different from the fine, sunburnt hands of the Delmaynes. He looked at Venetia and Zinnia – at their pink cheeks and sparkling eyes lit up by excitement – with a bored, languid, almost critical air.

He thawed slightly when Uncle Vane came out and talked to him. He answered in the quick, clipped voice that is often an affectation of the unselfconfident. Sometimes his sentences ended in a little dry cough. Aunt Emily made him partner Venetia in the first croquet match. I saw my cousin give a swift, rueful glance up at Charles as she bent to place her ball. Aunt Emily, too, saw the look, and frowned.

But soon there was a greater distraction, which put even Peregrine and Sir Rednall out of my head.

It happened when almost everyone else was absorbed in watching a close finish on the croquet-lawn; Charles and Theodore slogging it out at the last hoop, while their partners squeaked in horror or admiration at every shot, and everyone else cheered or gasped, as appropriate. Something made me glance at the house.

In the distance, through the open front door, I saw Zinnia's flounced skirt disappear, Giles's straight back follow, and the drawing-room door close firmly behind him.

Blind horror seized me. Oh, God, I prayed, don't let them do it again. Above all, don't let Aunt Emily find them. I looked at Cedric, on the other side of the lawn. He was gazing at the house. He looked green and wretched.

As inconspicuously as possible, I walked round the lawn behind the other spectators and stood beside him.

"Try not to worry," I muttered. "They wouldn't dare do it here."

He shot me such a look of fury and misery as I hope never to see again. I retreated. Aunt Emily was nowhere to be seen. I quaked.

"I'm going to blast you into the lupins!" roared Charles, taking aim.

"Not that, anything but that!" quavered Theodore, who was hugely enjoying himself – he was an ace at croquet and would probably win, despite whatever punishment Charles could mete out to his ball.

After a few minutes the drawing-room door opened. Giles and Zinnia stole out, holding hands, wearing seraphic smiles. Cedric plunged his hands in his pockets and turning his back on the match, stared blindly at the hedge. I thought wretchedly, How beautiful she looks.

Still holding hands, they came out to the garden and made straight for Uncle Vane, who was watching on the sidelines, gold watchchain across stomach, thumbs in the armholes of his waistcoat. Giles murmured something in his ear. Startled, he turned and followed them back to the house. Cedric, who had seen all this, looked sick. I was mystified.

But all became clear towards the end of luncheon when Uncle Vane produced an unaccustomed bottle of wine (hoarded since before the war), poured glasses for anyone over the age of sixteen, and held his up to propose two toasts: first to those guests who were off to the war, and then to the engaged couple.

Cedric raised his glass with the rest, and his thick red lips smiled, but his eyes did not.

Aunt Emily (who had been let into the secret before the meal) hugged the future bride and bridegroom, and wiped away a tear with her lace-edged handkerchief while almost everyone else was exclaiming at once.

"They're going to live at Riverpark," she told Sir Rednall, on her other side. "You know it, of course. A fine house – hounds often meet there."

Sir Rednall, who had preserved his customary silence, gave a faint smile that turned into a cough.

"Cedric, Cedric," called Louie across the room, "How d'you like being our brother-in-law?" And when he muttered "Excuse me," and blundered out, "What's the matter with him?" she demanded.

But nobody took any notice.

Aunt Emily, eyes moist, looked across at her husband. "This is a great day for us all," she said quietly, under cover of the general hubbub.

"Why, certainly," he smiled. "A grand chap."

She gave a little nod. "And the farm."

He seemed a trifle taken aback. "You haven't been worrying yourself about that, have you?" he said, quite low.

"No need to, now."

Because Giles was rejoining his ship the very next day, he and Zinnia drove off after luncheon to break the news to his parents and ask the Admiral's blessing. I couldn't help feeling rather sorry for Zinnia at having Aunt Letitia for a mother-in-law; but nothing could mar her happiness. She was radiant, sparkling, ecstatic. She pirouetted on the lawn, spinning round so that her full skirts billowed about her and the ends of her blue sash flew out.

When they had gone, the party continued. Cedric reappeared and glumly took up a mallet. Louie engaged Sir Rednall in conversation about life on distant planets. The twins challenged Cedric and Madge to a match. Charles and Venetia followed my aunt and uncle into the house. A few minutes later, having need of my forgotten handkerchief, I followed them.

The drawing-room door was not quite closed. From behind it came Venetia's voice. I was struck by its distraught, pleading note, so unlike Venetia, so different from the buoyant atmosphere of the day.

"But, Mother, you already know him nearly as well as you know Giles – "

"It's not at all the same," came Aunt Emily's voice. "I am extremely sorry, Charles, and we have nothing against you personally – "

"Well, you *have*, you must have," protested Venetia, near tears.

" – Let me finish, please," Aunt Emily's voice was rising. "The Delmaynes are an extremely old family, and I am afraid it's out of the question that they should ever be connected with a family who are in trade."

"I'm not ashamed of my family," came Charles's voice, very quietly.

"Nobody's saying you should be. But where marriage is concerned – "

I heard no more because at that instant I felt a heavy hand on my shoulder, and jumped with guilt. It was Uncle Vane.

"Cut along, Mary-Jane," he said, with a face like thunder.

I scuttled upstairs.

". . . And they've got to wait five years," ended Louie impressively out of the darkness that same night. "Mother said she must never see him again, but Father suggested five years. I think he quite likes Charles and couldn't bear not to give him an outside chance. But they're forbidden to meet for all that time."

"But that's so unfair!" I gasped, from the other bed. "Poor, good, sweet Venetia! And Charles is a most parfit gentil knight," for Louie had been reading stories from Malory to me after lights out.

"I think," offered Louie in her shrewd way, "that Mother hopes she'll get tired of him and want to marry Sir Rednall."

I snorted. "He's not a patch on Charles. Charles is truly, truly nice, and he truly loves her."

"I know. But he is in trade. His father has shoe-shops in Newcastle and Sunderland. I bet you wouldn't like to spend your life with someone who pushes shoes on to other people's smelly feet."

"If I really loved someone, I wouldn't care what they did," I whispered defiantly.

"If she married Sir Rednall, she'd have a title, and an absolutely huge mansion – oodles bigger than Riverpark, even."

"But he hasn't asked her. She's only just met him. And she loves Charles!"

"But don't you see, it simply won't do," said Louie, sounding so like her mother that I hardly knew whether to laugh or cry.

Footsteps sounded on the stairs.

"Sh, here's one of them," her voice sank to a whisper. "If it's Venetia, we'd better try to cheer her up. It is hard on her, especially the very day Zinnia and Giles . . . Bad luck, Venetia darling," she added aloud as the door opened.

In the light from the nightlight I saw Venetia's pink sash glimmer as she crossed the room. Her head was bent and one hand shielded her eyes. She did not reply.

12

The next three days were terrible.

First, Giles went off to the war.

"Couldn't I go to London to be near him until his ship sails?" Zinnia begged her parents at breakfast the morning after the party.

"Out of the question," replied Uncle Vane shortly. "Young ladies who value their reputation cannot walk alone in the streets of London."

"I've saved some of my pocket-money. I could live in a boarding-house for a few – "

"No."

She saw Giles off at the station and came back in floods of tears.

A little later Venetia disappeared without telling anyone where she was going, which was unusual. She returned late in the afternoon, looking very white, and locked herself in her room. Charles, too, had gone.

Venetia told me, much later, that she had gone alone to Newcastle, and waited in Grey Street, under the pillars of the Theatre Royal portico, for the regiment to pass by on their way to the ship. There had been a great crowd, waving their hats in the air and shouting and crying, and a band that played "Goodbye, Dolly, I must leave you", and she had had to stand on tiptoe to be able to see anything, and the soldiers had marched past so quickly that she hadn't seen Charles until he had almost passed her. "I don't think he saw me!" she said. "Lizzie, all that way and I don't think he saw me!" and she put her face in her hands.

I stroked her soft brown hair. "Doesn't matter," I tried to comfort her. "He loves you, and one day you'll marry him. You must!"

"I wish I'd run away with him," she muttered – dear, law-abiding Venetia, who wouldn't even borrow her sister's hairpins without asking permission.

"Why didn't you?"

"I did suggest it. But Charles said he wasn't going to do anything that would divide the family, however much we both longed for it. He said we must do what's right, and not make anyone unhappy."

"Except *you*," I said savagely, and she patted my hand.

After that Zinnia and Venetia spent a great deal of time shut in their rooms, weeping. It must have been doubly awful for Venetia, because at least Zinnia had her wedding to look forward to as soon as all the arrangements could be made and Giles got enough leave.

I felt pretty miserable myself, because Peregrine had gone home without even saying goodbye to me. Theodore took him to the station in the trap. The fact that they had gone shooting, forgotten the time, and had to sprint back half a mile back to the Old Hall, bedecked with guns and rabbits, in order to catch the train his father was meeting – all this was obviously a mitigating circumstance; but I couldn't help feeling sad and hurt, though I knew that there was absolutely no reason why he should want to say a special goodbye to someone so much younger.

Theodore, too, obviously missed him, and sloped off, head down and hands in pockets, on his own devices. Louie scribbled away furiously at *Is There Life On Mars?* murmuring, "Don't stop me – don't stop me – my Muse is on top form" whenever I approached. Zinnia took the trap without asking and went over to see Madge. Even Young Vane was busy, trying to catch up with the school-work he should have done at the start of the holidays.

I took comfort and refuge in the house itself. Alone, I crept through the secret door and up to the apple-room, to munch in melancholy through a tasteless, wrinkled leftover from the autumn, and gaze through the cobwebbed window at the sunlit triangle of Riverlaw where little Mrs Hothersall staggered away from the pump, bent sideways by the weight of a full bucket. I spent solitary hours changing the points in the train-room, often knocking my head on the slanting beams, and in playing Patience with the dog-eared cards in the schoolroom, warmed by the log fire and protected from the onslaughts of the world by the panelled walls. I discovered a little cache of toys in an oak box behind the drawing-room sofa, and set up a family of gentle-faced rag dolls in crinolines and dusty pantaloons. I crept on to the great four-poster, pulled the curtains tight, and imagined myself in a cabin at sea, bouncing on the waves. In short, I reverted, as ill or unhappy children do, to the habits and consolations of an earlier period of my childhood. But just to be in the Old Hall was its own consolation. I would rather be miserable there than cheerful anywhere else.

It was Hannah who, coming into the room with a carpet-sweeper, diagnosed my condition and chivvied me downstairs to offer to help Aunt Emily. My aunt's mouth tightened when she saw me; she clearly had other things on her mind. But she set me to stand in for her Lady Bountiful visits. It made me feel quite important.

I trotted several times to the village delivering soup in a milk-can for Mrs Hothersall, disgusting, malodorous scraps for the postman's hens, and pies and basins of trifle to assorted poor, who seemed pleased. "Thank your auntie for them," they said; I was mildly surprised to learn that everyone knew who I was. I encountered one or two of the village children, and greeted them politely; Dick responded with "Morning, Miss Lizzie," but Ivy, now a Junoesque creature with blonde ringlets, a large bust and a daringly short and tattered blue skirt, put out her tongue at me and giggled, which so disturbed me that I walked past her with my nose in the air, trying to ignore her taunt, "I know something you don't know!" Although it was familiar from many a playground battle in Newcastle, I felt it was childish and stupid and should not be addressed by someone like her to someone like me.

One night, three or four days after Giles and Charles had gone, I found it hard to sleep. The Delmayne girls had long since come to bed. Slowly the light around the curtains faded. I whispered "Louie!" into the darkness, but got no reply; only her peaceful breathing.

I lay awake, wondering where Charles and Giles and Henry were now, what their uniforms were like, whether they were in danger. I wished I were a man, to fight, too, for England. I hoped desperately that the war would end before Theodore and Peregrine were old enough to volunteer. Sir Rednall didn't seem to be going; but perhaps he had to look after his estates.

I wondered what the Old Hall would be like without Zinnia and, eventually, Venetia, always supposing she did not die of a broken heart before the five years were up. I would miss them terribly. I already missed Peregrine more than wild horses would have forced me to admit. I still felt the dreadful sourness of Cedric's distress, and the unfairness of Venetia's enforced wait before she could marry Charles. Most troubling of all, I was still haunted by a mental picture, like a photograph pushed in front of my eyes again and again, of Giles and Zinnia in the Riverpark conservatory. Suddenly, in the space of a few days, the world had begun to fall apart.

All at once I was aware of an almost infinitesimal noise from Zinnia's door, and in the same instant was aware that it was the door-handle turning. I froze.

The door opened and a dark figure came through. From its height I knew that it was Zinnia. She wore outdoor clothes and lugged a suitcase and a Gladstone bag. She tiptoed over to the landing door and in order to open it she put the case down gently on the rug. In the nightlight's glow I saw her stretch and contract her long fingers; the case must have been almost too heavy for her. She was wearing her best gauntleted suede gloves.

It was on the tip of my tongue to whisper, "Where are you going?" I was dying for someone to talk to, and consumed with curiosity. To this day I don't know why I didn't. There was, of course, the gap between our ages; she was old enough to be a married lady. But it went deeper than this. I already realised how differently Zinnia looked at people and things, unconsciously knew what a gulf lay between us. I could never be a risk-taker; to her, risks were life-blood. Perhaps that was why I loved her; beautiful, fascinating, exotic Zinnia, who was what I could never be.

So I lay there like a log of wood while Zinnia eased the door-handle round (with a worried look at sleeping Louie when a floor-plank creaked under her feet), opened the door inch by inch, and came back for the big leather suitcase.

Before she picked it up she stood for a moment, put her gloved fingers to her lips, and blew a silent kiss to Louie and me. And a minute later she was gone.

13

Apart from Uncle Vane, whom nothing and nobody could frighten, the person who came best out of the brouhaha after Zinnia's disappearance was Theodore. While Aunt Emily practically had hysterics and Venetia laid her head on her arms and wept, he stayed steady as a rock.

It was he who rode to the station with Bob. Venetia had found a note pinned to Zinnia's unslept-on pillow; infuriatingly, it gave no information but read, "Dearest darlings, have no fear, I will look after myself. Masses and masses of love and kisses always, Z." While she was showing it to her dumbfounded parents at the breakfast-table, Bob came to the open window, the roses dripping round his ruddy face as he leaned in with the news that the trap and the old grey, Starlight, were missing.

Without fuss, Theodore stood up. "She might have got the night train. Saddle up Copper and Prince, Bob, and I'll go with you to see the station-master."

Cravenly, I said nothing. But what could I have told them? Only that she had indeed gone.

Venetia, in tears still, was dispatched to see what clothes she had taken. Uncle Vane rode over to Riverpark, and came back inside an hour, looking dejected.

"Letitia knows nothing," I overheard him telling Aunt Emily. "Silly woman kept saying, 'But what a flighty thing to do!' It dawned on me that she doesn't entirely approve of young Zinnia. As good as said that she was too young to marry. She could be right, you know, my dear."

"Oh . . ." wailed Aunt Emily. "Poor, poor darling – all I care about is getting her back safe! Surely Giles must have arranged it with her. He must have led her astray. We must contact his commanding officer immediately!"

"I don't think we'd better do that," said Uncle Vane gravely. "We don't want to ruin his career. Wouldn't do little Zinnia any good if he were drummed out of the Navy."

"The Admiral – "

"My brother is in no state to be worried about anything," said Uncle Vane sadly. "I had to promise Letitia I wouldn't tell him. She told me Giles's ship is already at sea, but she gave me his postal address. I'll write straight away. God knows what I can say – don't want to worry the poor feller if he knows nothing about it."

Theodore appeared at the front door, wiping his face on his sleeve. Louie and I had been lurking outside the dining-room, listening; now we followed him in. He slumped on to a chair.

"News," he said. "They took single tickets to London. We brought the trap home."

"They?" demanded Uncle Vane, and "London!" exclaimed Aunt Emily, aghast.

Memory jogged me. "She once said," I told them, "that she would – "

A shadow fell across the door. It was Sir Rednall, sweaty and dishevelled.

"Madge has disappeared," he said in his clipped voice. He sat down, uninvited, and broke into coughing. As Venetia pushed a glass of water over to him, Theodore looked up.

"Zinnia, too. We know where they've gone," he said. "At least, we know they went to London. Come with me to find them?"

Aunt Emily leapt up. "You're too young, Theodore – "

Uncle Vane put a restraining hand on her arm. "Sit down, Rednall," he said. I thought that was funny because Rednall was already sitting down. "I can't go, because of the farm. And you can't very well go, Emily, because of – " and he inclined his head in the direction of Venetia, who was busy patting Rednall on the back, which had no effect at all on his cough.

"I think they've gone to join the Army," I piped up. Nobody took any notice.

"I'm afraid she may have gone after Giles," moaned Venetia.

"With Madge as chaperone," Aunt Emily brightened a little.

"That seems the most likely," agreed my uncle. He turned to Sir Rednall. "I'm writing to him today, and if he has no news of them, we'll think again."

But, of course, he had not. And because he was already at sea, in a distant theatre of war the location of which he was not allowed to reveal, his distressed reply took weeks to reach Riverlaw; and by then the trail, if there had ever been one, was cold. Letters from him kept arriving, addressed to Zinnia. They sat on the hall table, a continual reminder of her absence.

Rednall, too, heard nothing. He was always riding over to see if there was any news. Aunt Emily went to see his mother – all dressed up, Louie said, in a stunning peachbloom coat and skirt and a new hat from Fenwick's French Department in Newcastle. But it did no good; Lady Carroun was distant and formal, and said it was all very regrettable but what could one expect in wartime, and doubtless they would return soon. She didn't even offer Aunt Emily a cup of tea.

Uncle Vane wrote to possible contacts, and to the London police. Everyone speculated endlessly. Aunt Emily was distracted with anxiety; Zinnia was under age and, of course, had no bank account. She had taken her few bits of jewellery, which were not worth much. Rednall said that Madge had taken hers, which might be valuable, or again, they might not; nothing in their house had ever been insured. She had, he thought, very little money.

I knew all this from Louie's letters, for the day after the discovery of the girls' flight I had to go back to Newcastle for the beginning of the school term.

It was an anxious time. My mother was listless and querulous by turns. I couldn't bring myself to tell my parents of Zinnia's disappearance; paradoxically, I felt too close to it, and could not shake off a feeling of guilt that I had hidden the little I knew. I had confided in Louie before I left (though I could not bring myself to tell even her what I had seen in the conservatory), but she had wrinkled her brow and advised, "I wouldn't say anything. It would only distress the grown-ups more."

In fact, Aunt Emily had told my mother in a letter that Zinnia had gone, but my parents never spoke of it, so I had to endure my guilt alone. My father seemed to take more trouble to talk to me, but he worked long hours at his office and usually came home late and exhausted. I lay in bed at night, unable to sleep for thinking of Zinnia. My mental pictures of London were based on a recent horrified reading of *Oliver Twist*. I visualised her in a Dickensian slum, penniless and starving in the attic of a filthy tenement. Dear God, I prayed, screwing up my closed eyes and digging my nails into my palms, Don't let her die. Make Giles come back and marry her, quickly, and then everything will be all right. Dear God, let the war end soon, next week, tomorrow, so that he can come back.

But the war, far from ending, was churning on in the waterlogged trenches of Flanders. The deaths had hardly begun.

Louie, bless her, wrote regularly to cheer me up. Her letters were tantalisingly short, and mostly about the birth of calves, the horse sales, and other farming landmarks. One day she wrote that her English teacher had marked her latest short story alpha plus and said she ought to be an author when she grew up. We had always both assumed that this was what she would be anyway, but Louie was thrilled to have it confirmed by Authority. I could tell that from now on, much homework-time would be spent on *Is There Life On Mars?* and its successors.

The next letter brought even more thrilling news. A postcard had arrived from Zinnia! It would not have taken nearly so long, Louie explained, if Zinnia had not omitted to add 'Northumberland' to the address. It had been all round the south of England. Worse, there was no return address. All it said was, "Why haven't you answered my letter? Oh, perfidious family! No word from Giles, either. I am best bandage-roller in London. Write SOON, eternally yours, Z."

From this slender evidence the family deduced that she and Madge were working as V.A.D.s in a London military hospital. They must have falsified their ages (oh, naughty Zinnia!). Rednall and Theodore had gone to London to find them and bring them home, presumably in disgrace.

Three days after this news reached me, I arrived at Riverlaw to spend half-term there, because my mother thought I was looking peaky (all that lost sleep, no doubt) and believed the country air would do me good.

Venetia and Louie met me at the station. Venetia looked sad and thin, with dark smudges under her eyes. Louie, on the other hand, was running to puppy-fat; she was never going to be tall, but had grown outward. She looked pasty and exhausted.

The house seemed as quiet as a cemetery without Zinnia and Theodore. Uncle Vane was busy on the farm; his hinds depleted by the number who had volunteered for the forces, he had begun to do much more himself and was limiting his hunting to the unheard-of maximum of one day a week. He looked tired. So did Aunt Emily, who was clearly on edge.

When Aunt Emily sent Louie and me up to the doctor's house later that day to renew her supply of embrocation,

Louie confided that there had been a row about who should go to London. Uncle Vane could not leave the farm; Venetia had been forbidden because she was a girl – Louie thought that her mother was afraid Venetia would try to meet Charles in London.

("Is that where he is?"

"No, but he's training at Aldershot in Hampshire. It's not far past London on the map. Henry's near London, too, but he isn't allowed to tell us where. All letters from the forces are censored, you know.")

Aunt Emily wanted to go and find Zinnia herself, and maintained that Theodore was too young. But Uncle Vane won the argument. Theodore, of course, was dying to go and had gone off with Rednall in barely-concealed triumph.

"What's Sir Rednall really like?" I couldn't quite bring myself to omit the 'Sir', which impressed me a great deal.

"Oh . . . languid. Sort of . . . neglectful," Louie replied. "He's got a weak chest, so perhaps he can't help it. But his house is so tremendously grand and romantic. You must have seen it – classical beauty, pillars and balustrades and so forth. I'd just love to see it by moonlight."

"Have you been there?"

"Oh, yes, we're very thick with Rednall now. His ancestors go back to Charlemagne, you know. Mother has even met Lady C. Don't think they got on very well, though. She's very stiff and cold. Positively corpse-like, really. Luckily the house is so huge we usually don't meet her."

"Is it beautiful inside?"

"Bare and freezing cold, and smells of damp. And there's not much furniture. Perhaps they're selling it off, bit by bit, like Mother," she added with undisguised relish. "She sold a silver sugar-bowl in Newcastle last week."

"Isn't that Bert the postman going into our gate?" I asked as we began the gentle descent back, past the picturesque cottages round the village green.

"Our" gate. I realised my mistake as I said it. But Louie said nothing.

In that instant I admitted to myself that my heart would never be in Newcastle. It was here. This was my home.

It was indeed Bert. He had come up to the Old Hall with a piece of news.

All through the war Bert became a kind of sybil to the village. He knew the contents of every telegram before the recipient saw it, and we got to know by the look on his face if anyone in the village had received one. (Telegrams! For decades afterwards, I could scarcely bear to look at even their small orange envelopes.)

When we reached the front door Aunt Emily met us to break the news gently. Vin Baggs had been killed on the Somme.

I thought of his carroty hair and his red ears that I would never see again, and remembered his last words to me. He had died for England. It didn't seem right or just that he could never be rewarded for going to fight for his country – for us. All we had given in exchange was tea and black bullets and a pair of socks. I couldn't take in the finality of death. Vin, who had ridden his sledge like a bronco, who could sky a cricket-ball like nobody else. It couldn't be true.

That evening the sky clouded over. Rain began to beat on the old curved tiles above the sloping ceilings of Louie's room. It ran in archipelagoes down the window-panes so that the drooping roses outside looked as if they were under the sea. The door of Zinnia's room stood open. I kept hoping unreasonably that she would emerge from the shadows within.

From the day-nursery, three rooms away, came the faint, irregular ping of water dropping into buckets and pans. The sounds seemed like nails in the coffin of sleep. I tried to picture Vin and felt as though I would never sleep again. I couldn't quite remember his face.

"Why doesn't Uncle get the roof mended?" I asked Louie irritably as darkness began to close in.

"It's not him, it's the Admiral," she said. "He pays for repairs of buildings. But I suppose he hasn't been well enough to see to everything. Father says he needs a bailiff, but he won't get one. He says Giles will do it all when the war ends."

"But what has the Admiral to do with mending your roof?"

"He owns this house and the farm," said Louie in an odd, off-hand manner. "Didn't you know?"

I stared. Marooned inside the noise of the rain the room seemed very still. "But I thought – "

"Well, you thought wrong, didn't you? Father is only the younger son. Our grandfather didn't leave him anything in his will. The whole estate – Riverpark, the Old Hall, the village, the farms – is always entailed on the eldest son, and he looks after his brothers and sisters, if any. It's always been like that."

"What does entailed mean?"

"Oh, don't be stupid," burst out Louie.

I was grievously offended, hurt and taken aback at this attack from her, of all people. But it was so rare for her to be bad-tempered that after a few puzzled and miserable moments I realised that her thoughts must be full of Vin, and the rain, and the leaking roof, and the horrible war.

I held my tongue.

14

The day before I had to go back to school, I heard the sound of wheels bowling through the gateway. From all over the house came the noise of feet tearing downstairs and out to the garden. Aunt Emily, all flying pink silk, got there first, panting, as I was still rattling down from the schoolroom.

"Did you find them? Where are they? What have you done with them?" she demanded, her normally cooing voice sharp with anger, disappointment and fear.

"Give us a chance, Mother!" protested Theodore, jumping down from the trap as I burst out of the front doorway. "We've had a bit of a time, you know!"

"Did you find them?"

"Yes, but it took days. Come in, Red, and have a cup of tea before I take you back." I was amazed at his self-confidence. I realised later that those few days on his own with languid, indecisive Rednall had given him his first taste of freedom and independence. He had learnt to make decisions. Until now, it would always have been Aunt Emily who offered tea and home comforts. Until now, Theodore had been, if not exactly a child, a vassal of the house. Offering tea was an emblem of a larger development.

For a second Aunt Emily's lips pursed. Then, she beamed, shook Rednall's limp hand and swept Theodore into her embrace.

"Lizzie, dear, run and tell Cook to make tea," she said.

Zinnia and Madge had been tracked down through the headquarters of the Voluntary Aid Detachment organisation in Grosvenor Gardens. They were working in a temporary private hospital that had been started in a big house in Queen's Gate by a committee of noble ladies, one of whom was Lady Kerr, a distant acquaintance of Lady Carroun. The girls had gone to call on her the morning they had arrived in London, and she had immediately sent them along as volunteers.

They were being fed, clothed – in the prim, low-forehead caps and voluminous aprons of their new calling – and housed in a nearby building that had been commandeered as a nurses' hostel, but they had almost no money. The glamour of London dress shops had been too much for Zinnia, especially. She had rashly decked herself out at Derry & Toms, and was scrimping in order to write to Giles – who had not, of course, received any of her letters until weeks after they were written.

Aunt Emily's rosebud mouth was pursed tight, and I could see that she was being quietly furious about Lady Carroun's failure to contact her acquaintance, Lady Kerr, to ask whether she had heard from the girls. Aunt Emily, I knew, would have turned every stone to find them. But she said nothing about this while Rednall was with us, and I suppose Lady C could scarcely have been expected to write to every single person she knew.

Rednall and Theodore had turned up on the hospital steps just before Madge and Zinnia, at the end of the day shift, flew down in their scarlet-lined hospital capes. The meeting was tumultuous, with shrieks of joy. The four of them had gone out to dinner that night at the Trocadero and spent the rest of the evening in a music-hall (Uncle Vane and Aunt Emily had exchanged a glance, which I could not interpret, at this news). They had gone out on the town each night of their stay.

But once the girls had received the emergency fund that Uncle Vane and Rednall had provided, they refused to return home. They felt they were doing something for the war effort; they were rolling bandages and fetching drinks of water and emptying bedpans and generally helping to care for the poor wounded officers invalided from France ("Officers, thank heaven," breathed Aunt Emily). Uncle Vane groaned. "I'd have got them back," he muttered.

Rednall said he had threatened to reveal their true ages to the Matron. Looking at his averted eyes and weak mouth, I knew he wouldn't have done this; and he hadn't. But, as Theodore said, if anyone had hoped to spare them the sight of suffering, it was now too late for that. They had been blooded already in the wards. They were learning nursing as they went along; they were often horrified at the injuries they saw but they could bear it, and wanted to do whatever they could to help. And Lady Kerr had been kind and had several times given them meals at her house.

Aunt Emily's blue eyes brightened and her bosom heaved in a sigh. "Well," she conceded at last, "I suppose you were right to leave them."

Theodore gave a short bark of a laugh. "They wouldn't come back, Mother."

So that was that.

When Theodore drove Rednall home in the trap after tea, I went for the ride, my feet on Rednall's big, battered calfskin case with its gold initials under a coronet.

"You'll love the house," Theodore told me as we jogged along beside the quiet fields.

He and Rednall didn't say much; but in spite of the difference between their ages, they were comfortable with each other. Theodore had that effect on people. Since he had no affectations himself, people relaxed when they were with him. They told me about the Trocadero, and about *Chu-Chin-Chow* and a little about the music-hall, and Theodore taught me a song they had heard there; "My old man says follow the van, and don't dilly-dally on the way"; when I nearly knew it we all sang it, and then (when Rednall had recovered from laughing and coughing at the dust the horse kicked up) we sang it again, very loudly, and a whole covey of rooks shot up in alarm out of some elm-trees we happened to be passing, and circled round, cawing crossly. "That's the chorus-line," said Theodore to Rednall, and they laughed again. At the final bellowed "Can't find my way home!" we came in sight of twin stone lodges with wrought-iron gates propped open between them, and a long, grassy, weedy, tree-lined avenue beyond. In the tiny, tunnel-like aperture at its distant end was a row of honey-coloured pillars. As we approached the picture grew to include, first, the pillars' Doric capitals, the huge double door in the shadows behind, and the great architrave above; then the tall-paned first-floor windows over that, and the wide, shallow steps below; more windows to either side and above, crowned with the balustraded roof; and suddenly, where the trees ended, the whole enormous width of house and wings sprang at once into our vision, as long as a rugger-field, the curving forecourt echoing the symmetrical curves of the building, the enfilades of Georgian windows on either side flashing in the sun, the whole façade mottled and cracked and patched like a cliff of crumbling stone that has been withstanding wind and rain and neglect since the beginning of time.

Theodore drove round the pillars and into the tall, cool, shadowy *porte-cochère* behind them. He stopped the horse with accuracy at the front door, beside which shards of entablature lay on the flagstones where they had fallen.

"Coming in to see Mother?" said Rednall in his throw-away manner, as he stepped out. He turned to retrieve his suitcase, and I lifted my boots into the air to assist.

"Kind of you, but I think we'd better take Lizzie back, it must be nearly her bedtime." I was mortally disappointed at being denied the chance of seeing inside this palace.

"Oh, well. 'Night, Lizzie. Don't let this wicked man do anything rash."

"Try and stop me," said Theodore. "'Night, Red.

Thanks for not giving me away. I really feel life is opening out at last."

"Good." Rednall stood there facing us, his face and hair pale in the gloom in front of the dark panelled doors. "Just be careful, that's all. Thank you for coming."

"Thank you for everything. Fun, wasn't it?"

Unexpectedly, Rednall gave a little hop and a dance step. "Rather. 'Bye."

"Goodbye," I said. Theodore raised his hand and shook the reins and we bowled out into the weak, slanting sunshine.

I looked back longingly at the house, ignoring the weeds at its feet and the dark, green-freckled damp-stains, the guttering and downpipes orange with rust, the great crack like the border of Wales between two windows in the east wing; seeing only ghostly lords and ladies, embroidered and jewelled, bowing and curtseying to each other gravely under the massive *porte-cochère*.

"He must be rich," I said at last when the trees hid all but the sun-struck pillars.

Theodore laughed. "Hasn't got a bean. His father died years ago and the place went to seed. His mother doesn't do anything, she just sits there complaining. The house'll never be right, it's too far gone."

"I think it's wonderful."

Theodore fell silent.

"When I grow up," I said, "I want to live in a house like that. If I can't live at the Old Hall, that is. If you'll have me to stay I'll have you to stay."

"It's a bargain," and he spat on his hand, like an old man at a cattle-market, and solemnly shook hands with me.

"What will you do when you grow up, Theodore?"

Theodore gazed at the placid fields before us. "I'm going to be a farmer."

"Of course," I said, but he wasn't listening. His brown eyes had a dreamy look.

"I'm going to be the best farmer that ever was. My crops

will grow for me and my animals will love me, because I will love them. My stable-yard will be swept and my fences mended, and I'll do my best for the hinds and their families. I will be noble and honourable and true – " He broke off, looked round at me and laughed. His eyes were very bright. "All sounds a bit pompous, doesn't it? But I intend to have some fun as well."

Love for Theodore welled up in me. I wished I were his sister. Time alone with him seemed precious, a privilege.

The countryside was quiet. A distant cow mooed. The rooks were settling down for the night. The lane was in shadow now, and I put my hands under my armpits to warm them. Theodore noticed. He held the reins between his knees, took off his brown jacket, and draped it over my shoulders. It was heavy and scratchy, but warm from the warmth of his body. It reminded me of something.

"How's Peregrine?" I asked.

"Oh, flourishing. He likes you, Lizzie."

"I like him," I said, trying not to blush. I wondered how I could extract more information about Peregrine without arousing his suspicion, and decided I couldn't. But there was something else I was desperate to know.

"How was Zinnia, really, truly?" I asked.

"In great form. We had a very jolly time."

"Was she well?" I said cautiously.

"Yes, very." He started humming. ". . . And we join the mad rush that rides hard for the brush And we'll all go a-hunting today."

This was difficult. But dreadful anxiety, bottled up for weeks, was overcoming me. I came out with it.

"Theodore . . . Is she having a baby?"

Theodore's jaw dropped. He turned and stared at me with horrified interest. "No, of course not. What makes you think that?"

I was covered in confusion and fell back on questioning. "Are you sure? How can you be sure?"

He looked back at the road with its splodges of shadow.

"I'm quite sure," he said. "We had a great heart-to-heart. She wants to spend at least three more months at the hospital, because Giles can't possibly get more leave till after that. Then she'll come back home and prepare for the wedding so that whenever he does get leave there will be no delay. I'm going back to visit her after the harvest. It's all fixed up. While I'm there I'm going to – " He broke off. "Look here, Lizzie, what gave you such an idea? What do you know about babies anyway?" He grinned.

"I just know . . ." I felt myself blushing. At my school you couldn't help knowing, some of the girls were always talking about such things. "It was something I saw . . ."

"You *saw*?" He turned back to me, half-frowning, half-twinkling. "What did you see?" Suddenly, he slammed the whip down so that the unsuspecting horse jumped and clattered forward. "Lizzie! You don't mean – whoa! Whoa! – You don't mean Zinnia was doing something she shouldn't with Giles?" He broke into a grin again. "Well I'm damned!" he muttered to himself. "The naughty girl!" Inexplicably, he looked as if he were tickled pink. "Well I'm damned!" he repeated. The grin grew to a laugh.

The horse, who was (luckily) well on in respectable middle age, puffed and slowed.

"Don't tell Mother," gasped Theodore, still convulsed with mirth. I couldn't understand – then – why he was laughing so much. I didn't think it was funny at all.

"Of course not," I said, appalled at the very thought. "And don't you, either."

"Don't worry," he chortled. "Our secret, eh?"

Afterwards, I thought that I should perhaps have defended Zinnia's honour by denying the whole thing. But I am not a liar, and in particular I didn't think I could have told a lie to Theodore, of all people.

15

Next day I went back to Newcastle, and school, and the preoccupations of ordinary living.

My mother's health improved. I spent Christmas at home. At Easter we stayed with cousins of my father's near Ambleside, and I was distracted by the majesty of the Lakeland mountains – the first sizeable hills I had ever seen – and the utter imperative that I should climb to the very top of as many as possible. We returned there that summer, and the following Christmas I was confined at home for six weeks' quarantine because a girl in my class had caught scarlet fever.

I grew, upward and outward, and went to a bigger school, where I was inundated with homework and nearly drowned in Latin verbs. Amy Gutch, my new best friend, had a pointed, bony, white face and ginger pigtails and said it was elegant to bring French phrases into our conversation. She spelt her name Aimée and called me Eloïse. We went round saying *"Pas du tout"* and *"N'importe quoi"* and *"Tant pis"*, and thought ourselves the *dernier cri*.

That summer the scents of Riverlaw were what I missed most; the rich, drowning mock-orange, the clove pink and mignonette, the sugar-dark smell of wallflower and above all the warm sweetness of the coral-pink François Juranville roses that pervaded the south rooms and drenched the air outside them.

After a while, I stopped thinking about Riverlaw most of the time. I was too busy swotting for exams and learning hockey and tennis. Sometimes the other girls talked about boys and I would mention my cousin Theodore, and see in my mind's eye his sunburnt, rosy-cheeked face with the tongue of black hair flapping on his forehead, and see him grin, and over his shoulder would be the tall, slim, shadowy figure of Peregrine, raising one quizzical eyebrow at me and saying "Hello, Bundle," in his husky voice.

And sometimes I thought about the weddings to come – Venetia's and Zinnia's.

Venetia's was so far in the future that at the age of eleven it seemed to me impossible that the time would ever arrive. I prayed that the years would pass quickly for Venetia, who was as steadfast and noble, I knew, as Theodore. Her love would never change; and when I saw the long lists of casualties every day in the *Journal*, the bleak, black-edged columns of names of young men dead, I trembled for her and for Charles, who loved her and was worthy of her love.

But Zinnia would be married at Riverlaw as soon as Giles was given enough leave. He had come home once, that I knew, and had visited Riverpark for two nights and spent the rest of his seven days in London, seeing her at every possible moment. Rednall had arranged for him to stay with Lady Kerr, who had been enchanted with the young lovebirds. Then his ship had sailed for an unknown destination; but on his very next leave they would be married. Mrs Hothersall was to make bridesmaids' dresses for Louie and me out of some rose-coloured silk Aunt Emily had put by. We were to wear wreaths of myrtle-leaves, tied with rose-pink ribbons, and the silk was to be draped in the Grecian mode. Zinnia had sent a picture of a Worth dress she wanted copied for herself, with an elegant wrap-over skirt and triangular cuffs, in the new mid-calf length.

Zinnia wrote that she was nearly dying of excitement. They wanted two boys and two girls, and she longed for them all exactly to resemble Giles. "I do truly believe, dearest Louie," she wrote, "that he is a king among men, a natural leader, as beautiful as a golden Greek god; and I can hardly believe the extraordinary stroke of fortune that made him love ME! ME! ME!!! Nobody will ever know how desperately I love and long for him."

And the week after Louie passed on to me this letter from Zinnia, Giles's ship was torpedoed and sunk by a German U-boat, and golden Giles was dead.

Uncle Vane and Aunt Emily went to London and brought poor Zinnia home.

I wasn't invited to Riverlaw for a term or two after that, and I was quite glad, because I would have wanted to try to comfort Zinnia but I didn't know how. Louie told me much later that her grief was awful, terrible. I wrote to her, at my mother's suggestion; I didn't know what to say, so I just sent her masses and heaps of love. She didn't reply.

My parents went to Giles's memorial service and came back pale and quiet. The Admiral had taken it very badly, they said, and Aunt Letitia was prostrated and would see nobody. I thought, Poor Cedric, nobody thinks of *him*. I wrote to him and said I was very sad. But I couldn't bring myself to send masses of love to Cedric, of all people. I ended up "Yours sincerely," and felt mean, but I couldn't tell a lie.

A few days later I got a letter postmarked Sherborne. I couldn't think who it was from, and the small, wavery, sloping writing didn't help. When I slit it open I thought, Of course! Trust Aunt Letitia to pack him off to school again straight after the funeral.

Dear Elizabeth (he had written),

Thank you very much for writing. Yes it is terrible isnt it. I dont want to be a farmer but I have to now. I dont think I am cut out for it. I think Father and Mother will never smile again. I feel so cut off here and the other boys dont help. I hope you will come to Riverpark in the hols when you are staying with Venetia etc. The weather is poor we have had a lot of rain.

Yours sincerely

Cedric

"*Quel horreur!*" I thought. Wretched little snob that I had become, I couldn't warm to a boy of seventeen who couldn't cope with apostrophes.

By the time I returned to the Old Hall it was the summer of 1916.

I was met at Riverlaw station by Louie and Young Vane, both taller than I remembered. Young Vane was now a fine boy of fourteen with large blue-grey eyes in an oval Delmayne face. His chin was rounded and soft, and his expression dreamy, but his feet clumped in stout shoes and his hand was large and hard when he shook mine. Louie, who never changed except to heighten a little and fatten a lot, was wearing one of Venetia's old frilled muslin pinnies over a brown-striped cotton dress. She threw her arms round my neck and her big straw hat rocked back on its ribbons.

"Dearest Lizzie! *Centuries* since we've seen you! So much to catch up with!"

And all the way to the Old Hall, as Young Vane drove, she regaled me with precious news. Venetia had gone to London to be a V.A.D. in Zinnia's place, and Charles had had leave and ("Don't tell Mother, whatever you do") had spent most of it staying with a cousin in Kensington and had seen Venetia every moment he could. In February, as soon as he was eighteen, Theodore had joined the Durham Light Infantry (Theodore! And I hadn't written to wish him luck, I hadn't even known!) and after his training and his embarkation leave, part of which he had spent in London seeing Venetia and having a good time, he had been sent straight to France. ("I'll show you his letters. He doesn't say much, just that it's pretty awful.")

116

Rednall, too, had joined up, because of conscription; his chest couldn't have been so weak after all – or perhaps baronets could avoid having medicals. He was posted to Catterick – not too far from home. Henry was flying behind the lines in France, and wrote often. The coachman's son at Riverpark had won a medal when Giles's ship went down; he had been in charge of a lifeboat because all the officers had been killed, and had done so well that he had won a commission from the Ranks.

"What about Cedric?" I said.

"Can you see anyone following Cedric over the top?" said Young Vane scornfully.

Louie said mysteriously, "I don't actually think he's likely to join up at all."

"But he's nearly the age, isn't he, for Conscription?"

"Ah, but I happen to know . . . But I don't think I should tell you."

"Come on, Louie, spit it out," urged Young Vane.

"I don't think I ought. Medical confidences, you know."

Young Vane stretched out his big hand and tipped her hat over her nose.

"Ow! Oh, all right. I think he's got flat feet." Young Vane grinned. "Bob told me that was enough to get you off being conscripted. It's all that marching they do. Anyway, there's something wrong with him that means he can't fight."

"Flat head, I should think. What a swizz. Why should Theodore risk his neck when Flatfoot can sit at home on his fat bottom?"

"Vane!" reproved Louie.

"Where are the twins?" I said hastily.

"He's in Theodore's regiment, but in a different battalion. She's packing medical supplies in Durham."

"And the village?" We began the gentle descent to where the Old Hall gates gaped open, revealing a cool green expanse of lawn and a flounce-skirted figure in rose-patterned silk, sitting in a wicker chair with a basket of flowers on her lap.

"Dick was terribly badly wounded in Flanders. He had to have his leg amputated."

"Oh, no . . ." I remembered Dick, small and wiry, plunging after the cricket-ball. How would he ever work on the farm, which was how most of the Riverlaw men earned their bread?

"This horrible war, Lizzie. This disgusting, beastly war."

The trap bowled up the drive. The façade of the house was thick with full-blown roses, their scent wafting over us like smoke. Aunt Emily put down her flowers and hurried over to greet us, her arms wide. As she embraced me I sniffed the familiar violets, felt the petal-soft skin of her cheek and the warmth of her silken arms.

"Dearest Lizzie!"

I do love you, I do, I do, cooed the white doves across the lawn.

And I was home.

The house seemed strangely empty without Venetia and Theodore.

Young Vane spent most of his time helping to get the hay in, and we didn't see much of him; at supper he would arrive late, smelling sweaty, with hair tousled and shirt stained, and fall on the food, saying little.

I felt a little shy of Zinnia at first, as I had expected her to be in mourning still. But she wore her ordinary clothes (enhanced by her elegant London purchases) and didn't seem to have changed, although I fancied that her eyes were a little strained, the skin below them a trifle bluer and more transparent-looking than before. She and Louie spent a great deal of time knitting scarves, mittens and socks in khaki wool for Our Boys, particularly Theodore, who must have had the hottest feet in his regiment.

Rednall, Louie told me, had been very good to Zinnia before he joined up, taking her out and about to take her mind off Giles.

"That's a good thing."

"Well, it's better than nothing. I think she despises him, really – I mean, he's not half the man that Theodore and Peregrine are, even though they're much younger, and he hasn't much to say for himself. Still, he is a baronet, isn't he? She likes that, and Mother, of course, is over the moon every time he appears."

By circumspect questioning I established that Peregrine had joined the D.L.I. shortly after Theodore. I asked Louie if it would be in order to write to them both.

"Of course. Letters from home are just what they want. They're in the trenches and it must be ghastly."

I felt a terrible stillness envelop me. I had heard people talking about the trenches. There were rats, and mud up to the soldiers' knees, and the Germans shot at them all the time with huge guns. How did they eat or sleep? Still, Theodore being Theodore, he would cope. Would Peregrine?

"When I'm old enough I'm going to do war work," I said fiercely, to take my mind off trenches. "Maybe I could be a V.A.D."

"Some of the village women have gone away to work in the munition factory in Sunderland."

"I know about the munition factory. It turns your skin yellow."

"And one or two have gone to London, I'm not quite sure why."

"What do you want to do, Louie?"

Louie sighed. "What I really want is to be a teacher. But Mother thinks that isn't suitable, and I s'pose she's right, really. What I really ought to do is to get married and have a family. I can't abide the thought of spending my whole life at home, doing the flowers and taking soup to the village."

"But getting married is just what Venetia wants, and look what happened to her!"

"Ah, but she wasn't particular enough about the man she chose! We are the Delmaynes, you know. We can't marry just anybody." She must have read my thoughts because she looked away and added, "Well, I expect you're right, but in any case I don't suppose anyone at all will propose to someone as fat and plain as me."

"Rubbish!" I said. "You know I didn't mean it like that – "

"I don't know that I really do want to get married, anyway. Some of the girls at school are always sniggering about it – the going-to-bed bit, I mean. They're disgusting."

"I suppose if you really, truly love someone," I ventured, "you simply want to be part of them."

"I don't think I could ever love anyone that much. At least, I want to be noble and true, and fall in love with a great happy spirit, and 'walk with him along the white shore beyond the death-flood', like in *Shirley*. But I can't quite imagine it happening," she added doubtfully. "Not in Riverlaw."

"I think Theodore is a great happy spirit," I said. "When I grow up I might fall in love with him." Or Peregrine, I added to myself; but for some reason I did not want to say his name aloud.

A day or two later, Sir Rednall came home on a fortnight's leave and immediately proposed to Zinnia, and she accepted.

We heard this news through Madge, who was home on a week's leave from Queen's Gate and had come over to give felicitations to her future sister-in-law, and to issue an invitation to dinner from old Lady Carroun.

Aunt Emily was both thrilled and reproachful.

"Why ever didn't you tell us, darling?" she demanded of Zinnia. "I needn't tell you how delighted I am. I couldn't be more happy. But if we'd known – " It was clear that she was furious at having learnt the news only from Madge, who stood in the drawing-room looking smug, with a cheeky little feathered hat perched over one eye – she, too, had been to Derry & Toms. "And the dinner-party – of course, you must go."

"I never intended not to," said Zinnia. For a newly-engaged girl, she looked remarkably sulky. And it was evident that Aunt Emily was mortally disappointed at not having been included in the invitation. "Just imagine, I shall be Rednall's mother-in-law!" she exclaimed, and added, "If you can wait a moment, Madge dear, I'll just scribble an invitation to dinner here and perhaps you would kindly deliver it to your dear mother?"

The coals of fire were all too obvious. Zinnia looked daggers.

"Where did he propose?" asked Louie, as Aunt Emily rushed off to get a piece of the best writing-paper.

"Oh – down by the pond, when we were riding yesterday."

"Yesterday?" Louie and I looked at each other. "And you didn't tell us?"

"Rednall said he is going to come and ask your father formally for her hand," said Madge hastily.

"He won't refuse," said Zinnia.

"When are you getting married?"

"Not for ages. It's too soon after Giles. We don't want to rush into things. I rather want to live in London. There's a lot to get sorted out."

I couldn't help contrasting this caution with her headlong passion for Giles.

"Fancy being married to Rednall," said Louie later when Madge had gone home with the message, and we were alone. "She'll be Lady Carroun. Mother's thrilled, but what about poor Venetia, wasting away with love for Charles? And whatever Zinnia says, she'll live in that huge, spooky house with dreary old Ma Carroun."

"Does she really love him?" I wondered aloud.

"Well, you never quite know with Zinnia. She's not like the rest of us. I couldn't bear to marry someone I didn't love – marriage for me means being faithful unto death, as you know. But I wouldn't put it past her to marry for a title, would you?"

"Bit unfair to poor old Rednall."

"But I'll bet Father's pleased, and Mother's absolutely over the moon, you can see that. She's going to be the mother-in-law of one of the oldest families in the county."

16

Despite Aunt Emily's elation at the news of Zinnia's engagement, it did not seem to change our way of life much. Zinnia's pleasure seemed to be of a depressingly matter-of-fact variety. I never saw Rednall kiss her, apart from a peck on the cheek at his frequent arrivals and departures – they seemed quite like an old married couple. She still didn't want to live in his house; she did not get on with old Lady Carroun, but then nobody did. "She's always complaining," Zinnia complained. "Try to be your radiant and charming self," urged Aunt Emily, but Zinnia's answer was a most uncharming snarl.

An atmosphere of unease pervaded the house. Uncle Vane was not very well, and he was unusually silent. And Aunt Emily was deeply affected by every snatch of news from the Front. She had become twitchy and anxious, and she scanned the black-edged casualty lists every day as soon as the newspaper arrived. She read aloud to us Theodore's brief pencilled notes that said so little. He was not in the same battalion as Peregrine, but had met him in Amiens, where the men in the front line were sent back for rest. He said the men were very brave and decent about everything but he hoped conditions would improve for them soon.

Henry wrote regularly, at enthusiastic length, and these letters also were read aloud at breakfast. He said he wished we could see him in his flying-suit and gauntlets and goggles, sitting up in the sky with the wind rushing past him as he flew at eighty miles an hour. He was on reconnaissance, he could not say where, but he would have loved to be able to swoop over the Old Hall garden and wave to us all, but unfortunately there was too much sea in between. He did hope that Zinnia was feeling more cheerful now and Venetia was enjoying the Big Smoke. He missed us all a lot and sent love and best wishes to one and all.

"Oh God," exclaimed Zinnia, banging down the butter-knife, "I wish he wouldn't!"

"That's an awful thing to say," reproved Aunt Emily. "Poor lad, he hasn't had your advantages in life, you mustn't be nasty about him."

"I wasn't!" exclaimed Zinnia indignantly. "But since you mention it, I can forgive him his disadvantages but I really can't see that I have to endure such a bore!"

Aunt Emily sat bolt upright and looked scandalised. "Henry's fighting for our country!" she said. "You mustn't say such a horrible thing about anyone, least of all about him!"

"Your mother's right," Uncle Vane said quietly. He added, "However boring he is."

This was so unexpected from my mild, kindly uncle that I caught Young Vane's eye and very nearly burst into giggles.

"Cedric's coming over today," said Young Vane hastily.

Zinnia groaned. "Then I'm going out. Who's that crunching up the drive?"

We all turned towards the window. It was Bert the postman, with his hand closed round a letter.

He saw us and hesitated a minute. Instead of bidding us good morning and handing the letter over the sill, as he usually did, he went on walking towards the back door. I looked, too late, for his expression and caught only the bony, sunburnt profile, the corner of the mouth turned down, under his peaked cap.

Zinnia half-stood, hands grasping the edge of the table.

Her face was white. Aunt Emily said, "It's all right, dearest." But her blue eyes were wide and frightened. And then we heard Hannah's croaking voice calling as she hurried along the back hall. "Mr Delmayne! Mr Delmayne!"

She appeared at the dining-room door in her checked turban and her stained old washing-up pinafore. She looked distraught. The envelope in her hand was yellow, a harsh, impure yellow, a colour I have hated ever since.

Uncle Vane had started up from his chair and now motioned her back into the passage, following her and shutting the door. None of us spoke.

Louie put her spoon down on her saucer. It seemed a loud, intrusive sound. Time seemed to hang in space. I looked at the oak panelling of the room and the carved oak court cupboard, black as a hearse, that had seen many generations of Delmaynes come and go. There was a little black butterfly among the black flowers and leaves along its canopy. Oh, God, I prayed, let him not be dead. I stole a glance at Aunt Emily. She was staring into space, hands clenched, as if she had seen a ghost. Outside, we could hear Uncle Vane's quiet voice followed by Hannah's, but the words were unintelligible through the door.

Then it opened.

"Theodore's coming home," he said.

The Delmaynes had wonderful smiles. When they smiled, you couldn't be worried or unhappy. The room lit up with their relief and my held breath came out in a rush. Then I saw that Uncle Vane wasn't smiling.

He held out his hand as if he were stopping traffic, and said, "He is dangerously wounded. He is being repatriated to Millbank Military Hospital."

Aunt Emily put a hand to her mouth.

"That's all it says," he added in a desperate, choking sort of voice. He put his left hand on his chest and his face seemed to crumple. "Excuse me," he said politely, and blundered past Hannah, who was in the doorway looking gormless with her mouth open. I heard him going very slowly up the back stairs.

"Ee, mistress," moaned Hannah. I had never seen anyone wring their hands before, but I recognised the action instantly. "The poor laddie."

Zinnia stood up. "I'm going to visit him. Millbank Hospital is in London."

Aunt Emily looked as if she were sleepwalking. "I'll go too," she said.

There was a bang from somewhere above us, as if someone had dropped a heavy weight. Hannah squinted, startled, at the ceiling. She hurried out of the room.

"What do you suppose 'dangerously wounded' means?" Young Vane was ruminating. "Is it . . ." He didn't finish. We all looked at Zinnia. She had worked in a hospital. She looked grim and said nothing. Uncle Vane, having been in the Army, would know what it meant too.

Aunt Emily's eyes grew larger and larger. They were glistening. I knew she was going to cry and I couldn't bear to look. I turned to the door, and that was how I came to see Hannah as she clattered down the stairs in her clumsy boots and her dreadful old pinny, and ran down the passage, her red arms waving, her lips drawn back in a terrible rictus-like grin.

"Come quick! Come quick!" she shouted. "The master's been took bad! Oh, Mrs Delmayne, master and heir on the same day!"

It was a massive stroke.

With hindsight, nobody these days could be surprised that the Riverlaw diet – home-made butter and thick yellow cream, fat bacon, two eggs for breakfast every day, and the best fat mutton and beef (for it was then thought that fat meat had a superior flavour, and all the cooking was done with rendered fat from the carcass) – produced premature strokes in both the Delmayne brothers. But oh, bitterness, that Theodore's wounds were the trigger of Uncle Vane's tragedy!

I don't know how we got through that day; for there was worse to come.

I remember running up the village with Louie, my skirts bunched in my hands and my heart pounding up in my throat, to get the doctor – but when we got there his housekeeper took ages to come to the door and we stood there, our chests heaving (and I had a stitch in my side), until she arrived and told us quite crossly that he had walked down to see Mrs Hothersall, who had a chill.

We didn't even wait to thank her. We turned and puffed down to the familiar little door with the row of pansies beside it, and there he was, coming out with his Gladstone bag in his hand, and Louie blurted out "It's Father! He collapsed and he can't move down one side, and he can't speak!" and his tolerant smile turned to a frown.

"Come, come, can't be as bad as that," he said, patting her on the shoulder. But we knew it was. Louie grabbed his hand and pulled him round till he was facing the right way and walking along with us. "Hurry! Hurry!" she urged.

"It's Theodore too," I told him. "We just got the telegram."

One startled look and Dr Bond began to half-run towards the Old Hall gates, leaving us behind.

I was conscious of someone else's steps on the footpath a little way behind us, but I didn't feel like speaking to anyone else. We hastened on. Louie sniffed, felt for my hand, and pressed it hard. "Good old Lizzie," she whispered. We walked hand in hand towards the gate.

"You know what," I said, "that telegram was probably sent last night. He may be lots better by now. They wouldn't be sending him home, would they, if he were too ill to be moved?"

Louie sniffed again, louder this time. She bit her lip and bent her head and walked on. "Mustn't let the villagers see," she muttered. "Stiff upper lip."

We went on past the gardens with their cheerful rows of candytuft and dahlias.

"I keep thinking of that funny bit of hair that lopped up and down on his forehead," she blurted.

"So do I."

"And what about Father?" The tears came gushing. She fished in her pocket and dabbed covertly at her eyes with a grubby handkerchief.

Desolation filled me. I had followed the others up the stairs and had seen him, grey and sack-like on the floor beside the four-poster, in his stiff tweed suit with his gold watchchain lopsided across the waistcoat.

"He's very strong," I said stoutly, for my own benefit as much as hers. "He'll get better." I wished with all my heart that I believed it.

The clop of hooves and the rumble of wheels sounded in front of us, and between the pineapple gateposts the pony and trap appeared. Young Vane was driving, wearing his torn old harvesting shirt, his hair unbrushed as it had been at breakfast. Beside him sat Zinnia in her best coat with braided lapels, trying to fasten a suitcase on her knee.

"Good luck!" called Louie in a wavery voice. "Give him our very best love!"

Zinnia looked up and past us. She went white and put her hand on her brother's arm.

"Stop, stop!" she told him.

I looked round.

Behind us was Bert, and in his hand was a yellow envelope.

"Whoa, whoa!" cried Young Vane, and the pony put up its head and swerved to an awkward, clattering halt halfway across the road.

"What is it, Bert?" her voice was high and small. "I'm just off to see Theodore in London."

Bert pursed his lips. He looked down at the road sadly. Nobody moved.

"I think ye'd better go back tae the Haall a minute and see this," he said at last.

We got Aunt Emily and somehow we were all standing silently in the drawing-room among the watered-silk chairs, and she had the envelope in her hand and looked at it for a long time, and then she handed it to Young Vane.

"Open it, Vane," she said.

He slit it with his thumb, took out the telegram and began to read.

"Regret your son . . ."

But he couldn't go on, and after a few terrible seconds he handed it back. Aunt Emily held it in both hands.

"Two brother officers bringing the body home. Arriving Riverlaw station 4.35 p.m. Tuesday." She stared down at the piece of paper.

"That's tomorrow."

"Don't tell Father," said Aunt Emily. "We just won't tell him anything about this. We won't draw the curtains, or have callers, or anything."

And then Louie gave a huge sniff and a sob and suddenly we were all embracing each other and all I remember is Aunt Emily repeating, "Oh poor Zinnia, poor, poor Zinnia . . ."

"Poor all of us," said Zinnia, kissing her mother's hair.

I don't know what we would have done without Hannah. It was she who got us through the day, for Cook just sat in her rocking-chair weeping and scrubbing her eyes with her apron, wailing, "The master and the heir on the same day! The same day!"

It was Hannah who told the hinds, and asked Bob to put the trap in the coach house, and made sure everyone got on with haymaking in case the weather broke, and produced drinks and snacks at intervals to try to tempt us to eat, and rushed up and down stairs to attend to Uncle Vane, who was propped up in the four-poster, unable to speak, and looking like someone quite different who was inhabiting my darling uncle's wrinkly skin and white whiskers; a grey person, unreal as a cemetery Frankenstein.

I remember being desperate to get out of the house, and finding myself wandering round the orchard with Louie, and saying, "Things will get better. I promise you, Louie, they will get better, one day!" and Louie saying, as if she hadn't heard me, "Do you remember when Venetia played her harp here and we were all so happy? Oh, poor, poor Venetia, being far from home when the news comes!"

And every gate, every tree, reminded me of Theodore.

And I remember coming down the front stairs just as Bert was delivering the third and last telegram, and Aunt Emily, still in her rose-patterned flounces, holding it and looking at it, and I knew exactly what she was thinking – that perhaps, possibly, please God, there had been a dreadful mistake and Theodore was back from the dead. And she ripped it open in a sort of frenzy and stood there, looking at it.

And Zinnia, looking over her shoulder, read it out in a slow incredulous voice:

"Correction. The coffin will also be accompanied by Mrs Delmayne."

"But that's me!" whispered Aunt Emily. The paper rustled as her hand trembled. "What can they mean? Mrs Delmayne is me!"

17

It was at that moment that we heard a horse coming up the drive, and a moment later the front door opened. It was Cedric.

We all stared at him, aghast.

"I say, Zinnia," he said in a loud voice with what, for him, was a determined attempt at jauntiness, "Would you care to come for a jolly little ride?"

"No," said Zinnia. "Get off my back, you horrible creature."

She turned and rushed up the stairs. Cedric's jaw dropped, his thick red lower lip lolled, his eyes nearly popped out of his head with horror and hurt. He looked appealingly at Aunt Emily. She looked dumbly back.

Something had to be done.

"Come out in the garden, Cedric," I said.

We walked silently over to the summerhouse, through the scent of roses and mignonette, and sat down, and I told him about Uncle Vane and Theodore.

"Oh heavens, oh Lord, I'm terribly sorry," he said. "I'll tell them at home. Father isn't too good either, perhaps I won't mention it to him. I'm so sorry, Lizzie, it's awful for you too."

"Yes."

"I'll come over another day soon for Zinnia, perhaps it might cheer her up."

I looked him in the eye. I had come slowly to the suspicion that most unloved people, when you understand the difficulties of their lives, are less dislikeable than they may superficially appear to be. Basically, I thought, Cedric was perhaps quite a nice person. It was just such a dreadful pity he was so repulsive in looks and manner. I said, as gently as I could, "It's no good, Cedric."

He looked away at the flowers and said nothing for a minute, and then said in a low voice, "Yes, I know you're right. It's never any good."

"I'm so sorry." Being sad for Cedric was somehow, and inexplicably, the last straw. Theodore would have jumped up and suggested something marvellous to do. Uncle Vane would have patted my head and said, "Cheer up, Mary-Anne, things aren't as black as they look." But they were. I gritted my teeth and dug my fingernails into my palms, and still the tears gushed out.

"Oh, I say, here, have this," and Cedric thrust a huge monogrammed handkerchief at me. Clean, of course – it would be. I mopped and scrubbed till my eye-sockets hurt. In the dovecot behind us even the doves seemed to have changed their song; now they moaned, *The master and the heir on the same day! Same day!*

"What'll happen to the farm?" I hiccuped.

"It'll be quite all right. They'll get a manager, like us," but there was an edge of doubt, of insincerity, in his voice. I tried to picture Young Vane giving orders to the hinds. I couldn't.

"Theodore could have done it," I sobbed. Cedric had obviously not been thought capable of managing a farm, but Theodore could.

"He was a bit young," said Cedric gloomily, and when this set me off again, "Oh, Lord, now I've done it. I know just how you feel," he said in an embarrassed voice, "I felt like that after Giles. But try not to cry. It doesn't help, honestly it doesn't. It's better to feel you're *braver* than anyone else. It'll help Aunt Emily, too, and goodness knows she'll need someone with their wits about them."

"She's got Hannah," I said, and then remembered that

Hannah probably loved Theodore just as much as the rest of us did; she had practically brought him up.

"Well, servants hardly count," said Cedric in his old condescending manner, which nearly undid all the good his previous speech had done. I suddenly understood why Zinnia and Venetia had been so beastly to him. I wanted to hit his silly face. And yet, I thought, it isn't really his fault. It's just the way he's been brought up. Aunt Emily thinks about servants in that way, too.

I blew my nose and took a long, shuddering breath. Suddenly, I felt better able to face the world. Whatever Cedric said, having a good cry had helped. But . . . Braver than anyone else. Theodore would approve of that.

I stood up.

"Thank you very much for the loan of your handkerchief," I said, holding it out, limp and wet, towards him.

"No, you keep it. You might need it – but I mean, I hope you won't."

"I think you'd better go now, Cedric, but you've been a terrific help. I'm sorry I made rather an exhibition of myself."

"If you think there's nothing I can do . . . Tell you what, I'll ask Mother if she can come over and help with mourning clothes, and funeral arrangements, and so forth. And try to be brave. Things will get better."

He saw I couldn't reply, and he patted my hand awkwardly with his clammy palm, and went.

As he unhitched his horse and scrambled into the saddle I realised that I hadn't told him about the third telegram.

Well, it must have been a mistake anyway.

Although wild horses would not have dragged it out of me, it was Cedric's phrase, "Braver than anyone else", that got me through the next few days; that, and Hannah's brawny arms round me, and Zinnia's, and Young Vane's big grimy hand in mine, and Aunt Emily's silken, tear-stained, sweet-scented embrace, whenever any of us met around the house. I don't know which of us was the more stricken. But we surrounded each other with love. Aunt Emily said that perhaps I should be sent home, but I reminded her that my parents were away, so I had to stay. Even Cook helped, plying me with toffees and incantations of "Poor canny wee lass", every time I came into the kitchen.

An endless stream of people came to leave their cards and condolences, from Lady Carroun to Geordie (the villagers, of course, did not leave cards but trooped, cap before stomach, to the front door). Most of them were fielded by Aunt Letitia, who came over each morning and practically took over the running of the house, while Aunt Emily spent most of her time sitting with speechless Uncle Vane or weeping on her bed. Aunt Letitia's face was stern, but I thought I detected a sort of grim relish as she made arrangements and gave orders. She, too, suggested on her arrival that I should go back to Newcastle; it was Zinnia who hugged me and told her that my parents were away and I had loved Theodore too, and no more was said. I knew how to keep out of the way.

After much discussion on the night of the telegrams, Zinnia and Young Vane set off for London next morning to break the news to Venetia and bring her home for the funeral. Aunt Emily wanted her to help nurse Uncle as well. In mid-afternoon, Louie was sent over on the pony to the twins' home, Burgess Farm beyond Riverpark, with a note for their father, in the hope that he might be able to give advice about keeping the farm going (I believe he actually lent Bertram – who was on leave – and a couple of hinds till the hay was in).

At a quarter to four that day, Aunt Letitia had gone home and I was sitting miserably halfway up the back stairs when I suddenly realised that none of them could possibly be back in time to see Theodore's coffin arrive. No doubt that was exactly what Aunt Emily had intended.

At that moment I heard her skirts swishing through the dining-room. She came out into the back hall without noticing me, opened the kitchen door, and said in a wavery voice, "Hannah, please run to the stables and ask Bob to bring the brougham round for me to go to the station, and tell him that one of the men must take the wagonette straight there to collect the . . . the coffin. I want you to look after the master while I'm out."

"Very well, ma'am," came Hannah's voice, high and strained, and Aunt Emily went back through the dining-room to the front stairs, her black bustled skirts rustling behind her. It was strange to see her in black – almost as if she were a different person. And in a way, she was.

I was sure, then, that Aunt Emily had forgotten me, and I knew what I was going to do.

I figured that Hannah would need a minute or two to wash her hands at the sink and roll down her sleeves – she always did that before she went out of the house. I tiptoed downstairs, nipped out of the back door and ran round to the stable-yard. As I went a wain, towering with hay under the lowering sky, lumbered past me, with Harry at the horse's bridle; as long as the rain kept off, haymaking couldn't wait, even for death.

Harry nodded at me. "We're that sorry," he said, almost under his breath. I felt the back of my eyes pricking, and clenched my hands. *Braver*, I reminded myself.

There was an odorous, steaming stack of manure to one side of the stable-yard. It almost hid the empty stalls once occupied by Uncle Vane's hunters, the best of which had been commandeered for the cavalry early in the war. I tiptoed around it and into a cool, dark stable. I stood in the shadows beside the empty hay-rack, thinking of Theodore on a hunting morning, with his hand gentle on his mount's neck, his boots flashing and his stock beautifully tied, humming an old song under his breath:

> With horses and hounds on the way,
> And huntsmen in scarlet so gay;

Oh, we'll join the mad rush that rides hard for
   the brush
And we'll all go a-hunting today.

Cruel, really. I couldn't quite imagine Theodore enjoying
the kill; I certainly wouldn't myself. But all the Delmayne
children had been blooded, even gentle Venetia. To them,
hunting was great sport. I reflected miserably that perhaps
I hadn't known Theodore as well as I had thought I did.
And now it was too late.

I didn't emerge from my hiding-place until Hannah had
flip-flapped in her carpet-slippers along the yard and into
the tackroom, given my aunt's orders, and flip-flapped back
again, and Bob had backed Starlight into the shafts of the
brougham and driven slowly out through the arch on to
the drive.

I could hear someone else in the coach house, and the
jingle of harness. I crept round the manure and saw a man's
legs under the belly of Prince, the old wagonette-horse
whom he had backed between the shafts. I tiptoed alongside
the wagonette, skipped up the step gingerly, so that it
wouldn't tip, and sat down inside it.

The driver was the cowman, old Will Broughty, and
he didn't see me until he had led the horse out and shut
the coach-house door. Then he jumped as if he had seen
a ghost.

"Ee, Miss Lizzie, ye did give me a turn!"

"I'm coming with you to the station."

"Who said ye could?" he said uneasily.

"It's quite all right. I'm going to help poor Aunt Emily
to look after the officers."

It seemed to satisfy him.

That is how I was the only person – apart from the
officers – to be present when Aunt Emily met the other
Mrs Delmayne.

I hadn't thought much about the third telegram. I supposed it was a mistake, or even an attempted joke in the

most abysmal taste; Aunt Letitia was also Mrs Delmayne, and it was conceivable, though surely most unlikely, that someone who knew there was little love lost between her and Aunt Emily . . . No, surely not, for who could have done so malicious a thing at such a time?

On the way to the station, the inconceivable began to dawn on me. Theodore, darling Theodore, had been *married*.

I grabbed at this thought as a drowning man grabs a lifebelt. Anyone whom Theodore had loved enough to marry must be wonderful, brave, adventurous and funny and nice, just as he was himself. But why, why hadn't he told his family, who loved him so? The only reason I could think of was that he had had a premonition that he would die at the Front, and had married her in London on his last leave. He must have loved her very much indeed to do that. And although it was terrible to think that there was a part of his life he hadn't wanted to tell us about, I was desperately eager to meet the girl he had loved as much as that. She would be a ready-made friend; eventually, perhaps, when we got to know her well, it might be like having a piece of Theodore back.

My mind was still churning when we reached the station. The brougham was parked there, empty. I felt a sudden hollow sensation in my stomach at the realisation that Aunt Emily might not welcome my presence. I recalled that she had sent Louie off for the afternoon. It was now obvious to me that she wished to greet Theodore's body by herself. I was rather frightened. I wished I hadn't come.

Still, it was too late to go back now. I jumped down and hovered outside the main door, to one side of it so that she couldn't see me. Then I thought, "I should be comforting her," and I went in.

In the waiting-room three or four people were lounging round the ticket-window. She wasn't there. I went through to the platform and saw her standing alone, wearing a black coat and a big black hat with a veil, at the far end.

I walked nervously towards her, and when I was twenty yards away she started to pace slowly up and down, and her eyes widened behind the veil as soon as she saw me. I knew, wretchedly, that I was too young for this, that I had done the wrong thing. She came up to me, and my fears were confirmed; her mouth was set in a straight line, she was angry.

But before she could speak there was a distant rumble, and we both turned to watch the train chug in, and she said nothing.

Almost the whole train passed us, and when it stopped we were opposite the guard's van. I was turning, thinking we must walk along the carriages, when she took my hand and squeezed it. I could see the end of a long wooden box on the floor of the van. I had never seen a coffin before, but I knew very well what it was. Seeing it finally brought home to me the reality of Theodore's death.

The guard jumped out, and behind him came a tall, slim officer in khaki. He took off his cap and gave Aunt Emily a big hug. It was Peregrine.

He saw me and bent to hug me too. His eyes were tired and sad and his cheek was a bit bristly.

"The guard will see to everything," he told Aunt Emily. "I travelled with Theodore, but the others are a few coaches away," and he put his hand under her elbow, just as Uncle Vane used to, and we walked along the train.

Suddenly Aunt Emily stopped dead. She was staring ahead as if she had seen Death himself.

"It can't be," she said in a low voice. "I won't meet her!"

Peregrine put his arm round her shoulders. "I'm afraid it is," he said softly. "I tried to stop her, but she insisted on coming."

I looked where they looked. I saw a very young officer with red hair and freckles, wearing the same uniform as Peregrine, and beside him a flamboyantly-dressed young woman with a painted face and a large bosom, in frilly, bright purple with a feather boa and a hat heaped with ostrich plumes.

I looked again.

It was Ivy.

18

Aunt Emily stood stock-still on the platform. Behind the veil her mouth moved, her face worked as if her whole life were flashing before her eyes.

Ivy, in full sail, a grotesque and vulgar figure in her too-old, too-bright London clothes, stalked up to her. She teetered a little, and I realised that she was wearing very high heels and was unaccustomed to them. She looked both scared and defiant.

"What cheor, Moother-in-law," she said.

At the old dialect greeting, Aunt Emily visibly flinched. "How dare you?" she said.

At that moment the red-haired officer made a sign to Peregrine, who looked round. Both men muttered "Excuse me," and hurried back the way we had come, doubtless to help with the coffin. I stayed in the background, rooted to the spot, dimly aware that we had an interested audience beyond the thick glass of the train windows.

"Will ye not gimme a kiss?" demanded Ivy. "I'm fam'ly now, ye kna. I'm Mrs Delmayne."

"You know that's impossible." Aunt Emily's voice was small, and cold as ice.

"Why noa, I kna no sech thing." Ivy's cheeky affability had become injured indignation. "Teddy and I was married, in London, at a chorch. I got me marriage lines."

"You dare to come here, telling lies, at a time like this!"

"It's nae lie! I'm his widder!" Suddenly, appallingly, tears welled in her eyes and she began to cry noisily. Little trails of mascara coursed like dirt down her reddened cheeks. "I'm his widder and I've come to claim me place and me portion!"

"I'm afraid that's out of the question."

Aunt Emily, with great dignity, turned her back and began to walk, a little unsteadily, towards the waiting-room door. The engine hissed. In the distance Bob and Will Broughty and the two officers were carrying the coffin round the end of the station office.

Aunt Emily stumbled a little over the waiting-room step, and Ivy, sniffing loudly and wiping her nose with a finger, caught up with her. She snatched at Aunt Emily's black sleeve, but my aunt shook her off as one shakes off a fly, and strode on through the waiting-room with her adversary tittuping after her, heels clacking on the boards.

"Me an' Teddy was like that," and Ivy held up two twined fingers. "'E promised 'e'd see me right. You wouldna break a dead man's promise . . . Mrs Delmayne . . . You wouldna!"

"I know nothing about all that. If he meant us to look after you he would have told us."

"Would you want your son's wife going to court agin you to get a roof over her head?"

Aunt Emily, by now in the station forecourt where her son's coffin was being gently slid and steadied on to the wagonette, stopped and said quietly, "Would you please stop this disgusting exhibition and allow me to mourn my son in peace? I don't want to see you or speak to you ever again. After the funeral our solicitor will make enquiries and if you are expecting a child, as I imagine you must be, and if you can prove it is my son's, we will adopt it and have it taken care of, but you will never see it again."

"No, I'm not expecting. Definitely not, you ugly old hag!" But Ivy's eyes had flickered and I knew she was now frightened.

"Let that be the last word between us."

Aunt Emily turned away, her head high. But as she walked towards the wagonette, Ivy shouted after her, "And after all my Mam's done for you. Slaved all her life for the Delmaynes, she has! She loved Teddy like he was her own son. Bathed 'im an' all, when he was a babby, an' never 'ad a chanst to do it for me! She did more'n you ever did for 'im, I'll be bound!"

Aunt Emily walked on, a lonely black figure in the dusty forecourt. Ivy was screaming now.

"Teddy was the heir! One day I'll be mistress of that 'ouse and throw you out, you cow!"

And somehow my aunt and I were in the brougham, and it was rocking fast out of the station-yard with the wagonette swaying down the road at a most unseemly speed in front of it, and our ears ringing with Ivy's indignant and (in the circumstances) incredible last cry, " 'Ere, amn't ye goin' to give us a lift?"

Aunt Emily, who had kept a stiff upper lip throughout the whole dreadful encounter, was crying silently into her lace handkerchief, and I felt certain her heart was broken.

And through the little back window I saw Ivy's ridiculous purple figure, her hat-feathers bobbing wildly and her ruddy face screwed up with the intensity of her emotion, running ineffectually after us, stumbling and tripping over the thick frill of her skirt and holding out her arms to the brougham in a last, desperate entreaty.

Aunt Emily said nothing at all the whole way home; she seemed to have forgotten I was there. She pulled off her hat and put her face in her hands and rocked to and fro. I tried stroking her hair, but it did no good. Her grief was terrible to see, and I knew that there was nothing I or anyone could do.

Just before the first houses of the village I patted her shoulder and told her where we were, and after a minute she mopped at her eyes with her useless little handkerchief and put on the hat and the veil again, in case any of the villagers saw her.

When we got home she went straight to her bedroom. I felt shattered and didn't want to see anyone either. I went up and sat on the floor in the train-room, remembering how Theodore knelt by the rails to whizz the express round the outer circuit – "Hoot, Lizzie, hoot!" – with his quiff of hair dangling over his bright eyes.

I was weeping into the threadbare rose-printed curtains when the door-latch clicked. I tried to shrink back under the eaves; I didn't feel like speaking to anyone. Well, hardly anyone.

The door opened and it was Peregrine. It was obvious he and I had both come here for the same reason.

I didn't say anything; I just looked at him through my tears. He didn't speak either. He came and sat on the floor beside me and put his arm round me, and settled me in the crook of it with my head against his shoulder. I felt his bristly cheek on the side of my forehead. I can't tell you how comforting it was. It felt as if I had, without knowing it, been waiting for him to do that all my life.

I don't know how long we sat there. Neither of us spoke. There was no need.

At last, "Poor old Bundle," murmured Peregrine. He moved slightly and kissed my forehead.

"Poor old you too."

"I don't think you were meant to come to the station – it must have been awful for you."

"I'm afraid Aunt Emily will never speak to me again – but I had to go, for Theodore."

"I think she was glad you were there, in the end. But I'm sorry you saw that dreadful scene."

"Did he . . . Peregrine, did he really love Ivy? I mean, how *could* he?"

There was a little silence. I looked at Peregrine's long, slender fingers along my forearm. He was still wearing his khaki uniform, but had taken off the jacket and the Sam Browne. He had little silver cufflinks with a crest.

"No, I don't think he did. It was just because – he was curious, I suppose, and she was such a flirt, and played a fast game. I'm quite sure he didn't think of her as a possible wife, but perhaps he saw something in her that we can't. But she was no better than she ought to be. She set her cap at him – I should have realised and warned him . . . But above all he was honourable. You'll understand better when you're older. Try not to think about it."

"I can't help it. He didn't *really* marry her, did he?"

"Yes, I'm afraid he did. It all happened rather quickly, last time we were on leave. I tried to persuade him not to . . ." His voice trailed away and he muttered very low, as though he were alone, "Oh, God, I tried. I kept telling him he was too young. God forgive me, I lost my temper and told him he was an idiot. Perhaps if I hadn't . . . But there was so little time – a night. One night. He'd bought the special licence for the next day. And I think perhaps he had a premonition about . . ." He didn't go on.

A moment later he said in quite a different voice, "Good heavens, Bundle, you've grown since we last met. Let's have a look at you." He moved me round to look me full in the face. "Yes, your eyebrows have definitely grown."

"Do they beetle?" I asked fearfully – other people had commented on them too.

"Certainly not. They're not spidery either. And they wouldn't make a wig for your dear little ears – that's a nice smile!"

"I love you, Peregrine."

"I love your big blue eyes," and he gave me a huge, warm, all-embracing hug. We clung to each other. "I wish I had a baby sister like you," he said. "How old are you?"

"Twelve."

"Oh, Lord." He stretched and began to get up. "It must be supper-time, I think we'd better go down and see."

At supper the room seemed full of ghosts. There were only four of us round the table; Louie, myself, Peregrine and the red-haired officer, Con O'Conor, whose father was an Irish doctor with a practice in Durham. Con was in Theodore's battalion, and had been coming home on leave; volunteer stretcher-bearers had been sought for the hospital ship, and he had volunteered so as to be able to travel with Theodore. I asked him what it was like, but he shook his head. "Don't ask," he said, turning away.

Apart from that he spoke almost entirely in quotations; perhaps he didn't trust his own thoughts. He looked round at the open window where the Juranville roses nodded, and sniffed the air like a dog. "Nice here," he said. "The air Nimbly and sweetly recommends itself Unto our gentle senses."

"We're doing *Macbeth* at school," said Louie. "I hate it. Everyone in it is either nasty or weak."

"What do you like best at school, Bundle?" enquired Peregrine.

"Poetry. 'Forth darted Spurious Lartius, Herminius darted forth – '"

"'And side by side those chiefs of pride . . .'" Con caught Peregrine's eye and his gentle Irish voice tailed off. I remembered the next line, and could have bitten my tongue for reminding them of blood and death. A love poem might distract them, perhaps? "'So, we'll go no more a-roving, So late into the night,'" I said – oh, stupid Lizzie.

"'Though the heart be still as loving, And the moon be still as bright;

For the sword outwears its sheath And the soul wears out the breast . . .'"

"Oh, I can't bear it," whispered Louie.

I handed her Cedric's handkerchief, and we shared it.

Con left next morning to go home to his parents. It was the last night of my stay at the Old Hall. My parents were due to return home next day, and I would do the same. Because of this I would miss Theodore's funeral. The Delmaynes thought I was too young to go to it, and I dare say they were right.

I thought nothing more could happen. I didn't know – how could I? – that once or twice in a lifetime, Fate forces our destinies out of their true course, so that our lives are changed utterly for many years to come. I didn't know that on that evening something like that would happen to me.

Peregrine was incredibly kind to me all day. After we had seen Con off at the station, he took me for a walk down to the river. Louie had slept in – I suspected that she had been crying most of the night, and I did not attempt to wake her – but I was pleased to have Peregrine to myself. We talked little, but he was very observant, pointing out a badger's paw-mark, the tracks of various birds, and a red squirrel looking at us bright-eyed from a high branch. We wandered along the river-bank, skimming stones and seeing how many different varieties of wild flowers we could identify. Peregrine was scoring, but he lost count.

"I'm sorry, Bundle," he said. "I'm afraid my heart isn't in this."

"Neither is mine. Peregrine – "

"Mm?"

"I just can't stop thinking. I know I oughtn't to talk about it, but – do you know who Ivy's mother is?"

He turned his head sharply. "Here," he said. "Let's sit down." He sank on to a fallen tree and I perched beside him. "Look, try not to think about it. The solicitor is there now. That's why you and I are here, to keep out of the way till it's all over."

"But do you know?"

"Theodore told me. Do you?"

"Yes. I can't believe it, though. I just can't believe it. I knew she went to Fred's on her days off, but I never connected . . . I thought Ivy was Fred's daughter, not his grand-daughter . . . And how could Theodore . . .? It must have been all those days we thought he was out shooting . . ."

Peregrine put his arm round me. I looked down at his long, slender fingers, the silver cufflinks with the crest. "They didn't have a tremendous love-affair, you know. Just a bit of fun in the hay. And when he knew she was in London, he called on her to make sure she was all right – just as your uncle would call on one of his tenants."

I stared. "But you wouldn't marry someone because of that!"

"Well, she said . . . Look, Bundle, try not to think about it. I personally think that Ivy would say anything that came into her head to get an advantage. But Theodore was a very good and honourable person. Nobody seems to believe that except me," he muttered.

"Oh, I do! I do!"

"Anyway, it's too late now. The solicitor will probably sort something out. He'll probably give Ivy an allowance on condition she goes far away. I think that's what they usually do."

"But my aunt and uncle aren't rich. All their money comes from the Admiral. And what about Hannah? Goodness, we'll be related to her! Aunt Emily would rather die than that happen!"

"I think your aunt was thinking of giving her notice," he said gently.

I stared. "But that would be dreadfully unfair! Hannah's worked at the Old Hall all her life! She hasn't done anything wrong!"

"Well, I suppose she did when she had Ivy. She wasn't married."

"Wasn't she? But that's years and years ago! Oh, poor Hannah – it would be so unfair!"

"Life *is* unfair," said Peregrine sadly. "Oh, Bundle, life is sometimes just bloody awful."

The one, the only consolation, I thought, was that he was there with me.

Eventually we wandered back. A big black motor-car was roaring away from the house. Louie, I knew, had gone – under protest – to tea with Henry's elderly aunt, who had once been a schoolmistress at a school Aunt Emily had attended during her teens, and had asked to see Louie's stories. I imagine this was another pretext; she was kind, and perhaps she thought she might cheer Louie up a little.

Hand in hand, Peregrine and I looked into the kitchen, hoping for tea. Cook was alone, rocking.

"After all them years," she keened. "It's wicked. Wicked. Hannah's gone away, hinny. Your Auntie wouldn't even wait to let 'er say goodbye. They went in the moty-car with the solicitor."

"Where have they gone?"

"Cornwall. To live."

"Cornwall!"

"Aye. Half an hour to pack and say goodbye to Fred – poor Fred! An' then away for ever an' ever from 'er native soil. That wicked girl, ruining her good mother's life!"

"They say Cornwall's rather nice," ventured Peregrine.

"And it's in England," I added desperately. "She will come back to see Riverlaw again – she must!"

"And how would the likes of Hannah pay the fare?" demanded Cook. "'Tis hundreds of miles away! And as soon as the war's over the two of them will be given their tickets to America. One way. She's gone, hinny. They're not coming back." Tears ran down Cook's furrowed cheeks.

I couldn't take it in. Peregrine drew me away, and left me looking for sweets in the dining-room while he went off to see if he could help with the haymaking.

On the hall table there was a little pile of letters. I knew what they must be; letters of condolence had been arriving by every post. I picked them up. Several were

in good, crisp envelopes, addressed in the confident hand
of educated people. But the bottom one was of cheap
rag paper, addressed in pencil in a cramped, tall-looped
schoolbook hand, on lines that had been ruled on the
envelope as a guide. The postmark read B.F.P.O.

I thought they might warm Aunt Emily's broken heart
a little. I looked for her, the sheaf of letters in my hand.
I found her lying on her bed – red-eyed, her hair wispy,
her chest mottled and old where her crêpe front had come
undone.

"I don't want them," she said in a strange, strained voice.
"Throw them away."

"But can't we open them? They must be about Theodore."

"Take them away. Throw them away. Take those others
on the dressing-table and get rid of them, too. I don't want
anything to remind me of him. Who would have thought"
– and she rolled over and buried her head in the lace-edged
pillow so that her words were muffled – "that my lamb
would turn out to be a black sheep?"

"But, Auntie – "

"I don't want to hear about him ever again. Tell the
others I'll go to the funeral because I've made sure she
isn't going, but I don't want to hear his name mentioned.
Not ever."

"But, *Auntie!*"

"Go away. Please go away."

So I did.

But I couldn't throw the letters away.

I hid them under my pillow, plumping it up nicely so
that nobody would see.

Late that afternoon Venetia, Zinnia and Young Vane
arrived, tired, pale and silent. Dr Bond, too, arrived to
look at Uncle Vane, and said he must go to hospital and
he would make the arrangements. I felt it incumbent on
me to keep out of the way.

Peregrine was presumably haymaking, but I felt too

dispirited even to try to get a ride on the hay-wain. The clouds were dark grey and bulging with rain, so nobody would have time to deal with a girl too small to use a pitchfork.

I mooched round the orchard and gazed at the duck pond, and didn't feel hungry enough to go in for supper. I stole some peas from the kitchen garden instead, and despised myself for doing it. But Aunt Emily was too maddened by grief and fate to know or care.

My thoughts about Theodore and Ivy went round and round in ever more desperate and fragmented circles. But Peregrine had said Theodore was a very honourable person. Hang on to that, I told myself. The Delmaynes are like me, and like Peregrine; noble and honourable. That is what makes life worth living. That is what gives meaning and worth to our existence.

If I had known then what would happen on that overcast night in Riverlaw, casting its shadows over my life for years ahead, I would have thought differently.

Twilight, and the damp chill before the rain started, drove me back into the house, but it seemed deserted until I heard low voices in the drawing-room. I retreated. In the boot-cupboard I found an empty sweet-tin. Not bothering to take a candle (for I knew every inch of the house blindfold) I took it up to my bed and put all the letters in it. The ones that were open I read by the window in the half-light that came between the tattered clouds. They were from my uncle's and aunt's friends. They were full of helpless sympathy, and they made me cry. The telegrams were also in this bundle. I found myself holding them gingerly by their edges as if they were poisonous.

I nearly opened the last batch of letters but I decided not to. Aunt Emily was, perhaps – please heaven – only temporarily mad with grief; she might recover and change her mind about them. I, a twelve-year-old guest, couldn't very well open her post.

I got out my best blue hair-ribbons, and tied the sweet-tin

across and across, and finished with a beautiful bow. Then I tiptoed through Zinnia's room and into Venetia's. It was now nearly dark, but past the deep shadows under the eaves I saw that the train-room door was open.

Outside Venetia's bedroom window there was a faint glow in the sky; the moon was rising. I thought of the many times we had played Indians around the house, of Theodore tiptoeing through this very door to ambush unwary opponents. I moved silently; he had taught me that. His skill could live on. I would teach it to my children, and they would pass it on to theirs, remembering how Theodore Delmayne had been the best Indian of all.

I edged silently into the doorway of the train-room, felt with my fingers above it and to the right, and down, and found the hollow back of a massive tie-beam, the best hiding-place in the house, about which only he and I had known. Soundlessly I lowered the tin into its cobwebby nest. Nobody would destroy the letters, ever. They were Theodore's memorial.

Suddenly, in the darkness at the other side of the train-room, there was an infinitesimal sound, like the rubbing of flesh on flesh. An insect, perhaps; but I had the indefinable but definite feeling that there was someone there. I was rooted with fright. I didn't dare move.

I looked across the dim railway-lines, made out the dark lumps of stations and bridges, identified Theodore's favourite dark green and gold engine by the glimmer on its flank. Under the eaves in the far corner of the room, opposite the window, there was a dark, shadowy mass where I remembered only some torn cushions and the tattered blankets we had used, years ago, to make an Indian tepee.

But in the minute I stood there, petrified, the moon's bone-white edge rose above the windowsill. And in its eerie graveyard light I saw the two bodies twined together; saw the moon-pale breast and rose-grey nipple with the man's fingers splayed beneath, and his dark head buried beside it; saw Zinnia's parted lips and wide, tear-glittering eyes; saw his broad back, his other hand convulsively clutching hers, and the moonlight glinting on the neat silver cufflinks with a crest.

I started, and the board I was standing on creaked, and I heard the swift intake of breath and Zinnia's urgent whisper, "*Who's that?*"

And I turned and ran, through the three dark bedrooms, down the stairs, out of the front door, through the garden under great drops of rain and on and on, panting, my chest tight, tears starting from my eyes, into the rain-spattered orchard that was still silvery under the moon.

ONTARIO

19

The station-wagon purred north along the empty road, with country-'n-western music twanging from the radio.

We had driven through Bolton, Kleinburg and Palgrave. Black and white Holstein cattle stood in the fields, with occasionally a distant flock of sheep. The red-brick farm-houses had a curious air of having been lifted from a Victorian suburb; they had white-brick corners with long and short bricks alternating, and sometimes white window-edges to match. Some of them had a verandah on two sides with pillars and a sloping roof, and a garnishing of wooden, carpenter-gothic lace on the gables and round the top of the porch. At the sight of the gingerbread lacework I felt an obscure stirring of dread, and didn't know why, until I realised that what it reminded me of was the ridge of the Riverpark conservatory.

"Not far now," said Cousin Kitchener.

The road had been rising imperceptibly for some time, and now I saw blue hills in the distance. We swung left on to Highway 89. Here and there I saw wonderful views back down the valley.

"Funny you should be a farmer," I mused. "Did you have any brothers or sisters?"

"No." He gave me a quick sideways look. I felt uneasy; I had set a trap for him, and perhaps he knew it. I didn't want him suspecting that I doubted his story.

But ever since I had drafted my advertisement for the *Globe & Mail* I had wondered whether I had given too much away in it and in my long, excited follow-up letter in response to his answer. A smart operator could have got a lot more information about the Delmaynes from the Public Record Office in London, British regimental records, wills, Somerset House . . . I had taken care in my introductory letter to tell him enough to assure him that I was indeed his Cousin Lizzie and not some confidence-trickster trying to cadge a free weekend's lodging. I had outlined the families at Riverlaw during the first world war, named names, described details that outsiders would not know. He already knew from my letter enough to talk confidently about the place and the family. I hadn't kept a copy; I couldn't even remember now exactly how much I had told him. Perhaps I had said too much. He had said in his reply that his mother's marriage-lines had been left in England, and lost. His story was unsupported by proof. And it mattered . . . oh, it mattered.

"Tell me your wife's name?"

"Bernice."

"And the children?"

"Well, the grandchildren you'll meet straight away. Their mother is our daughter. She's married to Shad. Her name," he smiled, "is Venetia."

I felt a great stillness envelop me. All this time I had held something back; I had been unable completely to believe that this middle-aged Canadian really was who he said he was. I wanted to believe. Wanted, needed it so badly. But the evidence had been too tenuous.

But a grandchild named Venetia . . . Surely, surely . . .

"Shad and Venetia – matter of fact we call her Vicky – they've gone off to see *Twelfth Night* in Stratford – Stratford, Ontario. Afraid you won't see them. They're staying the night with friends there. I have a business in Toronto and we have a farm manager who looks after this place during the week," he went on easily, "but the family spend most of the summer here. I guess in Canada we like to stay close to the soil."

Vicky, I thought. My doubts flooded back. I looked round at the great tracts of pasture and corn, with now not a habitation in sight. It seemed a very long way from England. And I didn't even know where the nearest village was. I was entirely dependent upon this complete stranger to return me to civilisation.

He swung the car left on to a grassy track under the line of trees. There was an unfenced lawn, a few shrubs, a brick house with aluminium double-glazed windows. The glass-paned front door was covered with an ugly metal-mesh screen. Behind the house was a tall barn with a clapboard cottage near it, both sheltered by big, broad-leaved trees.

A plump, sharp-faced woman in her mid-forties appeared at the screen door. She wore a low-necked red blouse and a black cotton skirt. She had shoulder-length hair, dyed bluish-black, and wore more make-up than I had expected. I found her hard glance disconcerting.

"Why hello there, Cousin Lizzie," she said. She held out a brown hand. "Come on in."

"Bernice?"

"Right. How about a coffee, eh?"

"I'd like that."

"The bathroom is there," she pointed. On the other side of the hall I caught a glimpse of a big yellow kitchen with a vast, gleaming freezer and refrigerator, rearing side by side like false teeth or space-age tombstones. There was the sound of children's voices; small, absorbed children.

"We've always meant to go to England and look over the old home," said Bernice a little later as we drank our coffee from mugs in the family room (as they called it).

"But my mother just couldn't bear the thought," her husband chimed in.

"You mean she's still alive? I must see her!"

He looked surprised at my vehemence. "Why yes, but..."

Bernice pursed her lips and shifted in her seat and I was aware that she was trying to telegraph some kind of message to her husband. His eyes shifted from mine.

157

"Tell you the truth, she's a little bit reluctant to meet you."

"She has very bad rheumatism and she lives in a Senior Citizens' Home," said Bernice in a decisive way. "We told her you were coming, but she said she definitely didn't want to see you."

Kitchener saw my jaw drop, and added hastily, "I guess she has very definite ideas. And you know, she went back once to Riverlaw and asked to see old Mrs Delmayne, but the old dragon wouldn't see her. Not one word would she say to her."

"Aunt Emily wasn't an old dragon," I protested. "She was . . ." and then I remembered what she had done to Theodore's memory, and I fell silent.

"Mother-in-law always lived with us, so we had to consider her feelings," put in Bernice smoothly. "She didn't want to go back to England herself, and didn't want us to either. And as we were dependent on her to look after the children and the animals while we were away from home . . . Florida, yes. Britain, no," she said, with finality. I realised that she had steered the conversation with some skill away from the possibility of my seeing her mother-in-law. Well, if the old lady had refused to see me there was nothing I could do. It was only what Aunt Emily had done to her. But I felt hurt and nettled.

"Hi, Gramps!" A small boy and girl entered from the kitchen, each carefully bearing a plate of biscuits, still damp with haphazard blobs of coloured icing. I looked at the children eagerly. The girl had curly, ash-blonde hair, curiously inapt to her sallow skin. Her little face was pointed, elfin. Nothing of the Delmaynes there. The boy had an oval, rosy-cheeked face, curly black hair, a cowlick flopping over his warm brown eyes.

"This is Cousin Lizzie," said their grandmother. "Dean, Sue-Anne."

"Hi there," said Dean. "Have a cookie. The pink ones are real good."

I had to struggle with myself to thank him, level-voiced, and take one. Idiotic, really. Little boys are not to be identified by the way their hair has been cut. I had never seen Theodore as a boy of four. I had not seen him at all for fifty-four years. I possessed a mental picture that had been taken out, contemplated, put back again, a million times. It had grown misty, uncertain with use. I was in danger of seeing bits of it in every black-haired, oval face I passed.

"Did you ice these?" I asked.

"Sure. Sue-Anne helped." Sue-Anne put a flower-like hand to her mouth and giggled.

"Tastes good."

He took a bite. "You're right," he said, munching.

"What are you going to be when you grow up?"

"Farmer, I guess. A real good one, with a million cows."

My thoughts went back through the years to a country road, a pony and trap driving back from Rednall in the sunset.

"Why have you come here?" he asked.

"Partly to see you all, and partly . . ." But it was too early to show my hand. The words stuck in my throat. Luckily Bernice, at least, misunderstood me.

"I hear you've brought some family snapshots," she said. "Let's have a look at them."

"After supper, when these two are tucked up in bed," said Kitchener. "Say, Bernice, you remember that man who asked us whether we were related to the Delmaynes from Northumberland, years back?"

"Sure, I was just thinking of him. He said he was connected with the family. It was really strange because he was American."

"Where did he live?"

The children sidled out, still carrying the plate of biscuits.

"New York."

Who could it be? "Where did you meet?"

"We were on vacation, staying in the same hotel in Nassau, in the Bahamas. Was it the Nassau Beach or the British Colonial, dear?"

"Oh my, I can't recall, it's too long ago."

"We got quite friendly. He was there on business – he told us he was in the hotel business. We thought that might come in useful one day, and we exchanged Christmas cards for a year or two, and then we didn't hear, and I cut down my list – you know how it happens, you just can't keep up with everyone."

"You don't by any chance have his address?"

"No – yes, well I might have, in one of my old diaries. But they're back in Toronto. Can't do anything about that right now. Do you know him?"

"I'm not sure," I said, trying to sound calm, "but I think he may be my – "

"Gramps, Gramps!" Dean's soprano voice shrilled from the kitchen. "Sue-Anne's burnt her finger!"

Suddenly I was alone.

I still couldn't make up my mind about these people. Were they really my cousins? How could I tell? How could it be proved?

I had to know the truth.

For Cedric was dead. Cedric had broken the entail and willed Riverpark and Riverlaw outside the family, and it was being sold. The Riverlaw Delmaynes would be homeless, and almost penniless.

But if the will could be contested, and it could be proved that the entail still held good after all, I believed that the legitimate heir was Kitchener. Kitchener and Bernice would own the whole estate.

And I had something enormous to ask of them, and also something to give that would be priceless to the real Delmaynes, and to them alone.

NORTHUMBERLAND

20

Dearest Lizzie,

Mother sends love and says please will you send your
measurements, i.e. bust (goodness, have you got one?),
waist, hips, centre back of collar to waist, waist to ground,
shoulder to wrist, inside arm, length of nose, ear to ear,
etc., etc.

Why is this, you will ask. Well, Zinnia has changed
her mind (what AGAIN?) and decided that she wants to
marry Sir Rednall as soon as possible. Now it's Mother
who is saying no hurry, too soon after poor Theodore's
funeral, people will be scandalised, etc., etc. Zinnia says
(crossly), small wedding will do. Mother says (coaxingly),
why not wait till the summer and have big grand one with
beautiful striped marquee in the garden and maybe Lady
Carroun will ask Lady Trevelyan and even the Duke?!!!
but this not possible while we are in mourning. Zinnia
stamps foot, says she wants to get married and get shot
of it. Adds (artfully) that delay may make Rednall grow
sick of waiting. Mother caves in. I just don't know why
Zinnia should win all her battles when the rest of us
always lose. Still, the wedding will help to cheer us up.
It will be five months after poor, poor Theodore. How
I miss him, Lizzie. I think I will never properly laugh
again.

Enough of that. Venetia and Madge are to be principal
bridesmaids. YOU are to be the other bridesmaid!!! All
by your little self. I am too tall for us to be a matched pair

so I am Out. At least they had the tact not to say we are too different in BREADTH. I am as fat as a pig and hate myself for it but I get so HUNGRY. So YOU will have to stagger under the bouquet and trip over the train.

Mother is much better but between you and me not really herself. Poor Father came home from hospital in the horse-ambulance but still in bed and Bob's mother comes in to nurse him. He can talk a bit but not much and hard to understand. I said he needs teaching to talk again and was desperate to try but they wouldn't let me, said it might make him worse. I could see from his eyes he wanted me to; oh, Lizzie, it was awful. And Mother has forbidden any of us to mention darling Theodore at ALL. If Father asks we are to pretend not to understand, and if that's impossible we are to say he is at the Front. I can hardly bear the thought of deceiving ANYBODY, let alone darling Father who is as straight as a die, but they say the truth might kill him. Mother made poor Venetia collect all T's things and take them to the Vicar to give to another parish, not Riverlaw. She wants to pretend he never existed. Oh, darling Lizzie, my heart is sore and battered with missing him. But I try not to think about it.

We can't mention Hannah either, LET ALONE you-know-who. Cook keeps rocking and saying she is ready for death. Yes, Venetia and Zinnia had to do some of the housework after Hannah left and I laid tables etc. and helped to wash up!! But Gertie Hothersall (Mrs H's great-niece) came after a day. She is short and fat and sharp with Cook. I do miss Hannah, and keep kicking myself because I never realised how kind she was. Poor Fred looks so miserable, I saw him hoeing the cabbages with a big tear rolling down his leathery old face. But what can he do, his home goes with the job.

Oh, dear, here am I grousing. But not everything is black. I just couldn't finish *Is There Life On Mars?* – I had discussed it so often with Theodore, I just hadn't the heart for it. But I have begun a Novel called *The Ghost of the Moated Grange*. I shall put Lady C in it but don't tell a soul as I think she will prove to be the Villainess.

(Later) Much argument about who to invite to wedding. Lady Carroun appears to have NO friends and when Mother mentioned the Duke she said coldly, "Oh, I don't think so." Venetia said, "Henry and his aunt, of course," but Mother to our astonishment said, "No." Then SHE said, "All the Seymours, naturally," and Zinnia said, "Absolutely Not," which is terribly embarrassing as Mr and Bertram were so kind helping with the harvest when Bertram was on leave. At this rate we may end up with Rover the Dog as the only guest.

Aunt L and Cedric will be invited, of course, and your parents, and I suggested Peregrine and Con, not thinking there was much hope, but Mother agreed, adding that they probably wouldn't get leave. Venetia said bravely, "You'll have to ask Charles Dawson because he and Rednall are going to be brothers-in-law," but Mother gave her a terrible look and said, "That's very unlikely, I'm afraid." We are all agog to know who will be best man, but perhaps Rednall has no friends either. Theodore would know . . . oh, I wrote that without thinking and oh, Lizzie, you know how I FEEL and I know you do, too. All these wedding plans ring hollow without him and I think Zinnia thinks so too. I keep remembering how radiant she was with Giles and I really feel sorry for Rednall, who is quite a good sort really.

I am up to Chapter 3 of *Ghost of the M.G.* and must rush and write a palpitating midnight encounter –

Yours *avec beaucoup d'amour* (I hope to impress La Gutch if I ever meet her)

L

My dear Bundle,

Excuse pencil but I am writing this in a trench, with

my feet in a hole which a rabbit obligingly dug for me. Unfortunately he is not here to be thanked in person and since he left, it has filled with mud. It is raining which is lucky as a) I haven't washed for ages, but unlucky because b) it's the theory here that the layer of dirt keeps one warmer. There is also a lot of noise from the Huns' Guns, but apart from that, I suppose worse things happen at sea. I keep thinking of Riverlaw and trying to smell those roses on the front of the house. Have you grown? Can you speak French? I can, just, but the French people have prudently disappeared so I have nobody to practise on. What a waste of being in France. *Je veux beaucoup attendre le mariage de Mlle. Zinnia mais je* don't know if I can get leave. This is a feeble letter – hard to sleep or think here – but millions of things to ask you about. Shall we form a Friends of Riverlaw Society?

 Write soon,

Affectionately,
Peregrine Fenwick.

These two letters aroused in me the most bewildered, painful and clashing emotions. For I loved Zinnia in spite of her wickedness, which had been so startingly confirmed in that never-to-be-forgotten moment in the attic at Riverlaw.

I was both moved and thrilled, as any twelve-year-old would be, that she wanted me to be a bridesmaid. And yet I never wanted to see her again.

I felt desperately sorry for Rednall because I knew, as he did not, how cruelly he was being used. And the thought that their marriage might mean that I might never see my friend Peregrine again was almost a mortal blow. Reading between the lines of his letter, I suspected that he, too, feared that with Theodore dead and Zinnia married, nobody would invite him to Riverlaw ever again. But he, too, was being badly used. Zinnia's boldness in countenancing his possible presence at her wedding took my breath away. But the possibility that he might come to the wedding was the main factor that decided me against indignantly refusing to go to it myself.

At the same time, however, I could not forgive him for what I saw as a dreadful, perfidious betrayal of the friendship I thought we had sealed. I could see only too well how he must have been beguiled by Zinnia's charm, and seduced by her loveliness. But added to this was the bitter knowledge that she was not good enough for him. *I* knew his worth; he had been *my* friend, but these two people I loved had excluded me, had stolen each other from my faithful, loving heart in a way I could not comprehend; and I knew they were mismatched.

I tried to write lightheartedly to Louie, because none of this could be confided to her, or to anyone. I tossed and turned all night wondering how I should reply to Peregrine. Perhaps his letter was just a contemptible attempt to ensure my silence – but I knew in my heart that the man in the attic could not have seen me, though Zinnia might have done. But the explanation I preferred – though I could not be sure it was true – was that Peregrine, stricken by the news of Zinnia's wedding, was hoping for comfort from me, his friend. And I must give it.

I took up my pen; and received another setback.

Dearest Lizzie,

I was absolutely shattered to hear that your Mother said you were too young to write to a soldier. What bad luck that she found the envelope. It's too bad when I know you must have made an effort to do it out of kindness. Well, I suppose she just hasn't met Peregrine and thinks he might not be out of the Top Drawer.

I am absolutely up to my plait in homework AND I am stuck fast in Chapter 5 of *Moated Grange* as I have accidentally killed off the hero – he climbed a high cliff, pursuing the villainess by moonlight, and I (and he) just got carried away. I think I'll have to end the book there but it's very short.

Zinnia and Rednall are going to live in Rednall (the house, I mean) after the wedding, with his mother!!! Z is furious but there just isn't enough money to live in London and of course he has to go on managing the estate after the war. She suggested dividing the house (which heaven knows is big enough to hold a dozen families easily) but Lady C of COURSE wants all the best rooms. You and I would meekly give in, but not Zinnia. I went yesterday and tramped round the empty wings with her and you never saw so many dripping ceilings and furry wainscots. Zinnia says that when Rednall was here he just shrugged and said he didn't see why the three of them couldn't live together. Can you SEE Zinnia doing it? But my guess is she'll have to.

Still, no thorn without a rose – she will be Lady Carroun and Lady C (guess what!) will be the Dowager Lady Carroun, so that they don't open each other's post. And Zinnia's eventual eldest son will eventually be Sir. SHE says she will call him Zadok (out of the Bible, isn't it hideous?) because she likes names beginning with Z. None of us can make out whether this is a Tease or not, but it made Lady C hopping mad when she heard, as the eldest son is always called Rednall. (Must be very confusing for historians, and how very Unchristian to be named after a House?)

The Wedding is fixed for Jan. 8 provided R can get leave – the Vicar was difficult about the date on account of Advent, etc. – but Zinnia will wear Mother's ermine cape and YOU are to be lent a fur tippet to stop you from getting the Sneezles. Aunt Letitia is sending hothouse flowers, and we are saving rations like anything for the cake (nothing but rock-cakes for tea till Jan 8th, oh horror!)

Henry keeps writing but he is never allowed to say where from – he says he has flown over the enemy lines, though, so you can guess can't you, though I do wonder whether someone just TOLD him that that was where he was to take a rise out of him, like when Rover had rabies? But perhaps I am being Uncharitable. I am trying not to be, though when Cedric calls I am Sorely Tempted.

Ever your devoted cousin,
Louie.

On the evening of Twelfth Night I went to Riverlaw. My parents were travelling there on the day of the wedding, but I had to visit Mrs Hothersall first in case any last-minute adjustments were needed for my bridesmaid's dress.

The woman to whom I had been (rather hastily) entrusted by my father got out at the first stop with a cheery wave. I was alone in the carriage. The train was dim and smelly. I was startled by a moving shadow on the night-black window. Eyes, dark with horror, stared back at me; my own eyes, reflected in the grimy glass.

From time to time bulky figures passed down the corridor, searching perhaps for the guard, for it was very cold. I bent down to feel the heating-pipe under my seat; through the leather palm of my glove, it felt barely lukewarm. As I was returning to vertical a tall officer in khaki, eyes in shadow under his peaked cap, looked into the carriage. For a split second I thought it was Peregrine, and my heart leapt. But it wasn't.

He slid open the door, removing his cap as he came in, and plumped down beside me, heaving his long, booted legs to rest on the opposite seat.

"Fancy seeing you. What were you doing upside down?" he said.

It was Bertram, the male half of the Seymour twins.

"Oh, it's you," I said stupidly.

"There's a fine welcome for a soldier home from the Front," he said. "Gimme a kiss, can't you?"

I was startled. Unwillingly, for I hardly knew him except by sight, I held up my face and managed to avoid a

169

mouth-to-mouth encounter by turning my cheek at the last moment. There was a not unpleasant smell on his breath that I couldn't identify.

"I was seeing whether the heating was on," I said, bending down again in embarrassment to inspect the offending pipe.

"Are you going to the wedding?" he enquired.

"I'm a bridesmaid."

"I'm looking forward to seeing that."

I was troubled. I recalled a distinct impression that Zinnia had not wanted to invite him. Still, perhaps she had changed her mind. "I've never even been to a wedding before," I confided. "Are the others with you? Con and Peregrine, I mean. Did they get leave?"

"We all did. They must be at home by now. I spent a couple of nights in London on the way, painting the town red, y'know," and he gave me a knowing sideways look and a wink. "They're coming to the wedding on the day."

"Oh, hooray."

"What a nice smile you've got."

Suddenly I felt unaccountably uneasy.

I had never taken much notice of Bertram, partly because he was so much older, and partly because for years he had been a fat, rather greasy-skinned teenager who stood always beside his twin sister and said little. He went to a good school but had never achieved anything of note. His father's farm was substantial, their house was comfortable, solid and well kept; and now I saw that the Army had slimmed him down and given him a bold, authoritative eye. He looked as if he were accustomed to getting what he wanted. I didn't know what his wink meant, but I discovered that I didn't like him.

However, remembering my manners, I said, "And how are you? Are you still at the Front?"

His face altered. "Yes."

"Is it dreadful?"

"Worse than you could imagine. We do get taken out

of the line to rest – we only do three weeks at a time –
but each time it's harder for some of the men to face going
back. And some of them really aren't up to it. I've seen
men die in agony who should never have been soldiers.
The wire . . ."

"What about the wire?"

He looked taken aback, as if he had forgotten I was
there. "Oh . . . you're too young. Tell me about Venetia
and Zinnia."

"And Louie."

"Well," he laughed, "Louie's no beauty, is she?"

"Louie's a trump," I said fiercely. "She's a marvellous
person."

"That so?" Already bored by the thought of Louie,
he looked out at the dark fields glimmering by, already
scumbled by the first snow of the year. A few small flakes
blew against the outside of the glass. "Venetia still carrying
on secretly with Charles, is she? Your aunt won't like
that. The story is that she wants all the girls to be Lady
Somebody. And what about Zinnia, eh? That'll please
Mama, all right. But tell me," his large, roundish face bent
uncomfortably close to mine, the reddish skin shining and
the pale blue eyes glinting, "does she really love the fellow
or is she just marrying for the title?"

I thought I knew the answer to his question, but wild
horses would not have made me be disloyal to Zinnia. "It's
none of my business," I said.

"Ah. I always knew you were remarkably discreet, for
a girl."

"Who told you that?"

"Theodore, of course." A glow filled me. If Theodore
had said that, it must be true.

"I'm quite fond of Zinnia myself," Bertram went on in
an offhand way, sounding as if he wasn't really.

"Everybody is," I said stoutly. "She's lovely."

"Wouldn't want her to be unhappy."

"Well, of course not."

"Mm. Those Delmayne cousins of yours play a fast game, don't they?"

I had no idea what he meant, but I sensed that it had nothing to do with croquet and was not complimentary. I was suddenly cross enough to retreat into deliberate misunderstanding.

"Cedric is far from being a fast player," I said coldly.

Disconcertingly, Bertram snorted with mirth. "You're right there. But mind you," he added, "old Cedric's a queer cove. I shouldn't be surprised if one day he gave you all quite a nasty shock," and his head bobbed and his broad shoulders heaved at some inner joke.

The train slowed and clanged to a halt at a small, deserted station. Along the platform a door banged shut, and we chuffed forward again.

"I hope you have a good leave," I said politely into the air.

"Probably spend it heaving sheep out of ditches." We gazed out at the snow, now whitening the anthracite-coloured slates of a ghostly farmhouse. "Wonder how Young Vane's getting on with the farm at Riverlaw? My father did everything he could to persuade your aunt to hire a manager, but she didn't see the need. Between you and me, she's a very obstinate woman. Still, she'll have one less to provide for after the wedding. Fancy little Zinnia being a Lady. That Carroun's an odd chap – never know what he's thinking. We shall all have to mind our p's and q's and not say anything to get her into trouble with him, won't we." He swung his feet off the seat and stood up. "Left my bags at the other end of the train. I'd better get back to them before we get there. Somebody meeting you at Riverlaw?"

"Yes, it's all arranged."

"Good, because I'm getting out at Overriver, otherwise I'd have offered you a lift. 'Bye," and he stooped again to kiss me, rather perfunctorily this time because he was dredging with the other hand in the pocket of his khaki breeches. He straightened, slid the door open, looked back at me, and pressed something small into my gloved hand. "That's because you're a good, nice, discreet girl," he said, and disappeared down the corridor as the door slammed shut.

I opened my hand and there sat a shining golden half-sovereign.

I leapt up and battled with the heavy door. "Here, I can't take this!" I called. "It's too much! You've made a mistake and given me the wrong – "

The door opened so suddenly that I all but fell through. I ran down the corridor, bleating "Bertram! Bertram!" Grown-ups looked up, startled or disapproving, as I passed their carriages. The door at the end of the next coach was stuck. I stood in the half-dark on the shifting floor of the space between the coaches, heaving and rattling the brass door-handle. The walls were some thin concertina'd stuff and I could feel the freezing air and see at the floor's edges the dark ground rushing past below me. I was frightened.

I walked back to my carriage, looking at the gleaming coin. I had never had so much money before. My mother bought my clothes, and my pocket-money had always been measured in pennies. Dazed, I remembered that Hannah's wages – which I knew from having come down the back stairs at Riverlaw one Friday when Aunt Emily was counting the money into her outstretched palm – were seven and six a week (plus, of course, free board and lodging). Bertram's tip was a third as much again. It wasn't fair.

At Overriver, the station before Riverlaw, I didn't get out of the train, but pulled the window down and hung out. A snowflake settled on my nose. Bertram, followed by an old porter weighed down with scuffed leather cases, was coming down the platform towards the exit.

"Bertram!" I yelled. He looked up. "It's too much!"

Bertram grinned and waved his hand dismissively. "Remember what I said!" he called.

The train wheezed, doors clanged shut, the guard lowered his flag and blew the whistle. We moved off.

More snow fell before the wedding. Zinnia drifted round the house all day looking dreamy in Aunt Emily's loose wool-lace dressing-gown trimmed with marabou, with her hair in curling-pins under a pink silk turban. An elderly, distant cousin (the one with thirty-nine bedrooms) arrived from Oxfordshire to give her away, but he was staying at Riverpark and I scarcely saw him.

My parents' wedding-present, a remarkably hideous silver epergne suitable only for the Baronet who has Everything, was in my suitcase, dismantled and wrapped in my spare cardigans. The day before the wedding I dressed up warmly and went down to the Gorgon's shop, my half-sovereign cold and thin against my palm under my glove, to try to find a present of my own. The village shop, with its rows of huge glass bottles of gobstoppers, its bluebags and flypapers and black-leading, proved an unpromising source of elegant wedding-presents. In the end I bought a large jar of preserved ginger, partly because I knew Zinnia liked it, but mainly because the jar was pretty, with pale pink peonies trailing over a rich Chinese-blue background.

When I got back, clutching it, I met her on the stairs and pressed the awkward parcel into her arms. "That's my present for you," I said. "Many happy returns – no, that's wrong." We both giggled. "Happy wedding anyway."

She tore at the paper. Her eyes and lips opened with surprise and pleasure. "Oh, it's divine! You mean you bought it all by yourself?"

I felt myself colouring, and nodded.

"It's beautiful! Here – " and she carefully put it on the landing behind her and turning, gave me a great hug. She smelt of violets. I felt her stomach, fatter than I remembered, against mine.

She detached herself, held me by the shoulders, and looked

at me searchingly. "We're friends, aren't we? Always will be? You won't let me down?"

Under her gaze I suddenly felt like a rabbit in the dark, mesmerised by coachlights.

"Promise?"

I nodded.

"Lady Kerr isn't coming," said Louie, only her sharp nose visible, from the depths of her eiderdown. "And neither is Lady Lambton, because of the snow. They sent telegrams last night." Little plumes of steam rose as she spoke, temporarily clouding a rosebud on the wallpaper behind her bed. The dawn air was unnaturally light, and my nose felt cold as a dog's. "Oh, I hope, I hope most dreadfully that Con can get here. And just think, in a few hours from now Zinnia will be Lady Carroun! Thank you, m'lady. Very good, m'lady. She'll love it. I do hope she'll be happy. D'you think we'll ever be Lady Somebody?"

I listened to the profound, muffling silence of the garden, and heard the faint sound of boots trudging through snow.

"Who can that be?"

"Who can what be?"

I scrambled out of bed into the goose-pimpling cold of the room, and threw on my clothes.

"You're mad," declared Louie. "The wedding isn't till eleven-thirty."

"Can't sleep any more."

"You'll freeze to death. Your poor little toesy-woesys."

I grabbed my muffler and gloves, tiptoed downstairs (avoiding the squeaky boards, which I knew well), and opened the front door.

"Bundle!" whispered Peregrine, a great smile lighting up his face. He opened his arms and enfolded me. He was warm and solid and smelt of Harris tweed. Snowflakes were melting on his shoulders and cap and on his feathery eyebrows. His eyes sparkled and his face was deliciously cold and prickly. I felt happy, miserable, excited and dejected all at once.

"Nobody's up but me. Have you walked all the way from the station?"

"Yes. I came on the milk train. Look, don't wake anyone."

"You must be ravenous." I closed the door cautiously behind him and he sat on the stairs to pull off his boots, and stood up in his khaki socks. I led the way to the kitchen. "We'd better find some food quickly before Gertie gets up. She's a bit of a tartar."

"Lovely to see you," he threw his cap and muffler on the table and unbuttoned his greatcoat. "I wrote to you, but the post is very bad."

I couldn't reply, and was glad I was bent over the breadbin with my back to him, wishing I could explain but ashamed to condemn my mother.

"How's Zinnia?"

"All right." Fetching the butter from the pantry, 'He must be so miserable, I must try to help him to cheer up,' fought in my mind with, 'He and Zinnia are two of a kind, he loves her, they betrayed Rednall, they're wicked.' In the pantry I took deep breaths to calm myself. I hadn't realised that the sight of him, his warm, smiling assumption of friendship, would so affect me. I mustn't show it; stiff upper lip. But that wasn't much help either. All I could think of was the past.

Back at the kitchen table, I had to ask, "Does anyone else call you Birdie?"

He flopped on to a wooden stool and took a silver knife from the table drawer. "No." He stared at the marmalade. "Bundle . . . It's hard, isn't it? Walking down the village, I had the most extraordinary . . . I kept thinking he was there, somewhere just behind me, wanting to tell me something, but whenever I turned round . . ."

"I know." Suddenly I burst out, I couldn't help it, "Aunt Emily thinks Theodore was dreadful. It's so unjust. She can't face the thought of his having married Ivy. We're not allowed to mention him."

"That's terribly unfair!" I had never seen him angry before. "You and I know what he was like."

"He was honest and true and honourable. One day," I resolved, "I'll prove he was a hero. I don't know how, but I'll find the proof somehow, and tell the world. I don't know how, but I will."

Peregrine smiled. "He loved you, you know," he said.

'And I love you,' I repeated silently. 'And oh, poor Peregrine, you love Zinnia, and she's getting married today.'

But when one is twelve years old one does not say these things aloud. I said nothing and took the tea-caddy down from the dresser.

21

Strangely enough, I can't remember much about the wedding itself, except the strong odour of mothballs that wafted from Aunt Emily's ermine cape when Zinnia arrived in the church porch, and the odd-looking skirt of her dress, which stuck out in folds over her hips and tapered towards her feet. It was the latest thing, copied from the Russian Ballet which was all the rage in London, and it had an elastic between the ankles that made her walk in a stilted way that didn't seem like her at all. Her bouquet was vast and tadpole-shaped, with trails of maidenhair fern from the Riverpark conservatory. I wondered whether it reminded her of Giles; it certainly reminded me of what I would very much rather have forgotten, and I could not meet her eye.

My parents were late, and I was anxious in case they had been snowbound on the way. How could my mother cope with snow? (In fact they arrived safely and sneaked in by an aisle door). But when I heard the stamping of boots in the porch during the vows, I couldn't help turning round and seeing, past Venetia's white kid-covered elbow, a uniformed figure; Henry Grey. Oh dear, I thought, and he wasn't asked. But it was a nice surprise all the same.

The church was deathly cold and the very stone seemed to exhale ice. I felt my arms coming up in goose-pimples under the thin rose silk, and Zinnia's veil trembled slightly because I couldn't stop my hands from shaking. I tried to concentrate on the vicar's high, solemn monotone, but my attention wandered to the steam ballooning up from his narrow lips. I was too cold to think. Even the Delmayne monuments seemed dead, cold stone, irredeemably secular.

I shivered home in the carriage and dashed upstairs to throw off the useless fur tippet and put on a cardigan before joining the press of people in the drawing-room. Zinnia, in the ermine cape with the tadpole bouquet still clamped over her stomach, kissed me on both cheeks.

"What a good little bridesmaid! Are you frozen?" And before I could answer Rednall stooped to kiss me too. "Little present," he said, pressing something into my palm. It was an oval gold locket on a fine chain. On the front was the Carroun crest – a large hand, forbiddingly raised to the viewer, with the motto *Nemo me impune lacessit* below.

"Oh, thank you!" I turned it over. "What can I put in it?"

"The hair of your lover," said Zinnia archly. She looked quickly round the room, but everyone was talking; nobody had heard her but me. Rednall had turned to the best man, who stood next to him, tall and dark with amused eyes in a sharp, weatherbeaten face. "This is Chuck McIver," he said to me. "Meet Lizzie."

"Why, hello, Lizzie." I thought he must be Scottish; his uniform was unfamiliar. "My, what a beautiful gift." I was baffled. No gentleman, Scottish or otherwise, would say 'gift' – a shopkeeper's word. But Aunt Emily, approaching to embrace me in a cloud of scent under her vast, pink, ostrich-plume-laden hat, didn't bat an eyelid. "Lizzie dearest," she cooed. "You did so well."

"Shook like a jelly," smirked Young Vane with a quick peck on my cheek.

"Dearest, you looked lovely," my mother tweaked at my neckline. "What did the bridegroom give you? Oh, *far* too good of him."

"Hear the sound of bells, wedding bells," said Con, for

although we could not, of course, have the church bells rung, Venetia had bought a record of bells in London and borrowed the Seymours' gramophone, and the chimes pealed out now, rather scratchily, from the kitchen.

"What a sound of revelry their harmony foretells," echoed Louie at his elbow. "No, that's not quite right – "

"Bloody monotonous they are, if you ask me," Bertram put in. Zinnia threw back her head and laughed. Everyone else looked embarrassed and the group began to break up among the porcelain-blue chairs. "*I* didn't invite him," hissed Aunt Emily from under her pink ostrich-plumes to Lady Carroun, who was standing beside the piano with two men I had not met before.

Zinnia's mother-in-law wore an elaborate dress of mud-coloured gabardine trimmed with velvet swags. It had a bustle and had been very expensive some years before the war, when she had (apparently) been somewhat plumper than now. Her matching hat was a little worn round the brim; a piece of black wire protruded from a tear in the velvet binding. Her grey hair hung, lank and wispy, over her ears, and her pointed nose was red. Her watery blue eyes looked disapproving.

I thought that something must be done, if only for Zinnia's sake. I went over to her, curtsied and introduced myself. "Do look at this lovely locket," I said. "I've never had such a splendid present in my life."

She gave a creaky smile.

"What does the motto mean, exactly?"

"Nobody injures me without being punished."

"Oh."

"May I introduce – " she indicated the elder man; thin, with a pursed mouth, a face like stale pastry, and thread-like hairs carefully distributed over his bald patch. "Mr Brown, and his nephew Mr Leslie Brown."

"How do you do?" I had heard of the Browns; Brown senior was a Newcastle estate agent who advised Lady Carroun. There was a rumour that he had made her evict some poor old cottagers, and they had to go to the work-house.

Leslie Brown looked at me coldly. He was small, slight and colourless, perhaps seventeen years old, with a soft, oval face, a Roman nose, and close-curled, fairish hair. Silently, he put out a limp hand.

"Do introduce me," lisped Cedric behind me.

"Mr Brown, Mr Leslie Brown, may I present – " Louie had taught me the formula, with graceful hand-movements – "Mr Cedric Delmayne. Mr Delmayne, may I introduce Mr Brown, Mr Leslie Brown."

Somewhere behind me I heard laughter and Chuck McIver's voice saying, "Holy mackerel, how old is she?" and Peregrine's replying, "Thirteen, but pretty sensible." Pretty sensible. I glowed.

Leslie Brown was saying to Cedric, "Are you the Riverpark Delmaynes?"

"Yes."

His pale eyes flickered with interest. "I'd love to see it," and they moved away together. Brown senior was already making his way through the crowd towards the doctor, who was having a clearly uninspiring conversation with the Vicar. Lady Carroun gazed at the sun-stained silk curtains.

I looked round in slight desperation. "Have you met Dr Bond?" I asked her.

"Yes," she said, without moving.

"Or Bertram's father?"

"Thank you, I'm quite all right." She began to retreat around the piano, then looked over my shoulder.

"Oh, Lieutenant McIver, how are you getting on?"

"I'm having a whale of a time admiring the maids of honour." No, he definitely wasn't Scottish. "Madge I know, but who's the very pretty one?"

"That's Zinnia's sister Venetia," I explained. "She's in love with a soldier."

"Just my luck. And what relation are you?"

"I'm Zinnia's father's cousin once removed."

"I'm getting the picture. Are you Cedric's sister?"

"Heavens, no." My face must have betrayed my reaction, because he laughed; a nice, quiet, delighted sort of laugh. "Those are my parents over there."

"Guess I like to get these things straight in my mind. Well, I've met Zinnia's father's relatives, but what about her mother's? Which are they? Will you introduce me in that splendid British way of yours?"

"You know, it's a funny thing," I reflected, "but I've never heard of her having any. There certainly aren't any here." I looked round at the chattering guests; I knew, or could identify, everyone. "Louie," I grabbed at her plump and tightly-upholstered arm (I recognised the dress; it had been cut down from a rose velvet one of Aunt Emily's) as she edged past, eyes on Gertie's silver platter of cheese straws. "Has Aunt Emily any relations?"

Louie looked round, startled. "I think so, but we're not on speakers. They live somewhere up in north Northumberland. I think they cut her off when she married Father." The old bright, twinkly look came into her rather spotty and shiny face. "Rather romantic, isn't it? And fancy not approving of Father!"

I was impressed. Aunt Emily's antecedents must have been grand indeed. I was disconcerted for a moment when Chuck said, "That's real sad."

"Where do you come from?" I asked him.

"Nova Scotia."

"Goodness where's that?"

"Canada, at the right-hand side of the map, thirty-six hours on the train north-west of Toronto," he was clearly used to explaining it to the ignorant British.

"How on earth did you meet Rednall?"

"My father was Scottish. He emigrated to Canada soon after he left the army. When I was sixteen he made some big money and sent me over here to school at Harrow for a year. The other boys in the house were all friends already, but I guess Rednall was a solitary kind of person and we chummed up. When I came back to Europe to fight, it was good to see him again." He looked thoughtfully at the glass in his hand. "I'm glad I got leave for this wedding."

"Amazing, when you come to think of it, that all the boys managed to get here," said Louie.

"Charles didn't," said Venetia sadly over her shoulder. She was still wearing her bridesmaid's picture hat, of ruched, rose-coloured organdie, absurdly unsuitable for winter. She looked beautiful, but a little pale and withdrawn. It could so easily, after all, have been her wedding to Charles.

Madge, beside her, was already a little the worse for the wine, and her hat was askew. "Of course, that doesn't apply to Cedric," she said in a loud, high voice. "*Cedric's* here all the time, and we all know why, don't we?"

"Oh, don't be silly, Madge," said Venetia.

But Cedric had heard from across the room. I saw him look round, his glistening red lips stuck out in an angry pout, before turning back to Leslie Brown.

"I love your locket, Lizzie," said Louie, a little wistfully, fingering it. "Pity it's the Carrouns' crest and not yours. Do you think he bought it specially, or just happened to have it in stock? May I look inside?"

I remembered Zinnia's voice saying "the hair of your lover", and wondered, for a ridiculous moment, which of the men in the room would be my lover when I grew up. Of course, I knew it is wicked to take lovers, and I was sure I would never do that.

Much later, when everyone was talking twenty to the dozen and even Lady Carroun had mellowed slightly under the influence of sparkling white wine, I found myself next to Peregrine. My mouth felt cloyed and sticky inside with sarsaparilla.

"Do you think it would be all right to get a drink of water?" I said.

"I'd like one too. Come on."

We slipped out. Outside the door he said, "Don't let's go into the kitchen. I'm bushwhacked. Can't face being polite to Gertie and Cook, just for a little while."

"Schoolroom?"

He nodded.

We went upstairs and I got two glasses of water from the bathroom. When I entered the schoolroom Peregrine was seated with his head and arms slumped on the table in an attitude of utter exhaustion.

"When did you last sleep?" I asked him.

"On the boat, night before last. Oh, I don't know. So sorry to be like this."

I thought: Of course, it's because he loves Zinnia. I ached with hopeless love.

"Today must have been awful for you," I said gently.

"I can't stick it," he muttered into the red plush cloth. "None of those people could imagine what it's like . . ." His shoulders shook. "Human nature can only take so much. I love it here, I love you all, but . . . I wish I hadn't come." I wanted to say: You weren't the first, she isn't worth it. But that would mean betraying Zinnia, and even for Peregrine I couldn't do it. "No, that isn't true. I wish I could just stay here and never go back," he groaned. "Oh this war, this bloody, cruel, disgusting war . . ."

My hand hovered over his head, drawn downwards as if by a magnet. The effort not to stroke his soft hair made my whole arm feel almost disembodied.

"She won't be happy," I ventured. But it was no consolation to me and I knew it couldn't be to him either.

He looked up and stared at me for a minute. I couldn't read his thoughts, and his gaze was so direct and concerned that I had to look away in case he read mine.

"Here's your glass of water," I said.

"I reckon we both have our troubles," he murmured. "Lizzie, my friend, you're about the nicest person I know."

He stretched out his hand, and the silver cufflink flashed in the January sunlight.

Later still, after everyone had eaten and drunk as much as they decently could, and a little circle round Henry had pumped him about his adventures (I noticed that the soldiers present did not speak of theirs), and Young Vane had made him promise to land his plane in one of the Delmaynes' fields as soon as he was posted back to England, we waved Zinnia and Rednall off in the Carroun carriage with its discreet gold crest, just like the one on my locket. Gleaming leather suitcases had been strapped on the back, full of silk and lace underwear and silk stockings that Aunt Emily had saved since before the war, and the most elegant dresses Fenwick's French and Mrs Hothersall could provide, all packed in rustling layers of fresh tissue paper. "Twelve camisoles!" sighed poor Venetia, who only had three.

Rednall had to go back to his regiment at the end of the week, so they were not going away but spending the time at his home. "Fancy having Ma Carroun with you on your honeymoon!" snorted Louie; and indeed it did seem hard on Zinnia, whose relations with her mother-in-law were already barely polite. "You'd think he could afford three days at an hotel!"

Nevertheless, when she came downstairs after changing out of her wedding-dress, Zinnia looked terribly happy. She was muffled to the ears in a soft blue tweed ulster with a big, squashy fur collar, and a pert little fur toque was tilted over her shining eyes. Rednall's big driving-coat had been cleaned up for the occasion, and he had a camellia in his buttonhole. He looked proudly down at her as they walked, she on his arm like a queen, into the snow-whitened garden. I thought: He's happy too.

"Good luck, m'lady!" called Aunt Emily, lifting a lace handkerchief to her eyes.

"Goodbye, goodbye, good luck!" we all shouted as

Young Vane started to pour rice over Rednall's head and the happy pair fled down the drive to the carriage, with Young Vane and Louie and I in pursuit.

I stumbled over my long skirt and got left behind, so the last I saw of Zinnia that day was her laughing face as she tumbled up the carriage steps, her hand still in Rednall's. She slammed the door while he lifted the whip to the horses. They careered down the drive and through the pineapple gateposts into the future.

My parents took the train back to Newcastle later the same afternoon, and Chuck McIver went with them, *en route* for his regiment; but it was thought that the excitement of being a bridesmaid was quite enough for one day, and I was allowed to stay another night at Riverlaw.

By nightfall, everyone else had gone. The last to leave was Peregrine, and I volunteered to drive him to the station in the trap. To my surprise, Aunt Emily agreed (perhaps because the hinds had been celebrating in the stables with a barrel of beer and by then were possibly in no condition to drive).

There had been a slight thaw, but as twilight drew on the shallow snow began to freeze, so that the trap made a nice crunching noise as we bowled along. Aunt Emily had wrapped us in mufflers and faded tartan blankets and an ancient fur rug, matted and motheaten but still very soft. But even so, it was bitingly cold, with a sharp little wind that burnt my cheek like frozen metal.

The sky was darkening grey, and an eerie luminosity threw the stone walls into relief against the whitened fields, as if we were driving through a stage set. Bare, black branches creaked above our heads, occasionally tipping blobs of snow in our path. But gradually the wind petered out, and when I stopped the pony in order to negotiate a pothole, there was for three or four seconds a complete and utter silence.

"Back, back!" I chanted into the emptiness. "Whoa,

there! Gee up!" It was like driving in one's sleep, in a land of the imagination. The white shore beyond the death-flood.

Peregrine had been very quiet. He looked dreadfully tired. As the lights of the station came into view, "I hope she'll be happy," he muttered.

"So do I."

"But I have a feeling this might be the fall of the house of Delmayne?"

It might have been a question, but I didn't answer.

I looked at him anxiously. I imagined him crouched alone in a water-logged trench, staring along the sights of a rifle, with millions of snarling, grey-helmeted Germans charging towards him, bayonets drawn, while their great guns boomed and whining shells fountained death around his dear head.

In the station yard he helped me to put the brake on and hobble the pony, and lit the brass carriage-lamps with a lucifer. He heaved his case out and together we walked through to the platform. I thought of the last time I had met a train there, and he had been on it.

"I've always thought of Riverlaw as my second home," he said suddenly.

"So have I." The first murmur of the train emerged from behind the sledging hill.

"I keep thinking that there's no real reason now why they should ever invite me again."

"Don't say that." A mournful hoot, and the crossing gates clanged shut.

"I hope we meet again one day."

There were so many things I could have said. My heart was full. But for once I was tongue-tied. He was a grown man. He had been very kind to me. But I was a child.

I said nothing. Oh, stupid Lizzie!

The train chugged to a stop.

"Goodbye."

"Goodbye."

He pressed my hand, looked into my eyes for a moment, kissed me gently on the cheek, and was gone.

All night I tossed and turned and thought of Peregrine, and Zinnia, and Theodore, and the golden days at Riverlaw that would never come again.

The fall of the house of Delmayne, Peregrine had said.

Well, perhaps he was right.

And yet.

One day . . . (I told myself fiercely). One day, even if I have to wait nearly all my life . . .

I must have dozed off in the small hours. But I remember the dawn, that interminably empty time when one knows it is far too early to get up. I saw the roses on the wallpaper emerge one by one from the shadows, and heard an early cock crow in the stackyard.

Eventually I heard a sound downstairs. Someone was up. I slipped out of bed and dressed quickly.

In the dining-room I found Aunt Emily, wearing a voluminous white nightie and the wool-lace and marabou dressing-gown that Zinnia had worn the day before. Her hair was tied in a fat, wispy pigtail. She looked as if she hadn't slept either. She was gathering up the best silver and storing it away in its green-baize bags in the silver-cupboard in the panelling beside the fireplace. As she caught sight of me, her head jerked up and her pigtail and arm shook.

"Oh! How you did startle me, dearest."

"I'm so sorry. I couldn't sleep. Can I help you?"

"I couldn't sleep either. Must be all the excitement. You could put that cream-jug into its little bag – you have to find the right one, or it won't fit. That's right – pull the drawstrings tight, so that the silver won't tarnish."

"Auntie," I said – and I don't think I would ever have dared to ask the question if I hadn't been so exhausted with turning it over and over in my mind through the night – "When is Zinnia's baby due?"

188

Her face changed. She tensed, and looked both angry and fearful. "What made you think that?"

I couldn't look her in the eye. "She hugged me and I felt it."

"Oh, dear. Oh dear, oh dear. They were very naughty, you know, darling. But he's such a charming man and devoted to her, and very aristocratic. It isn't as if . . . And she knew he would marry her. It'll all be the same in a hundred years."

"But surely – "

"Babies can be very premature, you know, Lizzie dear. We must just say nothing about it. Don't tell anyone, will you, for poor Zinnia's sake. After all, she has made such a very good marriage, she's a Lady and going to be mistress of that beautiful house one day. And it's not as if Sir Rednall's baby was going to be born out of wedlock."

"But . . ." I tried to think how to tell her the truth.

"Don't worry about it, dearest. Everything's going to be all right."

But somehow I knew that it wasn't. In that bleak dawn, I suddenly saw with complete clarity a great moral principle. Evil actions have evil results. In the face of lies there is no truth, and to the consequences of wrong-doing there is no end.

But saying nothing was not a lie. And perhaps it was best that Aunt Emily should never know. Yes, obviously that was best. I couldn't betray Zinnia, let alone Peregrine.

As Aunt Emily and I were pottering about the dining-room and drawing-room, collecting a shining pepperpot here and an entrée dish there, and each lost in our own worries about Zinnia, we both simultaneously heard in the silence the distant, muffled clop of hooves and crunch of wheels coming quickly down the village . . . approaching the corner by the garden wall . . . stopping.

"Goodness, who's that arriving so early? It doesn't sound like the fish-cart. Dearest, you're dressed – would you run and see what they want?"

As I went out the cold air hit me like a blow, and I hurried down the drive over yesterday's rutted and footmarked snow. In the frigid half-light outside the pineapple columns I saw a pony-trap piled with luggage, with a lone figure sliding down from the driving-seat; a figure muffled in a big, fur-collared ulster, and capped in fur.

No word was spoken. I just stood there, my mouth open in dismay and disbelief, and Zinnia came to me and put her arms round me and rocked, and wept silently into my hair, and at last she whispered, "They've thrown me out. And for God's sake, if you love me at all, don't tell Mother!"

22

"We'll have to hide the trap right away," I said. "She's in the dining-room at this very minute. Stackyard?"

"No, no. Bob gets up very early. Get in, quick." Zinnia scrambled back up the step after me, and Rednall's stolid pony moved forward as she shook the reins on his back. "Why was she up at this godforsaken hour?"

I rested my feet on something shiny, and recognised it as the crocodile dressing-case with heavy gold fittings, luxurious but slightly soiled, that Lady C had given Zinnia as a wedding present.

"What will you do?" She was driving round the corner into the Riverpark lane.

"I can't stay here." Her voice rose, distraught. "Has Venetia gone back to London yet?"

"Yes. Not long after you left."

"I'm going back there to be a V.A.D. I can stay in the hostel with the other nurses. But I have to get into the house to collect my uniform first."

"Zinnia," I protested, "you can't do it! You can't desert Rednall! He loves you! You're his wife!"

Zinnia urged the pony at a trot past the gap at the bottom of the lawn, and pulled up just past the next bend, opposite the orchard in a place where we could not be seen from the house. Tears were glinting on her cheeks, but her jaw was set.

"I think if it had been just him, I could have engineered things so that everything was all right," she said. "I was so sure he would come round. But as soon as I took off my coat, his ghastly mother saw my stomach. She went rigid. 'Zinnia, you never told us!' she said. And Rednall went white and said, 'It isn't mine,' and she hit the roof. I've never seen such a rage. It was horrific. 'Out of my house!' she bellowed. She went on and on about how the name of Carroun had never been so besmirched, and *Nemo* impugned them *Lacessit*, or whatever it was, and I wasn't fit to lick Rednall's boots – or words to that effect."

"Blow *her*. You're not married to *her*. Didn't Rednall stick up for you?"

"No." She put her face in her hands. "Oh, poor, poor Rednall, who could blame him? But he'll never have me back. To tell you the truth, I was really surprised he ever proposed to me. I don't think he's really a marrying sort of man. He was very quiet and grim last night. I minded that more than all Lady C's storming. He persuaded her to let me sleep the night there, but he led me miles along a dark corridor to a horrible, dusty bedroom with a single bed, and the sheets were mouldy with damp. He kept coughing that little, nervous cough – you know we thought he had T.B.? Well, he hasn't. I tried to kiss him but he just turned his head away. He wouldn't touch me."

"You mean to say you spent the night alone? On your honeymoon?"

"Yes." She began to sob.

I was embarrassed, and my heart ached for poor, passionate Zinnia, so shellshocked by rejection that she had to pour out her troubles to a child. I couldn't bear it, and besides, my teeth were chattering with cold.

"Listen," I said. "If you're going to the station we'd better get a move on, or half the village will see you. Can I get the uniform and bring it out to you here?"

"What a brick you are!" She gave an enormous sniff and began to revive. "But no . . . I'm not sure where I put it. Tell you what. I'm awfully hungry, because what with all the drama I was never actually offered any supper, and I sneaked out down some back stairs this morning as soon as it was light enough to see. I was terrified some groom would wake and stop me from stealing the trap, because above all I didn't want Rednall and his ma to have the satisfaction of seeing me off the premises."

"So you've had no breakfast either."

"Exactly. Now, if we creep round to the back door, will you keep cavey for me so that I can slope upstairs and find my things, without anyone seeing? And while I'm there, could you get me some food – as much as you possibly can? Otherwise I'll starve to death by the time I reach London – and I must save money like mad."

"However will you manage when the baby arrives?"

"That's what I mean. Venetia will help me. But I'll need every penny I can lay my hands on. Buying unnecessary food is out."

"Zinnia," I said slowly. "Are you quite sure you want to do this? Go to London, I mean?"

"Heavens, yes. Anything – *anything* rather than face Mother!"

"I must tell you. She knows about the baby already."

Zinnia groaned and put her face in her hands again. "I'm sure Mrs Hothersall guessed. She must have told her. Lizzie, you won't tell a soul, will you? I know you never split on me over Giles. I trust you, Lizzie."

"Well, of course. But listen. Aunt Emily thinks it's Rednall's baby, but she was so thrilled that you married him that she really isn't too cross. And you still are Lady Carroun, aren't you?"

"I couldn't face her if she knew the truth. I just couldn't face her. Come on, we must hurry!"

"Very well." Trembling with cold and apprehension (for I did not relish the thought of being caught by Gertie in the act of stealing large quantities of food) I got down from the trap. "I'll get my coat and walking-boots too, and I can see you off at the station and then take the trap back to Rednall and walk home. I could leave it at the entrance to the drive and they wouldn't see it till I'd gone."

"Darling Lizzie, what would I ever have done without you?"

I held out my hand to help her down. For the first time that morning she turned on me her old, dazzling smile.

And then, looking back towards the bend in the lane that led to the village, her face changed completely.

I looked round.

There, hurrying towards us with her eyes fixed on me and not ten yards away, was Aunt Emily.

"Oh, thank God you're there, darling," my aunt burst out as she approached. She had thrown an ulster over her nightdress and dressing-gown, and galoshes over her slippers; her hair was still undone, and her face looked jowly and distraught. "When you didn't come back and the trap drove away, I got anxious – *Zinnia!*"

Gazing at me as she hurried forward, she had until this moment ignored everything else in her path.

But now mother and daughter stared at each other, aghast.

"What's happened?" One look at Zinnia's tear-stained face must have struck fear into her heart. "Why are you here? It's not – darling, it's not the baby, is it?"

"You're going to kill me."

"What do you mean? What's the matter? Where's Rednall?"

"Oh, stop asking stupid questions!" But immediately Zinnia added, "Oh, I'm sorry, you're only trying to help." She burst into tears. "But nobody can help, nobody. Oh, I'm in such a pickle," and she scrubbed at her eyes with her fur-gloved hand.

Aunt Emily looked at me, but I was not going to be the one to explain Zinnia's disaster. I went to the pony and felt in my pocket for the spare lump of sugar I usually carried for emergencies. If Aunt Emily hadn't been there I would have given it to Zinnia, not the pony.

"Has something happened to Rednall? Oh, poor, poor Zinnia!" Aunt Emily put her arms round her daughter but Zinnia shook her head violently and broke away.

"No, Rednall's perfectly all right. Oh, stop it, Mother. I can't tell you. Just accept that I can't stay there."

"Can't stay there?" Aunt Emily's blue eyes grew wide with horror. "But you're his *wife*! You've *got* to stay there!"

Zinnia sobbed anew.

"This is your great chance in life, darling! You're Lady Carroun now. You've taken on the duty of being nice to Rednall in exchange for the title and all it means. You've got to be loyal to him."

"You mean I've sold myself."

"Oh, no, no, darling, don't say that!" Aunt Emily looked searchingly at her daughter. "Did he ask you to do things you didn't like, dearest? I'm afraid you just have to bear it and try to – "

"No! Be quiet! You don't know a thing about it!"

"And the baby! You must bring up his dear little baby in its father's house, it would be wicked to – "

"The baby's not Rednall's," said Zinnia. She put her hand to her mouth in horror, as if the words had slipped out without her knowing.

There was a silence.

Aunt Emily's soft little mouth was clamped shut. A succession of violent emotions passed over her face. She drew the ulster round her and stood there in the snow, a pathetic, bedraggled figure that yet retained a kind of dignity.

"Who is the father?" she said at last.

"I'm not telling you."

"You must."

"No, I won't. Not ever."

"Do the Carrouns know who he is?"

"No."

"Perhaps you could get a divorce and marry him," I said miserably, trying to help.

They both turned on me and said "No!" with vehemence. I was taken aback and saw that I should have kept out of it.

"You mustn't think of divorce," said Aunt Emily. "You'd lose every advantage you've gained."

"Advantage!" sniffed Zinnia.

"Yes, you have. Listen, dearest, don't despair. It'll be all right in the end. You, Lizzie," she turned to me, "must promise never, never to speak of this again."

I nodded.

"And, Zinnia dearest, we will have to make some forward plans. I think you will have to go back to London for the time being. But in the end everything will be all right, I promise. Poor, poor darling, don't cry!"

And she enfolded her daughter in her arms.

23

After these events, and perhaps indirectly because of them, my links with Riverlaw became steadily more tenuous.

Oh, Louie's letters kept me informed; but, for one reason and another, I did not go there.

I went on holiday with La Gutch to Scarborough; I endured the mysteries and anxieties of puberty; I stayed at home to work for examinations, and later, far from being sent away when my mother was ill, I stayed to look after her. I grew.

In France, the war rolled on. The two armies reached a virtual stalemate in the sodden trenches. The black-bordered casualty lists grew ever longer. Almost every family had lost someone in the fighting or the air-raids. Shortages of food, household goods, materials, seemed permanent. I couldn't remember what bananas or oranges tasted like.

Meanwhile, a lot of things happened.

Zinnia had her baby. Louie wrote that it was officially premature but everyone was shocked to bits and counting the months on their fingers like mad, but as Rednall had been home when Theodore died, they sort of understood. Poor Zinnia, she wrote; what a life she had had when you thought about it, what with Theodore and Giles and being so young when he died. Perhaps, she added with a *soupçon* of the condescension of the experienced novelist, it was excusable to have comforted herself with Rednall at that dreadful time – though, of course, you and I (she assured me) wouldn't have dreamt of such a wicked thing.

And it was when I received this letter that I began to suspect that there was a connection between Louie's misconception (oh, appropriate word!) about the baby's parentage, and my failure to receive any further invitation from Aunt Emily. The official line, apparently, was that the baby was Rednall's. As usual, I knew too much.

The baby, born in a London hospital, was christened Zadok Rednall in the parish church at Riverlaw. Zinnia brought him home from London specially, and Louie was a godmother. The first I knew of it was when I received a note on thick white paper headed with a crest and two words engraved in large Gothic letters: REDNALL, NORTHUMBERLAND, crossed out, and RIVERLAW scribbled in Zinnia's flamboyant hand. I firmly relegated to my subconscious the fact that she must have stolen the paper – but perhaps she thought she had a right to it.

She explained that she had meant to ask me to be a godmother too, but Zadok had had a severe chill because of the journey, and she had had him christened straight away in case (she wrote) of accidents, and actually it was a very small affair as Rednall was at the Front and of course couldn't be there, and the Dowager Lady C had been busy that afternoon and couldn't either. From this I deduced that Zinnia had attempted a reconciliation with the Carrouns, which had (not surprisingly) failed.

I had told my mother the bare fact that Zinnia was expecting a baby. But now she had seen the crisp white envelope on the hall table, and some explanation was required. Besides, I was bursting with pride at having very nearly been a godmother. I read her the note, but all she said was that it was unheard-of for a grandmother not to attend the christening of the heir.

I didn't attempt to explain. But I naturally asked Louie, in my next letter, to tell all about the christening. She revealed, with many capitals and exclamation-marks, that although

Zinnia had written to Lady C she had not come, I could guess why, and Zinnia had been relieved because she was convinced that her mother-in-law would try to veto the name Zadok at the very font itself. (Battling with Aunt Emily, who also hated the name, had been bad enough.) The Vicar had been appalled at Lady C's absence, but Zinnia had sobbed, declaring that the baby was ill and might die; so he had performed the ceremony in hugger-mugger, and Young Vane had been proxy godfather in the absence of Chuck McIver the Canadian. (I did wonder whether Zinnia's choice of Chuck was by way of being a pipe of peace to Rednall.) The baby, stated Louie, had been perfectly well; it only had a little snuffle, which was now better. "We didn't even have a Cake," she added indignantly.

I imagined them in the draughty old church, surrounded by high oak pews and stone monuments and silence, and felt sad.

Something else Louie told me was even more disturbing. Aunt Emily, she wrote, had tried terribly hard to get Zinnia to send the baby away for adoption. She had even found suitable parents in a distant mining town. But (thank heaven) Zinnia would have none of it. Little Zadok was her very own and she couldn't bear to give him away. She intended, against the advice of Aunt Emily, Aunt Letitia and Dr Bond, to bring him up herself – in London.

I embarked on knitting a pair of blue bootees. It took a long time, and when they were finished I embroidered 'Z' in white silk on the toes. I sent them off to Zinnia for the baby, but she never replied.

Perhaps that was because, soon afterwards, Uncle Vane had another massive stroke, and died.

I begged to be allowed to go to the funeral, but my parents were being protective. They and Aunt Emily, they said, thought I was still too young for funerals. Besides, it was the middle of term and exams were looming.

I went to stay with La Gutch, two streets away, while my parents were at Riverlaw. She called me "*pauvre petite*

Eloïse", which was gratifying, but I couldn't help shedding a few tears for dear, white-whiskery Uncle Vane, and felt sure that all the girls he had ever called Mary-Jane were missing him too. In a way I had already mourned his passing; but his actual death was another signal that things would never be the same.

Soon after that, Louie wrote that Aunt Emily was bearing up fairly well, considering. She was managing the farm herself with Young Vane's help. Everyone wanted her to get a manager, but she wouldn't.

To be frank (she wrote), I don't think we could afford a manager, and where would he live? None of the village cottages is vacant, and a hind's cottage wouldn't do for a manager anyway. I believe the money the solicitor is sending to Hannah and You-Know-Who is making a big hole in the exchequer, and Mother is now having to help Zinnia too. Z sent an impassioned appeal to Rednall about being homeless and destitute though still his wife, and he sent her enough money to buy a little tiny house and she has bought one in St John's Wood, in London. She says she really loves it, but it only has three bedrooms and Venetia is living there as well, so there isn't even a spare room or a place for a nursemaid, and she has hardly anything to live on. I know she has borrowed from Mother, and I think it's ridiculous she should have to when Rednall has that huge house and all that land – if the Dowager ran things properly they would be Rolling, but their fields are all thistly and their hinds take no notice of her. This is for your ears only, dear Lizzie, and I know it's ill-bred to talk about Money but I know you are the Soul of Discretion.
Masses of love,
L.

The war rumbled on. The columns of dead and wounded in the newspapers grew longer every day. And even my memories of the golden days at Riverlaw were fading and vanishing away. I was still hardly more than a child, but I felt that war and wickedness and death had already robbed me of all that was precious; that never again would my life be affected by my favourite place and its people.

But I was amazingly, ridiculously, entirely wrong.

24

It was the custom during the war for Commonwealth soldiers on leave from the Front to be offered hospitality by British families. I think my father may have made some such offer to Chuck McIver while they were in the train together after Zinnia's wedding; anyway, a year or so after that historic day, he turned up one evening at the door of our house in Newcastle.

I heard the bell and looked over the banisters as the maid opened the door, and there was this dusty, exhausted figure in uniform, cap in hand, bulging kitbag beside him on the doorstep. He had travelled from Dover on a series of trains slowed by air-raids. He was on his way to spend his leave with Rednall and his mother but he had missed the last connection to Overriver. Could he possibly stay the night?

"You'd better telephone the Carrouns, otherwise they'll be anxious about you," said my father. Our telephone had just been installed and hung gleaming on the wall beside the front door.

Chuck grinned, a disarming display of tanned crinkles and perfect teeth.

"I guess they don't know I'm coming," he admitted.

"All the more reason to let them know," said my father sternly.

I went into the drawing-room, but I left the door open on purpose. As he telephoned, I watched the tall, rangy figure in khaki and, throwing manners to the winds, I listened to the deep, thrilling voice with its exotic accent.

When he had finished he came into the drawing-room like a prince entering a suburban street.

"I'm in a fix," he said. "A maid answered, and then went away for ages. The line was crackling and I could hardly understand her accent. But Lady Carroun's in bed with 'flu and Rednall's on leave, but he's shabby. What's shabby?"

"In this part of the world, in that context, it means under the weather. Ill," explained my father.

"That's what I thought. Anyway, she told me it isn't a good time to come."

"In that case you'd better stay here."

So Chuck spent the whole of his leave with us. He had his ration-book so food was no problem. And because my father had to go to the office every day and my mother was again unwell and kept largely to her room, he spent the time, in effect, with me.

My school holidays had just begun, and my parents liked Chuck (and I think his having been Rednall's best man was, for them, a passport to respectability). They were delighted to have my entertainment taken off their hands by a friend of the Aristocracy. "Put on your best dress and brush your hair properly," hissed my mother. "And don't forget a clean pocket-handkerchief."

Having just done well in the Easter exams, I was cheerful and raring to go. I showed him what there was to see of Newcastle, and when that was done we set out on day trips, by tram to Roker and Whitley Bay and by train to Alnmouth and Berwick. We sat on empty beaches making sand-forts with our hands, scrambled over rocks and discovered rock-pools previously (we told each other) unknown to man. We changed prudishly into our long-legged swimming costumes (mine had a skirt, for modesty) out of sight of each other in the shelter of sand-dunes, and raced each other into the waves, catching our breath and shrieking at the cold. Chuck showed me how to float and began teaching me to swim, and as he held me in the water with his large hands supporting my midriff and thighs, I felt an obscure excitement.

"I just love this," he said one day as, after a hundred-yard dash over the sand to get warm, we sat, huddled in towels and sucking black mint humbugs, in a sheltering fold of the dunes. "It reminds me of home."

"Honestly? I thought Nova Scotia was covered in forest?"

"Well, there are a good many farms like ours, but basically you're right. But the North Shore is very like this. Sand-dunes and marram-grass, and lots of shells on the beach like those ones in your pocket, and maybe some bigger ones too. And I'll tell you something. Suppose we were there now, we'd see maybe a cute little red and white lighthouse on that point over there, and a big shadowy island in the far distance – Prince Edward Island – and the water between is called the Northumberland Strait. How about that?"

"Not really?"

"Yes, 'really, truly absolutely'." He smiled as he imitated one of my schoolgirl phrases in a mock-Oxford accent. "You'd love it." He looked sideways at me in a funny way. "Maybe I'll take you there one day."

My heart leapt. Foreign travel, seeing the world – that was something only men did, as a rule; and with the war still grinding on, even they could only get abroad if the Army or Navy sent them to battle. But here was a chance, an unbelievable chance, and I seized it.

"Oh, yes, please! I'd simply love that."

"Right. It's a deal." And we shook hands on it. If it had been one of the Delmaynes or Peregrine I would have spat on my hand like a horse-trader, but I didn't quite like to do that with Chuck, who might not see the joke. Besides, I didn't really think for a moment that my parents would allow me to go with him. It wasn't just that there seemed no possibility of the war ending; even if there were a miracle and peace was declared, it wouldn't be *comme il faut* to travel alone with a man. Going on day trips was quite unconventional enough.

But anyone can dream. And if there were all that wonderful world out there to see, one day I would do my damnedest to see it.

On the following day, the last of Chuck's leave, we travelled north and changed at a deserted station on to a little train with only one carriage, divided into first, second and third class. We sat in solitary state in the first, among red plush and antimacassars, and curtains tied back with brass curlicues. The train proceeded at walking-pace down a long cutting lined with wild flowers, and I leaned out of the window and snatched an armful of bluebells stalk by stalk as we went along.

We got out at the next station because we smelt the sea. Walking down a narrow, stone-walled lane between fields to the beach, we saw in the distance to our left a great sandstone castle high on a rock above the dunes.

Chuck said, "Could we go to see it?"

"It looks a very long walk." It floated magically above a layer of heat-haze. I longed to approach; I had never in my life seen a place that looked more enchanted. But some deep instinct made me want to go alone. "And don't forget we haven't much time or we'll miss our connection back to Newcastle." *Fool*, I told myself. You want to see it, don't you? Missed your chance, now. "What's it called?"

Chuck fished the map out of his breast pocket, and unfolded it on top of the wall. "Shoreburgh."

"Oh! That's where Peregrine lives. We must go there, at all costs!"

"Who in earth is Peregrine?"

"You must have met him at Zinnia's wedding. He's a friend of the Delmaynes. A great friend," I added. "Peregrine Fenwick."

"Oh, you mean the guy who got an M.C."

"The Military Cross? Honestly?"

"Well, I guess there can't be two officers with that

name. Yeah, they had a very bad time in his section of the line. They came under very heavy bombardment and machine-gun fire both, and had to retire. They had a good sergeant, named Bonfire, and when they got back to the trenches they looked back and half the platoon were dead, and there was Sergeant Bonfire in the middle of them with his legs shot off, but still alive and moving. So what does Lieutenant Fenwick do but go over the parapet, in the middle of all this murderous Boche fire, and run to the sergeant and heave him up over his shoulder and carry him back to safety. They all said it was a miracle he survived and he should have got the Victoria Cross."

"He wasn't hurt?"

"Not that I know of. God, you don't know how brave that man was."

I felt just as thrilled and proud as if I'd done it myself. "Couldn't we just walk to Shoreburgh and see him?"

"Surely he's very unlikely to be on leave?"

He was right. Sadly, my excitement subsided. We continued on our way to the beach.

"I did meet him at the wedding, but only to say hello. I wonder how that marriage is getting on," said Chuck pensively as we walked.

"Didn't Rednall tell you?" I asked, astonished. But he was busy staring at the castle and couldn't have seen my face.

"Well, it's not something you ask. He doesn't write to me much – the odd postcard. Doesn't give much away, old Rednall. I guess it's your British reserve. I admire that."

"Didn't you know she left him the day after they were married?"

He smiled to himself. "You don't say! Maybe his upper lip is even stiffer than I thought."

Whether because of the revelation that Rednall had failed to confide in him, or whether Chuck McIver really preferred my company to that of his old school friend, I did not for a long time discover; but his leaves thereafter were spent with us. At first I was embarrassed about my parents' lincrusta taste, although it was then fashionable. "No, it's a real home with a real Mom, I love it," he said enthusiastically. It seemed odd to regard my mother, who seldom appeared except at meals, as a real Mom, especially compared with Aunt Emily. But Chuck, after all, had only visited Riverlaw when the house was crammed with wedding guests, and he had barely spoken to his hostess. As for Lady Carroun, he called her "the old dragon". "Staying at the Carrouns' palace sure is an experience," he declared, "but homey it ain't."

I discovered that his own mother was long dead and he and his father lived alone. On their house, and his life in Canada and at the Front, he was not to be drawn. I wondered if he were emulating Rednall's reserve. Whatever the reason, Chuck's amiable exterior concealed a peculiarly private mind. He simply didn't like talking about himself or his own feelings.

My school friends, of course, were all agog, and I was endlessly teased about my tall, handsome Canadian. Once or twice I had seen from my bedroom window little groups of girls hanging about after breakfast at the end of the street; when Chuck and I went through the garden gate for our daily expedition, they would whisper and giggle and run away. "Goodness, isn't he good-looking!" they would say to me, without preamble, when next we met. "Ripping blue eyes . . . An officer, isn't he?"

"Naturally," I replied, looking down my nose. "He's an Old Harrovian."

Gasps from the impressed audience.

I enjoyed all this immensely. When he went back to the war I didn't really miss him – not as I had missed Peregrine, of course – but I liked him a lot, and looked forward to his next appearance.

As the months limped by the war went sour on England,

and I dare say on Germany too. We saved coal, matches, clothes, blankets, string, even, thinking we might never be able to buy them again. Food had doubled in price. Some women dressed in breeches and drove buses and ambulances. Wheeled traffic in Newcastle was reduced by two-thirds. The East End of London was bombed and dozens of people were killed in their homes. I woke in the night from nightmares, my mouth dry, my face sweaty, imagining Zinnia huddled in the midst of a great explosion, sheltering her precious baby in her arms.

The war effort was dislocated by strikes at home, and by disputes among the Allied generals and politicians about the conduct of the offensive abroad. In March 1917 riots had broken out in Petrograd, and the demoralised armies of our Russian allies were crumbling before the Germans. Lloyd George said he was sick of being "a butcher's boy driving cattle to the slaughter". It was hard to believe that hostilities could ever be lifted out of the terrible stalemate that had already killed millions of soldiers on diverse fronts.

But just after Chuck's second-last leave, on the fourth of April in driving sleet and snow that sapped the morale of the weakened German divisions, a great bombardment opened at Arras, and five days later at five-thirty in the morning the Canadian Corps went over the top at Vimy Ridge. Chuck was among them. He told me long afterwards how by the beginning of the afternoon they had left behind them the churned mud, the rotting corpses and desolation, and for the first time in that campaign they stood victorious on the high ground and saw stretching before them a peaceful countryside that appeared untouched by war.

It was the beginning of the long journey to the peace we had so passionately hoped and prayed for.

It happened that at the Armistice in November 1918, soon after my fourteenth birthday, Chuck was on leave and staying with us. He and my father and I went down to Jesmond church to take our turn at ringing the church bells, and in the evening we joined the happy crowds milling across the cobbles round Grey's Monument. I stood between the two of them in the crush, and we crossed arms and with several thousand other people sang "Auld Lang Syne", a deep, grateful roar that went straight to the heart. I thought of Dick and Vin and Giles and Theodore, and the fathers and brothers of many people I knew, and swore to myself that there must never be a war again.

The trams were packed with people singing and cheering, some of them very drunk, so we walked home over the dark pavements lit at long intervals by wavery gas-lamps, our footsteps loud under the black sky.

"What will you do now?" my father asked Chuck.

"Go back to Canada. Gotta get back to the farm. Last letter from Pop said he wasn't too well, and he's not getting any younger."

"Will you ever come back to England?"

"Gee, I hope so. But not to live. But I guess you've all been real hospitable to me. Don't know what I'd have done without you. The Carrouns were kind, but I think I got across Lady Carroun some way."

"Everybody does," I told him.

He laughed and put his arm round my waist. "You've been real good company, little Lizzie."

"I'll miss you."

"And I sure will miss you. Maybe your father'll let you come out and visit with us."

My heart leapt. But not for long.

"I don't think that would be quite the thing," said my father firmly.

I think if he hadn't said it, I wouldn't have longed so passionately to go.

When Chuck said goodbye on the station platform next morning, I thought I would never see him again, and I put up my arms and we hugged each other tight and I kissed his bristly cheek as hard as I could, to show him how grateful

I was that he had fought for Great Britain. He kissed my cheek hard too, and when he let go of me his eyes were shining.

As the train pulled out he leaned out of the window and blew kisses and waved until only his khaki-cuffed hand was visible, and finally the curve of the rails carried him out of sight.

25

Venetia had waited patiently while Zinnia was officially engaged and married to Rednall. During the last part of the war she went on working as a V.A.D. in London, seeing Charles Dawson whenever his leave allowed. She ate her meals at the hospital, lived in Zinnia's house, and spent much of her free time helping to look after Zinnia's baby. She was costing Aunt Emily nothing, and – because in her quiet way she was looking after Zinnia as well – saved her mother a good deal of anxiety. After the war ended she came home to claim her reward.

The 'flu epidemic in the autumn of 1919 must have delayed matters; and Aunt Emily would never change her mind without a struggle. She must have insisted that they wait the full five years, because the first I knew of the plans for Venetia's marriage to Charles was when a letter from Aunt Emily arrived for my mother early in 1920, asking if I could be a bridesmaid.

I was delighted. The scruples my aunt had had about Charles's suitability as a suitor must have been overcome. Perhaps her widowhood, the struggling farm, the amount of money she must have been sending to Zinnia (and doubtless Ivy's allowance), helped her to a decision. Venetia's hospital work had ended with the war, and she was now twenty-five years old and trained for nothing except marriage. And there were now far fewer eligible bachelors. Many had married young in the haste and uncertainty of war, and the black-edged casualty lists had disposed of hordes of the rest. There was hardly a family without a death. But Charles had had a good war. He was now Captain Dawson, had been mentioned in despatches, and – unlike many more aristocratic officers – had come back to a steady job in his family's firm.

I was kitted out with a pale blue muslin dress and mittens to match (made of the offcuts), and despatched to Riverlaw three days before the wedding in the autumn of 1920, for Mrs Hothersall to construct my headdress with earphones of artificial flowers, and turn my hem up at the front and down at the back to match the bride's. Kind Venetia had asked Louie to be the other bridesmaid, and her hem had to be aligned with mine.

When I alighted at the station I found, to my astonishment, that Aunt Emily herself had driven alone in the trap to meet me, and clasp me comfortingly to her violet-scented bosom.

"They *all* wanted to come – but just this once I want you all to myself. So lovely to see you again, dearest, after all this time – and haven't you grown! Almost seventeen, aren't you? I do declare you're nearly as tall as me. You're going to look lovely in your bridesmaid's dress, and terribly grown-up."

As we bowled past the dear familiar fields, she brought me up-to-date on everyone. Vane had left school several terms before, because of the farm. Louie had left in July; nobody had decided what to do with her. "She wants to go to London and try to be a writer, but I really couldn't think of allowing her to go – two daughters far away is quite enough, I simply can't do without her. Besides, she is much too young and unworldly."

It was on the tip of my tongue to say that Zinnia had left home at seventeen, a year younger than Louie was now, and Venetia and Charles would after the wedding presumably be making their home near Newcastle – not exactly distant. But it seemed rude, and I forbore.

"She's clever. Couldn't she go to university and study literature?"

"Goodness, darling! – Gee up, Starlight, we'll never get there at this rate! – What would we do with a bluestocking? Besides, I'm afraid it would be terribly expensive. Since Uncle died, you know, we have had to be a little bit careful. Oh," she stretched across the trap and patted my hand, "it's so lovely to have you here, darling! Now there's just one little thing I want to warn you about. I know you're so sensible and grown-up now. Zinnia and little Zadok are staying with us for the wedding."

"Oh, hooray! I've been dying to see him. What's he like?"

"Very, very sweet. But I must tell you, darling. We have to be so discreet, and I know I can trust you. Can you keep a secret?"

"Of course."

"Do you remember that awful time when Zinnia rushed home from Rednall after the wedding?"

"Yes, I do."

"Well, she's never been back. Not yet. But I do tremendously hope that things will come right one day. I'm treating you as a grown-up now, darling. And the thing is, everyone assumes that Rednall is Zadok's father. I know that you and I know differently – "

"So does Rednall."

She made a little face. "Well, we don't see him now, and he and his mother are not the sort of people who would tell anyone. They wouldn't want anyone to know. And even Louie doesn't know, and I don't think she should."

"But everyone must know Zinnia left him."

"Well, nobody will be rude enough to ask why. Remember that she's been in London all this time. Hardly anyone will realise she left him so *soon*. I think we must both keep very silent on the subject, don't you, for Zinnia's sake?"

I wasn't going to contradict Aunt Emily, of all people.

"Naturally," I said.

"Promise me, darling?"

I conducted a short internal struggle between truth and love. But after all, nobody was actually suggesting that I should tell a lie.

"I promise."

The first time I saw Zadok, he was tottering over the lawn towards a peacock. He wore long shorts and a sailor blouse, a wide-awake hat, clean white socks and soft leather boots. He had a round, rather white face and a fine head of dark brown hair like Zinnia's. I searched for Peregrine in his face, but he was too young to have a pronounced likeness to anyone. He had large eyes, a small mouth, and did not smile, but pursued the now retreating peacock wobblingly but with determination.

The peacock suddenly honked like a klaxon, and Zadok retreated; but seeing the bird slow down and turn with a magisterial brush of tail-feathers, he cautiously advanced again. Zinnia, a few yards behind, rushed to enfold me in her elegantly-outstretched arms.

"Heavenly to see you! Look at him – isn't he just divine? And isn't it just glorious to be here again? It's almost the first time I've been home this year. I did make one flying visit to beg supplies from Mother, but I've been so busy with the shop!"

"The shop? What shop?"

"Oh, didn't you know? I started making hats in my spare time – such fun, and Mother's produced sacks and sacks of old bits of ribbon and feathers and lace scraps and lengths of silk. I sold a few to the V.A.D.s and then to their friends, and friends of friends, and it's gradually grown, and I've opened a tiny shop in Mayfair – all grey watered silk, and so elegant you wouldn't *believe*! People are coming to stock up for Ascot, and I sold two hats to Lady Bessborough, and one to Lady Ripon!"

"Whatever does Aunt Emily say?"

"Oh, she looks on it as just my little hobby. In fact, I

think she's rather pleased; she's asked me for a hat already. She says it won't make money so it's really quite different from being in trade. But it does – make money, I mean."

"She's got us all hemming silk and dyeing feathers," said Louie, who had come up behind me. "Oh, Lizzie, it's lovely to see you!"

"And you, too." I gave her a big hug, and stood back to look at her. She was now an adult, but still rather fat and spotty, sharp-nosed and sharp-chinned. Only the bright, intelligent eyes were attractive. Still, with nicer, less crumpled clothes and clean hair, she would look better. I wondered why Aunt Emily had not made her take more trouble; perhaps she had given up trying. Or perhaps this was the secret rebellion of someone who never openly rebelled.

"I must tell you, I've had a brilliant idea," went on Zinnia, bending to take Zadok's hand and lead him back to us. She was wearing one of her old blue skirts with a high-necked Gibson-Girl blouse that must have been handed down from Venetia. Her hair was escaping in fronds from a great, loose coil at the back of her head. And – oh, poor Louie – in spite of this, she looked perfectly beautiful. "I found masses of reels of binder twine in the barn, and some of it is a beautiful Prussian blue. I believe we could crochet it into little sports hats. Something with a rather deep crown and a rather charming little turned-up brim? Or no, perhaps the brim wouldn't stay up. A beret, perhaps, rather big and floppy, to wear on the golf course, with a big silvery brooch at the side? Lizzie darling, can you crochet? It would be terribly quick to do – I couldn't pay much, and then only if I managed to sell any – "

"Doesn't matter!" I said, thrilled at the thought of actually making money and helping Zinnia at the same time.

"Don't batten on the girl," protested Louie.

"Why not?" I said. "I'd love to try."

"Come on, Lizzie, I'll show you the headdresses. And Peregrine's here – just arrived on the train before yours – and Cedric's coming to tea," Louie chattered on as

215

we crossed the lawn, "and Bertram might too – did you know Bertram's rather keen on Madge Carroun? Not sure if she's keen on him, though – she's rather a flirt, one can't tell. We don't see her much since Zinnia's been living in London. Of course, we don't see Rednall at all now, it's a bit awkward. Theodore would have gone on being friends with him regardless – oh, how I miss him, Lizzie!"

"Me, too."

"Henry keeps turning up all the time – I suppose it's more fun here than at his aunt's. And I must tell you," her voice took on the old conspiratorial tone as we entered the house, sniffing the wallflowers on either side of the porch, "I'm writing a new novel. Don't tell anyone but I think it's going to be my best. I really want to succeed this time – I did finish one of my other books and actually sent it to a publisher in London, but I got a rejection slip – not even a letter, the brutes – and I was so discouraged I completely stopped writing."

"Oh, poor Louie!"

"But this new one is quite different from anything I've ever done. It's symbolic."

"What's it called?"

"*Out.*"

"Out?"

"Yes. Pretty stark and striking, I thought."

"Yes," I said doubtfully.

We rounded the corner of the stairs and I literally walked into a man. Before I knew it his arms were round me and my nose was buried in the fragrant Harris tweed of his jacket, and I felt him kissing my hair. Then he held me at arm's length and beamed at me. It was Peregrine.

"What have you been doing all this time?"

"I know," said Louie. "Hasn't it been an age? I kept harassing Mother to have her to stay, but there was always some great reason why it wasn't quite convenient."

I thought back to Aunt Emily's confidences in the trap, and everything clicked into place.

"But you're grown up!" Peregrine's grey eyes shone at me. They had the most delicious crinkles at the corners. "Have you left school?"

"Goodness, no, at least, not quite. Have you left the Army?"

"Yes. I've been at home helping around the farm."

"I was so worried in case you got wounded. Are you all right?"

"He got the M.C.!" said Louie.

"I told you not to embarrass me," grinned Peregrine.

"Chuck told me, it's absolutely splendid, I'm so impressed. Who else is here?"

"It's no good, Louie, we're not good enough for her."

"Oh, don't tease! What are you going to do now?"

"Have tea, I hope."

"No, I mean with your life?"

His sparkling eyes became serious. "Good question. My father wants me to be a farmer, but the idea of settling down without seeing the world first – heavens above, there are so many marvellous things and places to see! I have an uncle in Australia I could look up – 'What do they know of England, who only England know?'"

"You sound just like Con," said Louie, adding quickly, "How is he? He hasn't written. What's he doing now?" Her voice was carefully casual.

Peregrine looked down at her, then round at the landing where we still stood. "What are we doing here? I was on my way to find some tea. Come down to the dining-room and I'll tell you."

He looked worried, his dear, feathery eyebrows were nearly meeting over his straight nose.

We trooped into the dining-room. The table was half-set; the lace cloth was out and the Rockingham china on it, with plates of thin buttered bread and a chocolate cake and a plate of angel cakes, but the sandwiches and muffins and the silver tea-set hadn't arrived.

"Sit down," said Peregrine, drawing out a chair for Louie.

217

"Listen, Louie, Con's all right, but I'm afraid I have a bit of bad news – or have you heard already? I'm afraid he was wounded. Such rotten luck – only a week before the Armistice."

Louie stared straight in front of her. "No," she said in a little voice.

"His hand."

Relief flooded her face. "Oh, is that all!"

"A big shell-splinter." His voice was very gentle. "I'm afraid he had to lose it. He's coming to the wedding and he asked me to warn you all."

"Oh, is he coming? That's wonderful! Which hand?"

"The right."

"Oh, how dreadful," I said, "poor Con. What will he do?"

Louie said nothing, but her eyes showed the depth of her feeling.

"Hello, hello, anyone at home?" came a familiar voice, pinched yet fruity, from the front door, and Cedric walked into the room. Simultaneously, from the kitchen passage, came Vane, wiping his hands on the seat of his breeches.

"Hello, Lizzie! You're looking well. What a big girl! Well, look what the cat's brought in – hello, Cedric! Timed your visit, I see," with a glance at the table.

"Not very polite," commented Venetia, behind him.

Behind Cedric was a silent young man whom I recognised with difficulty as Leslie Brown. "Do have some tea, Cedric – Leslie," Venetia gestured to them to sit down. "Lizzie darling, what a long time it's been!" and she stooped to kiss me where I sat. "Goodness, you've grown. You might fit some of my clothes, let's have a trying-on session later." She was animated and obviously happy, with a bloom in her cheeks, and wore a simple, pale pink dress which suited her, and a diamond engagement ring.

"Well, so who else is coming to the wedding?" demanded Peregrine as everyone sat down, and Gertie came in with the silver tea-tray.

"Everyone!" said Venetia. "I couldn't leave anyone out. It'll be fascinating to see all the boys after so long."

"Henry's a hero," Louie told me. She looked a little white but didn't refer to Con again that day. I knew she was being brave. "He shot down five Hun planes and won two medals."

"Did you know he wants to be a coffee-planter in Kenya?" put in Cedric. "Rather an adventure. And he has a great plan to start an aeroplane service from Gibraltar to the Cape. He and a friend from the Royal Flying Corps are thinking of prospecting the route. Through desert and jungle and all that."

"I don't believe it," said Zinnia, who had appeared at the door while they were talking, with Zadok on one arm. "Can you see Henry, of all people?"

"Zinnia," said Peregrine, "you look stunning. The picture of motherhood. Come and sit by me," he patted the empty chair next to him. "Hello, Zadok old man, how about some of Gertie's delicious bread and butter to start with?" and he cut a sliver and popped it in the little boy's mouth.

It was as delightful a fatherly performance as I had ever seen. (Not that my experience was wide. My own father would merely have smiled absently.) A great ache filled my heart.

"Forgive my asking," said Cedric, "but are Rednall and Madge coming?"

Everyone looked at their plates.

"I don't think Rednall can," said Zinnia quickly. "Madge wrote and said she would but her mother can't. Might have had the politeness to answer for herself, the old hag. That reminds me, Lizzie, I must see you afterwards; there's a little job I'd love you to do."

The "little job" was nothing less than going over to see Rednall with Zinnia so that she could ask him to see – and by implication, accept as his son – little Zadok.

"I *can't*, Zinnia! What the dickens could I possibly do to help? I'll be completely *de trop*, whatever happens."

"Well, Cedric's question at tea decided me to try. Zadok needs a father. And I do so need a bit of support."

"Cedric's a tactless ass. And what about – " I hesitated, but I couldn't bring myself to name Peregrine directly – "the baby's father? Hasn't he any rights in the matter?"

"Goodness, no. I'm Lady Carroun – 'I am Duchess of Malfi still'," she added in a fruity actress's voice, striking a pose and making me giggle in spite of myself. "I am married to Rednall, after all. He can't take that away, unless he divorces me, which he won't. Now listen. I terribly need someone to go with me – "

"What about Aunt Emily?"

"Are you mad? She'd have a stand-up row and ruin everything. No, I need a charming, tactful person whom Lady C doesn't know, so that even she won't be rude to me in front of her. That's you."

"But she does know me. I was your bridesmaid, remember?"

"Come on, Lizzie, be a sport," said Zinnia with desperation in her voice. "You've grown up since then, she'll never recognise you. And you're the only one who knows the truth. You're the only one I can possibly take."

So the venture was arranged, greatly to my apprehension, for the following morning.

In the meantime everyone talked twenty to the dozen. Henry arrived, and was greatly teased about being a hero and a pioneer. It took him a moment or two to realise that it was only in fun – it was always easy to take a rise out of Henry – but when Venetia came to his rescue and told him that we all thought he was wonderful, he beamed and relaxed, and talked at great length about his forthcoming African adventure. His idea was that much of the route might be feasible with seaplanes, which could land on lakes, thus obviating the need to keep landing-strips cleared in the jungle. I thought this was brilliant; gullible old Henry had some brains after all.

He and Cedric were extraordinarily nice to me. Cedric dropped no more bricks; he went home after tea, and Leslie went with him.

"Why he lets Leslie trail round after him I can't imagine," said Louie pensively. She must have been feeling very low since the sad news about Con, but she had not mentioned it. She had contributed very little to the general jollity, but I had a feeling she was being brave in order not to cast a shadow over Venetia's happiness.

"They're two of a kind, aren't they?" offered Peregrine.

"I don't see that," said Louie. "Leslie is a snake of the first water. Cedric may be all sorts of idiot, but he's not an actual reptile."

"Very uncharitable," sniffed Venetia, but smiled as she said it.

"I think you'll find that Leslie Brown has quite an influence on Cedric," said Peregrine, offering the honeycomb sketchily to his neighbours before taking a spoonful himself.

"Where are you going to live, Venetia?" I asked.

"Charles has bought a house! It's small, but it's old and pretty, and the garden's going to be lovely when I'm finished with it – I'll have roses round the gate and honeysuckle over the porch, and Mother's giving me lots of cuttings. You must all come and see us when it's fit for visitors. Mother's giving me some furniture and the Dawsons are paying for a maid – everyone's so terribly kind."

"Heavens, I left Zadok with Cook," Zinnia leapt up and shot out of the room. The men rose politely to their feet.

"I'd better go and do some packing," Venetia rose with a smile.

"And I've just had an idea for my book," Louie made for the door.

"Oh dear, I suppose I'd better get back to Auntie," Henry said, unhero-like.

"Alone at last!" Peregrine struck a theatrical attitude. "Nobody wants us. Come for a walk, Bundle?"

So we walked down to the river, chatting comfortably of this and that, like the old friends we were; and in his company I was happy.

26

Next morning Zinnia dressed with the greatest care for our expedition to Rednall-the-house to see Rednall-the-husband next morning. Instead of her fashionable London clothes, she had extracted a white muslin dress from Venetia. I recognised it; it was the very dress she had worn the day she had sealed her love for Giles in the Riverpark conservatory.

"It's lovely," I said. "It suits you so beautifully. But isn't it a little bit . . . well, not faded, but . . ."

"I don't want to look *rich*," declared Zinnia, brushing her newly-washed hair vigorously. "I want to strike just the right note. Pass me that scent-bottle, there's a dear."

"Is Zadok coming?"

"Zadok? Goodness, no." She looked at me sideways out of her almond-shaped eyes. "Plenty of time for that later."

"Zinnia, excuse my saying so, but what do you hope to get out of this visit? Do you really think it's wise? He's given you a house, after all."

"Wait and see," she said mysteriously, licking a long finger to smoothe her lashes and eyebrows.

"Does Aunt Emily know?"

"Goodness, no, and don't you dare tell her." She peered into the mirror, pinched her cheeks, and carefully put her hair up with the aid of several combs that exactly matched it. "Now, will you get me the big blue hat with roses out of the top of Louie's wardrobe?"

"Zinnia, you *can't*! That's Aunt Emily's best."

"Get it."

So, weakly, I did.

As we bowled in the trap towards Rednall, the hat firmly secured, I reflected that Zinnia could never have looked prettier. She was nervous, but excitement had always made her eyes shine, and it did now.

"Someone coming behind us," I said, seeing the tweed of a man's hat bobbing above a high-banked wall after we had rounded a bend. "Riding, by the look of it."

Zinnia drew the pony to one side — traffic was so rare in the lanes around Riverlaw that everyone normally drove in the middle of the road.

The rider caught up with us.

"Hello, Leslie," I said.

"Morning. Where are you off to?"

"Rednall," I answered. "Are you going there too?"

I saw Zinnia glaring at me, I couldn't think why.

"Just going to pay my respects to Lady Carroun," he said in his high, light, monotonous voice, and spurred his horse.

"Oh – Leslie – by the way – Leslie – " called Zinnia in a fluster. But he was gone.

"Oh, hell's bells," she said angrily. "That's torn it."

I still couldn't see why she was so agitated.

"Tell me about making hats," I said, to take her mind off whatever it was.

"Later. Look, Lizzie, I want you to follow my instructions implicitly. When we get there, I'm not going in at the front door."

"Why not?"

"Never you mind now. We'll go up the back drive, and I want you to go in by whatever door we find open, and ask the first person you meet where you can find Sir Rednall. Then come back and tell me. There's bound to be maids and footmen and so forth about the place – the Carrouns may be poor but they do have quite a few servants."

"But, Zinnia – "

"Then I'll go in and speak to Rednall, and you follow at a discreet distance. The thing is, I need you as a witness if necessary, but I want him to think we're alone."

"But – "

"And if Lady C appears, it is absolutely and totally essential that you should come forward and be one of the party. I simply can't be left alone with her, I couldn't stand it – I'd probably murder her. Do you understand?"

"Oh, all right," I said.

The back drive of Rednall was farther from Riverlaw than the front drive, and twice as long. It was shaggy with grass and wound darkly under towering rhododendrons. It was unnaturally quiet because birds don't like rhododendrons. I don't blame them.

We came out in front of a huge stone arch with a clock set into a bell-tower above it. Inside, we found ourselves in a big, deserted courtyard lined with stables. This part of the vast house seemed in better condition than the façade. One or two nags put their long heads over the stable doors and inspected us.

Zinnia parked the trap by a hitching-post.

"How do I look?" She pressed down the crown of Aunt Emily's huge blue hat, tweaked the brim forward over her eyebrows, and brushed a curl over her ear with one finger.

"Ravishing."

A boy in a baize apron emerged from a door. He took one look at Zinnia, and goggled.

"Where can I find Sir Rednall?" she enquired in a manner that combined imperiousness and charm as only Zinnia knew how.

"He'll be in his study, m'lady. I'll take you round to the front entrance."

"Not at all, please don't bother. Tell us how to get to the study from here, and we'll take ourselves there directly."

225

"Sure, m'lady? In there, down the long corridor, turn right and left and you'll see the door in front of you."

"Thank you so much," and Zinnia and I swept into the house.

"He knew it was you," I whispered.

"Oh, probably. I should think every servant between here and Newcastle has been speculating as to what exactly Rednall did to me. Still, I don't care."

I followed her down a vast, stone-flagged corridor with a vaulted ceiling. On either side were framed architects' drawings and assorted views of the house itself, mostly brown with age. Through half-open panelled doors I caught glimpses of dusty rooms with mahogany furniture and dim, tattered damask curtains edged with elaborate bobble fringe.

I kept a few yards behind as Zinnia turned into a larger, carpeted corridor. The carpet was so old and neglected you couldn't see what colour it had been. In front of us, at a T-junction, was a life-sized, dirty-white marble statue of a man in a toga and laurel-wreath. Someone had hung an old golf umbrella over his eloquently outstretched arm.

Zinnia turned to me, winked, and disappeared round the corner to the left. I followed on tiptoe, keeping my distance. I heard a door open. There was a silence and the sound of a chair scraping, as if someone were rising slowly to his feet. Then Rednall's voice in wonderment:

"*Zinnia!*"

"Rednall, my dearest, it's been such an age."

"I – I don't know what to say."

"Rednall, you look so *handsome*. I was so afraid – you never seemed terribly strong – your cough – I've missed you so, I just had to see you to make sure you were all right. It's just lovely to see you!"

"It's lovely to see *you*. You look more beautiful than ever."

"May I sit down?"

"Of course – forgive me. No, come nearer where I

226

can see you properly. Oh, Zinnia, how can you ever forgive me?"

And at Zinnia's delightful laugh, like a string of pearls flung in the air, I realised that I was eavesdropping and retreated so far and so abruptly from the half-open door that I collided with the golf umbrella, and the toga'd statue rocked. I stood terrorstruck, both arms around its marble waist in an attempt to steady it. And it was at that moment that I heard footsteps approaching from the front of the huge building, and around the corner to my right came Lady Carroun and Leslie Brown.

"What are you doing here?" she demanded in a voice like grit-coated ice.

I quaked. My one idea was to play for time, so that Zinnia could make the most of her interview with Rednall; and so that Rednall himself would not hear and be put off by his mother's presence, I must keep the conversation as quiet as possible.

"This statue's very unsteady," I said in a hoarse whisper, still embracing it. "Oh, do help me, I think it's going to fall down on me."

"Nonsense, you must have knocked it. Do be careful, it's quite irreplaceable." She came forward and seized its outstretched arm. "Leslie, can you kindly assist us?"

"Hello, Leslie," I whispered. "If you could possibly grab hold of it lower down, about the level of his knees, we might – " I took a risk and rocked the statue a little more.

"Look out, do look what you're doing!" said Leslie. He steadied it.

"Do you know this young person, Leslie?"

"Of course he does!" I said hastily. Presumably Rednall and Zinnia were sitting close to each other, because their words could no longer be distinguished; but I could hear the rise and fall of their voices and – my heart lifted – Rednall's rare laugh. Play for time, I repeated to myself. "And I know Leslie. We know each other, don't we,

Leslie?" I said wildly. "And you and I have, in fact, met before, Lady Carroun. It's a small world."

"I saw you on the way here with Zinnia Delmayne," said Leslie. "Where is she now?"

At that moment Zinnia's laugh pealed out again from the study. Like tennis-players watching the ball, the suspicious faces of Leslie and Lady Carroun turned from me to the study door.

"She's in there with my son!" exclaimed Lady Carroun, her watery eyes popping with rage. "You were quite right, Leslie!"

"Don't worry, Lady Carroun, we'll soon deal with her," said Leslie in a sickeningly sycophantic way. "Let's go in now."

"You've been eating the Delmaynes' chocolate cake and listening to their private conversation," I said to Leslie, "and now you do this. I just don't know how you can be so frightful."

"May I remind you that you're trespassing on private property, which is a criminal offence."

"You're a sneak and a toady," I said.

Leslie went bright red.

"I'm afraid I must ask you to leave the house," said Lady Carroun, giving me a look that would freeze a hot bath.

I didn't move.

"Do what you're told," said Leslie.

I resisted with difficulty an impulse to put out my tongue at them.

Leslie took his hostess's arm and turned away from me. "I think we should just ignore her," he confided. "Let's go in. You stay outside," he added to me over his shoulder.

"Certainly not," I said, and marched into the room behind him, poking my foot forward so that he couldn't shut the door in my face without an unseemly battle.

Rednall and Zinnia were sitting side by side on a leather chesterfield, and his hand was in hers. Her hat had fallen off and she looked tousled and distractingly pretty. At our entrance Rednall leapt to his feet, looking guilty. Zinnia looked defiant, and a tiny bit frightened.

"I told you never to set foot in this house!" stormed Lady C.

I waited for Rednall to answer her, but he seemed struck dumb.

"Please don't speak to me like that," said Zinnia. Her cheeks were pink but she spoke quietly. "I am your daughter-in-law. I love my husband and I have every right to be with him."

It was a brave try. But Rednall was still looking, like a cornered animal, at his mother. "Zinnia," he said, pleadingly.

"I married you in the sight of heaven," went on Zinnia, but Lady C broke in furiously.

"You're a wicked . . . *strumpet*! Out of my house!"

"Mother," appealed Rednall.

"There's nothing more to be said! There's no place for you here, miss!"

"You'd better go," said Leslie importantly. I could have kicked him.

"Now wait a minute," pleaded Rednall; but I could see his faint resolve was weakening.

"Off with you!" Lady C was almost foaming at the mouth with rage. "We don't want people like you here!"

And suddenly, disastrously, I saw red.

"You've no idea what Zinnia's like!" I stormed. "You have no right to be so rude to her! Zinnia's a wonderful person! She's brave and she's enterprising and resourceful, and she's had more tragedy in her life than most people could bear, but she's always refused to be defeated! She'd never treat anyone the way you're treating her! I'm absolutely disgusted that you should treat another human being so badly, let alone your own daughter-in-law who loves your son so much that she was willing to marry him, let *alone* someone who is such a truly marvellous person as she is!"

I was conscious, on the fringes of my fury, that the

three of them were staring at me; Lady C actually with her mouth hanging open. I was suddenly silenced by the enormity of insulting her in her own house. Worst of all, I had disobeyed Zinnia's orders.

"I'm sorry," I muttered.

"Please go at once," said Lady C frostily, "both of you."

Rednall was gazing at Zinnia, and she at him.

"I'm yours," she said simply. I sensed it was a rearguard action.

"Mother – " said Rednall.

Zinnia picked up her hat and held out a graceful hand to Rednall, her eyes still on his. He took her hand and raised it to his lips.

She turned, ignoring his mother and Leslie, and we stalked out.

As Zinnia passed the statue she put out her tongue at it.

We went out into the sunny courtyard to a delicious smell of burning leaves. She put her arm in mine and hugged it to her side.

As we drove out of the gate she said, "What a snake Leslie is. I might have known he'd shop me. But good old Lizzie. You were amazing."

I had been dreadfully afraid, once my temper calmed down, that she might be angry with me for ruining her future. But she never uttered a word of reproach.

27

I was considerably shaken by this interview, and deeply troubled, mainly because I had ruined it by losing my temper; but also because although I had gone to it thinking that it was for Zadok's benefit, his name, as far as I knew, had never been mentioned. My prime consideration had been for Peregrine's happiness. Peregrine (I reasoned) loved Zinnia, and she him; they must be brought together; whatever anguish this might cause me, my own happiness was less important than that of these two people whom I loved so much. I had not really thought with any coherence about why Rednall must be reconciled to Zadok; presumably it would make it easier for Zinnia to get a divorce on her own terms – my ideas on divorce, a taboo subject among all the grown-ups I knew, were the haziest possible. But now I was not at all sure what Zinnia really intended, and when on the way home I asked her straight out, she gave her mysterious smile and said, "You've been a huge help, Lizzie dearest. But now we'll just have to wait and see."

I might have reflected further on this. But there was the wedding to get ready for, and Aunt Emily had us all, even the guests, scurrying about weeding the garden, putting up awnings, moving furniture, and even helping in the kitchen, in preparation for the next day's festivities. I spent a hectic afternoon, whipping batches of egg-whites in the big copper bowl, and decorating puddings with my best flower-patterns of almond slivers and sliced cherries and angelica. And it was at about six o'clock, when I was sitting in the schoolroom helping Aunt Emily to clean the family silver and plate, that something happened to put all thoughts of Zinnia temporarily out of my head.

On my aunt's direction I had covered the big schoolroom table with newspaper, and myself with an all-enveloping maid's overall. That it was dirty and stained was bad enough; but she also insisted that I should cover my newly-washed hair with a turban made from a frayed roller towel. I was mortally afraid one of the young men would see me, and I protested; but she had a point – if anyone had to wash their hair twice, there would be no hot water left for the bride – so I gave in.

I arranged all the cutlery, the silver tray, the tea-set, and miscellaneous cream-jugs, salt-cellars, pepper-pots and entrée dishes at one end of the table, and we set to for a long, messy session of polishing.

Halfway through, there was a knock at the door, and poor, half-witted Mary Broughty came in and said, in her lisping sing-song voice, "Mrs Delmayne at the door to see Mrs Delmayne."

"Who is it, Mary?" asked my aunt, who was covered in a big apron herself, and grey-handed from the polish.

"Mrs Delmayne, Mrs Delmayne, mam."

My aunt clicked her tongue and looked down at herself ruefully. "Could be anyone. Gertie's making pastry, is that why you came? Lizzie dear, it might be someone with a wedding present. Would you mind going down and saying it's not convenient for me to come at the moment? But thank them profusely."

Mary loitered in the doorway. "Iss Mrs Theodore Delmayne," she said.

My aunt's face changed.

"Thank you, Mary. Go back and finish the shoes," she said sharply.

When the door was shut she turned to me with a look of stone. "If it really is, send her away," she said. "Our

232

agreement was that she should never come to this house again." She was shaking.

Her words hung on the air while I hesitated.

"Go on. I won't see her. What is she doing here? Get her away." Trembling, she spat out the phrases.

I rattled down the back stairs and through the dining-room. Luckily there was nobody about. Ten to one Ivy would have come to the front door. I opened it a crack, my heart thumping. She had. In her purple dress, too. I saw a vertical segment, an inch wide, that included some bedraggled purple boa, a fresh pink cheek and one eye, frightened and baleful and older-looking than when I had seen her last.

"I want to see Mrs Delmayne," came the defiant voice I remembered so well.

"I'm afraid she can't see you," I said tremulously.

"I'm 'er darter-in-laa!"

"I'm sorry, it's not convenient."

"'Oo are you, then? Divva ye kna ye're workin' for a proper bitch? I'm off to Ameriky and I canna stay, or I'll miss me ship at Liverpule, or I'd wait now and force the bloody wumman out to face me an' see what I've got 'ere. But, by God, I'll get back at 'er one day!"

I dared not open the door further in case she put her foot inside it.

"She won't see you. Please go."

"Oh, aye. But tell 'er I'll haunt 'er till the day she rots in hell, the auld witch – and may that be sune!"

I thought it prudent to close the door, and I heard footsteps retreating over the gravel.

After a couple of minutes I re-opened it a crack, and finding nobody on the other side of it, I cautiously stuck my turbaned head out, hoping that if by chance Peregrine or Henry were still weeding, they would fail – as Ivy had done – to recognise me.

I saw a purple-clad figure at the end of the drive, and a second later it had disappeared round the gatepost.

But not before I had registered that over her shoulder she was carrying a bonny, pink-cheeked, dark-haired little boy.

It is humbling to think how strong are the powers of custom, vanity, and the fear of being seen to be ridiculous.

On any other day I would have picked up my skirts and run after Ivy, demanded to see her son and know his name; required her to give me her address and her destination in America. I could ask old Fred, who would surely keep in touch with his granddaughter; but he was as close as a mussel and quite capable of resisting enquiries. A moment's thought would have told me that if Ivy could not be coaxed into telling me, I might well lose touch for ever with Theodore's child, in whom for an instant his father's likeness, as his little face above her shoulder looked back at me, had pierced my heart.

But I knew I looked ugly and absurd in my overall and turban, so like Hannah's; and the instinct to conceal myself, for fear that Peregrine or any of the other young men were looking out of a window or somewhere about the grounds or the village, overrode every other. I hesitated. I dashed up two flights to tear off my servile trappings and run a comb through my hair. I couldn't find the comb, and embarked on fruitless upturning of the contents of my suitcase and grovelling under the bed before I saw it on my pillow. As I slammed the bedroom door, the handle came loose in my hand, and I wasted another minute working the door open again and dragging a chair across the room to prop it open so that Venetia wouldn't be locked out of her bedroom, where her wedding-dress hung, tenderly shrouded in new tissue-paper.

I dashed downstairs again. I fumbled with the heavy front door-handle. I sprinted down the drive and round the gatepost.

And Ivy was gone.

Only a small shabby closed carriage, of the kind that plied for hire at rural railway stations, moved in the village. As I watched, it passed the doctor's house and proceeded at a brisk trot round the first bend towards the station, and out of sight.

28

If ever I smell woodsmoke and roses together, it brings back the morning of Venetia's wedding day.

There was a little September nip in the air, and Gertie had risen early and lit the dining-room and drawing-room fires. They were drawing as Louie and I came downstairs. The flowers in the church were our special charge, and when we went out to the garden the lawn glistened, and the dew on the flowers and leaves diamonded our ankles and sleeves as we stooped to pick great armfuls of purple and mauve and white Michaelmas daisies for the windowsills, and Venetia's favourite roses for the altar.

All the way up the village the scent of woodsmoke pursued us from the Hall's tall chimneys and mingled with the sweet, acrid smell of burning leaves – Fred, perhaps, tidying the kitchen garden with an early bonfire in case any guests strayed there – and with the rich scent from the trugs of roses over our arms.

When we had finished our flower-arrangements and admired each other's, cleared up the cast-off bits of stalk and leaf and put back the spare vases in the vestry, we hurried back to the Old Hall. The quilled petals of the fading Juranville roses on the house were still pearled with great, shiny drops of dew and their scent was drowsy and deep. The woodsmoke was a faint, warm note above it, and out of the dining-room window drifted the welcome breakfast-smell of hot buttered toast; and when we went in, there were Peregrine and Zinnia smiling at us.

The wedding was at eleven, and Venetia looked so happy in white silk with a great cloud of veil fastened by real jasmine. Vane was wearing his father's grey morning-dress, with a grey topper in his hand; it was almost a shock to see that the suit fitted perfectly, but Vane was now eighteen, tall and well-built. Venetia, gliding down the aisle on his arm, was not so tall as her brother. Louie and I followed them in our blue muslin and floral earphones. I tried to look straight in front, but I couldn't help sliding my eyes to left and right as we approached the altar. Everyone I had ever been fond of seemed to be there, and many others besides, and they were all looking round and smiling at us.

I listened to the vows, and took in what they meant, and joined in as the congregation sang the old hymns Venetia and Charles had chosen. *Ransomed, healed, restored, forgiven* – for perhaps the first time, I began to realise that there is no circumstance of life for which the Church has no balm. In the front bench, Aunt Emily dabbed her eyes with a lace handkerchief in the shadow of her blue, rose-laden hat-brim. Behind her Zinnia, slim and elegant between Peregrine and a dark, well-groomed man whom I did not remember seeing before, had stopped singing and was biting her lip. I prayed silently, Dear God, make her happy.

After the service we walked back down the village. The entire population was out to see us. The stone pineapples had been mysteriously draped with garlands of roses, and as we approached them, all the village children clustered round the bride and groom and Charles threw handfuls of pennies for them, holding Venetia's hand and laughing at their eager, rosy faces.

So many people had been invited that they could not possibly all be fed inside the Old Hall; but Aunt Emily had gambled on fine weather and won. There were trestle-tables on the lawn, covered with white cloths hung with garlands, and the men had carried out every chair and bench from the house. There were cold meats and salads, and trifle and fruit salad and meringue pyramids, and white wine to drink, and everyone moved round talking to everyone else, and the church-bells rang a triple, and a happier party you never saw.

Halfway through the dessert I felt a hand on my shoulder, and a man's voice in my ear said, "Elizabeth."

It was Henry.

"You look very well dressed, Henry," I said, for something to say. He had certainly taken care over his appearance; but he was wearing a celluloid collar and a made-up tie.

"I'm so glad you think so," he smirked, and I felt obscurely ashamed of my polite lie. "I say, Lizzie, come into the kitchen garden for a minute."

I was mystified, but allowed myself to be ushered between the twin urns, now overflowing with tumbling roses. Once beyond them he tucked my arm into his as we walked down the path between miniature box hedges.

I grew uneasy. What was this?

"Something I want to ask you, Lizzie. I've watched you grow up into a lovely girl – oh, yes," as I made some demur, "I've had my eye on you for a long time. I won't deny it's been a sad day for me each time one of the Delmayne girls has married. But I see now that it was all meant."

"What do you mean?" I felt uncomfortable with the way he was clasping my arm to his side, and tried unobtrusively to loosen it, without success.

"You're very young. You know I'm going off to Africa in a year or two, as soon as I can get financial backing for my seaplane idea."

"Ye-es?"

"I hope very much that it may lead to a good career. I want to make a lot of money and I think I'm on the right track. But there's more to life than money, Lizzie."

"Of course there is."

"I . . ." He stopped on the path, and turned to look at me, still with my arm in his, so that our faces were very close.

His was sweating slightly and his eyes were very bright. We were now out of sight of the lawn and the ground-floor windows. He seized my free hand in his hot, pink one. "I . . . Lizzie, I shall be quite a long time building up my fortune, but . . . oh, hang it all, what's a fellow to say? . . . I'll need a home, and a . . . Not quite sure where it'll be, but I intend to make a cosy little nest – all I need is a . . . Lizzie will you wait for me?" came out in a burst at the end.

"How do you mean?" I said.

But I knew really. Because his sweating face was closing on mine, his eyes shut, his lips protruding slightly. I could see the reddish hairs in his nose. He was going to kiss me. I couldn't feel anything but disgust.

I scrambled somehow out of his arms. "I'm sorry," I muttered. "Terribly sorry, I think I'm a bit too young." It was the first thing I could think of that might be less hurtful than the truth.

His eyes opened. They did look dreadfully hurt. "But I'm not asking you *now*. It may be a few years."

"That's just it, Henry, I'm tremendously honoured, but I – " I cast around wildly for an excuse. "I think I'm not mature enough to think about that sort of thing yet."

"You *look* mature," and he glanced down at my bosom, and went red.

"I'm still at school. And I like you a great deal, of course I do, but not . . . not like that."

We stood there, awkwardly facing each other.

"I've shot down all those Huns," said Henry miserably, "and this is worse."

"I'm so sorry, so terribly sorry," and, not feeling able to bear another minute of his hot, pink gaze, I turned round and ran back down the path and on to the lawn.

I felt so shaken at the thought of having so narrowly escaped sharing a cosy little nest with Henry that I unwisely took refuge in a third glass of wine and went in search of less threatening company.

Peregrine was watching me from across the lawn.

He was tall and slim, but broad-shouldered, and he looked in his pale grey morning-suit exactly how an English gentleman should look. His eyes glowed and his brown hair fluttered a little as he moved over the grass towards me, quite slowly, threading his way through the chattering company as if he were deliberately savouring the way the distance between us was decreasing. His topper and gloves dangled in one hand, and one of Aunt Emily's best Waterford wineglasses was in the other, as he sauntered to where I stood beside a table and smiled into my eyes. I felt quite faint with happiness.

"That blue matches your eyes," he said in his lovely, husky voice. "What's it like being an experienced bridesmaid?"

"Well . . . It's fun being in the vestry when they sign the register. Everyone kisses you."

"That so? Some people have all the luck." I felt myself blushing, I couldn't help myself. He put his glass down on the table and his hat and gloves on a chair beside it. He looked round. "Bit public," he said enigmatically, and picked them up again. "Now tell me, what's the latest news from your school? Come on, make me laugh!"

So I did my best; and soon we were teasing and joking in the old way, and that strange electric moment, when we had silently watched each other through the crowd of unheeding guests, was gone.

"Cedric looks in good form," he remarked when my store of funny stories about school was exhausted. "But who asked Leslie Brown?"

"Oh Lord, I don't want to meet him."

"Do you think he's Cedric's Svengali? Good heavens, look at Bertram! He must have been at the wine," and I turned to see Bertram Seymour seated with Zadok wriggling on his lap. Bertram was trying to feed him with a sponge finger. He poked it at the small mouth and missed. Zadok turned his head, champed at it and spat it out. Bertram made a face, and mopped at his stained lapel with a large white handkerchief. Louie, who was at the other side of the table chopping some cold beef on a plate, leaned over to wipe the small, flower-like mouth with a napkin. I was touched to see this maternal action, and wondered if it was partly for the benefit of Con, who sat next to her, his bandaged stump of a hand hidden Napoleon-like in the breast of his jacket.

Bertram put Zadok down on the grass. "Run along," he said. He looked up at Peregrine and me. "Greetings!" His face was rather red. "Tell me, who's the Jewish fellow with Zinnia?"

"His name's Nathan," said Peregrine. "From London."

"All that way to see little Zinnia? Mrs Delmayne won't like that. Don't suppose she's ever had a Jew in her garden before."

"Lady Carroun will be most interested to hear about Mr Nathan," said a high, monotonous man's voice behind me. Peregrine turned.

"Brown," he said quietly, "if you go telling tales about Zinnia to Lady Carroun, I'll break your teeth."

"Well said," Bertram half-rose from his chair. "Shall we do it now, just to make sure?" He grinned and began clumsily to take off his coat. In the middle he lost his balance and had to grab at the chair-back.

"Don't be silly," put in Louie, and at the same time, "Don't be absurd," said Leslie hastily, and made off at a swift walk. I couldn't help laughing. Peregrine, obviously tickled pink at his success in frightening Leslie, broke into a huge smile.

"Come on," and putting his arm round my waist he turned me towards the house. "Let's go and see if Gertie needs a hand with carrying things out."

It was the first time for years that Peregrine had touched me, and I felt an electric thrill go through me. I couldn't think, I couldn't speak. I went dumbly beside him to the front door. Instead of going towards the kitchen he went up the first flight of stairs and I floated up beside him. On the first step of the next flight, where nobody coming in from the garden could see us, he paused, pushed me gently up another step, put his hands on my shoulders and turned me round.

"I think I'm probably drunk," he whispered, and kissed me.

Oh, how he kissed me! He held me tight, and his eyes were shut, the long lashes dark on his hard, sunburnt cheeks, his mouth moving on mine. I was out of breath, swooning, in heaven.

"Shouldn't be doing this," he muttered against my cheek. "You're too young. But oh, you darling, I always feel happy with you," and he fell to kissing me again so that I felt myself tremble with joy, and Peregrine felt it too and held me even closer against his body, and I was dizzy with love and delight, and –

"Lizzie!" came my aunt's voice, calling melodiously from the lawn. "Photographs!" We sprang apart and it was at that moment that I remembered Zinnia and felt the most dreadful pang of guilt and despair. We must both have been drunk. Peregrine would die of embarrassment when he sobered up. He'd never face me again. And I had been disloyal and treacherous to Zinnia, who loved him.

"Oh, hell." Peregrine grinned ruefully. "Bad timing." He sounded a bit out of breath. He smoothed my hair and straightened my earphones and brushed at the crumples in my skirt. I couldn't meet his eye. I tingled all over with the memory of his closeness. I knew now that I was in love with him and would love him for ever. But I mustn't. I must cure myself, for Zinnia's sake.

"Off you go," he said.

And I trotted downstairs obediently, and forced myself not to look back.

By the time the photographer had come out from under his black cloth and tenderly packed up his heavy glass slides and his mahogany camera, I was clear in my mind about what I should do.

I had got to forget about Peregrine. It was going to be the hardest thing I had ever done. I was going to have to build an imaginary wall right through the heart of my life. I just stood there, wondering how I could possibly bear it, until I realised that the wedding celebrations were still going on and I mustn't spoil the day by looking conspicuously miserable.

Louie was still sitting beside Con. The flower earphones and the bridesmaid's dress suited her; for the first time, the world could see part of her pretty legs. She was leaning very close to Con to cut up the pastry on his plate, and they were laughing. I changed my mind about approaching them. I looked round and saw that Cedric was making for me across the lawn.

"I say, you're looking stunning today, Lizzie," he said. "Didn't realise you were grown up till I saw you coming down the aisle beside Louie."

"I'm not really," I said hastily, remembering Henry's onslaught. I dredged for an uncomplicated subject of conversation. "How's Riverpark? And the Admiral? What a pity he couldn't come and give Venetia away."

His face clouded. "He hasn't left the house for ages. He isn't a bit well."

"I am sorry. What are you doing these days?"

"Oh, I try to run the place. I'm not very good at it. I say, who's the smooth-looking fellow beside Zinnia? They look very thick, don't they? I saw him in church but she didn't introduce him. Bit tricky, what, with old Rednall still on the horizon?"

"His name's Nathan, and he's Jewish," said Leslie, appearing between Cedric and me with Madge Carroun at his elbow. I enjoyed the look on Cedric's face when he saw that she must have heard him mention Rednall. Madge was dressed to the nines in acid green frills, and looking daggers.

"Oh, good," I said. "I've never met any Jews but they sound splendid on the whole."

"Don't say that to Lady Carroun, or to Aunt Emily," warned Cedric. "Jews and foreigners to her are a red rag to a bull."

"I don't believe she knows any," I said recklessly. "Except Chuck McIver – he's a foreigner, well a sort of foreigner, and she likes him."

"Canadians don't count as foreigners. They're decent chaps."

"Is Chuck here?" I grasped at his name like an angler pulling in a fish. If I couldn't think about Peregrine, almost anyone else would do. That's right, concentrate on Chuck. "I did hope – I know it's an awfully long journey but he told me he'd come back soon – "

A male arm stretched round me and refilled my wineglass, and I took a grateful swig.

"You like Chuck, don't you," said Madge sweetly. A saucy green hat dipped low over one of her eyes; the other did not meet mine.

I remembered my schoolmates' envy with satisfaction. Here, at least, was a kind of consolation. I felt a base and inexplicable urge to discomfort Madge.

"I *love* Chuck," I enthused. My head was beginning to swim a little. "He's my boyfriend. He's stayed with us so often and we've done *everything* together. I'm going out to Canada to see him. But look here," I added, regretting the extravagance, not to mention the inaccuracy, of what I had just said but not knowing how to put it right, "you never said who Zinnia's friend was. What's his other name? What does he do?"

I turned to ask whoever had filled my glass. It was Peregrine.

He was standing there, very still, the decanter drooping from his hand. He was looking at the ground and his lips were pursed in a straight line. Cedric was staring at me sadly. Through my misery I heard Madge announcing, "He's called Jacob Nathan, and he helped her to set up the hat-shop. I believe he's in the clothing trade and very well orf." Her lip curled as she said it, and her plucked eyebrows rose. Then she looked round conspiratorially, and lowered her voice. "He sees a great deal of her."

"Don't let's beat about the bush," said Leslie. "She's his mistress."

"What do you know about it?" said Cedric. I could see he was half-horrified, half-fascinated.

Suddenly I was furious with the whole world; with myself for my rash words about Chuck, with the way Madge's and Leslie's voices were edged with malice, with Fate that had made Peregrine kiss me while he was drunk; oh, cruel Fate, that had made me love and hope too much.

He didn't look drunk now. I wanted to turn round to him and say, "I'm not like them! I like Chuck, but I don't love him – don't think that! And it can't be true about Zinnia – she wouldn't be unfaithful to you! I know she married Rednall, but that was different! Don't be unhappy! Don't think badly of her! Horrible Leslie – what he says just can't be true!"

But I didn't say it. How could I, when they would all have listened and drawn their own conclusions?

And at that moment Venetia and Charles, who had been changing, skipped laughing out of the house, hand in hand, in their going-away finery – Venetia, in a rose-coloured velvet costume and petal hat, looking like a rose herself – and we all rushed over to wave them off to the station in the carriage.

Venetia, laughing with happiness, hugged her mother and sisters and Vane, and seeing me near her, rushed over to my delight and hugged me too.

"Be happy," I said, and she answered with the old Delmayne dare that reminded me, with a terrible pang,

of Theodore, "I will if you will!" And as the two of them
climbed into the carriage in a shower of rose-petals, she
turned back to the old house and held out her arms as if
to embrace it. "Goodbye, dearest Riverlaw!" And Charles
tapped the horses' backs with the whip, and they bowled
out of the gate.

We rushed out after them and waved them all the way up
the village and past the doctor's house and out of sight.

As we trooped back through the gates, many of the guests
were already queuing to say goodbye to Aunt Emily.

I felt a dreadful emptiness. I needed comfort. I looked up
the rose-laden side of the house for inspiration, and found
it at the sight of the attic window.

Theodore would understand. I could – I must – look at
the hidden letters about him. Nobody else need know.

I felt a tap on my shoulder. It was my father.

"If you get your things now we'll catch the next train
back to Newcastle."

"But I thought . . . I've always stayed here, before!"
Oh, the things I had meant to do and see here, the chats
I had promised myself with Zinnia and Louie and above
all, in spite of everything, with Peregrine! And the letters.
Always, before, I had been too grieved to look at them. But
now, in my new wretchedness, I felt an urgent imperative
to do so.

"Emily's been very kind, but we can't impose on her.
She's had a tiring day and she must be longing to get rid
of us all and have a rest. Your bedtime isn't seven o'clock
any more. You're old enough now to arrive home late in
the evening."

"But..." I looked round wildly for Zinnia, for Peregrine.
Neither was in sight.

"Come on, get your things together and say goodbye
quickly – I don't want to miss the train, or your mother'll
be exhausted."

I saw it was useless.

And so my last farewell to Riverlaw for many years was

hasty and perfunctory; and my last image of it was of my blue-hatted aunt in the middle of a crowd of silken and morning-suited wedding guests, in front of the rose-covered wall of the house and directly under the attic window, blowing kisses to us as we drove away.

29

In the train on the way home from the wedding my mother said casually, "I wouldn't go back to Riverlaw for a while, dearest. Louie seems so wrapped up in that poor young man, and I'm afraid Zinnia isn't quite as nice a person as we thought."

Indignantly I demanded, "What makes you say that?"

"Oh, one discovers these things when one's older. Poor Emily, she has enough troubles as it is. Goodness, I'm terribly tired. I'm afraid I must stay in bed for a few days, another attack would finish me. Do try not to worry me, dearest."

I saw my father's lined, worried face. I didn't go back.

For a time I felt, with that dreadful finality that one feels in youth, that my life was to all intents and purposes over. But, of course, it was not.

I badly wanted to go to university, and above all to Oxford. But grants had not yet been invented; I knew that my parents would never agree to my trying to earn a living, and I would be entirely dependent for living expenses and fees on my father. And when I asked him he looked troubled. "To tell you the truth, Elizabeth, I'm a bit pressed at the moment," he admitted. "It's not so very long till I retire, and I haven't saved as much as I hoped to. And I'm very worried in case your dear mother becomes a permanent invalid. I should have taken out health insurance years ago, but I didn't. If I should have to pay for her to spend years in a nursing-home . . ."

So, deeply troubled by this, I made another plan; I would go to France with Aimée, whose purpose in life was to live in Paris and study to be an artist. I was dependent on my father for funds, but we could save money by sharing a room – two could live almost as cheaply as one, surely – and I could study and improve my French enough, I hoped, to enable me eventually to earn a living by teaching it.

But my parents were horrified.

"Not Paris," said my father. "Den of vice. Not suitable for a girl."

"Oh, darling!" said my mother. "Do remember that as I get older I'll need you to look after me. You don't want a" (knitting of forehead lines, flare of nostrils) "*career*, do you? And you're certainly not going to find a husband in France – at least, I sincerely hope not."

There were still many girls who were expected to stay at home, waiting for Mr Right. The world was full of dutiful daughters, arranging the flowers and embroidering and knitting and ordering the meals and running little messages for Mama.

I didn't fight. I knew a battle would hurt them, and hurt me more, and I knew (seeing my mother's lips set in a firm line, hearing her send me upstairs that very moment for a rug she needed to cover her legs against imagined cold) that it was a battle I couldn't win.

"Mr Right will come along one day, you'll see," she said kindly later, when she saw I had given in.

I hadn't told her about Peregrine, and now I couldn't. Not ever.

I saw Aimée off at the station for London on her way to France. She had no chaperone. She had fought her parents, and won. Elegant in black, with her red hair bobbed under a deep cloche hat that half-hid her eyes, she hugged me on the platform. She smelt of Chypre.

"*Au revoir, chère Eloïse.*" She was already well into the persona of a *femme fatale*. "It's too devastating that they

won't let you go. Just shows what a nice person you are.
Come and visit me."

"Wish I could."

"I bet you when we next meet I shall have – " her voice
sank to a thrilling, conspiratorial purr " – a *lover!*"

I thought of Venetia's wedding and almost flinched, but
smiled and held up bravely.

"Goodbye. Quick, they're shutting the carriage doors,
better get in. Good luck!"

"Goodbyee!"

And the train rolled out with Aimée's black-gloved hand
waving madly from her carriage window in a halo of steam
that rose and hung in the station roof as the last few carriages
rattled away into the distance.

I trudged back home and sat in my room, wondering
how to make enough money to escape.

I was, of course, making a little by my efforts as an
outworker for Zinnia. Every now and then I would receive
a packet of silk or a parcel of straw brims with cryptic
instructions, "Please backstitch round edge close tog as
many lines as poss", or "Bind edge narrow velvety ribbon",
or "1-in pompoms any bits self-colour wool you can scrape
up". I was thrilled when payment arrived, though when
I eventually started timing my work and dividing the
hours it took by the pound-notes Zinnia sent, it seemed
a disconcertingly small amount. I had already crocheted
so many golfing berets that Zinnia wrote that she couldn't
sell all she had in stock and would I mind stopping? I tried
selling my next one to the Newcastle milliners, without
success. I wrote an article on knitting golfing berets and
submitted it to the *Journal*; it was returned with a printed
refusal.

I pored over the small-ads. But the War to End Wars
had not produced a World Fit for Heroes. There were
not enough jobs to employ all the ex-soldiers, let alone
women, let alone women – girls, rather – without qualifi-
cations or experience. Carefully omitting to tell my parents

where I was going, I set off one day for Grey Street and methodically tried every office; but nobody wanted a clerk. Footsore and humbled, I went round the shops. If Zinnia could be in trade, I could too. But I was obviously not the first. "Got any experience?" they would say, and when I shook my head, I hardly needed to wait for the answer.

All this time there shone at the back of my mind a golden, leonine castle, floating palely in the distant sky like the Grail.

Soon after Venetia's wedding I wrote to Peregrine.

I had thought long and carefully about what I should say. I admitted that I had been drunk at our last meeting. I said that what I had said about Chuck was an exaggeration and not true at all. I said I was very sorry to have behaved so badly but I loved him very much and missed him terribly.

I sent off the letter, addressed to Peregrine Fenwick, Shoreburgh, and bit my nails for days. I could hardly bear to wait for his answer. Would he think even worse of me for writing? But any reply would be better than none.

But what actually happened was worse than anything I had feared. A few days later a fattish envelope arrived, addressed to me in a hand I did not know. Inside was my own envelope, folded, with a terse covering note. "Please do not write again as my son has emigrated to Australia." No signature. My envelope had been slit open, my letter unfolded and doubtless read. Peregrine's parents would know I was a drunkard and a liar.

My life went on like an unhappy dream from which there is no escape.

But even in my lowest hours, hope kept breaking through. Peregrine had said he wanted to see the world. But he would come back, wouldn't he? One day he would come back and I would somehow see him again, and make things right between us. All I had to do was be patient.

I took over the household accounts; I did charity work at the church; I tended the garden.

Eventually, through a friend of my father's, I got work as a bank-clerk (lowest grade). It was not an exciting job, especially as women in the bank were restricted to the most boring work and their pay was lower than that of the men who did the same. However, it was good to be able to contribute to my upkeep and pay for my own clothes. Above all, I could save. I put aside something every week.

More than a year passed, and one lunchtime I went down to the shipping-office and found out the cost of a steamer ticket to Australia. They couldn't tell me how much it would cost to stay in a modest boarding-house in Sydney, but they promised to find out. On the way home I called in at a jeweller's and sold the locket with the Carroun crest.

Before the shipping-agents received a reply, Louie sent me some news.

In his club in Newcastle, Charles had made the acquaintance of a D.L.I. officer, and in the course of a conversation about what had become of their brother-officers after demobilisation, had learnt that Peregrine Fenwick had settled permanently in Australia. The reason for this was that he had married an Australian heiress. Bertram Seymour had confirmed this news after consulting the regimental magazine.

When I read these words in Louie's spiky black writing, some part of my inner self shrank back, turned away from the light, and died.

I wrote guardedly to Louie, and thought up excuses to refuse her invitations to stay. I had spent my life keeping other people's secrets. Nothing would have induced me to betray my own, even to Louie. She was still at Riverlaw and being the youngest daughter was more or less trapped there, in much the same case as I. But she did not resent it, because she was still totally immersed in writing *Out*. It was written in the stream-of-consciousness style and was about a day in the outdoor life of a backwoodsman in Canada. ("I want to get down to Real Essentials – the essence of Life Itself.") Dusting the drawing-room and collecting the eggs and feeding the poultry and the other little jobs Aunt Emily found for her were, she declared, done in a dream; her life took place among the mighty redwoods ("Please DEAREST Lizzie go to the Public Library and find out whether there really are Redwoods in Canada & also everything you can discover about Logging and Beaver Dams – so irritating no public library here, I will Dedicate the book to you when it's published I promise").

Conscientiously I spent hours in the library most evenings and every weekend, and became the only expert in Newcastle, I dare say, on Beaver Dams.

In the encyclopaedia there was a picture of a lake in which were reflected amazing snow-capped mountains. I decided I liked the look of Canada. I think it was the idea of freedom, of ranging over a vast, empty country, unshackled by the requirements of ageing and dictatorial parents, that attracted me most. I desperately wanted a new beginning, and Canada was the perfect symbol. I would turn into our gate and enter our dark lincrusta'd hall with increasing desperation. There *must* be more to life than totting up columns of figures at the bank, and knitting and crocheting and fetching a clean hankie or a pill-box for Mama.

And one March day, as I was upstairs tidying her cardigan-drawer while she lay on her bed giving directions in a tired voice ("Fold the brown one and put it at the back, the mauve one goes on the pile for the church bazaar, the green one isn't too bad, darling, would you like it?") the front-door bell rang.

Even in such a modest household as ours, we had a living-in housemaid and cook; but it was Thursday, their weekly half-day. I rattled downstairs, eager for any distraction, and flung open the door.

A tall, slim, sunburnt, handsome man stood there smiling.

It was Chuck.

"I did write," he explained as we sat in the drawing-room in front of the Venetian-blinded and aspidistra'd window, "but I guess the letter took longer than me to arrive. Should have written sooner, but I guess I'm not much of a hand at writing."

I beamed at him. In five years he had grown even better-looking than before; brown, weatherbeaten, with a certain hardness to the mouth. His hands were rough, his hair tipped with grey above the ears.

"I've thought about you a lot," he mumbled. "Outa sight wasn't outa mind, eh?" We both laughed at this, and then my mother's anxious pipe floated down the stairs. "Who is it, Elizabeth?" I jumped up.

"Will you have a cup of tea?" And then, realising that at all costs I wanted to keep him near me, "Will you stay a few days?"

"I would very, very much like to visit with you," he said gravely.

"Then that's arranged. Where's your luggage?"

"At the station."

"Then let's go and get it."

"Elizabeth, Elizabeth!" came peevishly from above.

"Excuse me a minute." I tore upstairs.

"Who is it?"

"Chuck McIver."

"Who, dearest? Could you get me my other spectacles, from the very back of the first long drawer, please?"

"Chuck, all the way from Canada!"

"Oh, the Old Harrovian." She was pleased.

"Yes, I've asked him to stay."

"Oh dear, the spare room isn't very – "

"I'll see to all that," I said impatiently, slamming the drawer. "We're just going to get his luggage from the station."

"Get him a cup of tea, and one for me too," but I was out on the landing and galloping downstairs as her voice floated after me.

"Why did you come over?" I asked later as we got out the trap.

"To sell some wool – I did that already at the warehouse in Liverpool when I got off the boat. And to buy some pedigree rams, and get one or two other little things I need."

My heart seemed to jump to my throat. For he had given me a sly, sideways look, and I knew as surely as if he had said it aloud that among the other little things he needed was a wife.

"How long are you here for?" I said at last as the trap bowled down the mews.

"Well, that depends on you."

We sat knee to knee. His legs were long and relaxed. His nearness had a powerful effect on me. I longed to be interesting and witty, but I felt bereft of speech.

"What about your farm?"

"Got to get back for the planting in May. But until then Pop can hold the fort."

"I would have written to you," I said apologetically, "but in this country it isn't proper for a lady to write to a man she doesn't know well." I blushed, thinking too late about the implications of this speech. But Chuck was delighted. He grabbed my hand and held it tight. I realised there was no turning back to mere politeness. We sat in silence, clutching each other, and there was no longer any need for conversation. Which was just as well, because for once I couldn't think of any.

We went by train to Kelso the next day to the ram sales. It was good to have company, and I thought back to those other pleasant expeditions when he had been shy and glamorous in uniform and I had been a schoolgirl in a long gym-tunic, blazer and straw boater, showing him round Northumberland in, I saw now, a comically proprietorial way. Now he wore a worsted suit with a waistcoat, and a collar a little higher than the fashion. He seemed quieter than I remembered, and less fun; but perhaps the things we had laughed at had mostly been my school jokes and what seemed to him the oddities of English life. The gap between our ages seemed greater than before, because now he was a man of thirty who had been through the war and run a farm.

I wandered about the pens looking at the woolly, baaing monsters while Chuck chose his rams and bid for them at the breakneck auction and sealed the bargain with a handshake. The farmer was obliging and arranged to keep the animals until it was time to dispatch them by rail to Liverpool docks to catch Chuck's boat in just over three weeks' time.

"Three weeks!" I said on the way back, as we sat in the empty carriage with the stone-walled fields of Northumberland rocking past us. "What are you going to do for three weeks?"

"See everyone I know, I guess. May I telephone Rednall?"

"Of course." But at Rednall's name I felt a dreadful pang of longing for Riverlaw, for the Delmaynes, for Zinnia in darkest London, for Cedric, even; and most of all, impossibly, for a sight and touch of Peregrine, whom I must not love, and whom I had for ever alienated by my stupidity, and would never see again.

"Say, if I can go to see him," said Chuck, "will you come?"

I was flooded for an instant with delighted anticipation at the thought of being so near Riverlaw. And then I remembered my last visit to Rednall's house, and his mother's furious face as the statue rocked. Besides, I was now seventeen and could hardly go visiting with Chuck without a chaperone. I hedged.

"I don't think I can. I don't think it would be quite proper to go travelling with a man."

"Oh, come *on!*" Chuck was both amused and incredulous.

"No – honestly. Anyway, Lady Carroun doesn't like me because I stuck up for Zinnia. She still lives in London, you know."

"They never got together again?"

"No, and never will, if Lady C has anything to do with it."

"It doesn't surprise me. I guess Rednall isn't the marrying type. Say, Lizzie," he burst out, clutching my hand, "are you the marrying type?"

Again my heart leapt to my throat. I looked at him – the lean, sunburnt face, the hard mouth, the blue eyes intense with longing. He certainly was the handsomest man I knew, and this opinion had been endorsed by my schoolmates' envy.

I thought of the dark, dull house in Newcastle, of my mother lying with the blinds down issuing peevish commands, of my bleak and featureless future. I thought of redwood forests and beaver dams and spectacular mountains and the great, exciting world I had never seen.

"Yes," I muttered. "Yes, I am."

"Lizzie," he turned awkwardly as the train rocked, and took me by the shoulders and gazed into my eyes. "Will you marry me?"

I closed my eyes and saw Peregrine, whose eyes would have twinkled and whose arms would have hugged me and in whose warm embrace I would have moaned with love. Peregrine, who now belonged for life to someone else. Peregrine, whom I supposed I would never see again.

And Chuck was nice. Chuck was good-looking and he loved me. He would look after me. I wanted to have children; I felt I had a better idea of how a family should be brought up than my mother. I thought Chuck would be a good father. We could make a go of it together.

"Yes," I said. "Yes, Chuck, I will."

Chuck had planned the timing carefully. There were just three weeks till the boat sailed; just time to call the banns. He had even, incredibly, brought a letter from his local minister in Stewiacke County, Nova Scotia, to certify that there was no impediment to his marriage.

Lying awake in the middle of the night, I began to have doubts. Had I done the right thing? Once or twice I actually wanted my mother to feel unable to do without me. But no. She said it was an excellent match. Bravely, she feigned delight. "He's so handsome, and he has hundreds of acres!" she said. "A big farm, just like Riverlaw. And he's an officer and an Old Harrovian. You couldn't do better, darling. He's just what I've always wanted for you. There isn't even a mother-in-law – he told me she died when he was a boy. So there won't be any problems for you at all. And he's promised to bring you over to see us whenever he needs new rams."

I told myself that this order of priorities – rams before wives – was simply a misunderstanding by my mother. I told myself that I was being idiotic. Hadn't I always longed to see the world? Wasn't he terribly handsome? Wouldn't my classmates be jealous? I looked at the ring he had given me – his mother's ring, a trio of diamonds in a heavy, old-fashioned setting – and imagined Peregrine slipping it over my finger, and laughing (as Chuck had not done, for he seldom laughed) because it was ridiculously loose.

This thinking about Peregrine, I told myself, has got to stop.

And indeed, through a combination of determination, common sense, and despair, I did succeed eventually in banishing Peregrine deep, deep into the farthest reaches of my subconscious.

Meanwhile, preparations for the wedding rushed on.

I wanted terribly to be married at Riverlaw, but my mother vetoed it.

"In April? Goodness, dearest, we couldn't possibly ask

Emily that. They'll be up to their ears in the ploughing and sowing. Quite the wrong time of year for them. Besides, it'll probably rain and it would be much more awkward to have the reception in the house. Anyway, you surely want to be married from your own home?"

A frank "No" would have hurt her beyond measure. And now that I was to go far away, it was extra important not to hurt; it would be remembered for ever. I gave in.

Our drawing-room was not large. The list of potential guests had to be ruthlessly cut. All sorts of distant friends of my parents, whom I hardly knew, had to be included. "They'll give you a nice present, dearest," said my mother soothingly when I protested. Aunt Emily, Venetia and Charles, Zinnia and Louie and Vane were obligatory, of course; but when I put down Zinnia's friend Nathan he was firmly crossed off.

We had a short battle over Cedric.

"He's not a close relation," objected my mother. "And we really must ask the Vicar and his wife."

"Cedric really *will* give us a nice present," I said nastily. But that wasn't the reason I wanted him at the wedding. In spite of everything, I was fond of him. I felt he had been treated unfairly by life. I knew nobody else would think this; but I was sorry for Cedric and wanted somehow to tell him so and say a fitting goodbye.

A week later, I got home from a fitting at Fenwick's French to find a letter on the doormat, with Louie's familiar scrawly black writing on the envelope.

The letter was quite short because Louie was, at the time of writing, in the middle of a sizzling chapter ("How lucky, dearest Lizzie, that you will be able to do some of the research for my book *in the field* and I am compiling a list of questions for you to take with you and if poss. answer by return of post as soon as you get to the Wild West or at least the East of the West if that is how one can describe where your Exile will be??? Golly, we will miss you!")

On the back of the letter was one of Louie's long postscripts.

P.S. Zinnia sends much love and hugs and kisses and is dreadfully sad she can't come to wedding as little Zadok has chickenpox and she feels she can't leave him, and anyway daren't risk passing it on to The Bride. And listen to this – Henry is most frightfully hurt at not being invited. Don't you think you could be merciful and ask him? He came round here in an awful state having heard news of it from his aunt's cook who is Gertie's cousin. He went on and on about the etiquette of invitations and poor old H, I think he must have had a *tendresse* for you what a lucky escape you had there! He looked quite haggard and talked a lot about going to Africa soon and Mother got fearfully upset and said it was bad enough *you* going so far and she was afraid we'd never see Peregrine again either, and with Henry threatening to cross the world too things would never ever be the same.

Tons and tons of love dearest Lizzie, and be happy.

I put this letter in my purse, and it went across the Atlantic with me. Sometimes I got the feeling that the whole world was scattering into fragments, and at such times the sight of Louie's writing, and even just the scrawled heading, "Riverlaw", were a kind of comfort.

NOVA SCOTIA

30

Nothing in my life had prepared me for marriage to Chuck.

Certainly not the ceremony. Standing in the chilly church in Newcastle in my white lace dress (hastily run up by my mother's dressmaker), I had breathed *love, honour, obey* with all the heartfelt sincerity at my command. After the reception, my parents' guests shook hands and said goodbye (Chuck had no guests, as although he had invited the Carrouns they had pleaded a previous engagement). But the whole family went with us to the station, and my cloche hat was soon covered in confetti, and crooked from all the hugging and kissing on the platform. Even Cedric pressed my hand and said, "I say, Lizzie, I'll miss you." I thought I saw tears standing in his eyes, but perhaps it was only the sparkling white wine my father had provided.

"Take care of yourself, Cedric," I said. "Don't let anyone . . ." I suddenly wanted to say, "Don't let Leslie dominate you," but it seemed impertinent and silly. Cedric had telephoned to ask if Leslie could come to the wedding; luckily, my mother had taken the call. "Don't let anyone tell you how to live your life, Cedric," I said.

"Right. Same to you, Lizzie." His large, cow-like eyes shone, perhaps only with earnestness, and his hand was clammy.

The biggest, most loving hugs came from Louie and from Aunt Emily, resplendent in her huge, blue hat with roses, the sight of which brought back such memories of Riverlaw that I nearly howled. I stood there, enveloped in her soft, rose-silked arms and the smell of violets, biting my lip and quite unable to speak.

"Dearest Lizzie," whispered Aunt Emily. "I couldn't bear it if you didn't come back to see us. You're very like me, you know," a revelation which so astounded me that I was able to compose myself for the last farewell to my parents. I didn't doubt that Chuck would bring me back to see them all quite soon.

"I'll write and tell you all about everything," I assured Louie.

"Mind you do my research," she said. "The nearest library should be the place. Goodness, we'll miss you!"

"Maybe you'll be the next bride," I said. "I'll come to the wedding, cross my heart."

"He hasn't asked me yet," she said. She pulled a funny face, but her eyes were bleak.

As the train drew up majestically to the platform in a great hiss of steam, I looked at Chuck, who was busy brushing confetti out of his trouser turn-ups. How lucky I was to have a handsome husband! He looked handsomer than ever today, in a new suit he had bought, he told me, specially to be married in.

I hung out of the carriage window till the last minute, waving and blowing kisses to all my darling relations as their festively-dressed figures diminished along the curving platform and finally disappeared behind the great curve of the train.

I had expected that we would be alone in the carriage, but the train was crowded and a family with bawling children emerged from the corridor and joined us. Chuck and I hardly spoke all the way to Liverpool.

The boat sailed that evening. I had hoped that some of the family, at least, might come to Liverpool to wave us off from the quay. But it would have meant a night in an hotel, which I suppose made it too expensive for the Old Hall contingent, or perhaps they did not like to intrude on our honeymoon; and I had overheard my mother telling my father on the platform at Newcastle that the day had utterly exhausted her and she wanted to be taken straight home to rest.

We went down to our cabin. On the way I sensed the sinewy strength of Chuck's tall figure behind me, and thought suddenly of Giles and Zinnia *en déshabille* in their strange ecstasy in the Riverpark conservatory, all those years ago, and felt an almost unbearable excitement and curiosity. But there were two narrow bunks. Chuck looked at them.

"Guess we've plenty of time," he said. "I'll take the top one. I won't disturb you. I'll just go and make sure those rams are tucked up safe and sound."

From my bunk, later, I watched him undress. I felt half-shy, half-eager. He left his clothes on the floor, but I didn't care. I waited for him to sit on my bunk, hold me in his arms, whisper words of love, stroke and tease and cajole me into surrender. But he started to climb straight up to the top bunk, and I had to interrupt his climb to ask for a good-night kiss.

I couldn't understand it. What had I done to offend him or put him off? Surely a husband on the first night of his honeymoon would at least kiss his wife good night without being prompted by her outstretched arms?

But for the rest of the voyage he seemed to be more concerned about the rams than about his as yet unravished wife.

After the first excitement of being on a ship at sea, the voyage seemed very long and boring. The ship was primarily for cargo and there were only a dozen or so passengers. I found myself looking forward eagerly to mealtimes when I could talk to them. One was a smiling young Irishman called John O'Grady who had a fund of old jokes. He was going to Halifax to work in his uncle's shipping agency. Sometimes when I was swopping puns with him I caught Chuck looking at me, and he wasn't laughing.

After the midday meal my husband would find deckchairs and rugs and tuck me up in one, sitting down in the one next to it.

"What shall we talk about?" I would say.

"No need to talk about anything."

"But it's boring, just looking at the sea. I'm going down to find a book."

"You don't need to read all the time. Have a rest now, there's plenty to do when we get home."

"Tell me about it. What does the house look like? How many bedrooms has it?"

"You'll see soon enough. Have a nap now."

Love, honour, obey.

I closed my eyes, but I found it hard to sleep. Even at night I lay awake, listening to the slap of waves that were taking me farther and farther from Riverlaw and all the people I loved best.

The McIver Place (it was so isolated as to need no other name) was in a remote branch of the Upper Stewiacke valley in Colchester County, Nova Scotia, and it took something over an hour and a half to walk from the McIver house to the nearest human habitation.

Not that the intervening land was all owned by the McIvers. Much of it had been, once; but it was forest, and years before I arrived Major McIver, Chuck's father, had sold it to a timber company for the price of a year's education at Harrow School. They had cut the best timber, left the rest to grow, and gone away. I often reflected that his action had been (to put the best interpretation on it) hasty, for he could surely have sold them the timber rights for a few years, and kept the land for himself; but when you got to know Major McIver you understood how this rash deal had come about. I had ample opportunity to get to know Major McIver, for he and Chuck were the only inhabitants of the McIver Place besides myself.

Can I ever forget my first view of my new home as

Chuck and I lurched in a neighbouring farmer's old Ford over the muddy, deeply rutted, branch-enclosed dirt track through the woods, the evening after our ship had docked in Halifax harbour?

Halifax was sombre, fog-bound, and partly ruined by the recent explosion of an ammunition ship, so that gaunt remnants of houses loomed at us through the mist, and broken or boarded-up windows made the buildings seem like threatening faces in a fantasy of hell. I had expected log cabins and torrents and beaver dams, even perhaps redwoods; not this grey, shattered fortress of a city hanging over the huge, grey arms of water in the fog-bound dawn.

The road from Halifax had seemed eternal. First, we were the only passengers in an ungainly omnibus that strained up the long hill, while Chuck made me look up to where the citadel should be visible and I watched obediently for a break in the fog, only to be profoundly disappointed by its hard, grey, prison-like walls. As we climbed to higher land the fog gradually dissolved to shrouds and then wisps of mist as we rumbled on and on, through endless stunted spruce and birch. We passed farms that seemed carved out of the forest, their small fields almost enclosed by walls of dark trees, with – set back from the road behind strips of grass – big barns, each flanked by a small weather-boarded, basemented house whose corner-boards and door- and window-frames were painted black or dark green, so that in the distance they looked like nothing so much as a child's drawing of a house.

At Brookfield – a place so small and dispersed as to be scarcely recognisable as a settlement – we left the bus and ate pies and tea at a cheap hotel. The woman who brought them to us stared at my clothes – and, indeed, my fashionable low waistline was something the few Canadian women I had glimpsed did not seem to have adopted.

Chuck was restless and kept going to the door and looking down the road, and by and by an old Ford with a hooped hood drew up, coughing and belching. My hand was wrung by Jed Macalister, a grizzled and ruddy farmer with a wall eye. He and Chuck loaded up the back of the car (he called it an automobile) with the big boxes of wedding-presents and as much of my extensive luggage as there was room for, and the rest was put in the charge of the hotel until we could return for it. And we set off along the Collector Highway (as over-optimistic a label as one could imagine) for Middle Stewiacke, Upper Stewiacke, and the unpaved roads past Glenbervie. Finally, in late afternoon, we came to the end of these and at a desolate crossroads we lurched into a narrow track, and then another, bumpy and rutted with churned mud, scarcely wide enough for the Ford and closed in by fly-infested trees. It was cold, but Jed (who had spent much of the journey in an earnest discussion with Chuck about fatstock prices and cow disease), drove with the driver's celluloid window unfastened – "so's we don't be pizened by the engine fumes," he explained; "they make me pass out some." I found myself swatting flies and buzzed-about by mosquitoes, and I watched the red weals of bites emerge under my new silk stockings and had to grit my teeth to stop myself from scratching and tearing them.

The cobwebby trees crawled by for ever, with behind them more trees, and more and more to everlasting blackness, until I felt trapped by an unending prison of trees. And then far ahead, above the roar of the engine and the rustle of the forest, we heard rushing water; and soon we crossed a small river by a rough, wooden bridge, stopping a moment to admire the foam churning over the rapids above; and a few minutes later the road turned and petered out in a waste of mud, and before us was a big clearing that led down to a curve in the river and there, backed by half a dozen fields and entirely surrounded by the all-embracing forest, was a tiny, shabby board house, the same size as the hinds' cottages at Riverlaw, with a high stone chimney, a few brown chickens picking at the mud among the dusty stones outside, a couple of tall barns behind, and an upright, red-faced, purple-nosed elderly man standing in a collarless shirt and braces at the open doorway.

31

For most things in life there is a reason; and in most lives, as one looks back, one sees that a pattern begins to emerge, a pattern of loss in one direction that leads to blossoming in another, of appearances being belied, of seeming waste and actual growth and gain.

Just as in the Old Hall gardens the flower-petals faded and dropped and were dug in, with the manure from the stables, to enrich the dark soil and make next year's roses huger and more prolific and beautiful than ever before; so in life nothing is wasted. But when I first arrived in Canada, I was young. I did not know that.

The first shock was the place itself. I had somehow expected Chuck to have a house, if not like Riverlaw (though that hope-against-hope had, of course, been hovering at the back of my mind all the way across the Atlantic), then at least corresponding to the British home of the average prosperous Old Harrovian. He had in no way prepared me for a two-up-two-down where we ate in the kitchen, and went to the lavatory in an outhouse a few yards outside the back of the house, with a door that didn't even shut properly. There were two bedrooms upstairs, and no bathroom. Having been brought up in the habit of modesty, I could not for a long time contemplate the thought of the tin bath in front of the kitchen fire which the men used, and I lived in terror in case I inadvertently walked in on the Major while he was in it, or – worse – vice versa.

The other downstairs room – not counting the basement

where we stored vegetables and the snowshoes and other impedimenta, and hung the washing during the winter – was a square parlour beside which my mother's dim drawing-room was positively elegant. Oddly enough I rather liked the home-made hooked rug and the rocking-chair and the tinkling glass prisms on the mantelpiece, although Zinnia would have thrown up her hands in horror at these simple attempts at home comfort. But the rug was dirty, the furniture ringed with stains, the door smeared with handprints and the wooden walls spotted with flaking paint in a kind of dingy ginger colour that I had seen only once before, through a window of a notorious public house in the Newcastle docks, on the ceiling of its four-ale bar.

The second shock came the very first evening of our arrival.

We roared up to the kitchen door in a cloud of midges, and my father-in-law looked up and said in a rich, whisky-laden growl, "You've taken your time. I plucked a chicken for you and you only need to cook it. Everything's on the kitchen table. Be as quick as you can, I'm hungry and he must be too."

Stunned at this welcome, I stood there, beating tiredly at the midges and brushing little black-winged corpses off my expensive two-piece from Fenwick's French.

"Get those bloody trunks off the wagon, Chuck, where the devil are we going to put them all?" roared the Major. "And get in there, woman, and rattle them pots and pans!"

I scuttled into the kitchen. It was a small, square room with a blackened kitchen range across the wall to my right and a stone sink in the opposite corner. The whole room was filthy and every flat surface was littered with the unwashed remains of rudimentary meals. Gobbets of mouldy bread and stinking meat lay on the first plates that met my eye. Chuck had been away from home for six weeks or more; it appeared that his father had left all the washing-up for Chuck's wife. A further clue emerged when I looked down at the floor and saw empty bottle after empty bottle. The

Major must have drunk approximately a bottle a day of whisky, and he had left them where they lay.

On the draining-board was a raw chicken. It looked horribly naked and the legs and wings stuck out. Beside it was a heap of potatoes, a cabbage, and some gnarled cooking-apples.

I had done very little cooking; we had always had a cook-general at home, even during the war. I had automatically assumed (and so, obviously, had my parents) that on an Old Harrovian's two-hundred-acre farm there would at least be a kitchenmaid to help. But here, equally obviously, we were too remote for any household help at all. I was willing to do anything; but if only Chuck had warned me!

I rolled up my sleeves and began peeling the potatoes. I had seen cooks do it, but it was much harder than it looked. After a few minutes the laboriously-peeled potatoes, and my hands, were filthy with the mud that clung to them. I realised I needed water and went back to ask about it.

"Pump's not working," barked my father-in-law. "Take the bucket down to the stream."

I got my best French high-heeled shoes wet in the stream as I heaved at the heavy bucket among clouds of blackfly. Why couldn't the men do it?

Somehow, I produced a meal.

But the chicken I had laboriously cooked was disgusting. As the Major pointed out, I had left the giblets in. I had also burnt the potatoes. I imagined the giggles these calamities would have produced at Riverlaw, and giggled myself in an attempt to laugh it off. This was a cardinal error. To these two humourless men, tired from unloading the luggage, my lack of housewifely qualities was a disaster of colossal dimensions, not to be mocked.

"What did you think I married you for?" asked Chuck.

That hurt. The more I thought about it, the more it worried me.

"I'll learn," I said humbly. "I promise."

"You'd bloody well better," said the Major. "My God,"

he added, tripping over a Gladstone bag that had fallen off the pile of my luggage stacked, for lack of a better place, inside the narrow hall, "why the hell did you bring all this stuff? There'll never be room for it! What's in that trunk?"

"My party-dresses."

"Hah! You won't need party-dresses here."

Looking around me at the cramped house and the endless forest, I could see he was right.

That evening, while the men put their feet up with loud declarations of exhaustion, and I struggled unaided to scrub the disgusting dishes and pans with a lump of gritty soap and the small amount of water left in the bucket, black despair seized me, so that silent tears dripped down my nose into the dirty sink to mingle with the scum. The whole of my life, my whole precious future until I died, was to be spent in this godforsaken, flyblown, friendless outpost with only these two unkind strangers for company.

And I had vowed to be faithful to Chuck. There was no escape.

Although I never did and never would like the Major, when I really thought about it it was obvious that his life had got on to the wrong track, and he was too old and set in his ways to alter it.

He had come to Canada years before, no longer young but full of hope for a new life. He had married a Toronto girl who was staying in Onslow with friends of her parents, and they had settled in this remote, half-cleared, abandoned valley because it was cheap. They never meant to stay; he had hoped to make his fortune and go back to England a rich man. But he was both lazy and impulsive. He could not manage money, and he lacked the brute strength and patience to improve his farm and clear his forest. His wife, for whom I felt acute pity, had died of pneumonia one winter not long before the war; if only the doctor had been nearer, they thought, she could have been saved.

Depression and grief had driven him to drink. He loved Chuck and depended on him; when he was away, the Major went to pieces. The two men had fallen into a rough, basic, slovenly, bachelor way of life. The Major was never slow to criticise, and it became clear that he had been nagging Chuck for years to get a wife.

A mature and capable woman might possibly have pulled them out of it, and as over the course of time I met what neighbours there were within reach, I gradually learned that I was not Chuck's first choice of wife. He had taken the first hesitating steps towards courting two or three unmarried women in the district; but when they met the Major and saw the primitive isolation in which the McIvers lived, they backed off.

Chuck was handsome and presentable; but what my seventeen-year-old inexperience had failed to perceive was that he had not a spark of humour or wit. He had a nice smile when there was something to smile about, but he could not contribute any gaiety of his own. He was a dull, unenterprising, silent man, customarily uncommunicative.

And there was something even worse.

I was deeply romantic. I was ready and willing to try and forget my old life, and put all my heart and energy into making a success of the new. I had assumed that Chuck would flirt, tease, whisper sweet nothings, declare he adored me. I was ready and willing to flirt and tease back, to be wooed, to make his concerns my own, to give my last and greatest gift; myself.

That first night, in the plain and dirty bedroom (the Major having obligingly moved out of his double bed to Chuck's old room the day before, without, however, shifting his possessions from the bulging press or his empty bottles from under the bed), Chuck turned to me and performed his matrimonial duty quickly, roughly, and without a word of love.

The next day, and the next, I worked so hard that I

had no time to think. In the interstices between burying bottles and embarking on the daunting task of tidying and spring-cleaning the little house, I studied Mrs Beeton. When the Major barked, "Aren't you going to feed the hens?" I asked him to show me how to do it, and tried to be an attentive pupil. I discovered that he liked having someone to teach. When he was sober one could see that he had once been able, and quite attractive to look at; he was bald, but he had bright blue eyes under bushy brows, a military moustache, and a tall, broad-shouldered frame that was now paunchy and slack except for the sinewy hardness of his sunburnt arms and hands. He had been to a minor public school in England, and his Canadian way of speech still bore traces of a bourgeois Englishman aspiring to be something grander – "Quaite naice but rarther refeened," as Zinnia had unkindly described a dancing partner who wasn't socially up to scratch.

I wondered why the Major had left the Army, but never dared to ask; but something about the fury with which he met any suggestion from Chuck or myself that he might do the farm accounts made me wonder. Somewhere under the gruffness was a once-ambitious man, curdled with disappointment, loneliness and frustration, and perhaps remorse. His impulsive decision, years before, to give Chuck a year at Harrow had been the last flowering of his longing for a better life. I felt sorry for him, sometimes. But he was very difficult to live with.

Among Chuck's luggage were several cases of Scotch whisky; to the Major it was more precious than the pedigree rams.

I worked from dawn to dusk, and after. I cleaned the oil-lamps, scrubbed the grimy floors, and washed the clothes and sheets on a washboard in the old sink. Everything took so long and was so tiring because I had never done manual work in my life, I wasn't much good at it, and I hated it. And it was done in a silence and isolation more oppressive than anything I had ever known. The men were out in the fields or the forest all day, and came back too tired to talk. In the evening you couldn't even see the sunset. Out of doors, when I looked around me, the horizon was charcoal-black with tree-trunks, with behind them more, and more, blacker and blacker to infinity. I was closed in on our little island of fields by an eternal ocean of trees, their trunks as black and impenetrable as my despair.

But I was married. I had vowed in church to love, honour and obey, as long as I lived. If I didn't make the best of it I might as well be dead. By hook or crook I must grow to love this country.

Although my new home was obviously never going to be like Riverlaw, I determined to improve it, to plant a proper garden, and to run the house as efficiently as I could. In the end I became a successful and thrifty housekeeper, but I learnt the hard way.

To cheer myself up when I was alone I sang, I recited poetry, I composed speeches, I declaimed what Shakespeare I knew at the top of my voice. There was nobody to hear.

"Where's the next farm?" I demanded one evening the first week, after the Major had retired, a bottle under his arm.

"Oh – an hour's walk, I guess," said Chuck, wolfing down leftover potatoes as I washed the dishes. He never offered to help me, but then, I never expected him to – I don't think my father had ever even entered our kitchen. "It's quicker as the crow flies, but there's no way through the forest."

"I'll go in the buggy," I declared.

"Whatever for?"

"They haven't called on me," I said, "and I know it isn't etiquette, but I'm going to call on them."

He stared. "Waste of time. He'll be out in the fields."

"I'll make friends with his wife. What's their name?"

"Van Tyghem. And there ain't a wife. He's an old

276

bachelor, and he's Dutch. He doesn't speak English. I wouldn't bother to go, if I were you."

"But . . . Chuck, it's so lonely here."

"Nice and quiet. You'll soon get used to it. Anyway, you'll meet the neighbours Sunday. We'll go to church."

"Hooray. Chuck, we're running out of candles."

"Right. You make some."

"But I . . . Look, where's the nearest shop?"

"Now don't fret. We go to the store twice a month, usually. It's in Upper Stewiacke."

"Is that a big place?"

He grinned. "Big for here, I guess. It's got a store."

"Only one?"

"Stewiacke has three, but that's a fair way."

"But where do I get clothes? And books? I must have books!"

"What you need more clothes for? You *got* clothes. We buy them from the Eaton's mail-order catalogue, but only when the old ones wear out. And Pop's got some books beside his bed. Read those."

"I've seen them."

"The church has a lending shelf."

"I'll need a lot more than that. And what about meeting the other people here and making friends?"

"We meet them Sundays after church. And there's the school concert, and the school picnic in June. Everyone goes to that."

"You should have told me we'd be completely isolated!"

"Nonsense. There's the agricultural exhibition once a year in Stewiacke – "

"Oh, riveting!" I hadn't meant to be sarcastic. It just slipped out.

"What's the matter with you?" shouted Chuck. "You're never satisfied!"

I was devastated to be shouted at by the man I thought had loved me. I tried oblique tactics.

"If I write home," I said, "how soon can I get a reply?"

Chuck stopped shouting. "A month, I guess. But if you think you're going to try buying stuff from England, forget it. I spent more'n I should getting you here. Money's tight."

"A *month*?"

I knew already, of course. But I was young, and in the excitement of marrying, it hadn't sunk in.

I lived for letters. The farm was so remote that it did not even have a letter-box on a stick at the gate like the other farms. I went to look in our box at the crossroads every few days, and always on Fridays, despite Chuck's protests that he didn't want the bills so soon, and twice a month had always been quite adequate for his parents, and that there was plenty of work to be done on the farm without wasting time and tiring the horses driving around Nova Scotia.

From Saturday to Thursday I itched with impatience. If on Friday there was nothing in the McIver box, I was wretched.

I still remember my delight the day I felt in the box and my hand closed on a thick, laid-paper envelope bearing several stamps. It was from my mother, and told me nothing about anything except the weather, which had been nice, she said. Still she sent love, and that was what I needed most.

But, of course, traumatic though my first days in Nova Scotia were, there were also new sights and experiences, and places and people of whom I gradually grew fond.

Every Sunday we drove through the forest to church. The service was strange and simple, the sermons yawningly long, the hymns often unfamiliar, the wheezy harmonium primitive when I remembered the resonant organs of the Northumbrian churches I knew. But it was comforting. There was something very moving about being united in prayer with these good people in this remote corner of the world. And afterwards people came up to me and introduced themselves, and clearly expected to be told anything about myself that I cared to reveal.

There was a smiling woman of about my mother's age – Mrs Macateer, tall, soberly dressed, in an old but once charming straw hat with blue ribbons; I took to her at once. There were the minister, the Reverend Campbell, and his wife. There was a highly intelligent spinster, skinny with grey-speckled red hair, who was the teacher in the one-room school and knew more about human nature than most people learn in a lifetime. There was Janet McWilliam, a young wife with three children, sturdy, cheerful and kind; she lived on the road to Upper Stewiacke, and became in time a rock-solid friend. There was also a gaggle of old gossips, and in the ensuing months I became used to eyes flicking down to my belt and the concerned enquiry, "And are you feeling well, dear?" At first, I didn't know why they kept asking me.

The gathering after church was a landmark in our week, and I looked forward to it. But it was quite different from the short and casual chatting that took place after Sunday service at Riverlaw. Here, it was a serious business, and the sexes were almost segregated. I didn't like that at first. I found it hard, when Chuck left my side to hobnob with the farmers and tradesmen he had known at school, not to follow, but to "consort with Godly matrons" as the minister had solemnly bidden the female half of his congregation; especially as many of the matrons seemed either ancient or frumpish. However, in time I learned to look beyond their home-sewn clothes and outmoded hats to the warm hearts within.

On the third Sunday, Chuck and I were invited to a quilting bee at the McWilliams'. I didn't even know what it meant; but Chuck was pleased.

"My mother was making a quilt," he said. "I'll ask Pop if you can finish it. You can sew, I suppose?"

So the following Saturday, I armed myself with the irregular piece of patchwork and a pillowcase full of templated patches, and we drove in the buggy to a farm near the crossroads, and while Chuck yarned with the husbands in the parlour, I sat with the wives round the big kitchen table.

I didn't need my late mother-in-law's quilt, because Janet McWilliam's almost-finished one was stretched out over the big kitchen table and eight of us sat round it, each quilting the section in front of us with tiny stitches in an elaborate leaf pattern. I learned that on each subsequent Saturday night we would work at a different house on a different quilt. Eventually it would be my turn. I felt both delighted at the chance to confound the Major by giving a party, and ashamed that my new friends would see inside the McIver house.

"Could you get a painter to come and paint it?" I begged Chuck.

"Whatever next? Money's tight, I told you, and it would cost a lot to get a workman from Stewiacke to come all the way out here. He'd have to camp out nights. I don't know who we could ask."

I looked at the flaking ginger walls.

"Couldn't you do it, Chuck?"

"Good God, woman, you think I have time to spare?"

I couldn't work out why Chuck in Canada seemed so different from the amused, urbane-seeming soldier I had thought I was marrying. Eventually I discovered the key. At home, he was greatly under the influence of his father. Being thrown together with him had made Chuck speak in the same way; as the Major had coarsened with solitude and whisky, Chuck had unconsciously fallen in with his ways. In England he had been on his best behaviour, remembering his days at Harrow, and trying to adopt English good manners. It was quite a long time before he told me that he had hated Harrow; he had been unbearably lonely and Rednall, his only friend, had been the only person to take any notice of him – and that, he suspected, was because Rednall was so weak and solitary himself that the other boys despised him. When Chuck returned to Canada he tried to forget Harrow and the miseries of the war. His time in the trenches had further blackened his picture of Europe. He never spoke about what he had seen during the fighting, but sometimes at night he cried out in his sleep about the mud and the guns, and groaned and shook, and shouted with fear at the touch of my hand on his shoulder.

At all events I realised that Chuck was unwilling to do anything to improve his home; it had been like that ever since his mother had died and he was used to it. And since my admission that I could sew, the two men had produced a backlog of mending that must have gone back for years. Most evenings I turned cuffs well into the night by the eye-aching light of an oil-lamp.

However, I was desperate to make friends, and quite determined that Janet and her cronies should not write me off because of the state of the McIver house. On my next visit to the store I spent some of the small savings I had brought with me from England on paint and distemper, brushes and turpentine, sandpaper and filler – the last two on the advice of the shopkeeper who saw my ignorance and took pains to explain what I should do.

Next day, as soon as the men had left for the fields, I began on the parlour. It was hard work. By the end of the morning I had barely finished the preparation; but as soon as the first creamy brushfuls of paint were on, I realised that I hadn't enjoyed doing anything so much since I left England. I was in a fever to finish it, and yet I had to stop to prepare the men's dinner. I had saved some cold meat from the previous day, but when they tramped into the kitchen the potatoes still weren't ready. But I managed to brave their irritation, and neither of them went into the parlour.

That evening I kept them out of it by saying that the

floor was wet (which was not a lie; I had spilt a little paint and had to wash it to try to remove the smell of turpentine). And by the next evening the whole topcoat was done, in a beautiful pale grey which set off the bright colours of the rag rug.

I had washed the curtains, which were stiff with dust but proved to be a pretty Indian red, and found an eyelet-embroidered tablecloth (castoff from my mother's linen-cupboard) for the little round table. Aunt Emily's wedding-present had been a number of silver photograph-frames. In them I put photographs of my parents and cousins, and one of my deceased mother-in-law. They looked splendid on the table and on a handsome chest, which I further adorned with a jug of wild flowers.

A bright cushion or two, the covers improvised from a torn old quilt that I found on top of a wardrobe, cheered up the sofa and rocking-chair, and after a lot of hard polishing I discovered that the blackened poker and coal-scuttle were copper, and the best lamp silver-plated. It took hours, but I made them shine.

On the third evening I made the men stand in the hall, and I flung open the door; and was rewarded when Chuck threw his arms around me.

"Didn't I tell you, Pop?" he demanded. "Didn't I tell you there was a whole lot to this girl?"

"Yes, you did," grunted the Major. "And I didn't believe a word of it till this moment."

And that was only the start.

I turned the kitchen into a vision of white and pale green – I even painted the floorboards, though the labour of scraping them first nearly made me give up the whole idea. I coaxed Chuck into putting up extra shelves. I couldn't persuade the Major to do without his whisky, but at least he agreed to leave the empty bottles on one of the new shelves, and I made a lace-edged curtain so that they were out of sight.

Not all my work was as perfect as I wanted. The edges of the window-panes in both rooms were smudged with paint, and I couldn't get it all off. But at night, with the curtains drawn, I felt delighted at my creation.

Later, I would transform the bedrooms and the dingy hall. In the meantime I lived from Saturday to Saturday, when I listened to the other women talk about their families, swop recipes, tell stories of their lives. They were all older than I, but not much older; kind-hearted, shrewd, church-going people of Scottish descent, whose conversation was the best possible training for the hard life of a Nova Scotian housewife. Long before the winter came I knew what to expect, and how to cope with it; what stores to lay in, how much salt and tallow, how many sacks of flour, how many home-salted hams and crocks of eggs and jars of beans I must prepare, how much feed for the animals who were doomed to six months indoors in the big barns.

When the great day came for me to entertain the quilting bee party – seventeen in all, including the Major, whose whisky I had hidden in the cowshed for the night – the cakes I was cooking for second course came out of the oven sunken and burnt nearly black. At that moment Janet and her husband arrived.

In a panic, I took her into the kitchen and pointed to the charred ruins. "What'll I do?" I whispered.

Janet, bless her heart, never turned a hair. "Scrape off the black bits, turn them upside down and ice them. Here, give me a knife. Got enough powdered sugar? Put it in that bowl and add a tiny bit of water out of the kettle, and stir like mad. We'll just slap it on anyhow and call it Lizzie's Snow Cake."

"Quick, I can hear a buggy coming – oh, oh, I've put in too much water!"

"Hey, let's put in more sugar and make them layer cakes as well," and we stirred and giggled and slathered the frosting on at top speed, and Lizzie's Snow Cakes were a great success.

So was my transformation of the house; and so was the quilting bee. And eventually I finished my quilt and put it proudly on our bed. Chuck was pleased.

And it was at about that time that I discovered I was pregnant.

32

I was astounded by the length and coldness of the winter. I trudged round McIver's Place in the snow, feeling ugly and ungainly in my borrowed smock and clumsy boots and the Major's shabby old Army greatcoat. I envied Janet and her friends, because their husbands didn't take it for granted that they would spend whole days at a time shovelling snow, whereas mine did. I found it a huge effort and never really got used to it. Dragging myself to the outhouse in a freezing blizzard was almost more than I could face, especially at night. I was troubled in case the deep cold might affect my baby; and frightened in case the old woman who acted as midwife to the community might not get to the birth in time. I thought about Chuck's mother, slowly dying in the cruel cold and waiting and praying for the doctor to come, until she could wait no more.

Irrationally, I wished I could have comforting, impersonal Dr Bond to see me through the birth.

"Don't worry, we'll manage somehow," said the Major with unconcealed relish, which of course made it worse. No doubt he would volunteer to deliver the baby; he kept telling me it was just like dropping a calf. I rehearsed ways of politely declining his help. But could I manage without? And how would I know when it was about to arrive?

In the event, there was no doubt. I woke in the night with a great ache that swelled and ebbed away. I lit a candle and timed the delay till the next one. Then I woke Chuck.

"It's coming! Get the midwife!"

By the time the next pain came, he was dressed and out in the freezing, moonlit whiteness, and a few moments later I heard the clop of hooves and jingle of harness as he set off for Upper Stewiacke.

I walked cautiously down to the kitchen to make myself a cup of tea. While the kettle was heating on the hob I drew back the curtains and looked out at the maples in the yard, loaded with lumps of snow like ungainly blossoms, and up at the moon, cold above the iced blackness of the forest beyond the farm. That same moon, I comforted myself, is looking down on Riverlaw, and on Cedric at Riverpark, and on Zinnia in St John's Wood, and on Henry Grey in Africa, and even – yesterday or tomorrow, perhaps – on Peregrine. Oh, Peregrine, wherever you are, I whispered as the next pain rose like a great wave and filled me, if only this child were yours!

My labour was long, and until Chuck returned with the midwife I was so tense, and terrified in case he did not find her, that I suppose the pains were worse than they need have been. I don't know. I only recall that when she eventually arrived at my bedside I was crying and near the end of my strength, but quite proud that I hadn't woken the Major. I expect he was in a drunken stupor anyway.

But she was in time. The baby was a girl, with dark hair, a calm little face, and bright eyes. I called her Zoe, because it means joy.

I will not attempt to describe the happiness of watching Zoe develop into a person; every parent knows what I mean, and knows too that it is a peculiarly private joy, never quite to be communicated to others.

Time, when a loved child is growing, takes on a different perspective. I now saw McIver's Place not as exile, but through Zoe's eyes, as the centre of the world. As she grew, each step was an adventure, each discovery of interest or beauty among the things around her was a revelation for me too.

With her I searched for the first mayflower buds when the snow went, and sniffed their marvellous fragrance when they burst into flower after a few days in a sunny window. I noticed the petals and stamens of the summer flowers, saw the sumac leaves redden, heard the music of the wind in the maples and the creek-water rushing over the stones, with an intensity I had never felt before. Together we picked blueberries in the forest and came home with purple hands, and weeded among the neat rows of carrots, parsnips and cabbages in the vegetable-garden. Together we searched in mid-March for the sap flowing up in the maple stumps, and rushed to get buckets and spiles, and went out – Zoe importantly carrying the brace and bit – to tap the trees. We stalked the bobolink and song sparrow, and listened rapt to the hermit thrush in late evening, and the owl that hooted under the moon.

The impenetrable wall of tree-trunks that I had once thought of as prison bars was now ambiguous. The trees might engulf a lost child, but they were also a barrier against evil. Inside them we had our safe and private world where no stranger could intrude.

In church I listened with Zoe's ears to the simple sincerity of the prayers, and noticed the tender smiles of the old people whenever they saw her trusting blue eyes and flower-soft little face. Even the Major melted when she curled her fingers into his rough hand. Chuck was grave and formal with her, but I saw again in his eyes the amused look that long ago had drawn me to him. He might be undemonstrative – nothing, I bitterly knew, would ever make him otherwise – but he was immensely proud of his daughter.

He persuaded the Major to help him build a little extension behind the hall of the house, with a dining-room below and a bedroom and shower-room above, and even a lavatory – I tried for a bathtub too, but you would think I was asking for a gold-plated ballroom; they turned on me with roars at my extravagance, and I retired defeated. Still, to do them justice, they worked hard at it, digging out the basement that was necessary in that forbidding climate, installing a bigger boiler for the extra heating, and lining the walls with pine – we had plenty of that – to save the expense of plaster.

So the years passed in the McIver Place. I taught Zoe to read, cutting the letters out of pastry so that she would feel their shapes and remember them by the delicious taste of the home-made jams and maple sugar I spread on them. I borrowed a wild-flower book and wandered through the valley beside her to seek and identify many species, and later to press them and make delicate pictures. We played counting games with pretty pebbles from the creek, and planted roses together in the garden I had made, and covered them carefully against the deep frost. I answered her questions patiently and truthfully. There is a moment in every child's life when it is ready for the next piece of learning, and longs for it. I tried to catch those moments.

"The kitchen floor needs a good scrub," said Chuck sourly one day.

"I know, but I've been busy teaching Zoe geography," I said. "We made a map of Canada on that bare ground by the creek."

"We'll speak to the schoolteacher – if she's able for geography, she should go to school."

The tiny mixed-age school was in Upper Stewiacke; a long drive, but Chuck had gone there as a boy and the teacher had educated him to a standard not unacceptable to the Harrow of those pre-war days. Other children whose homes were on the route attended it, so Zoe joined the rota. Each weekday I drove her to Janet's house, and I collected her from there after school. Often I had to lift her sleeping body, thumb in mouth, from the back of Janet's buggy into ours. On Fridays it was my turn to do the whole journey; I delivered five assorted children to the teacher and went on to do my shopping at the store. Usually I took my sewing to fill in the remaining time, and an apple or two in my pocket to munch sitting on the river-bank in the warm weather. When it turned colder, I went to the one cheap hotel a little way down the road and sat there writing letters to England and making a glass of milk last until it was time to go back to the school. (I had offered my services free to the red-headed teacher, but she preferred to be sole empress in her own domain.) Finally, having delivered my other charges to their homes, we would wend our way between the darkening walls of forest to McIver's Place, where I would have little enough time to prepare the evening meal for us all.

In the depths of winter Zoe couldn't go to school at all. I prepared for our snowbound weeks by getting her a work-programme from the teacher.

The silent, monotone world never lost its wonder for me. Great claws of snow hung on the drooping branches of the conifers, against a winter-white sky. When the snow was deep the rooms would darken as it piled up outside the windows. Twice a day Chuck would set out like a Polar explorer into the blizzard, scarcely visible under his layers of clothes. Shovel on one shoulder, a sack of turnips slung over the other, he would feel his way across by the rope fence to the invisible barn, to milk the cows. Sometimes he wouldn't come back for ages and I would muffle myself up and set out in search of his, perhaps, injured or frozen body – only to find that he had done the milking and forked down the hay and straw and then sat down for a nap in the odorous warmth. The barn stank, because it wasn't mucked out until the thaw; but the cows' warm bodies and hot breath made it much warmer than the house where Zoe and I cooked and cleaned and toiled over irregular verbs, while the Major snored by the wood stove.

When the weather allowed, we went out snowballing or snowshoeing, and one winter I nailed together a toboggan. Every time I looked at it I saw again the hill outside Riverlaw, and strained my ears to hear the excited cries of Louie and Zinnia, Giles and Theodore and Vin and Ivy, as they swept down over the snow.

I gave Zoe a censored account of the family; she was fascinated, especially by the thought that her first-cousin-once-removed, Zinnia, had a title.

"Is Zadok a Sir?" she asked.

"No." I hesitated, then remembered that although Rednall was not his father, he had not publicly disinherited the boy. "He may be, one day."

"Sir Zadok, my, what a stoopid name!" for like Chuck, she had no trace of the Major's English accent.

I wrote letters feverishly, pouring out demands for news. Aimée Gutch sent glamorous accounts of life in Paris, where she was soon involved in a circle of aspiring writers and painters. But one day, after a series of letters full of a young painter named André, her letters stopped. Perhaps she became his mistress and dared not admit it; perhaps she married him; perhaps she was dead. I asked my parents to try to find out what had become of her, but they never did, or if they did they chose not to tell me.

I missed the Delmaynes more than I can say. They all wrote to me, but not even Louie's vivacious letters could quite bring them alive.

And then, quite suddenly, the fun went out of her letters. Con had married the nurse who had looked after him in the military hospital.

At first I had not wanted my cousins to see how we lived; but when this news came I wrote at once to invite Louie to stay. It was some time before she replied.

Dearest Lizzie what an angel of mercy you are, and how I would have loved to! But a lot of Vane's barley was laid by high winds this June and couldn't be harvested properly because of that and the rain. Afraid we are having to economise madly this year. The main other news is that Cedric is getting married to Madge Carroun!!! It is in *three weeks* – rumour has it that *she* proposed and actually bought the Licence, so as to tie the knot quickly before he can change his mind. Looking back I think she has had her eye on Riverpark for some time – she once told me she thought it was a very "suitable" house, she didn't say what for but now we know. Poor Cedric hardly knows what's hit him – he looks half the time as if he's being pursued by hounds, and my guess is that he has only not thrown her over because he's afraid she might sue him for breach of promise. He specially asked me to tell you that he wanted to invite you and Chuck to the wedding but he knew you couldn't get here in time. Zinnia is not being asked, in order not to embarrass Rednall and Lady C. Leslie is to be Best Man, imagine. He is now Cedric's full-time Farm Agent & does all his Accounts and even answers for Cedric when you ask C a question. Vane says Madge will say, "Come to bed, Cedric" and Leslie will answer "It isn't convenient tonight, would you make an appointment please".

Poor Louie! Poor Cedric! Marooned thousands of miles away behind an impenetrable barrier of trees, I ground my teeth with disappointment at missing the wedding.

Eventually Louie sent me a cutting from the *Newcastle Journal*. "Northumberland's Wedding of the Year", said the headline. In the photo Cedric looked as if his collar was too tight, and Madge, wearing a very tall and ugly diamond tiara, carried a sheaf of gladioli. All the presents were listed; Aunt Emily had given a silver champagne-cooler. The bridegroom's present to the bride was a pair of Purdey guns. I am sure this was Cedric's idea of a joke, but feared Madge would not see it.

At first, I waited confidently for Chuck to tell me when we were to visit England again.

"See you in a year or two," I wrote to Louie, "but I can't go while Zoe is a baby."

I waited patiently. When she was five or six, "When can we go home?" I demanded of Chuck.

"This *is* your home."

"But you said . . . Next time you needed rams . . ."

He laughed. "Won't need no rams for a long, long time."

With an eye on Zoe, who was playing with a home-made doll in the corner of the kitchen and pretending not to listen, "Won't need *any* rams," I said unwisely, adding, "They didn't teach you much grammar at Harrow."

"I hated Harrow. I never asked to go there. I loathed the war, too. I guess I don't want to go back to Europe ever again."

I was aghast. A great yearning for Riverlaw and its inhabitants welled up in me, like a river bursting through a dam. It must have been churning away for years inside me. "Don't want to go – ever?"

I had taken for granted that it was a promise. My sort of people don't break promises.

"Gee, Lizzie, you know we're still paying off the cost of the house extension, and we had a poor harvest these last two years. How can we throw money away on steamer tickets? And you know Pop ain't well enough to cope with the farm alone now."

" 'Well enough' isn't how I would describe it. A lot too much of your money ends up as empty whisky-bottles in the kitchen. It's bad for Zoe to see it."

"Cut it out!" He turned away, his brown, handsome face a petulant mask.

Desperately, "If you don't want to go, why don't Zoe and I go in her summer vacation? My parents would so love to see her – "

"Nothing doing. We need you here at cutting-time. And I told you, money's tight. If you're so frantic to get away, why can't they pay your fare? Pop and I'll look after Zoe. Go in the Fall, and she can quit school a while."

"You know we can't do that. She's missed too many

classes already when the snow's been too deep. If she misses more, she'll get behind and maybe never catch up. Anyway, my father's retired now. I could never ask him to pay our fares out of his pension."

"Well, there you are."

If only he hadn't given that smug grin as he said it.

Chuck was not a bad husband. His chief faults were meanness (which was perhaps partly justified, for the farm was hard to work, the climate in winter was terrible, the markets far); and the lack of physical love and tenderness, which had been such a shock to me when we first married. What, I used to ask myself in desperation, was marriage *for*? Chuck resolutely parried all my attempts to increase our intimacy. I was never really close to him; often, I despaired of even knowing him well, and as the years passed he became increasingly silent and irritable by turns. But in his own way he was loyal, he was a good father to Zoe, he worked hard. Many women fared worse. I had made my own bed and I must lie on it. And I enjoyed being mistress in my own domain. I became a good housekeeper and home-maker; and I came to be very fond of the wild free country and of the intrepid and self-sufficient women who became my friends.

In short, I made the best of it.

My parents wrote regularly, but dull lives usually make for dull letters. My mother's referred to her obscure malaises by subtle graduations – "I haven't been feeling very well lately" was not so bad as "I haven't been at all well"; this was less serious than "I have been quite poorly," and "rather poorly" was worse, though none of these meant "very ill". I was irresistibly reminded of Hannah's simple definitions of ill-health; an invalid was either "shabby" or "very shabby". The only alternative was "The poor thing's got away", which meant that he or she was dead.

Poor Hannah; she had indeed got away, though I sincerely hoped she was not dead. It was odd to think that we were on the same continent. I even contemplated finding out her address and trying to visit her. But when I suggested it to Chuck one day, he grunted, "You know very well we can't leave the animals. Father couldn't manage on his own now."

This was true; the Major was careless and chronically bad-tempered, and spent much of his time sunk in his chair.

"Why don't you get a hired man, like everyone else we know?"

"Where would he sleep?"

"We need another room anyway."

"Oh, sure. You build it."

"Right," I said in sudden exasperation, "I will, if you'll pay for the materials." I had never done carpentry, but I could learn, couldn't I?

"Don't be stupid," and he turned away, took a whisky-bottle out of the Major's store under the table, and went out, slamming the door.

As time went by I pondered on the past at Riverlaw. I realised that although I was now grown up, a married woman and a mother, there were things I did not quite understand about Theodore, about Zinnia, about Cedric – even about Aunt Emily and Uncle Vane; but however much I thought about them all, I could never quite put my finger on the answers. All I knew was that I loved them and missed them terribly.

Louie was my most faithful correspondent, and kept me up-to-date with news of almost everyone who had ever come to Riverlaw.

Soon after Zoe was born, Louie's letters were full of scandal about Venetia and Charles, of all people. What Louie called "their dear little Love-Nest" was next to a Roman Catholic church, and they had made friends with the priest in typical Venetia fashion, by offering him cuttings for his bare garden. In no time they were going to

Mass. "Darling Venetia is such a sheep, she does anything Charles wants to," wrote Louie. "We daren't tell Mother because it would upset her so."

Barbara Seymour was engaged, to a farmer three villages away. Bertram had found it difficult to work with his father and rejoined the Army until such time as his father should retire and hand over the reins. Later she wrote that Bertram, too, had married. His bride was the daughter of a farmer from a village two stops down the railway-line. ("Not One Of Us," wrote Louie darkly, "and she wears a lot of Rouge as Bertram will doubtless discover.")

Then came the news that Venetia was at last *enceinte*; and in due course she had a baby girl, called Anne.

And would you believe, they had her Baptised as a little Papist! Just before the Christening we still didn't know the place and time, and they brought the baby over for Sunday tea in the drawing-room, and when we asked about the arrangements they looked at each other in a very odd way, smiley and secret, and Charles said, "We didn't tell you before because we thought it would be rather a shock, but a few weeks ago we were both received into the Roman Catholic Church."

Well! I was really afraid Mother would have a seizure, she looked totally stricken, but then Charles said, "My parents are so angry they've stopped speaking to us," and she cheered up a bit and said "Well of course *I* wouldn't do that." But if he hadn't said it, it's exactly what she would have done. I'm sure by the way Charles gave Venetia a little sideways smile that he knew it too. "Nobody in our family has ever been a Papist," Mother said. "Won't you think again? It's a fearful disadvantage to a child, you know. They only marry each other."

But Venetia and Charles just held hands and smiled, so Mother said "I expect she'll change her mind as she gets older," and went on pouring the tea.

Henry, she informed me soon afterwards, had made an epic flight southward from Cairo, but had crashed in Kenya. The plane was a write-off, but he liked the country and had accepted an offer to go into partnership on a big coffee-plantation. "Perhaps we'll never see him again," she added gloomily. "Poor Henry." I felt sad that his great plan had failed, but faced the possibility of never seeing him again with equilibrium. Nevertheless I wrote to him occasionally, and he sent back long, boring letters full of details about the coffee harvest, and at Christmas we received large bags of coffee beans and, once, an enormous pineapple which had gone soft and disgusting during its long journey. I hadn't the heart to tell him so in my thank-you letter, but Louie did – he had dispatched a pineapple to the Old Hall too. "Too sad and wasteful," she wrote in her next letter to me – "I simply had to tell him in case he did it again next year."

For a long time I heard nothing more about Cedric. But when I wrote to ask Louie for news of him, she was unaccustomedly serious.

He doesn't seem happy at all (she wrote), but then I suppose he never did. Madge is always ticking him off – she treats him like a moron. And that snake Leslie clings to him like a leech. Cedric was always rather hopeless about running the estate, anyway now he depends on him entirely. Leslie goes round Riverpark giving everyone orders, and the hinds hate it, or so I hear. He ticked off Nibbs the coachman for some footling thing and Nibbs gave notice, which is pretty disastrous as they'll never get anyone so clever with motor-cars. Nibbs was really rather wonderful in his way and his son got a commission in the Navy and started a business – something to do with wirelesses – with his demobilisation money, so I expect Nibbs will be all right, it'll be Cedric that'll suffer. And Leslie's absolutely servile to Aunt Letitia and of course she loves that and thinks he's wonderful. He says she's asked him to live with them but I do sincerely hope he's just twisting her words – he's a genuine Twister, he'll have Cedric on toast for breakfast if he goes to live there.

Vane did not write to me, but always added a message in his rather childish handwriting at the end of Aunt Emily's Christmas letter each year. Vane never married. I never discovered whether this was because he never found a suitable girl (which was quite likely), or because his manner was too blunt, or because he simply never got round to it. It occurred to me that although Venetia and Zinnia – and Theodore too – had had the force of character to get away from Aunt Emily's powerful orbit, Louie and Vane had never managed to do so. They were too straightforward; they could not have manipulated her, even if they had wanted to.

My aunt's letters were loving, concerned and emotional, always anxious that I should take good care of myself in the winter and wear a shady hat in the summer. She sent me many presents – a blue silk scarf, a case of apples from the orchard, a little phial of Worth scent, a tin of violet oatmeal for my complexion (the very smell of which made me almost weep with nostalgia). "I'm so sorry this is such a small present," she wrote, "but things are not going very well with the farm"; but she could scarcely have sent me anything that would have given me greater pleasure.

In 1929 Louie sent news of the death of the Admiral.

"Has he left you any money?" was the first thing Chuck said when he heard.

"Don't be silly, I only spoke to him about twice." The thought of profiting from the death of someone I had admired was repugnant. Everyone had liked the Admiral, in spite of his brusque manner.

"I suppose that idiot Cedric is now rolling in wealth."

I felt an urge to spring to Cedric's defence. "It's not his fault!"

Chuck stared at me. "I didn't know you were so fond of him."

"Of Cedric? Don't be ridiculous!" Absurdly I felt myself blushing.

"My God," whispered Chuck, "is it the money that attracts you?"

I thought of Cedric – pathetic, unloved, physically repulsive – and of his lonely bravery. I felt my cheeks burning with anger.

"He's a better man than you," I shouted.

My husband's lips set in a straight line. His eyes glinted with dislike as he turned away.

33

Once every few months, to my delight, I heard from Zinnia
– usually only a picture postcard with a few exclamations
on the back.

> Just got my hair bobbed! Mother will be so scandalised
> she won't speak to me! Zadok is a DEVIL – pulled
> his teacher's hair at school today and very nearly
> EXPELLED – I had to PLEAD! Hats selling like
> hot cakes – stitched stiff silk brims (try saying that
> six times quickly) all the rage.
> Ever thine, Z.

Her cards made me smile, and I longed fruitlessly for her
company.

Once, in a brief letter on thick, deckled, handmade paper
with her address elegantly engraved in red, she had scribbled
"Utterly DISTRAUGHT. Nathan has upped & left me on
my uppers again, oh Lizzie wish you were here to help with
my new Plan!" After a few minutes of panic I calmed down
when I realised that she couldn't be too seriously poor –
not, certainly, as poor as me – if she could afford the heavy
paper and its matching envelope.

I was further encouraged by receiving a postcard of a
pillared, palatial country house with, on the back, the
words of a song even I had heard on Janet's crackly
wireless-set:

I've danced with a man
Who danced with a girl
Who danced with the Prince of Wales!
Loveissimo, Z.

Her next card was posted in Cannes and showed a large yacht on a very blue sea. "Sailing to the Riviera with Miles. Everything divine. Feels a long way from Riverlaw." That first Miles postcard was followed, at irregular intervals, by others from Monte Carlo, Bordighera, Naples and Venice, and, much later, by a card of a rococo salon in Schonbrunn, succeeded by a postcard-backed photograph of a snowy mountain with a barely recognisable Zinnia in trousers and a bobble hat, shouldering skis, beside a tall, tanned, male skier – "Carl and I at Kitzbuhel," it said, without even a signature. Later still, there was a view of the Pyramids – Miles again – followed by an impressive panorama taken from Table Mountain.

It took me quite a time to realise that Miles was Lord Barbary, and longer still to discover, from a cutting from the *Tatler* that Louie enclosed with one of her letters, that he was a twice-divorced millionaire on the fringes of the Prince of Wales set.

Poor Rednall, I thought. I wondered what had happened to the devil, Zadok.

Zinnia never mentioned Peregrine at all. But as the years went by and Chuck's attitude to me became colder and colder – so that at night I would lie awake for hours in our room, listening to his even breathing beside me and feeling the warmth from his handsome body, willing him to turn to me with words and actions of love, and later, simply wishing he would put his arms round me or give some token of, at least, affection – as these longings proved to be in vain, I thought more and more of Peregrine.

I hated myself for it. It was asinine. It was disloyal to Chuck, and it was also disloyal to Zinnia, who with her desperate affairs was still, I felt certain, trying to compensate herself for losing the soul-mate with whom she had been united on the never-to-be-forgotten night of Theodore's funeral. Peregrine must have known she would never contemplate divorce, or he would never have married his Australian heiress – a man as passionate as Peregrine could not die a bachelor.

What I had thought was his love for me must have been nothing more than a drunken flirtation.

In any case, I would never see him again.

I thought of the slim, elegant figure in a morning suit threading his way between the wedding guests towards me. I conjured up his bright eyes under their feathery brows, the straight nose; I strained to hear in imagination the quiet voice with a little, husky break in it. Again and again I relived every conversation we had ever had, the carefree days with Theodore, the terrible meeting on the station with Ivy, the bonds of sympathy we had forged on our long walks round the farm together. And then I played out again in my mind our last encounter on the stairs at Riverlaw, that magnificent kiss, and my fatal, idiotic, drunken stupidity that had taken him from me for ever. And great tears fell from my eyes and slithered down my cheeks and my nose; because even if he had loved me, I would never have been able to betray Zinnia.

Love was great, but honour was greater. Golden Giles, her first true love, was dead; and it had not been in me to deprive poor, gallant Zinnia of the chance of one day winning the man she must now love most in the world.

But gradually, as Zoe grew into a tall, slim, quiet girl with straight dark hair and shining eyes, I became almost reconciled to my life. I came to love the deep silence of the snow, the endless trees sparkling with ice, the sudden flowery springs and the hot, sunny summers, the sense of nature untrammelled, and most of all the people; blunt, kind, humorous, and better suited than I to the hard physical toil that was our common lot.

Out in our Nova Scotian backwoods we scarcely knew what was going on in the great world across the ocean. The *Advertiser* told us the fatstock prices and the news from Halifax – who had died in the province, what brides had worn and who had given what as wedding presents – and gave us a rough idea of what was going on in Ottawa and Toronto; but if war had broken out in Europe it would have been mentioned, if at all, in a small paragraph at the bottom of an inside page. We knew about Prohibition – Temperance was a strong thread in the lives of many Nova Scotians, to the Major's disgust. But (although my father wrote sometime in 1931 that he had hoped to send me the fare to England, but his shares had gone down recently) the Wall Street crash was something I didn't hear about until years later. I did notice a small item at the back of the paper one day about a politician called Adolf Hitler in Germany, but I didn't take much notice.

More high, square Ford cars appeared on the roads. Lots of people had the telephone, but we were so remote that Chuck would have had to pay part of the wiring costs, and he wouldn't do it. A farmer near Stewiacke started using a traction engine for ploughing; then first our taciturn Dutch neighbour, and later Chuck, saved up and bought a tractor – or rather I saved for it, for he reduced my housekeeping money until it was paid for.

Afterwards, he kept it reduced. "You managed well enough on what you had," he mumbled when I raised the subject, and every time I asked for the previous allowance to be restored, he turned away without answering. I wouldn't have minded if he had been open about our finances; if I had known exactly where we stood, I might have suggested further economies; but he and the Major regarded money as men's business and women as profligate spenders. Men did the farm-work, went their reasoning, and they would enjoy the fruits of their labour. I threatened to stop looking after the vegetables, but their absence would have made our diet so plain that I couldn't do it, if only for Zoe's sake.

For several years, when the harvest was good, I cam-
paigned for a washing-machine or an icebox to be bought
out of the money he had saved after the tractor, and got
neither. I was so furious and disappointed that for the first
time I told some of my troubles in my next letter to Louie,
and then felt ashamed. Until then our letters had usually
been jokey, full of news and description, but I had felt I
must be loyal to Chuck and our marriage, and had never
written anything to denigrate him. But it was true that he
was mean, wasn't it? Why should I conceal the truth?

I suppose I had always been rather secretive – I would
have preferred to call it discreet. Zoe, too, became shy and
secretive as she got older. I tried hard not to spoil her, and
perhaps my strictness made a distance between us. I remember with anguish times when I refused to let her accept a
rare invitation from other children because she had already
promised to go to tea with the minister's wife or read to
some half-blind old lady in Upper Stewiacke after school.
Chuck might break promises; Zoe must learn never to do
so. When I insisted on this, Zoe didn't throw a tantrum;
that was not her way. She obeyed, but refused to speak to
me for days. She had some of Chuck's sullenness. She was
a taciturn girl, wasting no words; but when she smiled it
was like a room suddenly flooded with sunshine.

She wasn't very old when Chuck decided that she could
ride alone to Janet's on school days. I missed my daily chat
with Janet; I even missed checking for letters in the mailbox
at the crossroads. Zoe did that now. Still, it gave me more
time to work on my gardening and sewing. I made more
quilts, largely because it was an excuse to attend – and hold
– more quilting bees. There were dances and hoedowns and
sleighing parties up in Stewiacke, and I longed to go, but
Chuck wouldn't. He didn't like dancing – and perhaps he
was afraid of meeting the women who had once rejected
him. All his life he had been used to the isolation of
McIver's Place, and that was what he liked – that, and

his father's company. With a sinking heart I noticed that Chuck had started drinking with the old man. The Major was frequently crotchety or maudlin – justifiably, because he was now in worse physical shape than he had ever been. He was racked with gout and his bent, bulging frame and purple, ravaged face were a pitiable sight as he limped about the fields. But the two of them took pleasure in their small triumphs on the farm – a field well ploughed, a big crop of oats or cow-corn, a ewe sold for a good price – and they got on well together, because they always had. I was the outsider, the interloper, the woman imported to minister to their needs. I had no say in anything.

"I do wish we weren't so isolated," I said to Janet one day while Zoe and I were drinking tea in her untidy kitchen on the way back from the school on my shopping-trip day. "I'd love to have tea-parties, and raise money for the Ladies' Aid and the missionaries and the hospital, and bridge sounds such a good game, and it would be wonderful if you could drop in on me as I do on you – poor Janet, heaven knows I owe you more teas than I can count!"

"No you don't, Lizzie. I'd go mad without your visits. Zoe, why don't you go and find my children? I think they're building some kind of store in the barn, they may need help."

"What can I do to help you?" I asked after Zoe had leapt up and gone out.

Janet's freckled forehead wrinkled as she considered. "Well, we could shell the peas."

"I used to do this at my cousins' farm in Northumberland," I told her as we sat with the basket of pea-pods between us. "Oh, I do miss them all."

"Why don't you go back and visit them?"

"Well . . . It's difficult."

Her kind hazel eyes looked at me searchingly. "Chuck won't go?"

I nodded, wanting so much to confide in her; but I couldn't be disloyal. I knew if I said even one word against

Chuck, all my troubles would come tumbling out, and sooner or later the whole valley would know. I said nothing.

"I guess he won't want to leave the farm – his father couldn't cope with it alone now. But Lizzie, Zoe's almost grown up now. She's clever and capable, and you've taught her well. She could manage the housekeeping, couldn't she, if you went to England for a few weeks?"

"I wouldn't want to go without her. It's so sad for her not to know any relations. I'd love her to meet mine, I adore them."

"Well, she'll do that one day. There's lots of time. And she's never known anywhere but McIver's Place – she's used to it. But you're different." She pushed back her chair and brought the kettle over to top up the big brown teapot. She stood there in her flowered pinny, her eyes worried. "Have you considered that one of these days the Major may need a lot of looking after?"

"Yes, I know. I'm dreading it." Looking after the Major, doubtless soon to be bedridden, would fall to me, and a thankless task it would be. I would never let Zoe do it – it was difficult enough as it was to shield her from the worst results of his gradual descent into a vile-tempered, drink-sodden old misery.

"Well, then. Isn't now the time to go and visit your family? Zoe can call on me for help and advice any time, and I'd never let her down, you know that."

"I know. You're a brick, Janet. Goodness, I'd so love to go . . ."

"Well, why don't you?"

I did try to make some money in order to save up the fare. Although I begged him, Chuck could not or would not provide it, and when I suggested that I should get work he laughed. "Who'd employ you here? Any rate, I don't want my wife working. And you're needed here." Not even, "I need you."

I wrote some children's stories and sent them to the

Advertiser, but they sent them back with a nice note to say that they showed great promise but were unsuitable for their columns – they didn't say why. Perhaps they were too British.

I thought of trying a book; but there were no book publishers in Canada that I could discover. Besides, none of Louie's books had ever found a publisher. She never mentioned them now, and I think she had given up trying. If Louie couldn't achieve publication after all the millions of words she must have written in her life, how could I, who had had no practice at all?

I did wonder whether I should try inviting some of my relations to visit us. My mother, obviously, would never come, and my father would never leave her. But what about the Delmaynes? I mentally rearranged bedrooms and practised asking Chuck or the Major to sleep on the sofa, without much hope that they would agree. But it was no good. Even if we could fit them in, even if any of the inhabitants of the Old Hall could afford the return journey, I realised that I simply could not submit them to the company of my silent husband and drunken father-in-law, in this godforsaken place, for weeks on end. It could only cause trouble which, eventually, might make my life even worse.

So I prayed, and tried to be a good housewife and mother, and scrubbed at my washboard and plied my needle and cooked the food Chuck liked, and kept my passport up-to-date, just in case.

And the months and years went by; until, one summer day, something extraordinary happened.

Zoe had always been good at school work, and eventually the schoolmistress asked her to be a pupil-teacher to help cope with the increasing population of the little school. Zoe seemed delighted – mainly, I suspect, because it brought her a little pin-money.

One Friday I took her in to school in the buggy, under

an arching blue sky, for Handicrafts Day. I walked around the classroom, making sure to praise aloud (as we had plotted together) the things made by the less confident or adroit children. I admired the embroidery and the wooden book-ends and the quillwork, secretly so proud that my Zoe had brought out so much talent in her young charges.

I went on to do my own not very extensive shopping, and ate my sandwich sitting on a stone by the riverside, watching the weeds and the eddies and brushing away the flies, as I had done so many hundreds of times before. Afterwards I drove to the little hotel near the crossroads. In the dingy bar Mrs Levitt, the fat proprietress, brought me a glass of milk before I asked for it. I took it out to the porch where her thin, downtrodden husband had put out a couple of tables and chairs for the summer. I took out my writing-paper and fountain-pen and, as I had done countless times before in that place, started a letter to Louie. I wrote quickly, pausing only to wave away the flies.

After a paragraph or two I was vaguely conscious that a large vehicle of some kind had come down the road from Stewiacke and parked outside the hotel; someone passed behind me on their way in. It was a few seconds before, still scribbling away with my head bent over the paper, I registered a whiff of delicious scent, rich and lingering. I smelt Europe.

I turned round to look at the automobile. Along the previously still and deserted road there were now small oases of movement, as people emerged in their work-clothes from fields and shacks to have a look.

It was a large, maroon-coloured Rolls-Royce.

It was dusty from its journey over dirt roads, but its polished brasswork glinted blindingly in the August sun. Behind the wheel sat a brown-haired man, his face hidden behind the map he was studying.

The violence of my sudden longing to speak to this man and his wife, for it must have been she who had gone into

Mrs Levitt's bar, astonished me; it was a measure of the loneliness I had tried so hard to conquer all these years. My second reaction was one of shame. I looked down at my faded, well-darned, blue cotton dress. I wore no make-up or stockings; my hair was clean, but I had tied it back with a rag torn from one of Zoe's outgrown dresses. I must look a complete peasant. I had never felt so far from Fenwick's French. I knew with despair that they would never speak to the likes of me.

The screen door swung open behind me and I heard the tap of high heels and Mrs Levitt's booming voice – excited as I had never heard her – saying "She's right there on the porch! There's a visitor here looking for you, Mrs McIver!"

And before I could even take this in, a hand tapped me on the shoulder and I half-turned, and saw the fine, inlaid leather shoes, the silk stockings, the svelte linen dress, the slender, ringed hand, the shady straw hat with a green bow that said Paris, the oval face, the sparkling almond-shaped eyes . . .

"We just called here to ask the way," she said, in a voice full of laughter.

"It can't be – " I choked.

"But it is!"

And Zinnia gave me a hug that knocked her hat off and sent my pen flying.

34

Breathless, almost delirious with joy and astonishment, "How long are you here for?" I gasped. "Where are you staying? Do stay with me! – No, oh Lord, I'm not sure whether my father-in-law – Zoe could give you her room, but – "

"Don't worry, I booked here, in case. Oh, darling Lizzie, it's so divine to see you! Only here for a tiny time – Canada's much bigger than we thought! We had to hire the car in Halifax to get here at *all*. But just you wait – and *guess* who's here with me!"

"Oh, Zinnia, can it really be you?" I gazed at her. In all these years she had scarcely changed. Her complexion was creamily perfect, her hair elegantly cut and waved. Her eyes seemed larger, more hypnotic than ever. Minute creases at their corners were half-covered by hat and hair.

"Really, truly. Now guess."

"Miles?" I ventured.

"Try again."

"Nathan?"

"No, no, someone quite different."

"Not Vane?" I tried, before I realised with huge disappointment that he would never leave the farm in summer.

"Not Vane, no. I say, Lizzie, I've so much to tell you, it's so glorious to see you – "

"I know, it's been a lifetime, I can't really believe it's you! I can't guess who it could be. Not Henry over from Africa, I suppose?"

"No-o . . . Goodness, look at the chap, he's completely absorbed in that stupid map. Turn round and look at the wall. Yes, that's right – now don't dare *move* till I give you permission!" I gazed obediently at Mrs Levitt's peeling grey clapboard as Zinnia's high heels tap-tapped down the steps. Mrs Levitt's moon-face, intense with curiosity, shone behind the window. The car door opened and slammed and two sets of feet hurried back to me. Zinnia was giggling. A pair of large, warm hands covered my eyes from behind.

"Guess who?" said Zinnia, delighted.

"Oh . . . It couldn't be my father?"

There was a snort of male laughter, hastily muffled.

"Sorry – no!"

I couldn't imagine who it could be. Out of my subconscious came Theodore, grinning, the cowlick flapping on his forehead. I pushed the memory away. Who else?

"Rednall?"

"Goodness, no, haven't seen him for years. Getting warmer, though," Zinnia was enjoying herself.

"Not Cedric? Dear Cedric!"

Hoots of laughter. An infectious, joyous laugh that I would never forget. "Dear Cedric, eh! I never knew you cared!"

"That's not Cedric . . . Oh, glory, is it who I think it is?"

And the hands dropped to my shoulders and spun me round and gathered me in, and it was Peregrine.

"After that embrace, my dears," said Zinnia as we went towards the car, "your reputations in Nova Scotia won't be worth tuppence. The she-dragon in the hotel was behind the window with her eyes popping out of her head."

"Oh, pipe down, Zinnia," said Peregrine cheerfully. "I must say – " looking at me – "I half-expected you to look worn out with childbirth or something, but you haven't changed an atom."

"Neither have you. Much more sunburnt. A few distinguished grey hairs at the temples."

"Hah! She puts it well, doesn't she?" He lifted an eyebrow to Zinnia beside him. He wore a well-cut, summer-weight suit and polished shoes of good leather. He and Zinnia made a handsome pair.

Conflicting thoughts rushed in and out of my brain, alternately making my heart thump with incredulous joy and sending it plummeting to my boots.

"I thought I'd never see you again," I stammered. "If I'd known you were coming I wouldn't be dressed like this."

"I think you look lovely." He sounded as if he meant it. But then, the McIvers had made me unused to good manners. "Here, sit beside me. We'll put her Ladyship in the back."

I sank into the soft leather, admiring the suede-lined door and the battery of dials on the walnut fascia in front of the steering-wheel.

"I look forward to Zoe's face when we arrive at the school in this," I said. "We're nearly there, slow down now . . . So however did you both come to be here?"

"I was going round the world with Miles – you know about Miles," said Zinnia, leaning over from the back seat in a waft of scent as Peregrine parked outside the little white clapboard schoolhouse, "and we'd got to Singapore and it was suffocatingly hot and he was so impossibly bad-tempered, and I suddenly realised that it was no fun, no fun at all! And then I remembered I'd got Peregrine's address in New South Wales – "

"Just next door, really." Peregrine's voice had that husky, ironic tone I had never been able to resist.

"But Louie tried to get his address for me, and had no luck."

Peregrine's head turned sharply when I said this, but Zinnia was in full flood. "Well, I knew that from Louie so I got Mother to write – you know the kind of thing,

'My daughter Lady Carroun who is travelling with a party on Lord Barbary's yacht' – and, of course, back the address came. A title is some use, after all!"

"Good thing you turned up," said Peregrine. "I'd been feeling so low ever since Linda died. I badly needed someone to cheer me up and drag me away."

"We both wanted to go back to England, and luckily he could afford it," laughed Zinnia. "Otherwise I'd have been up the creek without a paddle, wouldn't I, Perry?"

"Oh, you'd have muddled along somehow," and Peregrine turned in his seat and looked at her admiringly.

During this conversation my heart had continued its yo-yo progress as more and more facts had interrupted my first rapture. Who was Linda? Peregrine and Zinnia had travelled together from Australia – were they married? If not, the journey in itself defied convention; ladies did not travel alone with men to whom they were not married. And worse, he had paid for her ticket.

My thoughts were interrupted by the clanging of the school bell.

"Look at those little darlings rushing out in their pinnies, clutching their home-made rabbits," exclaimed Zinnia. "Which is Zoe?"

"She'll be out last – she's the pupil-teacher."

Peregrine turned and looked at me intently. "You don't look much older than a pupil-teacher yourself!" He gazed into my eyes and smiled. My knees turned to water. I looked away.

This won't do, I told myself firmly. He belongs to Zinnia and I belong to Chuck.

I opened the car door, displacing a small crowd of children who were gazing with awe and delight at the Rolls. "I'll make sure Zoe knows it's us."

"Want to sit inside?" enquired Peregrine, through the open window, of the nearest pupils. In a moment the car was thick with beaming children, who stroked the leather and opened and shut the ashtrays and cocktail cabinets before yielding their places to others.

Zoe, in a pink frock, came out of the door marked "Girls", and stared.

"It's Cousin Zinnia from England," I said.

As I said it I suddenly wondered, for a fleeting second, whether Zinnia was a suitable person for my pure, good, country-bred daughter to meet. Then, Ridiculous! I thought.

"Oh, Mom – is that Zadok's mother?"

She took my hand and smiled her sunshiny smile at me. We walked to the car together and the children fell back respectfully. Zinnia and Peregrine were standing beside the driver's door, Zinnia looking as near to a fashion-plate, I dare say, as any inhabitant of the Stewiacke Valley had ever beheld. She held out her hands to my daughter.

"The whole family has longed for years to meet you!" she declared, and kissed her.

"And this is Mr Fenwick," I said.

"Delighted to meet you," and Peregrine took her hand between his. "Hop in now, and we'll take you both home."

"What about the buggy?"

"Mrs Levitt'll look after it till we can get back to collect it."

"What made you come here?" asked Zoe as we drove along, raising clouds of dust behind us.

"Actually," said Zinnia with a sideways look at me, "it was a letter your mother wrote to my sister Louie. She showed it to me, and we thought one of us must try to come and pay you all a visit, to cheer her up."

"But that was ages ago!" I said stoutly, in case Zoe suspected me of being downhearted.

"Well, I told Peregrine, naturally" – and again I felt the jangling in my head of joy and despair – "and we made a little plan to come and whisk your mother away, Zoe, for a little holiday."

I felt so happy I could scarcely believe it. "Could you come too?" I asked Zoe.

"Oh, no, term begins in a week or two. Anyways, I'll be fine. Don't you fuss, Mom. Maybe I have plans of my own. Where are you going?"

"We'll have to break it to Lizzie," said Peregrine, guiding the car gingerly over the increasingly stony track, "if she's got over the first shock of seeing us. We're not staying here long."

"We got your ticket in Halifax," said Zoe, "or rather Peregrine did. And we're going the day after tomorrow, the three of us."

"So soon?" I heard myself squeaking with delight. "Where to?"

"England!"

Chuck took little pains to conceal his fury that his wife was being so high-handedly removed without his prior permission.

"It's only for six weeks," I protested.

"Only!"

"I'm sorry it's so sudden," said Peregrine, "but we came by train from Vancouver and we had no idea how often boats go from Halifax until we actually got there. When we arrived, we only just managed to get berths – everyone wants to go to Europe, it seems. I'm pretty anxious to get there myself – it's years since I was home. Look, Lizzie will want to pack and make arrangements – d'you want any help on the farm while I'm here? I'm a farmer too, you know!" He took off his jacket, removed his neat gold cufflinks and put them in his pocket, and rolled up his sleeves.

Slightly mollified, Chuck led him out to help with the milking.

Cufflinks, I thought. Why does the sight of Peregrine's cufflinks make me feel so devastatingly unhappy? And then I remembered why.

So stupid, I scolded myself, to mind after all this time. Concentrate on something else.

I led Zinnia upstairs and showed her the wardrobe. She riffled through my clothes while I dragged a suitcase from under the bed.

"That's a pretty blue . . . Heavens, I remember you wearing this at Riverlaw!"

"Yes, I took up the hem. It's done a lot of good service, that dress."

"This one's pretty," she said, putting an emerald-green wool on the bed. "Do bring it. Did you make it?"

"I made them all, except the old ones from Mrs Hothersall or Fenwick's French, and they've mostly gone under the arms. It's hard to get dress-preservers here."

"Lizzie darling, where do you keep your best clothes?"

"You're looking at them. That's all I have."

She sat down rather suddenly on the bed. "Oh, Lizzie! You *are* in the backwoods, aren't you? Don't you change for dinner?"

"Change for dinner?" It was my turn to collapse – with laughter.

"Haven't you a little silk dress you could wear on the ship?"

"Afraid not."

"Let's look at your hats then."

"Nary a hat – except these," and I fished down my rather battered summer boater, and the knitted helmet I wore in winter.

"Oh, darling!" Zinnia's face betokened tragedy. "No pretty things?"

"No pretty things. Chuck doesn't give me pocket-money – he doesn't see any reason for it. It's all I can do to keep Zoe clothed and shod."

Sitting on my home-made quilt, Zinnia wrinkled her brow, and then brightened. "I'll tell you what. I've never been broker, but one thing I do have is a lot of clothes. I can give you some of mine on the voyage, and when we get to Riverlaw I bet Mother'll give us some of her old silk dresses to cut down for you. She's so much fatter than you, it'll be easy."

"Will I have to wear a cream embroidered front?" And at the memory we both fell about laughing.

"Oh, Lizzie darling, it's too divine to see you again! Has it all been awful, all these years?"

"Well, not awful. The people round here are so genuine and kind. Canada's a great country – I just wish I could see more of it. And watching Zoe grow up was wonderful. But oh, I don't know . . . I just can't convince myself that I was born for this life. The thought of looking after Chuck and the Major till I die . . . Oh, I've missed all the Delmaynes so much!" It was on the tip of my tongue to add "And Peregrine," but I stopped myself. I had no business missing Peregrine.

"Oh, poor, poor Lizzie! Life is a puzzle, isn't it?"

"What about you? Are you happy?"

"Me? Well . . . Off and on. I love my little house, but when the lease of the shop came to an end and I had to close it down I had no visible means of support, so I've had to let the house and throw myself on the wide world."

"What about Zadok?"

Her face shadowed. "Oh, he went off when I took up with Miles. Couldn't stop him – he's grown up now, after all." She traced a patchwork flower with one manicured finger, and began again, in a jauntier voice, "It was tremendous being with Miles – he's so rich. He gave me such topping presents – remind me to show you my cigarette-case with the emeralds. But, you know, everything has its price."

I fell back easily – so easily! – into the jokey, half-mocking tone all the Delmaynes had once used to each other. "Were you a rich man's plaything?"

"Oh, absolutely!" Suddenly, she became serious again. "But it isn't enough. In the end he was quite ghastly. I swore I wouldn't put up with him another minute, and then he found a photo of me with Carl, and I found myself dumped on the quay in Sydney with my luggage and only the money I happened to have in my handbag. It was a relief in a way, but rather scarey wondering how I'd ever get back home to Riverlaw."

"Goodness, what did you do?"

"Well, I sold a ring Nathan had given me years ago – not a very nice one, garnets, actually. And luckily I'd got Peregrine's Australian address, just in case we went anywhere near. He lives on this colossal sheep station that belongs to his wife's family, with hundreds of managers and hinds and so forth, out in the wilds. By the time I got there I didn't have the price of a meal, or of the taxi that brought me from the railhead, and I was praying like mad. Seeing this huge, tree-shaded, verandahed bungalow appear in the dusty distance and gradually get nearer was like arriving at Valhalla. And he was absolutely sweet. By coincidence he'd been meaning to go to England ever since his wife died."

"His wife? Was that Linda?"

She nodded. "She was having a baby, and the baby died too."

"Oh, poor Peregrine."

"Yes, it must have been terrible. Devastating. Mind you, I gathered while I was there that Linda was a bit difficult. Rich and autocratic."

"Them as marries money pays for it," I said gloomily. It had been a favourite saying of Hannah's. I realised that I was not entirely sorry that Peregrine's wife had not been perfect – and immediately felt ashamed of this unworthy thought.

"Well, his Australian uncle died and Peregrine was his heir. I'm sure he didn't marry for money. From her photos she was very pretty in that rather bouncy Australian way. Which reminds me – Zoe is a lovely girl. Terribly like Chuck, though, not really your type at all."

"I do wish she could come with us."

"Perry invited her again when we were all downstairs. I

don't know her, of course, but I don't think she actually wants to come. Something tells me she has other fish to fry. D'you think she's in love, by any chance?"

I was startled. "I don't think so. If so I can't think who it could possibly be. Nobody takes her out – she's so young, anyway!"

"Don't you count on it. How old were you when someone first made a pass at you?"

"Heavens, I'd forgotten. Sixteen. It was Henry." I remembered so vividly the kitchen garden, and the hairs in his nose.

"Henry!" Zinnia rolled on the bed, hooting with laughter. "Oh, poor Lizzie! Who else?"

I couldn't tell her about Peregrine. "Well, Chuck proposed to me soon after that."

Serious again, she lay back and watched as I folded cardigans and undies. "Are you happy, Lizzie?"

I was unprepared for this. "Well . . ."

"Chuck's changed a lot since we last saw him. He takes you for granted rather, doesn't he? I mean, I was quite shocked to hear him contradicting you and ordering you about. Why don't you stand up to him?"

"I can't stand rows. It's easier if I just give in."

"I don't know how you stick it. But he's still very good-looking, I suppose. Is he a marvellous lover?"

What an embarrassing question, I thought. And then: Why should I be embarrassed with Zinnia, of all people?"

"He isn't a lover at all," I admitted. "Not for years. Not since Zoe was born."

Zinnia stared in horror. "Not at *all*? Oh, you poor, poor Lizzie," and she held out her arms and suddenly I was clasped to her bosom and weeping, weeping for all the nights over all the years when I had lain awake beside Chuck and hoped in vain that he would love me.

Zinnia said nothing. She stroked my hair and rocked me as Aunt Emily would have done. In time I managed to blink away my tears and with a bit of sniffing and the help of Zinnia's lace-edged handkerchief, I calmed down.

I went over to the window and looked out from the shelter of the curtains. There had for months been an ugly line of weeds spreading along the side of the big barn. Peregrine, stripped to the waist, was cutting them down with broad, easy sweeps of the big scythe. The muscles on his back moved like a piece of brown silk touched by a passing breeze.

"Do you know," Zinnia said quietly, "when we were crossing the Pacific Peregrine told me something that explained a great deal about my marriage to Rednall. You know Rednall and Chuck were great friends at Harrow."

"Well, yes. I don't think they were really great friends, though. I think, in a way, they were both outcasts and that was why they were drawn to each other."

"You think that was why?"

There was a long silence.

"It was odd, wasn't it, that when Rednall's mother was there they didn't get on so well? She was desperately possessive, you know. She couldn't share Rednall with anybody. He's completely under her thumb. And in his own peculiar way he's devoted to her."

"But what's that to do with Chuck?"

"We all thought during the war that Chuck stayed with you because he'd fallen in love with you. But could it be that he stayed because after his first visit to Rednall, old Lady Carroun realised that Chuck had a homosexual relationship with her son, and turned him out?"

I stared.

"I don't believe you," I said. But I did.

Years of uncomprehending misery fell into place. In a way, I had known about Chuck almost from the beginning.

"But if Peregrine knew about them," I said as it slowly sank in, "why didn't he stop me from marrying Chuck?"

"He didn't know. At least, he wondered but he wasn't

sure. And something you said at Venetia's wedding, apparently, made him think he was wrong."

"Something *I* said?" And then, clear as a hunting-horn my drunken words echoed back to me, "He's my boy-friend. He's stayed with us so often and we've done *everything* together."

"But Peregrine's brother-in-law had a friend who was at Harrow. After Peregrine married Linda, this man visited them in New South Wales, and Peregrine asked him whether he remembered Chuck and Rednall. And he did, vividly. There was a terrific scandal and Chuck was sent down. It was all hushed up."

"Chuck and the Major never told me he was sent down!"

"Well, they wouldn't, would they? You'd be bound to ask why."

I put my head in my hands.

"You and I are in the same boat, in more ways than you'd imagine," she said softly. "And that's one reason why I was determined, dear Lizzie, to come to your rescue."

It seemed uncanny, dreamlike, to be sitting at my own kitchen table that evening opposite Peregrine, with Zinnia beside me. I hardly noticed Zoe, Chuck and the Major – the men were customarily monosyllabic at meals anyway, and Zoe looked and listened as she always did. But I was aware all the time of Peregrine's eyes on me.

Over the celebratory lobsters we had bought in Upper Stewiacke, Zinnia relayed news of family and friends.

"Tell us more about Zadok," I said.

"Oh, he's grown up now. He's tall, dark and handsome! He left home last year, of course. He wants to be a rich entrepreneur like Nathan – I hope he succeeds. Perhaps seeing me struggling with the hat-shop made him think he could do it better!" She sounded jaunty, but there was an undertow of regret, and I wondered whether their parting had been acrimonious.

"Where is he now?"

Zinnia looked away. "I don't know."

Zoe looked embarrassed and shifted in her seat.

My eyes met Peregrine's. I saw that his shock, sadness and sympathy for Zinnia were identical to mine. I felt a kind of complicity, a deep bond. I had to look away in case the others noticed.

"Who's looking after the hat-shop now?" asked Zoe.

"The lease came to an end. I sold most of the leftover hats to Whiteley's and took the best ones home for Mother and Louie."

"How's Louie getting on?" I asked eagerly.

"Oh – fat and forty, poor dear. She never made the best of herself, I'm afraid."

"What about Cedric?" I saw Chuck's mouth tighten, but I didn't care.

"Oh, didn't I tell you? Madge went off to Italy and left him! And – listen to this – she came back for a few days months later – for her things, I suppose – and she had got tremendously fat and it got about that she was having a baby! Think of Cedric being a father! Then Gertie heard – via the Carrouns' stable-boy who's some relation of hers – that it was a boy, called Rupert. But poor old Cedric, he's never seen his son as far as we know. It's a bit worrying, too, because the Admiral's will left the whole estate to Cedric for life, but after that . . ."

"Oh, no! What'll become of the Delmayne family when Madge's son inherits? Or will he?"

"Well, I can tell you exactly." She fished a piece of paper out of an inside compartment in her enormous crocodile purse, and read aloud. " 'To his first and other sons successively in tail male' – that's the entail, you know, there's always been one. The whole estate always has to descend to male issue, so when Cedric dies his son gets it all – "

"But how do you know what's in Cedric's will?"

"We don't. This is from the Admiral's grandfather's will. He tied it up for generations – entail's like that, apparently.

After Cedric, the entail goes on just the same. It can go to such of Cedric's male issue as Cedric appoints, but none of us can see Cedric marrying again, let alone having any more children. When this Rupert has a son it'll go to him. Failing that it goes to 'issue in equal shares for stirpes' (whatever that means), and failing all that, generally as whoever-is-the-last-owner appoints by will."

"But what will happen to Aunt Emily – if she lives that long – and Vane and Louie?"

"You may well ask. That's the awful thing. They have no savings, you know, and they've never contributed to a pension. I don't think they've ever paid any National Insurance, or only the legal minimum. They paid it for the hinds, of course; but paying for the family always came last, and usually Vane had no money left."

"And where will they live if they have to leave the Old Hall? Think of Aunt Emily being thrown out!"

"Unthinkable," said Peregrine.

"Perhaps they'll be able to make some arrangement with Madge – although I can't think what. But although I know she was a friend of mine, she's a bit of a cadger by nature, and never had a bean. I don't even know where she is. I thought she might get in touch with me, but she didn't. Louie said she thought she'd gone off to foreign parts with a millionaire."

"Taken a leaf out of your book, I suppose?" The words were tart but Peregrine had a twinkle in his eye as he said them.

"Oh, shut up, Perry! I've had enough of all that. My ambition now is to settle down in a comfy little house in rural England with a good, steady husband."

"A likely story!"

"True, I swear!" And they looked at each other with teasing affection.

After supper, when I had waved Peregrine and Zinnia goodbye as they set off in the Rolls to spend the night in Mrs Levitt's hotel, I was again assailed by a jangle of emotions.

Zinnia's news about Madge's son and the entail had been deeply worrying, but I pushed it to the back of my mind. One glorious fact was uppermost; the arrival of our two guests. I felt a dreamlike astonishment, excitement and delight that they were both so near. It was like waking up gradually, after a long sleep, to a sunny day on which great things were to happen.

But at the same time, I saw in my mind's eye a darkened attic long ago, a shaft of moonlight, the flash of a cufflink, bodies entwined.

I had not asked Zinnia whether she and Peregrine were sharing a room at the hotel, because I thought I could not endure the answer.

35

Early next morning Chuck and the Major left the house, in their disreputable working clothes as usual, for a distant field. I cleared up, and sat down at the kitchen table to write a letter.

Dear Cedric (I wrote),

I am so very sorry to hear from Zinnia that Madge has left you. I am very distressed to imagine the unhappiness for you both that must have led up to this. I do send my most heartfelt sympathy, and I hope things will resolve themselves in whatever way is most conducive to your happiness.

Meanwhile, don't let things get you down.

I am tremendously looking forward to coming back to the dear Old Hall very soon, and longing to see you. All news then.

Love from
Elizabeth.

I wrote Cedric Delmayne, Esq., on the envelope.

At that moment I heard the Rolls and rushed outside to welcome our two guests as they emerged, elegant, bright-eyed and eager, from the car. The sky was blue, the sun shone.

Peregrine immediately went over to the barn and began to sharpen the scythe.

A little later, while Zinnia was behind the barn admiring

the progress of his weed-clearing programme, Zoe caught me alone in the hall.

"Don't go to England, Mother. I don't want you to go."

Taken aback by her vehemence, "But I thought you were pleased they had come!" I protested.

"Sure, I knew you'd love to see them. They're real nice. Lady Carroun is so elegant, and Mr Fenwick is so kind and twinkly and he has a lovely sense of humour. But it's not a good time to go to Europe – don't do it!"

I had had enough opposition from Chuck, and I hadn't bargained for difficulty from my own daughter. No doubt he had put her up to it. I felt suddenly furious.

"I've never had a holiday in all these years," I said. "I've never asked you to take charge even for a week. You're perfectly capable of doing my chores for a few weeks – in fact it'll do you good to be in charge of the house."

"Why do you have to go now, at such short notice?" she said, with a fierce glint in her eye that I hadn't noticed for years. "If it's me who has to do all the work when you're away, why couldn't you have consulted me?"

"Look," I said again, in an attempt to pacify her, "it may be my one chance, ever, to see my parents again and all the people I love. Won't you come? Mr Fenwick did offer to pay your fare."

"No." Her face took on the old, secret, closed-in look I knew so well.

"If you come, I think your father would manage, though he wouldn't like it. But if you stay, you must help him a little, at least, when you come home from the school and at weekends. You won't have to do all I do. You can leave all but the most urgent mending till I get back. The garden won't need much more work before winter. I've made enough jam already to last months, and Janet'll come and help with the late apples if I ask her — "

"Oh, you don't understand!" She beat the air down with her hands. "Where will you be, anyway?"

"The Old Hall, of course. You know the address — "

"No, I don't! I don't want you to go!"

"Well, your father knows it. I'll write it down for you if I have time. Go and set the table now, dearest, I've got to get the chickens fed and the stew into the oven," and I hurried out to the chicken-run, feeling upset and harassed both by her inexplicable intransigence and by my own tactlessness in taking offence so easily. But I was utterly determined to go. She must see that; and how hurtful to try to stop me after she had refused to go herself! I realised that in some ways I hardly knew Zoe.

Already I was beginning to see that I had perhaps been too anxious to dismiss her objections without examining them. Was I, I wondered, being selfish? Had she sensed that only one of us could go? – for however rich and generous Peregrine might be, the cost of a return steamer ticket was enormous by Zoe's, and indeed by my own, standards. Should I suggest that she should go in my place? But the truth was that, having been presented with this golden prospect not only of seeing Riverlaw and the family but of a whole Atlantic voyage in Peregrine's company, I could not bear the thought of turning it down.

The chicken-feed had to be mixed in the barn. I crossed the yard along the line of posts that in winter held the rope fence. The barn door was ajar.

I went in out of the sunshine to the shadowy, hay-scented twilight.

I moved the bucket over to the big heap of meal and was stretching up to get the meal-shovel off its hook when out of the corner of my eye I saw something move against the dim wall of hay to my right.

A man's brown-silk torso, hands at his belt, the broad shoulders gleaming, the face in shadow.

I stood very still. I was afraid that if I allowed myself to move, I would fly to him. He was looking at me – I could see the faint glow of his eyes. He must know, he must. But, *love, honour, obey* – my duty was to Chuck, my loyalty to Zinnia.

For an endless moment we watched each other. Then Peregrine put up his brown arms to the cliff of hay above him, stretched, and whispered, "Well, Mrs McIver?"

And because he said that I knew he remembered everything, including the barrier between us.

I must be very careful. At all costs I must defuse the electricity I felt, shake off the desperate longing.

"I'm just getting the chicken-feed," I muttered. My voice was shaky. "Didn't expect to see you here."

"The Major told me they'd be fed around now." So he could have come, couldn't he, on purpose to see me alone? My chest suddenly felt tight, my heart seemed to beat audibly.

"Bundle, I have to know," he said softly, "are you happy? By and large, and apart from being hard up, I mean?"

"I'm used to that," I said. "Money isn't really important." It was a philosophy I had cultivated deliberately, because I had to; and I believed it. No amount of money would be fair compensation, for instance, for never again seeing Riverlaw and the people I loved.

"I need to know – are you happy?"

Zinnia was in the house only yards away. At all costs I must get this conversation on to a less intimate level, or I might say something that would ruin her life and Peregrine's too. "It's just wonderful to see you and Zinnia. And I'm over the moon at being able to go back to Riverlaw. It's so kind of you," I added formally, politely. "Well, I must get on or the chickens'll get night-starvation," and I turned away and reached for the shovel and dug it into the meal so vigorously that the dust flew up. There was no sound from Peregrine behind me, so that it was with total astonishment that I felt a gentle grip on my forearm and saw the brown hand and bare arm, and felt his other hand creep round my waist and his cheek pressed, warm and sandpapery, against mine. He said nothing. He smelt deliciously of good soap and fresh sweat and I longed with all my being to melt into his arms and tell him that he was the only man I had ever truly loved. His face turned to mine and his grave eyes were looking straight into mine and his mouth was seeking my lips.

How could I have resisted? Again and again in the following months I reflected that perhaps if I had, I might have persuaded myself once and for all that my love for Peregrine was a thing of the past. But with his warm hip pressed against mine and his strong arms enfolding me and his hair tickling my forehead . . .

I wanted his kiss to last for ever. His mouth moved on mine and his tongue penetrated my lips, and his eyes closed, and he shifted closer so that my hand was caught hard between our thighs and I dropped the shovel.

He exclaimed, opening his eyes and looking down to where the shovel lay across his foot, and he laughed and pressed his laughing mouth again on mine, and pulled me down into the loose hay behind him so that I was sprawled over his body and felt his warm chest and his hard strength under me. He twisted a thigh over mine and began to turn me so that the whole length of our bodies was pressed together. He shut his eyes again.

"Oh, darling, darling!" he half-moaned, half-smiled, and detached a hand to press me more firmly against him, and began gently to rock me.

And at that moment, in the very pitch of ecstasy, I remembered Zinnia, and Mrs Levitt's seedy hotel, and imagined him doing the same to her.

I brought up my hands to his chest and pushed with all my force against the silky muscles, and kicked his leg away and scrambled to my knees. One of his arms was still round me and he grabbed my arm with his other hand, not hurtfully but gently, and raised himself up to try and kiss me again. And all I could see was his hurt, astonished eyes.

And I turned my head away so that the best he could do was to kiss my cheek, and I undid his fingers from my arm and pushed him away, and I ran out of the barn and down to the creek so that nobody would see the tears pouring down my face; and down in the creek-bed I sat on a flat stone out of view behind the bushes and sobbed and scrubbed at my eyes and sluiced my face, until my chest had stopped heaving and my tears flowing; and then I washed my face again and dried it on my skirt, and straightened my wild hair as best I could, and looked down at my wavering reflection in the water to check that nobody would suspect, and walked back to the house.

And the next day we went to England – Peregrine, Zinnia and I.

I remember turning round as the hired Rolls purred discreetly up the field track, and seeing the Major already shambling into the house in search, no doubt, of the first whisky of the day; and I remember blowing kisses to Zoe who stood waving, so tall and pretty in her pink dress, beside Chuck, whose hands were in his pockets. I remember hearing his last words – "Good luck, you two" – and realising that they were addressed not to me but to Zinnia and Peregrine, as he stood there, stiff and handsome, outside the front door. And the picture that the house made is engraved on my mind for ever, bigger and better-painted and neater than when I first came, the maple trees taller and branchier and my rose-garden flourishing at last after so many killer winters.

So many years of my life I had given to that house and those people, and only Zoe had a place in my heart.

"See you in six weeks," I called to her through the open car-window, waving wildly, my heart glowing with love for my daughter.

But I didn't see her in six weeks. Because things never happen quite as we expect.

And for years I was haunted – at first constantly and then, when I thought that at last I had laid that ghost, in dreams – by the voice of, of all people, the Major. For I had heard that gruff, whisky-sodden Canadian voice with its overtones of British-Army gentility, grumbling under his breath behind me as I came out of my own front door that day, saying to my shy, solitary, sparky, shining-eyed girl as she held my hand for the last time, "She'll never come back, you know . . ."

And I could have replied, laughed, reassured her, given her my promise. I could have done that.

Standing out on the upper deck that first day at sea as the S.S. *Boadicea* churned and swooped through the North Atlantic swell, with my hands on the moist mahogany rail, my hair blowing wildly and the fierce wind chilling my cheek, I mulled over what Zinnia had said about Chuck. No wonder I had been unhappy. And yet he must have been unhappy too, living against his nature. I had tried to do my best to be a dutiful and faithful wife. And perhaps marriage was the best that could be done; a way of making a go of things, a *modus vivendi* that compensated for imperfections, and helped the unhelpable.

And yet . . . Peregrine's presence had a powerful, an overwhelming effect on me. When he was there I could think of nobody else. I ached, I burned to be able to show my love; and seeing him laughing with Zinnia was almost more than I could bear. For the first time in my life I shuddered with resentment and self-hate. For again and again I saw in my mind's eye the conservatory at Riverpark, and the attic at Riverlaw, and Zinnia possessed by a passion I had never known.

Marriage was not just a way of making a go of things. Marriage was this mutual possession, a fusing of heart and body and soul, and I had never known it. I should be married to Peregrine.

Instead of which I was tactfully making myself scarce

on the foredeck of the S.S. *Boadicea* so that the presence
of a proper and dutiful married woman – myself – would
not inhibit him and Zinnia. They had separate staterooms
– as a façade of respectability, I supposed – but they would
want to be together.

Peregrine had bought all the English newspapers in
Halifax, though they were ten or twelve days old, and
I had found him in the saloon with a great pile of them,
waiting to show Zinnia a gossip column which had some
story about Lord Barbary and the Duchess of Windsor.

"Things look bad in Germany," he said. "Don't go,
Bundle. Look at this. I haven't seen a newspaper for
weeks, have you? Hitler's been going back on his word
and threatening the Poles. This editorial's talking about
war. War! Don't they remember what it was like last
time?"

"Perhaps things will have calmed down by now," I
suggested. "Journalists always expect the worst. That's
quite an old paper. What's the date today?"

Peregrine frowned.

"The fourth of September."

"Think I'll get some fresh air," I said, because Zinnia –
radiant in a lipstick-red Schiaparelli jacket Lord Barbary
had bought her in Paris – had appeared across the saloon;
and I hurried out by another door.

Outside, the horizon tilted to the left and then the right,
and I worked my way aft holding tight to the rail with one
hand and my scarf with the other.

Looking out at the featureless panorama of waves, I
reflected that it wasn't his fault, or Zinnia's, that I could
hardly bear to see them together.

He never referred, even obliquely, to our encounter in the
barn. On the ship he was his old delightful self; looking at
me, talking, joking, sympathising, exactly as he had always
done. At meals, and at the dances that were organised on
a couple of evenings, he shared his attention punctiliously
between Zinnia and me. The three of us spent half our time

laughing, the other half reading or playing cards or taking the air on deck, in companionable silence.

In those few days the years at McIver's Place receded and soon they seemed just an episode in my life. Peregrine was the same as ever, his company an eternal essential to my happiness. I felt he was part of me. And yet, I would always have to be the outsider, watching Zinnia in her elegant French clothes gazing into his eyes and laughing.

These Delmaynes, I thought. I can't be myself without them. And yet there was something about them that I could not grasp or dominate. Even darling Uncle Vane, whom even the servants loved, seemed almost too perfect to be true. Almost all of them, each in his or her different way, had something about them that I did not, as yet, understand. Perhaps, I thought, it would always be so. And looking far over the rail to the bleak horizon, I wondered whether I ought to try to break with them once and for all, for I could see no hope of happiness without Peregrine, and perhaps it would be better for us all if I never saw him, or any of them, again.

And then I pictured them, one by one as they had been in Aunt Emily's photograph long ago, with Peregrine among them like a nonchalant Greek statue, on the lawn in front of the dear Old Hall with its foam of roses; and I knew in my heart that to the end of my days I would still feel the old enchantment.

I imagined myself as an elderly lady, white-haired perhaps, still fascinated by my country cousins from Riverlaw; ranging the world to try to solve the mysteries that seemed to come in their wake, as the maelstrom of foam whirled and churned in the wake of the ship before it dissolved in the limitless ocean.

ONTARIO

36

. . . And that evening in 1970, in the white clapboard farmhouse in rural Ontario, I unpacked the flat cardboard box into which, as an afterthought half-an-hour before I was due to leave for Heathrow, I had shovelled a few loose photographs from each of the albums that sat on a shelf in my bedroom. And round the kitchen table, those strangers and I looked through the faded pictures of my life and the lives of the English Delmaynes; they, seeking the thread that would tie them to an unknown past; and I, reliving the strange turns of Fate that had brought me like a beggar to their door.

The very last picture in the box was the biggest, for I had had it enlarged years before from the negative, which Louie had given me. There we all were, lined up on the lawn at Riverlaw, with the kitchen window behind us, and looking out of the window a turbaned face.

"That's Hannah," I said, pointing with the wrong end of my Biro.

"Is that . . . Is that some relation?" asked Bernice.

Her husband Kitchener said nothing.

"Well, that surely was fascinating to see them all," said Bernice briskly, and went out to where the children were playing. I didn't think she had been fascinated at all. She had looked carefully at the photos of the house and the village, but had scarcely glanced at the people.

I put the last photograph into the box, and closed the lid.

"I'd like to go and see your mother tomorrow," I said.

"As you know," he replied, not looking at me, "she's old, and not too well just now."

"I've come a long way. I'd really love to meet her again."

"Love" was not the right word. She would know that.

"I'm afraid that's not possible. She really isn't what she was. She doesn't want to see you. I guess meeting you would upset her."

"But why should it? Look, I'd like to convince her that nobody bears her the slightest ill-will. Heavens above, it's fifty-four years ago. D'you think anyone would bear a grudge that long?"

He grinned. "She might!"

"Least of all me. I was a child when it happened. But I did know her and I'd like to see her once again before I die. After all, we are related, and I loved the whole family. I knew her mother too, don't forget. And there's something I want to tell her that I think will make her happy . . . I'd rather see her than Niagara," I added desperately.

A long silence. He looked at the floor, out of the window, anywhere but at me. Finally:

"Well," he muttered. "I'll try."

Later that evening, as Bernice and I sat with the children round the kitchen table, I half-heard him in the next room, making a telephone call. It was a long conversation. Faint and shorn of the Canadian accent, there was something about the tone and pitch of his voice that I thought I had heard before. But fifty-four years is a long time.

Overnight, my doubts increased. Kitchener's mother had obviously not wished to be confronted with me. Perhaps her son was up to no good and she wanted no part of it.

But the next morning, he announced, obviously with misgivings, that she had agreed to see me.

It was a ten-minute drive. On the way, I wondered how on earth I would know whether a woman in her seventies, in poor shape, was the same person as a girl I had known only in the most superficial way more than two generations ago. I could hardly even remember what she looked like. The more I thought about it, the more I realised that in my letter and my long conversations with her son, I had given away all the information I might have used to test the authenticity of their claim. She might have jibbed at meeting me, but she only had to pretend that her memory was failing – perhaps it was anyway – and I would never know the truth. I wondered, too, why a woman not far past seventy years old was in an old people's home. Surely she was scarcely old enough to have taken such a final step? Everything I had heard seemed to make it all the more likely that her son was not really the man he claimed to be.

The Senior Citizens' Home was in a wooded area where there were a few widely-spaced homesteads; a long, low building in impressive grounds. Several cars were parked outside. The entrance was clean and modern. We walked in, past a big, airy lounge where groups of old men and women were playing chess or cards, and down a wide corridor.

"Seems a nice place," I observed.

"Oh, sure. People put their names down years in advance to come here. It's very well run, and there's full nursing care and a real happy atmosphere." He hesitated. "We would have had Mom live with us, but she's very independent, even now. Always been used to paddling her own canoe, I guess." Was it my imagination, or was he on the defensive?

He knocked at a door.

"Come in, whoever it is," said an old, cracked, Canadian voice.

We entered.

Immediately I saw why the old woman inside the room had come to live in such a place. She was bent almost double with some affliction of the spine. One hand, gnarled and swollen, was on a metal walking-frame. Her hair was grey and wispy and fastened in a knot at the back of her head. She lifted her face as far as she could to look at us. It was pale and lined, the eyes faded blue, the mouth twisted as

337

if by pain. I gaped at her. As far as I knew, I had never seen her before in my life.

"Sit down, sit down," she rasped. "Please excuse my appearance, I'm not the girl I was when we last met."

I had expected to hear the dear Northumbrian lilt in her voice. But there wasn't a trace of it. What could I say? In spite of my doubts, which should have prepared me for this, I felt utterly taken aback. And afraid. What conspiracy were they planning, and how could I forestall it?

Not for the first time in my life, I played for time.

"I've come a long way to meet you," I said.

"I didn't really want you to see me like this. I'd rather people remembered me as I was. It's a long, long time since I saw any of your family. Not since around the time of the funeral, I guess."

"Some of them were very bitter," I said cautiously.

"Right. So was I. Oh boy, was I bitter. That's the other reason why I didn't want to see you. Didn't want to be reminded of it. Guess I put the whole thing behind me years ago. Turned over a new leaf, for his sake," she nodded at her son as best she could.

So this was the line they were taking. It was perfectly plausible. But I recalled that it could have been deduced from what I said in my letter.

"And as for you, Miss Lizzie . . ." And suddenly, the lined face crumpled even further, the sunken eye-sockets creased, and she broke into a huge cackle. "Do you remember the time when your knickers fell down at the cricket-match? Droopy-drawers lost her drawers, eh?"

And Ivy stretched out her gnarled hand for mine, and pulled it to her mouth, and kissed it.

"Well, Ivy," I said, moved and disconcerted at this display of affection, "I'm sorry to see you in this pickle." I was appalled to remember that she was only a few years older than me.

"Well, I'm used to it. I've had a hard life, Miss Lizzie,

and a bad beginning. Them cottages at Riverlaw was damp, did you know that? Water down the walls, half the year. No wonder the rheumatism got me in the end."

"I'm very sorry. Do they look after you properly here?"

"Oh, aye." The Canadian accent was peeling away, revealing the Northumbrian residue underneath. "And how are they all? How's Miss Venetia? She was always so pretty and quiet."

"Happily married, and living in a lovely stone house up on the moors near the Roman Wall. She's very houseproud, and she's made the garden beautiful. They'll never leave it. They just had one child – at least, she's a woman now." I hesitated. "She's become a nun."

"You don't say! Best ask her to pray for me."

"I will. Then Louie – you remember Louie?"

"The little fat one?"

"That's her. She never married. She lives at the Old Hall still, looking after Aunt Emily."

"There's a waste of a life. What about Master Vane? Did he marry?"

"No. He's still running the farm. He and Louie are rather like an old married couple – bickering sometimes, but united like a pair of old shoes. They're really very happy, they love the place," I added, remembering Aunt Emily's dictum, "Never gossip with servants." But Ivy, I reminded myself, wasn't exactly a servant. She was Theodore's wife.

"What about Miss Zinnia? She was a one!"

"Married twice. She used to be Lady Carroun, but now she's plain Mrs." I felt it wiser to add nothing to this.

"Any children?"

I hesitated. "One, from her first marriage. But he went off to make his fortune, and they lost touch." Ivy said nothing – perhaps she had long ago become reconciled to losing touch herself. Kitchener, bored perhaps by all this talk of people he didn't know, slipped out.

"What about you? You got a family?"

"I had a daughter. But she . . . she died in a fire." Even after all these years, it was still difficult to say it.

"Poor lass." I couldn't tell whether she meant Zoe or me.

"And Mr Henry lives in Africa – in Kenya. Mr Cedric married Sir Rednall Carroun's sister, but they parted." I didn't tell her what I knew about Madge's son.

"That's no surprise. She was a spiteful little thing."

"Do you miss Riverlaw, Ivy?"

She shifted again on her chair, and groaned. "What I'd give to stand on the village green, where we used to play cricket, like, and see the cottage gardens and smell the roses from the Old 'all, and feel the cool wind on my cheek!"

"That's just how I feel."

"But it's no good. I'll never get on an aeroplane again. I'm stuck in here," and she lifted up her gnarled hand and tapped her pitifully bent back.

"You never wanted to go . . . earlier?"

I couldn't see her face. "The money would have stopped if we had. We had to sign, like, for the solicitor."

"Ivy," I said gently, "tell me about Hannah – your mother."

"She died of pneumonia in the winter of 1930, God bless her."

"I am so sorry. I've wanted all these years to see her, and thank her. She was a fine woman, and very good to me when I was little. I always felt Aunt Emily treated her shockingly in the end."

"Aye, Mother was a fine woman. Just the one lapse, when I was born. I couldn't have survived in Canada without her, not with the baby, in spite of the money from England. She got work in Toronto, cleaning in a hospital, and the three of us lived in one room. We didn't have warm enough clothes, that first winter; I was afraid for the baby. But she got promotion to housekeeper. They thought very highly of her. She got me a job there when my son was old enough for school. As for your aunt, Mother had always hated her."

I stared. I couldn't imagine anyone hating Aunt Emily. No, that wasn't true; I could well see that after she turned Hannah and Ivy out, they would loathe her. But always?

"Why was that, Ivy?"

She shifted impatiently on her chair. It occurred to me that she must be in pain. "If you don't know, I'm not telling you," she said tetchily. She had been looking up at me awkwardly. Now she looked stubbornly at the floor. I felt she was tiring, and I should go. But I had something to say first.

"Ivy, I specially wanted to see you, because I found some letters. They were written about Theodore after he died." The swollen fingers moved in her lap. "I felt Theodore's son should have them, but there was one in particular I wanted to read to you myself, before I give them to him." I took out of my bag the old sweet-tin that had spent so many years hidden behind a rafter at Riverlaw, and began to open it.

"Aye, I'd like to hear it, but he has no right to them," she said.

"Of course he has! Theodore's son — "

"He wasn't Theodore's son," she said.

I stopped, my hand in mid-air.

"You have other children?"

"No, only the one."

"But . . ."

"Teddy didn't know. He was innocent. He thought it was going to be his child. But I was expecting already."

I had a sudden vision of a billowing purple dress, a feather boa streaming down the front. And a faint picture, seen for a fraction of a second, of a woman in purple disappearing round a stone gatepost, a little boy over her shoulder. A little boy – surely a little older than one might have supposed he would be?

"I couldn't bring myself to tell Teddy it wasn't his. He was a gentleman, he insisted on 'making an honest woman of me', as he put it. And I had visions of being the lady of the

The Old Enchantment

manor. I knew he wouldn't let me starve. I was frightened, and greedy mebbe ... And when he was killed, I thought it was a judgement on me."

I gazed at her, appalled. Ivy's revelation had upset my great scheme for restoring Riverlaw, had negated my reasons for coming to Ontario at all. If Kitchener was not Theodore's son, he could not be the heir. And worse than that; Theodore's great, noble gesture had been in vain.

"Who was the father, Ivy?"

She grinned. "Vin Baggs, I think. A bit of a one, he was." She smiled at the ground.

"But he had red hair!"

"Aye, but me father didn't. Me mother told me his was black, once."

"Your father . . ." Somehow, I had never thought of Hannah's production of Ivy as involving a father. "Who was that?"

"I dursn't tell you."

"Did my aunt and uncle know?"

She smiled again, a witch-like splitting of dry lips. "Yes, they both knew. I don't know how Mrs Delmayne could have me mother in the house. But mebbe there was some reason why your uncle could do what he liked and his wife couldn't complain."

"What do you mean, Ivy?"

"Never mind. It was just something me mother said to me once. But she loved me father. She loved him and served him all her life, till she was turned out from his house."

"His house?" I repeated stupidly.

Again, images flashed through my memory. Hannah's sturdy, womanly figure and curly blonde hair. The terrible moment when Uncle Vane had fallen in the bedroom and Hannah hadn't hesitated, but rushed up the stairs to help him. My aunt's dreadful, unnatural reaction to the news of Theodore's marriage.

It all fell into place.

I took the crabbed, swollen hand.

342

"Ivy," I said, "you're not just my cousin-in-law. You're my second cousin. You were Theodore's half-sister. You're a Delmayne too."

"Aye," she said. "And I'd like to put a curse on them all."

After I had said goodbye to Ivy, I walked back down the hospital-like corridor and through the orange-carpeted foyer of the Senior Citizens' Home, under the inquisitive gaze of some spry old ladies loitering round the notice-board. I found Kitchener leaning against his car in the shade of a maple, smoking a cigarette.

Somehow I couldn't talk to him about my discovery.

"It was amazing to meet her after all these years," I told him. "Her mind seems perfectly all right. But it's quite a small room to live in all the time. Does she ever," I chose my words carefully, "go out for a drive, for example?"

His reply came quickly. "God, no, she'd only complain." Then he smiled at me. "She's quite an outspoken old lady. It's very hard to please her. It really got my wife down, which is why we thought she'd be better off here."

"It's obviously a good place," I said diplomatically. I wondered whether my daughter Zoe would have thought me hard to please, and whether she would have put me in a home.

I looked at my watch.

"I've got to make an urgent phone-call to England," I said. "Is there anywhere . . . ?"

Kitchener looked put out. "Here, I guess. You could call collect maybe?"

With an apology, I turned back to the office. I explained, and was directed to a dark little telephone-room. When the operator put me through I listened to the crackles and the distant burr-burr, burr-burr, praying that Zinnia would be in.

"Hello?" came her bright voice at last. "Good heavens,

343

Lizzie darling, I was just making tea, will you have Indian or China?"

"Zinnia," I said urgently, "I found Cousin Kitchener, but he isn't Theodore's son. I was hoping so much to be able to persuade him to contest the will and live at Riverpark and leave the Old Hall alone. I spoke to Ivy — "

"Heavens, not really!"

"And she told me the truth, and I believe her. So if we discount Madge's son Rupert, Vane's the heir — isn't that marvellous?"

"I'm afraid," her voice came gently and clearly along the line, "it's no good, Lizzie."

"But couldn't we prove somehow that Cedric wasn't Rupert's father? I mean, I don't believe he was, do you?"

"I'm afraid we can't. But it's not just that. There've been developments here, and things are looking rather black, I'm afraid. I phoned Leslie Brown, and he said the same as he told Mother at poor Cedric's funeral — that he had Cedric's will, and the entail had been barred, and Cedric had made him sole executor and left the entire estate to him. Vane's been to inspect the copy of the will at Cedric's solicitor's office in Newcastle, and there it was — everything was left to Aunt Letitia, and after her death to Leslie."

"Well I knew that, but — "

"And Leslie says he's got an offer for the whole estate — Riverpark, Riverlaw, the Old Hall and everything — and the contract's being drawn up on Thursday next. Apparently the buyer doesn't care about searches or surveyors or anything, and he's paying cash, which Leslie needs so that he can pay the estate duty. He's a scrap-dealer from Newcastle — a dreadful fellow, Vane says."

"Oh, how could Cedric be such a fool?" I groaned. "How could he trust Leslie of all people?"

"And he's told Mother she has to get out. At her age! She's got no money — I just don't know what they're going to do, Lizzie." Even through the Atlantic crackles and rumbles I could hear the desperation in her voice.

"Look," I tried, "why don't we try and track down Madge? Surely as Cedric's widow she has a claim – and surely she wouldn't turn Aunt Emily out?"

"Don't bank on it. I know she was my friend, but . . . And they were divorced years ago. She has no claim at all."

"Zinnia," I said, "there's one last outside chance. I'm going to see if Kitchener could be persuaded to put in a rival bid for the Old Hall. There's a reason why he might be interested."

"But would he let Mother stay there?"

"I don't know," I said unhappily, "but there's only one way to find out."

ENGLAND

37

On the way back to Kitchener's farm I thought again about Zoe. I kept carefully in an inviolable corner of my memory that picture of her – young, dark, pretty, with that strange, closed-up look – standing outside the door of McIver's Place waving goodbye, at the beginning of autumn 1939.

For the millionth time, I went over in my mind the events of that season. I remembered with what love I bought her English postcards of the castle and the Theatre Royal in Newcastle during my visits to my parents, and of Riverlaw at the Gorgon's (still alive, and gratifyingly delighted to see me so that the forbidding furrows round her mouth turned, for the first time in recorded history, to smile-lines), and posted five at once so that she could have some idea of the place and of how much I missed her. I remembered rattling down the stairs of the Old Hall at the sound of the postman's feet on the gravel, and moaning to Louie that perhaps the ships were taking longer because war had just been declared (I didn't, then, care much about the war; it could surely not touch Riverlaw, much less Zoe, and Peregrine would doubtless go safely back to his property in Australia).

I recalled the letters – friendly, appeasing, apologetic – that I wrote to Chuck, and the slight unease I felt when he, too, failed to reply.

A ship was torpedoed in the North Atlantic, and then another. Nazi U-boats were rumoured to be controlling the northern routes. Liners were commandeered, and convoys assembled, for children who were being evacuated to Canada and the States. The general feeling that the war would be over by the end of the year began to evaporate. And still Chuck and Zoe did not write. McIver's Place still had no telephone – another of Chuck's little economies. I waited with increasing anxiety for some sign of life from them. I was almost physically afraid of Chuck's reaction to my last letter, which told him that the ship on which I was to return had been commandeered for evacuees, and I had been advised that for the present I should not try to travel.

While I was waiting for news from the shipping company I got into the way of spending a couple of days with my parents in the ossified gloom of their house, and spending the rest of each week at Riverlaw, where I loafed about, running messages for Aunt Emily, cutting down two silk dresses and a rose-red tweed suit she had given me, cleaning the depleted silver, and weeding and deadheading the flowerbeds.

The Juranville roses on the garden façade wafted their delicious scent, grew fat, and crumbled into papery beige balls. The leaves fell, the white doves cooed elegiacally.

"Don't go back, darling, until you hear from Chuck," commanded Aunt Emily – fatter now, her face pouchy and hair mostly white, but otherwise quite unchanged – from the porcelain-blue sofa where she reigned over the silver tea-set.

"It's Zoe I'm worried about. I don't really care about Chuck."

"You mustn't ever say that, dearest. He was a good catch. A lot of girls would give their eye teeth for a handsome Harrovian with two hundred acres." Obviously, Louie hadn't shown her my incautious letter about Chuck's parsimony.

"Did you love Uncle Vane?" I asked her.

She looked up quickly, shocked, the cream-jug arrested

in mid-air. "Of course. He was always terribly good to me. One has to count one's blessings and work at one's marriage, always."

This dictum being unwelcome, I made my excuses and went to see Cedric. He had called to say hello when I had first arrived, and had joined our group after church on Sunday, but we had not spoken alone.

As I walked along the lane to Riverpark I was haunted by memories of the many times I had gone that way before. The dawn encounter on the day after Zinnia's wedding; the walk in the rain with Zinnia the day she gave herself to Giles; the ride with Cedric and Aunt Letitia the day of the Admiral's first stroke – each stone in the dry walls on either side of the lane, each tuft of sea-pink and half-hidden gleam of wild strawberry, had witnessed a turning-point of my life.

Cedric was sitting at one end of the huge mahogany dining-table at Riverpark with a Crown Derby cup of coffee at his elbow, frowning over a column of figures. Behind him, through the tall windows, the clipped lawn stretched uneventfully down to the river. The mud-coloured velvet curtains looked exactly the same as they had looked when I was five.

When the servant showed me into the room, he sprang up as spryly as his ponderous frame allowed. His hair had receded from a worried forehead. His face was redder and more mottled, his thick lips purpler, than I remembered. He wore tortoiseshell-framed spectacles, and a thick tweed suit with waistcoat and dangling watchchain.

"Elizabeth, what a lovely surprise!" He came up to me, hovered with hands waving uncertainly, and then, deciding perhaps that the moment to kiss me had passed, drew out one of the severe, leather-seated Chippendale chairs.

"How are things, Cedric?" I said as I sat down.

"Oh, not too bad. Actually, we're doing quite well here. It's been a good summer and the corn sold well."

"That's funny. Vane told me he was very disappointed with the harvest this year."

"Between you and me and the gatepost," he confided in his fruity voice, "we all love Vane but he isn't the best farmer in the world. Leslie says he should have more hinds but he can't afford them. And he doesn't mend his fences."

"I noticed." In fact, I had been appalled and saddened, on my first walk round the farm, at the tumbledown buildings, the drifts of waist-high weeds, the poor state of field after field that had once been a pleasure to look at.

"He's a dear fellow, and as straight as a die, but he's not the farmer Uncle Vane was. Leslie says we ought to get him out."

"Cedric, you *can't*! He can't help it – he was never taught farming, don't you remember? He took over when Uncle had a stroke and he had to pick it up as he went along. And what about Aunt Emily? What about — "

"Oh, I know, I know. Don't worry, I'll see what I can do. Blood's thicker than water, and all that. Ah, here comes your coffee. Lovely to see you, I've missed you a lot over the years. How's Zinnia?"

"Looking a picture. I left her in London, threatening to join the Wrens as her contribution to the war effort. Of all the women's services they have easily the nicest uniform."

"Typical. Has Zadok turned up?"

"No, she hasn't heard from him. Privately, Cedric, I think she's pretty desperate about that. What's he like?"

"Charming, very able, but definitely got a bit out of hand. He started running away with girls at seventeen. But can you blame the fellow? He was always left with the cleaner's aunt or a retired nanny, while Zinnia was off gallivanting with some tycoon. He probably thinks it's normal. Needs a father, if you ask me, but I expect it's too late. But not to tell his mother where he is – that's naughty."

"Yes, poor Zinnia. They had a terrific row, apparently, when she told him she was going round the world with Lord Barbary, and he stormed off shouting that he was leaving England too and she'd better forget about him."

Cedric grunted. "But what about you?"

"My no-letters problem seems rather minor by comparison. But I'm a bit worried because I haven't had any word from Chuck and my daughter."

"Probably delayed because of the U-boats. But your letter reached me all right. Very nice letter, and the only sympathy I got for the wretched business. It came last week."

I stared. I remembered writing the letter. But I had left it on the kitchen table at McIver's Place. I hadn't even had time to write the envelope. In the flurry of packing and leaving I had forgotten all about it. What would Chuck's reaction have been if he saw it? He hated Cedric. And if Zoe read it, what might she think? Had I sent Cedric my love? Might that be misunderstood? Which of them had forwarded it? I had brought my address book with me, and had an absurd fear that Zoe might not even know where to write to me, but Chuck would know.

"You don't by any chance still have the envelope do you?"

"Matter of fact I do. One of the farm boys collects stamps." Cedric took a fat and battered crocodile wallet from his pocket, and after a moment's search among its contents he produced an envelope with a Canadian stamp. My letter was inside. The address was in Chuck's cramped, schoolboy hand.

"Any enclosures? No letter from Chuck, for instance?"

"No."

I looked at the postmark. "Well, he was alive six weeks ago."

"You don't sound very concerned."

I turned the letter over in my hand. I had an odd feeling about it. Perhaps it was the last time I would see Chuck's writing – no, that was idiotic. I dragged my thoughts back to Cedric.

"Were you very unhappy when Madge went off? Where is she now?"

"In Italy, I suppose – she has an apartment in Fiesole. Well, it was pretty ghastly, but more because of the baby than because of her, I'm sorry to say."

"Of course, the baby! Poor Cedric. When was he born?"

"June 1938."

"Have you seen your son?"

"Not *my* son," he said pointedly. "There's no way it could be *my* son." He looked down at the Turkey carpet, and went red, or rather redder.

I was dumbfounded. "Do you know who the father is?" I said at last.

"She won't say. But I'm pretty certain."

"Close to home?"

"Rather too close to home for comfort."

"Oh, Cedric!" It was hard to imagine Madge as Lady Chatterley. Who could her lover be? Gardener, chauffeur, footman – surely not. "Could you get rid of him? Not murder, of course, I don't mean that – but send him away?"

Cedric put his tweed elbows on the shiny table and put his large face in his hands. "I tried to, but it's all too difficult. Unless Madge owns up I have no grounds for accusing him. Mother thinks he's wonderful, and he has, I admit, virtually run the place for years. He knows far more about our finances than I do. And he's a trustee, and a lot cleverer than me. I'm stuck with him."

Leslie! I had seen them together at Venetia's wedding, all those years ago, and thought no more of it. "Perhaps it isn't him," I floundered.

"'Fraid so. You warned me, years ago. You were perfectly right."

"Cedric, do you have a good lawyer?"

"Well . . . Leslie found me a friend of his, in Newcastle. Don't like him much, but he's always affable."

"Get another. Get a London lawyer from one of the famous old firms."

"You really think so?"

"Yes."

Cedric sat up straight and looked me in the eye. "Right. I will."

"I'm thinking of leaving my husband," I said. It was entirely unpremeditated. It astonished me. How could I be confiding in Cedric, of all people? He drew back his chair and looked at me compassionately.

"Poor Elizabeth. Life is bloody, isn't it."

"Yes. Well," I thought of Peregrine's infectious laugh, his kind eyes. "Not always. Trouble is, I love my daughter and I'm worried for her. It would be a terribly bad example, wouldn't it, if I just didn't go back? And I don't know how the dickens I would support myself. Zoe's a pupil-teacher, and her principal told me she'd recommended her for a scholarship to training college next year, so perhaps she won't have a financial problem. But I hate to leave her. It seems selfish."

"She sounds well able to take care of herself."

"Oh, she is. But . . . Oh, I don't know. I feel a moral obligation to look after my father-in-law. He's an old drunkard and quite soon he'll be a stretcher case."

Cedric stood up. "Lizzie, we can't have you looking after old drunkards."

"Well, it's the Christian thing to do, isn't it? But I must say I can hardly bear the thought."

"Come and look at my latest motor-car. It's a Bentley. Do you drive?" he asked, all formal politeness, as he opened the door and ushered me through.

"No, we don't have a car."

"But I thought you lived at the back of beyond."

"We do. But Chuck is happy as we are. Apart from buying the groceries and selling the farm produce, which he does with a tractor and trailer, we don't go anywhere. The truth is," I burst out, as we set off across the lawn towards the coach house, "he's a miser. It isn't that he's grindingly poor – I know what he got for sixty acres of oats last summer, and for his prize ewes. He was too mean to pay a housekeeper so he got one free by marrying me. He's always been too mean to have a hired man to help on the farm as the other farmers do, much less a hired girl to help me. He's far too mean to buy a car."

"I think," said Cedric, "that you should stay in England for a while. Perhaps that'll bring him to his senses."

38

So I stayed.

History was in suspension. England was rearming and training, waiting for Germany to pounce. In Newcastle and Riverlaw alternately, I made blackout curtains, sometimes while wearing my gas-mask for practice in case of Nazi attack (though the thought of how the housewives who were doing this all over England must look, reduced me to giggles, which misted up the eyepiece and made a shambles of the whole exercise). I stuck adhesive tape in geometrical patterns across window-panes to minimise the effect of blast (as described in the Air Raid Precautions leaflets); I untied knots in string in case string became unobtainable; I knitted dishcloths, I preserved quantities of eggs in isinglass, I peeled bucketsful of apples for jam and chutney and dried apple rings – anything that would keep – against future shortages. My index finger was calloused and my hands begrimed from the constant peeling.

Whichever house I was in, listening to the nine o'clock news became a ritual. My father had an Anderson shelter built in the middle of the front lawn, with a bunk for my mother, a bench for himself and me, and a cardboard box containing a first-aid kit, a supply of tinned food, and a Winchester of water. When the air-raids started, refinements – spare torch batteries, a book of crosswords, knitting-needles and wool – were added. There was a paraffin heater and it was quite snug in there, but dank and smelly and very small, and the bangs and booms overhead never ceased to be alarming. "You're perfectly all right unless a bomb's got your name on it," my father would say as he went up the steps to the lawn in the middle of a raid, despite my mother's pleas, to look up at the echelons of planes roaring overhead.

I helped him to Dig For Victory, rooting flowers ruthlessly out of the back garden and replacing them with winter vegetables. Even my mother did her bit by knitting balaclavas on the chaise-longue. My father had aged most. Retirement, rather than advancing years, had made him an old man; a trip to the pillarbox on the corner was a morning's task, to be planned in advance, talked about, dressed for, and mentioned afterwards with a sense of achievement. My mother, on the other hand, was completely unchanged; she resumed her constant instructions to me ("The beige cardigan, please, from the third long drawer on the right, behind the vests – and when you're up there, could you bring me the hairpins from the little glass dish on the dressing-table?") as if my absence in Canada had only lasted an hour or two. It was now clear to me that, barring accidents, she would outlive my father.

And every week I wrote to Chuck and Zoe. My letters to Chuck got shorter and shorter, but to Zoe I sent a sort of serial word-picture of Britain under the Nazi threat. When Peregrine telephoned to say he was rejoining his old regiment, I poured out my fears and sadness to Zoe, and to her alone. But that letter, of course, I burnt. I gazed into the flames as they licked at its edges, and wished they could consume my guilt too. That evening I wrote an extra nice letter to Chuck, reminding myself that he had never been unfaithful, that he had worked hard, partly for my benefit, for many years; that he had done his best.

I had been told at the post office that non-essential airmail deliveries to Canada had been suspended, and I had no means of knowing when or how often sea mail crossed the Atlantic. One couldn't any more look up the sailings in the newspaper and write the ship's name on the envelope. But I kept on writing off into the void.

When Christmas came and went without so much as a card, I became seriously alarmed. Had Chuck forbidden Zoe to write to me? Had my letter to Cedric been misunderstood? I tried continually to recall exactly what Zoe had said before I sailed. Had I seemed cold or unresponsive? Had she been afraid, or even angrier with me than I realised? Or had she been trying to tell me something?

I told myself that McIver's Place must be snowed up by now. The postman wouldn't be able to get through to the crossroads, and Chuck certainly wouldn't allow Zoe to brave the drifts simply to empty the postbox. It could last for weeks. I pictured them stoking the stove, feeling their way hand-over-hand along the rope fence, coming out of the blinding whiteness into the dark, odorous warmth of the barn. Zoe was a bright girl, brought up to the deep winters of Nova Scotia. She wouldn't come to any harm.

More weeks passed. Louie was deeply involved in writing a War Diary, so many of the daily tasks at Riverlaw devolved to me when I was there. I roamed the Old Hall, dismayed by the evidence of woodworm and decay. I patched up a loose cover here, a torn Persian rug there, and tried to persuade Aunt Emily to get a builder to mend the roof over the train-room, but she wouldn't. "Another time," she said dismissively. Aunt Emily never talked about money; it was ill-bred.

And then, one day, a fat letter arrived for me with a Canadian stamp. The handwriting wasn't Chuck's or Zoe's, or even the Major's. On the back of the envelope was written J. McWilliam.

Dearest Lizzie (Janet had written in her small firm hand),
You may be surprised at hearing from me rather than the family, and it grieves me to be the one to tell you this. I want you to go and sit down now, as you read this,

and think of me as if we were sitting together in your kitchen, because I am the bearer of bad news, Lizzie, and I hardly know how to break it to you.

We have had a long, hard winter here and the farms beyond Upper Stewiacke have been snowed up for many weeks. The school was closed long before Christmas and stayed closed longer than usual in New Year. Your old neighbour Mr Van Tyghem was very ill in the Fall and we got him into the hospital in Halifax and my Jim and the Reverend went and got his animals so as to be able to feed them in our own barns. None of us saw Chuck or the Major or Zoe all through the snows, and we didn't expect to. It seemed odd they didn't show up at any of the Christmas services, because the snow wasn't too deep then, but we guessed maybe the Major wasn't any too well and they didn't like to leave him. The Reverend was going to go over there one morning, but that day the blizzards started. After Christmas the drifts were eight feet and more and there was no way the postman or anyone else could get through that last part of the track. We didn't worry because you're a good housewife, Lizzie, and we knew you'd done a lot of bottling and killed a pig or two last summer, and they'd got a barn full of fodder and cows and sheep there, so they wouldn't starve.

But then the thaw started and when the people at the store said they hadn't seen Chuck nor Zoe for weeks, we began to be concerned. We realised that if there had been any disaster, with Mr Van Tyghem's farm being empty nobody would have seen or heard anything. Eventually Jim and the Reverend drove up there and went to your home.

This is where it gets hard to take, Lizzie. Because when they got there they couldn't see the house, and then they saw it had burned down. It must have been right at the beginning of the winter and they thought from what they saw that it had happened in the night.

Chuck was in bed and maybe he just never knew a thing about it. We wondered if maybe the Major knocked over a candle, in his sleep perhaps.

The one glimmer of hope in the whole thing is that they could find no trace of Zoe, and when I spoke to the schoolmistress she told me that, contrary to what we had all understood, Zoe didn't show up at all last term. She had sent a nice note just before the term started, apologising that she wouldn't be coming, so Miss P wasn't too concerned. She had a word with Chuck about it after church one Sunday in October, because she thought Zoe would have looked in to explain, but Chuck wasn't disposed to talk about her. He just said that Zoe "had gone off somewhere, he didn't know where". She gathered it was a sore point and she suspected Zoe might have quarrelled with him and run away – she would have received her check for the last semester's work, so she had money.

We didn't know how we could get hold of you because, of course, all your papers were burnt along with the house. I had two lovely postcards from you but you didn't put your address on them. Then we thought of looking in your mailbox at the crossroads, and it was stuffed full of letters and cards from you. None from Zoe, though – I checked, oh, so carefully, Lizzie.

Jim went to Truro and showed the station-master Zoe's photo from the school group last summer. He thought maybe he might have seen her on the Toronto platform sometime in the Fall, but he couldn't be sure. We told the police and the Youth Fellowship, but Miss P says Chuck seemed more annoyed than worried when she spoke to him that time, and she fears that Zoe couldn't have been gone for long or they would surely have heard, and the police said that we must assume she had gone back home.

The Reverend gave the three of them a real good funeral, with an oration and everything you would have wanted. I have a list of wreaths and will send it, with the cards that were attached. When you come back we'll have a Memorial Service with all the hymns you'd like.

Jim asked Mr Moore the attorney in Truro what you should do if Chuck's will was burnt with the house. He says McIver's Place is effectively yours and if you come and see him on your return he will fix everything. The Bank Manager told him that the McIvers were not quite as hard up as you may have thought. However, there is now, of course, no house to stay in so you will need to think about having one built, and they asked me to ask you if the place was insured and if so by what company.

Dear Lizzie, I would give anything not to have to tell you all this. Come and stay with us whenever you like, for as long as you like.

With our love and deepest sympathy,
     Janet.

In time I knew this letter by heart, and I would wake up whimpering from nightmares in which I waded through charred shards and blackened bones in the ruins of my home, desperately seeking to save my daughter but knowing that I would find no relic of her among the sodden ashes.

McIver's Place was not, of course, insured – that would have been too much to expect. And Janet, in her kindness, had jibbed at telling me about the animals, which had met a miserable death in the barn, unwatered and unmilked. The Reverend wrote on behalf of his whole congregation to send their sympathy and to tell me that a team of volunteers had cleaned the place up. The Attorney, Mr Moore, wrote me a helpful letter, and at my request he put the whole property up for sale. Because of its remoteness and lack of a house, it went very cheap, to (Janet told me) a shaggy ex-waiter from Tennessee who talked to himself in a loud, nasal voice. Mr Moore warned me that the money would take a very long time to come through, and I asked him to give two per cent of the sale proceeds to the church funds as a goodbye present. I would miss them all, especially Janet, but I didn't want ever to see McIver's Place again.

While this correspondence – protracted because of the slowness and unreliability of the mail as the U-boats in the Atlantic became more pugnacious – was going on, I tried to come to terms with my loss.

I was so numbed that my father's sudden death from a heart-attack scarcely seemed to touch me.

My mother took to her bed. I looked after her for a while, but I found it a great strain; I missed my father more and more, and felt in retrospect that he must have been an angel to put up with her so patiently. In the end it was she who, dissatisfied with my limited nursing ability, asked me to arrange for her to go into a nursing-home.

Racked with guilt, I combed Newcastle and found a small, very comfortable, very expensive one in Fenham. I trudged there daily to sit and listen while she complained about the nurses, the doctors, the food. Gradually it dawned on me that perhaps these targets were symbols for something else.

One day, "You were a great disappointment to us," she said, *à propos* of nothing, as she reclined against a mountain-range of pillows, her spoon hovering over a plateful of pink blancmange. "You never seemed to like your own home. All the time you were hankering to go to the Delmaynes. I don't think they did you any good at all."

"Why ever not? They were terribly kind, always."

"Well . . ." For once, she seemed at a loss. "Young Zinnia wasn't . . . suitable company for you. Emily wasn't quite what she seemed."

I pressed her to explain, but she started criticising the blancmange.

And the next night a great chevron of German bombers flew over Newcastle. When the sirens went I didn't bother to cross the lawn to take solitary refuge in the shelter, so that when I heard the whine of the engines in the dark, and the first explosions so alarmingly near, I regretted my bravado and dived into the cupboard under the stairs – the only place in the house out of reach of flying glass if the windows broke. There, in pitch darkness among the brooms and carpet-sweepers, I listened to the racket as wave upon wave of planes roared overhead; I heard deafening booms down the street and the tinkle and crash of glass very near, and felt the floor beneath me shake in sympathy. When the planes had gone I crept out, briefly mourned the chandelier that crunched under my feet in the hall, postponed an inspection of my broken windows until daylight, and went round to see if I could help my stunned neighbours. It wasn't until the next morning that I learnt that my mother's nursing-home had received a direct hit.

As soon as I felt able to face the world, I sold the house and invested the proceeds, put the furniture in store, and joined the Wrens. To my great surprise, the mere mention of Zinnia's name as my referee got me a commission. Her title had almost certainly helped her at the beginning of her naval career, but it was her dash and efficiency that had allowed her to rise like a rocket, and before long she was in a position of command and influence in the Service.

I discovered just what a difference this had made to her halfway through the war, when I was sent on temporary secondment as a liaison officer to Bath, where she was stationed. I saw a good deal of her there – but mostly around conference tables and during working lunches. She would sweep in, crisply chic in her brass-buttoned navy uniform and tricorne hat, with a couple of minions in tow; and a tired table of men would sit up, straighten their ties, and look cheerful and expectant. She galvanised people into efficiency. She was a born decision-maker, and nothing alarmed her. When some earnest committee got bogged down in futile discussion, "I have a plan," she would declare with a light in her eye; and I would be for an instant transported back to a stone-walled lane among nettles and sea-pinks, and wish with all my heart that Giles could see her now.

I was only there for a fortnight but before I left she asked me to a party in a beautiful Georgian house where she was billeted. I was terribly impressed by the gaggle of admirals she seemed to know by their Christian names. (Years afterwards she told me that she had been match-making for me.) Strangely enough, the man she singled out for most attention herself was a middle-aged RNVR captain called Al, with bright brown eyes and a gentle but confident manner. I only spoke to him for a few minutes but he seemed extremely nice. He was a wireless expert, which was unusual for a naval officer of that rank. There was the faintest touch of the north in his voice, and I wondered where he came from, but I was dragged off to meet somebody else before I could ask.

ONTARIO

39

All these memories went through my head, in the telescoped way memories do, as Ivy's son Kitchener drove me through the broad Ontario landscape on our way back to his farm. But now we had reached it, and I came to as we drove up to the house and he parked out of the sun under a big shady tree. His wife Bernice came out to meet us, the screen door banging to behind her.

"How did you get on?" she called. "She's rather a difficult old lady, I'm afraid. Changes her mind once a minute."

"She never was very easy," I said diplomatically.

They led me into the lounge and she brought coffee. The children, she told me, were playing at a friend's.

"I found that man's name and address for you," she said, and handed me a folded piece of paper. I would have looked at it there and then, but I was suddenly conscious of a tension about her. She sat down on the rocking-chair and looked at her husband expectantly, and then at me.

"Now I think we ought to get to the point," she said.

We all looked at each other. I don't know why, but I felt a sudden menace in the air; nothing tangible, but I was aware that somehow they were turning the tables on me.

"We have an agent working for us in London, England," she said. "We know that Mr Cedric Delmayne died recently."

"Yes, it was very sudden." He had had food-poisoning, and it took him one lonely night to die, without even Aunt

369

Letitia to hold his hand, for she had died of a thrombosis two or three months earlier. Poor Cedric.

I had rehearsed this moment in my mind. They would say, "What's going to happen to the old home now?" and I would reply, "The trustee has put it on the market. You, Kitchener, are a Delmayne yourself. Would you – could you – buy it and restore it for the sake of posterity? Would you – could you – let the Riverlaw Delmaynes live there till they die, so that your children can have it in its glory, and their children after them?"

But it didn't turn out at all like that.

"We didn't tell you," said Bernice, "but my husband is a property developer. We've done quite well building condominiums and apartment blocks on the outskirts of Toronto, but there's a lot of competition here. We want to extend our operations and become an international company. Our information is that England is a good market just now. We were particularly interested in Northumberland because there didn't seem to have been much development there; we thought it might have potential. And also, of course, because of the family connection. So we were very interested indeed to hear about Mr Delmayne."

"You said you had an agent?" It began to fall into place.

"Sure. When we saw your ad, we guessed why you were looking for us. If we might be due to inherit in England, it makes sense," put in her husband.

"Due to inherit? I'm afraid not."

They looked at each other.

"Well, we'll come to that in a minute. Our agent spoke to a Mr Brown. Mr Cedric Delmayne's will says that a life interest in the whole estate goes to Mrs Letitia Delmayne – who I gather is dead – and failing her, to the trusted manager, Leslie Brown, and after his death Mr Cedric Delmayne's son Rupert Delmayne, of Casa Bella Vista at Fiesole in Italy, inherits outright."

Oh, foolish Cedric! The will had doubtless been drawn

up by Leslie's Newcastle lawyer friend. Vane had told me that it had been made in 1938, and Cedric had obviously signed without question whatever Leslie had put in front of him.

"Our information," Bernice went on in a cold, business-like tone, "is that a big rural area would be served by a supermarket and shopping mall with ancillary housing on the land in the Riverpark estate around the village of Riverlaw. Our agent says the whole village has practically fallen down anyway, it's ripe for demolition, but the roads are okay, and if the Old Hall were demolished too it would make an excellent site for the supermarket. We could bring a lot of employment to the area, and it sounds as if it needs it. And Mr Brown wants to sell."

I sat there, stunned.

"You can't do that," I said. "Those houses are people's homes. Their fathers and grandfathers lived there before them."

She laughed briefly. "Without bathrooms or main drainage? We can build better ones and they can buy them."

"These are really poor people. And I should think the houses are all listed as of historical interest. The County Council would never give planning permission."

"They aren't listed. And our agent says the County Council is left-wing now, and they'll give permission for anything that will bring more jobs to a depressed rural area."

"But you can't just demolish houses where people live! They could take you to court!"

"So what? We get fined, maybe a coupla thousand pounds. What's that against the profit from the whole deal? Peanuts! Anyway, it takes money to mount a court case, and you say these people are poor – they won't do it."

I thought bitterly of my reason for coming to Ontario at all – a last, desperate attempt to find a rich Delmayne who would be able to finance the restoration of the village and the Old Hall. And here indeed were the rich Delmaynes, not rescuers but bent on destruction.

I must play every card I had, and more.

"I'm afraid you can't do that," I said. "Mr Rupert Delmayne would scarcely agree."

"We've written to ask him. We can buy his reversion. He's not going to say no to a large sum of money!"

"You don't know that," I said desperately. "And Mr Leslie Brown has no legal right" – I was improvising now – "to sell without Mr Rupert Delmayne's consent."

"If Mr Rupert Delmayne doesn't consent," she said calmly, "we'll go to law. We also discovered that the Riverlaw part of the estate has always been entailed on the descendants of the eldest son. So whatever the will says, we are heirs twice over." She gave a wintry smile. "Once because Ivy is the daughter of the late Mr Vane Delmayne — "

"I'm afraid not. Ivy was illegitimate – and the entail goes in the male line. Mr Vane Delmayne has a son still living."

" – And once because my husband is the son of Theodore Delmayne."

"He isn't," I said sharply. "Ivy just told me Theodore wasn't his father at all."

"Then why was your grandmother sending money to support her all those years? Ivy always said that he was Theodore's son. Theodore may have been a sucker, but that's neither here nor there. What court would take any notice of her changing her mind in her dotage? And if it does come to court, she'll say what we tell her to – considering that we support her, she'd be a fool not to. No, I'm sorry if it's a shock to you, but you can't prove it, and we'll be coming over soon to look at our property and hire labour and machinery to get the demolition started. Once the Old Hall site is cleared I guess getting planning permission will be easy."

NEW YORK, FLORENCE

40

Ivy's son dropped me with my suitcase at Toronto Airport. I waved goodbye briefly and stood there on the sidewalk among the limos and the anxious, hurrying people, thinking that I loved Canada and I felt deep affection and admiration for most of the Canadians I had known well. It was just my bad luck that the only ones who could directly affect my life were the exceptions to the rule.

It was afternoon. My host had gone back to his Toronto house to prepare for an early start at work next morning. I had booked a modest hotel room in Toronto so that I could go to evening church and see more of the city before I caught the overnight plane to London on Monday night. I could phone Nova Scotia for a chat with Janet – I really looked forward to that. Maybe I'd even go to Niagara, if there was time.

But things were different now.

I went into the big, glass-fronted foyer to find the Alitalia desk. But on the way I decided that I needed to visit the ladies' room. I needed that anonymity after the awful revelations of Bernice's plans. I needed to pull myself together, smarten up, take stock, just for a minute.

I stood in a row of women in front of the mirrors, and felt in my pocket for a comb. My hand closed on the folded slip Bernice had given me at the farm. I'd forgotten all about it. Well, there wasn't time to do anything about it now. I had to get to Fiesole, if possible before Bernice's letter reached Rupert Delmayne. I didn't know what I could do there, but I had to see him. I would think of something.

I dragged at my hair, scratched a parting, washed and put on fresh lipstick. Change my Heathrow ticket for a Milan one – that was all I needed to do; businessmen did it every day. I felt tired, but that was normal for a woman my age. I could sleep on the plane. The great thing was to get to Italy.

I put comb and lipstick back in my purse. The folded slip could go there too, until I got home to England. Whoever he was, I could write to him. The purse snapped shut, and I set off for the door.

And thought better of it. Who was he? I might as well know now. Maybe I could phone him while I was still in North America – I might have quite a wait for my plane. I opened the bag, fished out the slip of paper, and unfolded it.

The name on it was Zadok Carroun.

The man at British Airways frowned at his computer terminal. "Milan tomorrow's okay, but New York on a Sunday's difficult. Try Eastern, over there."

I lugged my bag at a run to the Eastern counter.

"New York right away?" A pretty girl in uniform picked up the phone. She made three calls. After the first two she pursed her lips. After the third she smiled. "You're in luck, they had returns. You've got an hour before takeoff." She scribbled on the ticket form, checked a number, clicked my Amex card on to the machine. "Sign here. Check-in over there. Have a nice day now."

I galloped back to finish buying my Alitalia ticket and pay – recklessly – the extra, then crossed to the check-in. Thank heaven I had got a visa, just in case I was re-routed through the States – there had been a Canadian airline strike recently and the travel agent had advised it.

Where were the telephones? Oh, heavens, why hadn't I phoned before I'd bought the ticket? What if I couldn't get hold of him? Suppose he was away, or had moved and left no address?

The first phone I tried was out of order.

What if an Ansafone answered? What if the number I had was his office, not his home?

I went into the next booth and, trembling, dialled the number written on Bernice's scrap of paper. I found myself holding on to it for grim death in case it blew away. A girl answered.

"Mr Carroun's office."

"May I speak to Mr Carroun, please?"

"The office is closed. He's been in but I'm afraid he's just on his way out. It's Sunday," she said reprovingly.

"Oh please, I'm in Toronto airport and I'm only going to be in New York for one night!" (And where are you going to sleep, you idiot? I asked myself.) "I'm going to Italy tomorrow! Do try — "

"Hold, please," and I heard the clatter of high heels running and her voice calling some distance away, "Mr Carroun! Someone in Toronto wants you urgently!" She came back. "Who is speaking, please?"

I hesitated. He wouldn't know my married name. "Tell him it's his cousin Elizabeth, from England. Tell him . . . tell him I was nearly his godmother."

There was a silence — she had put her hand over the receiver. And then a man's voice.

"Who is this?"

"I would have been your godmother, Zadok, but you were christened in a great hurry."

"And where was that?" His voice was American, rich, deep — and guarded.

"In the church at Riverlaw. Zinnia brought you from London specially. I remember seeing you on the lawn at Riverlaw," I gabbled on, "chasing a white peacock. Zinnia and Louie and Venetia were my cousins — "

"Cousin Lizzie! Is it really you?"

"Yes, it is. Can I come and see you?"

"What, tonight?"

"Yes."

There was a pause. "Well, I don't know," he said slowly. "I have to think about this. Where are you?"

"Toronto airport. But my plane for New York leaves in less than an hour."

"You've got your ticket?"

"Yes," I said, almost testily. "I've only got one night," I added desperately. "I have to fly to Italy tomorrow, and I'm not coming back."

"Well, I'd like to see you, but . . . I'm not sure. There are other considerations."

"What other considerations?" I could hardly keep the indignation and despair out of my voice. "I bought the ticket just so that I could see you. I'm sorry I couldn't let you know before, but — "

"Look." He was placatory. "Give me twenty minutes to track someone down and make a phone call. I have to consult someone."

"If it's your wife, I'd really love to meet her — "

"No-o, no, it's not that. Just give me twenty minutes. Have you got a pencil? Write down this number," and he dictated it while I fumbled a pen out of my bag and wrote on the back of my chequebook. "Call me there. I can't promise," he warned. "It won't be an easy decision. But call me," and the line went dead.

Decision? What decision?

I had done the wrong thing. I should be on my way to Italy. Maybe Rupert was at this very moment posting his answer to Bernice.

I used the twenty minutes to telephone Janet. It took that long. I'll never forget the shriek of delighted surprise, and the pleasure of hearing her kind, no-nonsense Canadian voice. We had written, of course; but it was better than letters to hear her chatting on about her children, and about the neighbours; who had died, who had married, where new houses had been built and new stores opened. McIver's

Place, she said, had been resold, to a Dutchman with a nice wife. They were good farmers, and were restoring my garden.

I was telling her my own news when I looked at my watch. I promised to write soon, and said goodbye.

I rang the number Zadok had given me just as the sound system broadcast the last call for my plane.

"Zadok Carroun, quick," I said, and a woman's voice said, "It's okay," and gave me an address on Central Park West. "Got that? Be there at nine tonight," she added.

"New York? Gate 23, fast," the man said, jamming a boarding-card into a ticket pouch. "Have a nice — "

But I was already on the way.

It's not easy, when you're sixty-five, to hurry. I threw my bag on to an empty trolley as I passed it, and charged up the corridor as if I were pursuing an escaping pig. Gate 23 was an age away. There was a press of people, going slower than me. "Excuse me, excuse me," I panted, and they all turned round with expressions ranging from irritation to outrage. A mad granny, they were thinking. Except that I wasn't a granny. I'd have loved to be; I thought I'd have made a good one. Grandmother – grandchild is the nicest relationship in the world. Every time I saw a child, I felt a glow of affection, and at the same time this little sad ache of memory. Oh, Zoe! If only . . .

I made it to the departure lounge just in time.

As I fastened my seatbelt on the plane, "You're mad," I said aloud.

The neatly-suited young man next to me, with worried blue eyes behind hornrimmed glasses, gave me a startled look, ostentatiously opened his newspaper, and bent his head to read it.

This whole wild-goose chase . . . what will a New York hotel cost? I asked myself. And I forgot to cancel the Toronto one, I'll have to pay for that too. "You're insane," I mumbled, and Hornrims looked up again. I realised what I must sound like, and grinned at him, and he looked relieved and grinned back.

Insane, maybe. But I was doing this for Zinnia. There was no way I could let her down.

By the time we got to Kennedy I had made friends with the young man, and heard about his Wall Street law firm and his girlfriend in Toronto. He doubted whether she would make a good wife. She had another boyfriend and was unwilling to say goodbye to him.

"Maybe he's platonic?" I suggested.

"I can't believe that," said Hornrims.

"Give it time," I said. "Take out some other girls. Forget about marrying for a little while. See what happens."

For the first time his eyes were cheerful. "I just might do that."

We talked about London, and about New York, which I had never seen, and I confided my anxiety about arriving alone in New York City lateish in the afternoon. Where could I eat that was safe for an elderly lady alone who needed to kill a few hours until a nine-o'clock appointment? He suggested we share a cab. It sounded expensive, but by that time I was past worrying about expense.

At Kennedy we went to the carousel together for our luggage and came out on the big circle of futuristic terminal buildings. By the time I had gazed around at the swooping cantilevered roofs, he had hailed a cab.

We swept out of the airport and on to the thruway. As the laconic, elevated road-signs rushed by with their strange yet familiar names, I began to feel the scarey magic of America.

I looked again at my talisman, the sliver of paper stashed away safely in my passport. "Zadok Carroun." That was magic, all right.

Wilbur (for that was his name) was sweet. He told me I reminded him of his Mom. Every now and then he mentioned his girlfriend; and from these increasingly elegiac asides I gradually realised that he had proposed earlier that day and she had turned him down. I could see why; he was a little earnest, a little lugubrious; transparently trustworthy, but far from exciting. He reminded me slightly of Henry Grey. He was kind, and he needed cheering up, so I did my best.

He seemed in no hurry to go back to his empty apartment. As we sat in the yellow cab he directed the driver on a scenic tour of Manhattan. "This is my treat," he insisted when I worried aloud about the fare. He showed me the Empire State Building and the United Nations Building and the World Trade Center and Greenwich Village and SoHo and St Patrick's Cathedral and its staggering reflection in the glass side of a skyscraper. We ended up having sandwiches, pastrami on rye, at a deli in an elegant shopping street behind the Carlyle. Wilbur told me his life-story, and we wrote down each other's addresses and telephone numbers in case we were ever in each other's neighbourhood.

"You've been very kind," I smiled at him.

"Well, you've been very understanding. I guess I couldn't have talked about it to anyone I actually knew, but I felt pretty low when we set off from Toronto. You really helped."

"D'you feel a bit better now?"

"Much better now. Look, it's getting on for nine. I'm going to escort you to your date. No, no," he waved a dismissive hand at my protests, "I'm getting a cab, and it can take me back home afterwards."

The address was a big, grey, old-fashioned apartment block on Central Park West. On the way I looked south at the incredible skyline where a million lights glittered.

It wasn't far. When the driver drew up I shook hands with Wilbur and wished him luck.

"Take out a few girls," I said. "Go to theatres, have a bit of fun."

"You really do remind me of my Mom," he said.

I smiled. "Then give her my best wishes."

"I can't – she died last year. Hey, write to me some-time."

I was touched. And if Wilbur wanted a surrogate Mom, he should have one. "I promise," I said. "You, too." He told the cabbie not to go till I got safely in the door. As soon as it opened I turned and waved goodbye, and they drove off into the night.

There was a big, black, uniformed caretaker behind a desk. I showed him Bernice's scribble.

"Mr and Mrs Carroun, right," he said. "Wait, please." He lifted the phone and dialled. "A lady here to see you . . . What name?"

"I'm Mr Carroun's Cousin Elizabeth from England," I said. "From Riverlaw."

The caretaker grinned. "You're expected," he said. "This way, please."

He took me up in a lift lined in brown suede. On the top floor, the lift doors slid open.

I was aware of a wide, white-walled hall, a thick blue carpet, a couple of good modern abstracts. A man stood in front of me. We gaped at each other. He was tall, running to fat a little, fiftyish, with a pale, roundish face, receding grey hair, a small mouth and strong jaw, and large, dark, smiling eyes under thick brows. Almond eyes like Zinnia's.

I took both his hands and kissed his cheek.

"I can't believe this. Have you seen my mother? How is she?"

"She's very well, and she's wonderful."

"How did you find us?"

While I was reminding him about Kitchener and Bernice, he took my elbow and steered me to a long, book-lined room with a grand piano at one end and a couple of deep, comfortable sofas at the other. A slim woman with long, blonde hair got up from one of the sofas and came over, smiling, towards us.

"My wife Karen."

"I'm so glad to meet you!" she said. "Ever since I met Doc I've been dying of curiosity about the rest of his family. Have you eaten? Would you care for coffee?"

"Thank you, I've eaten but I'd love coffee."

"I'll get it."

"Tell me, Zadok," I said as she walked gracefully out and we sank into one of the sofas, "do you have any children?"

"Sure. Two sons, married to very nice girls. They all work in the business with me. And a daughter – she's younger, seventeen."

"What are their names?"

"Jim and George, married to Jane and Fay. Our daughter's Dru."

"I long to meet them, Zadok."

He grinned. "Call me Doc, everyone does. One of the things I had against my mother was my name. How is she, truly?"

"She's great. She has a wonderful husband and they live in her house – your old home in St John's Wood. She doesn't know I'm here, but she'd really love to see you again." His eyes hardened a little. "What do you do for a living?" I went on hastily. I didn't want him to have a chance to refuse contact with Zinnia.

"We're in the hotel business. We've done rather well."

A door buzzer sounded. He jumped up. "Excuse me. You know I said I had to make a decision?" He strode across the room. "This may be a surprise to both of you, Cousin Elizabeth, but — " He was in the hall now and I heard him say through the intercom, "Is she here, Ezra? . . . Right, show her up!"

The lift whirred, the lift door slid open, and a woman came into the room.

"Mrs Williams," said Zadok.

I turned to look at her.

Mrs Williams was suddenly standing stock still and staring at me. She was dark and slim, and there was something familiar about her face. She was the woman whom I had glimpsed on the flat roof of the City Hall in Toronto.

I stood up. I looked at her long hands. I had seen those hands before. Her expression was tentative, self-contained, her nose straight, her eyes reminded me . . . It came on me like a clap of thunder. They reminded me of my own.

"It can't be," she said. She took a step towards me, and hesitated.

I couldn't stop gazing at her. Oh God, I implored inside my head, make it true.

"I don't believe it." I knew that quiet voice.

"You're supposed to be dead," I told her.

It couldn't be.

She said, faintly, a gleam of incredulous delight growing in her widening eyes, "What was your address in Nova Scotia?"

"Oh, Zoe, my darling love," I whispered, and burst into tears in her arms.

And that night, looking out on Central Park and the lights of Manhattan, they told me their story.

What nobody had known except themselves was that Zadok and Zoe had been penfriends for a long time before they met. Zadok said it started when his mother first went off with Lord Barbary and he was left with an old nanny in charge of him. He was bored and lonely and fed up, and assumed, of course, that Zinnia didn't love him ("Oh, if only you knew!" I interrupted) and he wanted to find an overseas penfriend. He had heard his mother talking about me, realised Zoe was about the right age and found our Nova Scotia address in Zinnia's address book. It never dawned on me that Zoe was getting letters from anybody, let alone Zinnia's son, because it was always she who emptied our mailbox on her way to school; and in London it was easy for Zadok to rush down to the front door when he heard the postman and grab Zoe's letters before the nanny got there.

Then Doc (as I learned to call him) got an evening job as a barman – strictly against school rules, of course, and he was under age; but he saved up enough to get to New York. By that time he had impressed an American customer who offered him a job in his hotel on Park Avenue. All this time he was writing to Zoe, and they poured out their hopes and unhappinesses to each other.

Meanwhile, Zoe was restless and anxious to see the world. I was stricken, as she told me about it so many years after, by the realisation that I had been an over-protective mother who never guessed that while I felt penned in and frustrated by being broke and isolated, Zoe was feeling exactly the same.

She poured all this out in her letters to Zadok, and he invited her to come and see him in New York. She was thrilled, and a little fearful too, and she promised him she would come on the first day of the Fall semester in 1939; she planned to post a note to the school the previous morning so that nobody would realise she had disappeared till the end of the day.

("What a naughty girl, imagine!" said Zinnia when I told her all this some time later – and her indignation suddenly turned to a mischievous smile. After all, she had once run away too. "What an adventure!")

The arrival of Zinnia and Peregrine to carry me off to England really mixed her up. She thought Zinnia was marvellous, but that made her feel even more guilty because she knew, or thought she knew, that Zadok hated his mother. And she was desperate to stop me going, partly because she had read an article that said there would be a war in Europe; but also because she had read my letter to Cedric, and both she and Chuck suspected (ridiculously) that I was going to run away with him. Chuck actually put the idea into her head, and she was devastated. She remembered the Major's cruel words, "She'll never come back," and realised that I had not contradicted him. She felt as if the bottom had fallen out of her world.

And it was in this frame of mind that she ran away to New York; and this was why she was in no hurry to write. She couldn't get in touch with me in England, anyway, because – as I had feared – she didn't know the address.

"But why ever didn't you write to Zinnia, Doc?" I said.

"I told Doc that his mother had a new lover," said Zoe.

"Oh, good heavens – not Peregrine?"

She nodded.

"It was too much," the pain of it was there in Zadok's face. "I had had the father and mother of a row with Zinnia before she went off with Lord Barbary. I guess I said some very hurtful things. I couldn't bring myself to write after that. I can't tell you how often I used to go over and over the memory of that fight, cursing myself for losing my temper. But I was just almost ready to write and apologise, when I heard about this man Peregrine that she was travelling with."

"But you could have written to me, Zoe!"

Zadok shifted in his seat. "I wouldn't let her. I thought we'd got to make our own lives. If she wrote to you, you'd tell my mother where we were, and it would all start again."

Zoe crossed to the window and looked out at the glittering wall of skyscrapers to our right across the park.

"It wasn't only that. I did manage to get a job in the end, helping in an infant school, but for the first few weeks I was dirt poor, and the only place I could sleep was in Zadok's room. Oh, it was very respectable! He found out soon enough" – they smiled at each other, and he took Karen's hand – "that I wasn't the sort of girl he'd kinda hoped I'd be. After that – to do you justice, Doc dear! – he was like a big brother to me. He gave me the bed and he slept on the floor – but I was very worried in case you and Dad discovered, and thought we were living together as man and wife. The church congregation in Upper Stewiacke wouldn't have stood for that, and I reckoned you wouldn't either!" She gave me such a droll sideways look that I laughed aloud. "But I never thought the break would be permanent. And what really scared me was what Dad would say. I was afraid if he found out where I was, he would come and get me, and horsewhip me or something. And then I got my job, and I met Brad and fell in love."

"Much to my relief," put in Zadok drily. "It was nice having someone on the spot to wash my shirts, and we've always been good friends, but it kinda cramped my style with the other girls. Of course, it's been different," he added hastily, "since I married Karen," and he looked lovingly into his wife's eyes. It was easy to see that Zadok had once been an accomplished ladykiller; he had Zinnia's vitality.

"When Brad proposed," went on Zoe, "I longed to introduce him to you, and I wrote to you and Dad to invite you to the wedding, and I would have written to Doc's mother too, but I knew the invitation wouldn't get there in time. But the letter I wrote to McIver's Place was returned, and the envelope was marked with one word – 'Deceased'."

"No! Oh, poor lamb! But how — " And then I realised how. It must have been the ex-waiter from Tennessee who bought the farm after the fire. Janet had told me in one of her letters that he wasn't exactly on the ball.

"The news arrived the day before the wedding," said Zadok. "Poor Zoe – and it was pretty hard on Brad too. After that it seemed we should all just forget the past, and get on with our lives without allowing ourselves to be hurt by anything else."

And they had done well. They must have worked like slaves.

Brad was a Canadian country boy who had come to New York to make enough money to fulfil his life's ambition of opening an elegant restaurant in Toronto. He met Zadok when they were both working in the Park Avenue hotel, and the two of them saved up and bought a run-down restaurant and persuaded Zoe to come to work for them. They made a success of it, sold out at a big profit, and bought a shabby hotel and did it over. A couple of deals later, Brad felt he had made enough money to fulfil his ambition in Toronto, so he and Zoe now owned an elegant establishment – which they had virtually created themselves – off York Street.

"So it really was you I saw at Toronto City Hall!" I exclaimed.

"Oh, Mother, I just couldn't believe my eyes – all weekend I was wringing my hands because it might have been you and I hadn't even come up to you and asked! And then when Doc called me and said I'd got to catch the next plane to meet someone – I knew it was the wrong city, but I was hoping against hope and praying there'd be a seat left, and desperate in case it was you and I got there too late – but it's just incredible, after all these years of thinking – knowing – you were dead!" And she gave me a great hug that told me that never again would there be coldness between us.

"Women!" groaned Zadok. "Don't you want to know what happened to me?"

Zadok had stayed in the hotel business. He told me he had just made a big profit on a country club near the Finger Lakes, and was thinking of going over to England to, as he put it, turn around some charming down-at-heel old country house hotel that needed a bit of Yankee knowhow.

At this point I remembered why I was in North America.

"What about the Old Hall at Riverlaw?" I suggested, with my heart in my mouth.

"Oh, gee, I remember it," sighed Zadok. "Peacocks on the lawn, and the whole place smelt of roses. But isn't it on the small side for a hotel?"

"How many rooms do you need?"

"Oh . . . fifty bedrooms minimum, I'd say, to make it worthwhile."

My face must have fallen, because Zoe said quickly, "But may we come and visit there? You must meet Brad and our children — and Charles, our eldest, is having a baby soon, or rather his wife Mary is. You'll have a great-grandchild! Maybe we could all come?"

There was an instant's silence. "Don't look at *me*," said Zadok. "Leastwise, not if my mother's going to be there."

I couldn't believe that I could have got this far, only to meet with such a setback. I looked at Karen.

"Oh, go on, Doc," she coaxed. "I really like the sound of those peacocks."

"You wouldn't if you heard them," I found myself laughing. "Remember, Doc? But they're white, and they really look gorgeous."

"I just couldn't meet her, not after all we went through." Something about his set face tugged at my memory.

"You know, Doc," I said slowly, "I've known your mother much longer than you have. And there are things about her early life that I bet you don't know. You have more in common with her than you realise. Did you know that when she was about the age you were when you came to America, she ran away from home and it was months before she was found?"

Zadok stared. "No. I didn't."

"White peacocks," sighed Karen. "Wouldn't I just love to see them." She winked at me. That wink gave me courage.

"She was quite a tearaway, you know. But very vulnerable always. I think the truth was that she needed more than most people to be loved and looked after, and it wasn't till she was quite old that she discovered her own strength. Sometimes, she would do something she thought would be disapproved of, and I can remember her saying to me," I searched my memory for the words, 'For God's sake, if you love me at all, don't tell Mother!' "

"No! Oh, no!" and Zoe, darling Zoe, collapsed in peals

of laughter. "What a family we are! Doc, would you ever believe the irony of that? After this, Doc, you've just *got* to come!"

There was a long silence.

We all looked at him.

Zadok shook his head. And with a rueful smile, he said something that took me back, back through the years to a cold dawn in the Riverpark lane, as I shivered in Rednall's trap with my feet on a crocodile dressing-case . . .

"Anything, *anything* rather than face Mother!"

I stayed the night. ("You can have the Heads of State suite in the hotel, or this chesterfield and the put-you-up in my study down the hall," Zadok had said; but there was no doubt in my mind about the answer, and Zoe's good-night hug in the study told me I was right.) We talked a hundred to the dozen, and I learnt enough about my grandchildren Charles, David and Mary-Anne Williams, and Zadok's children Jim, George and Dru Carroun, to make me feel I knew them. We all made plans to meet soon. They pressed me to stay longer, but I knew I had to go to Italy, and quickly. When I explained why, Zadok phoned Alitalia and reconfirmed the flight. Zadok was a man of action; every inch his mother's son.

And before I went to sleep, I sat down at Zadok's own desk in his study, and wrote him a letter about Zinnia. I put all the gentle persuasion I could muster into that letter, because it would be my last chance to mend a quarrel that had marred two lives for half a lifetime. I left the letter under my pillow, where Karen would find it after I had gone. I felt she and Zoe would be my allies; and that gave me hope.

After an early breakfast together, I kissed Zadok and Karen goodbye, and Zoe borrowed Karen's car to drive me to the airport.

"Good luck, Mother," she said as she pressed my hand

outside the Departures gate. "I hope you save the house at Riverlaw. I can see how much it means to you. We would help, but we have to take care over our enterprises, because the children are partners and work with us. We can't lose too much, or the boys might find they couldn't afford families."

I found her earnest maternal caution deeply touching.

"It's so wonderful to have found you," I said.

"It's so wonderful to have found you!" There were tears in her eyes.

"Goodbye, dearest. Take care."

"Goodbye, Mother," and she threw her arms round my neck. "See you very soon!"

I was on the plane and fastening my seatbelt, thinking about them all as I fumbled with the clasp, when there was an announcement on the public address system. Out of, as it were, the corner of my ear I heard that someone was being asked to make themselves known to the stewards.

After a minute the announcement was repeated, and this time I listened.

It was for me.

Amazed, shocked, a little fearful – was it an accident to someone I loved, a death even? – I made my way along the aisle and spoke to a black steward. He looked at me and grinned.

"It's a radio message. You been gambling, ma'am?"

"Me? No, why – "

He handed me a scrap of paper. Slowly I unfolded it. It read:

"Okay, you win! Love from us all, Zadoc."

I couldn't sleep on the plane for thinking about them.

By the time we reached Milan airport I was dreadfully tired, and wondering again about the wisdom of my journey. I didn't even know whether Rupert Delmayne would be there. I wouldn't know him if I saw him. And what could I possibly say? My brain whirred round uselessly like a moth beating itself against a light.

I summoned my rudimentary Italian to change one of my dwindling travellers' cheques at the airport. Then I grabbed a taxi, drove in to the city to the grandiose train station, and caught the next train to Firenze. A nice American tourist next to me saw that I was jetlagged and volunteered to wake me when we arrived. Once there, I wove my way through throngs of young, rucksacked travellers in sloganed T-shirts and cut-off jeans, to find a taxi.

We curved up the hill towards Fiesole. Looking back, I saw Florence shimmering below; the dome of the Baptistery pale above the jumbled roofs and towers, the silvery Arno serene in its bowl of hills.

Up in Fiesole the air seemed clearer and lighter, the view more ethereal. Light and ethereal seemed to describe my brain, now fragile with exhaustion.

The taxi-driver stopped at the bottom of a path that led straight up the side of a hill, and pointed.

When I had counted out the lire into his hand, he turned the taxi with one swift rev of the engine, and shot off down the hill. I was alone.

I picked up my case. It seemed very heavy. I set off slowly up the steep path, resting every few yards. I passed three or four houses, and began to think I would never manage to go further. But after one more effort, there was the sign, Casa Bella Vista in elegant blue lettering, on my right.

I rat-tatted with the iron knocker. The house was small, colourwashed pale yellow, with only one little top window. The other windows must face the view.

Nobody came. It was extraordinarily quiet. I thought, All this way for nothing? I knocked again. "Hello?" I called, ridiculously English.

"*Momento*," called a man's voice from inside. There was a snapping of bolts, and the door opened.

The man facing me was small, balding, tanned. He had a narrow face, with pointed features that gave him an almost elfin look. He wore paint-smeared cotton trousers, and a gold neck-chain over his bare chest.

"Mr Rupert Delmayne?" I said uncertainly.

"You're speaking to him."

"I knew your mother years ago," I said. "You're like her." I told him my name. "And I've visited Riverpark many times."

He hesitated. "You'd better come in."

He led me through the main room of the house. It was not large, and the walls were lined with stacks of canvases. There were easels and a battered table with more canvases, tins and tubes of paint, mugs of brushes, rags, and all the other enticing impedimenta of the artist's life. Most of the pictures faced the wall, but those I could see looked like Old Masters. I thought I glimpsed a Raphael, but I couldn't be sure – anyway, what was a Raphael doing here?

The whole further side of the room was open to a wide balcony overlooking a staggering view of Florence.

There was a white table and cushioned basket chairs on the balcony, but Rupert Delmayne didn't invite me to sit down. "And what can I do for you?" he enquired.

I felt too tired to beat about the bush.

"You may be getting a letter," I began, "from someone named Delmayne in Toronto," and I went on to explain, haltingly, as best I could, why it was desperately important to me and to the Riverlaw Delmaynes that he should not give leave – to Leslie Brown, Bernice Delmayne, or anyone else – for the Riverpark estate to be sold.

He heard me out in silence. At last:

"You're too late," he said.

LONDON

41

Early that evening I arrived in London.

I took a taxi from Heathrow to Zinnia's house, and rang the bell. She opened the door herself, crowed with delighted surprise as she hugged me on the doorstep, and led me into the cool, white hall with its curving Georgian staircase. Her white hair was softly knotted at the nape, her face beautifully made up as always.

"I like the suit," I said.

She grinned. "Not as rich as I look. Last day of the Chanel sale in Sloane Street." She led me up the stairs. "The lord and master's away on business, so we'll have a lovely lot of time to sit and gossip. Put your things in the spare bedroom, then come and tell me the news before you sleep off the jetlag."

So we sat in her pretty blue drawing-room with its Georgian furniture and chintz sofas and leafy view, and I told her about Riverlaw and our Canadian cousins.

"The sods!" she exclaimed when I had finished. "Do you think they'll take the law into their own hands and just pull it down?"

"They want to."

"You don't think we could enlist Leslie as our ally? He's so crafty, he might be able to stop them."

I smiled. "Machiavelli would be proud of you. But don't forget that Leslie's been trying to sell the place. All they've got to do is offer him more money than the scrap-dealer and he'll take it and run."

"God, what a situation! We're between the devil and the deep blue sea. Poor Cedric must be turning in his grave. Left to Leslie, indeed!"

"There's just one thing that might be useful," I said. "I went to Italy today — "

"No!" Zinnia threw up her hands in admiration. It was easy to see why so many men had loved her; her ability to make other people's very ordinary actions seem clever amounted to genius.

"I looked up Cedric's son Rupert. He's a painter. But there's something slightly odd about him. He tried very hard to persuade me not to tell anyone about his painting. I wonder if he's a forger. Anyway, he thawed out a little when I admired some of his pictures, and he suggested I might like to have a look at some of his mother's old photo albums. He even offered to give them to me – obviously he doesn't care two jots about the family. Well, we were sitting in what had been her bedroom, surrounded by albums and old letter-files and general mess – and he went out to answer the phone, and I did a dreadful thing. I saw in one file a bunch of old British passports, and I stole one."

"You *what*?"

"Well, I couldn't bear the thought of Leslie's manufactured will being so totally against what Cedric would have wanted. And look," I opened my purse and took out the passport. It was dusty, and one corner was clipped off. It was strange to see the old, good-quality British passport that gave us such confidence in Britain.

Zinnia opened it wonderingly.

"It's Madge's. She'd be spitting mad if she knew. You shouldn't have done it, Lizzie."

"I know. But it's worth nothing. It's useless. And it's our proof, don't you see? It only proves the truth, that Rupert wasn't Cedric's son at all."

She turned the pages. "But how . . . ?"

"Look at the entry stamps."

"But there are hardly any. She went to Italy in February

1937 – that must have been when she left Cedric – and didn't come back till April 1938. Then, here's Rupert added on, born June 1938 . . . Oh, Lizzie, I see what you mean!"

"I bet you Cedric never left England. If we can find his passport – if he had one – we can prove it. And I bet you Leslie Brown spent most of his holidays in Italy. Wouldn't he have wanted Riverpark left to his son?"

"You're right." She leapt up with excitement. "You're right!"

"But it doesn't really solve our problem," I added. "Rupert's fairly hard up, I think. He told me he'd signed away his reversion to Leslie in exchange for a quarter of the profits of the sale of Riverpark and Riverlaw."

"So we're back where we started," Zinnia groaned. "I knew Cedric was dim, but I hadn't thought he was quite dim enough to make a mess of his will, of all things." She paced the room. "What can we do?"

"I could produce a little money – but not nearly enough to buy the place. And the Old Hall repairs would run well into five figures, and we couldn't restore it without doing something for the villagers as well. Bathrooms and damp-courses and main drainage all round – it'd cost a fortune. We might get local authority grants, but we'd have to match them, and they might well say the whole place was too tumbledown and they'd build council flats instead. It'll fall down of its own accord if something isn't done quickly. But we just couldn't afford to buy and repair it between us all."

"Even if Leslie gave us the estate for nothing, which he certainly won't, these wretched people would come over from Canada and say it was theirs," Zinnia pointed out. "Could we finance a lawsuit that we'd have almost no chance of winning? I suppose we could get Ivy over as a witness – "

"She couldn't travel. She'd have to make a sworn statement in Canada. And they would tell her what to say, and make sure she said it. I don't think they're very nice to her."

Zinnia sat down and clasped her hands behind her head. "We've got just one hope. We need a good lawyer, and we also need to know exactly what Cedric put in his will."

"Right. Well, before we go down to Somerset House to find the official copy, there's one more thing I'm bursting to tell you," I said. "I left it till last to cheer us up. The Canadian Delmaynes gave me the address of a man they'd met once who, because their name was Delmayne, asked them if they knew a village in England called Riverlaw. He lives in New York and I went to see him on the way home."

"You went to see him? When all this was going on?"

"And I'd happened to catch a glimpse of a woman in Toronto, and she reminded me of somebody." I couldn't help smiling to myself. "And when I heard the man's name – this was the man they'd told me about – of course I simply had to see him."

"Well, what was his name?"

"And meanwhile he'd phoned her in Toronto and she caught the plane after me, and walked into this flat on Central Park while I was there, and it was the same woman. And they're old friends and they're both married and they've got three children each — "

"Lizzie darling, who in heaven's name are you talking about?"

"They gave me the most incredible welcome and sent masses of love and they're coming over to see us soon. You see," I said, my bottled-up happiness bursting out at last so that I had to fish for my handkerchief before the tears came, "I told you the woman I saw in Toronto reminded me of someone, and that someone was myself. Her name is Zoe, and the man who found her for me is Zadok Carroun!"

After Zinnia had hugged me and wept and jumped up and down with delight and been restrained with difficulty from rushing out with only her handbag and getting the next plane to New York, and after I had phoned home to report my safe arrival and declare the great news all over again, we went to bed.

And then the phone rang.

Zinnia must have answered it in her bedroom, next to mine. Even through the solid wall and the panelled Georgian doors I heard her shriek of surprise.

I thought it must be Zadok phoning from New York, so I turned over and went to sleep again, smiling.

Next morning, over coffee and orange juice in her little white kitchen, she was still exclaiming.

"It's incredible! I still can't believe it! After all those years! But why ever didn't they write to us?"

"I gather you had the father and mother of a row with Doc – Zadok, I mean – before you went away with Miles."

"Yes. He said some very hurtful things to me. They haunted me for years. I expect they were all true, but I was livid with him. I can't tell you, Lizzie, how I used to go over and over the memory of that fight, cursing myself for losing my temper and driving him away."

"I think you'll find he thinks exactly the same himself. He didn't write because of what you'd both said to each other, and he wouldn't even let Zoe write to me, at first, because he knew I'd tell you where they both were. But he blamed himself just as much as you."

Zinnia, pouring Frugrains into pottery bowls, said nothing.

"I don't believe they ever thought the break would be permanent – Zoe certainly didn't. And he's longing to see you, Zinnia. He and Karen are devoted to each other – I know you'll love them. You'll see them soon. They were already thinking of coming to England to, as Doc put it, turn around some charming down-at-heel old country house hotel that needs a bit of Yankee knowhow."

"Goodness," beamed Zinnia, "is that my son?"

There was a rattle at the far end of the hall, and Zinnia leapt up and literally ran out of the kitchen and over the Persian rug to the letter-box. I envied her her energy. If she hadn't woken me with early-morning tea, I could have slept the clock round. I was too old to disregard jetlag; I felt distinctly bleary.

"It's come! It's come!" She waved a huge buff envelope. "Vane rang me last night. He wouldn't tell me the details – really, he's getting very mean over phone bills. But I think you'll find this interesting!"

"What is it?"

"Come into the dining-room," she commanded, leading the way, "and we'll have more room to look at it properly." For a second, I saw a dark-haired girl in a long, blue skirt, sixty years earlier, effortlessly taking over the organisation of a cricket-match outside the pineapple-topped gateposts at Riverlaw.

We sat side by side at her mahogany table.

"Well, open it!" I said, a touch testily.

"Are you feeling strong?"

"No. But it can't be from Vane – look, the postmark's London. I expect it's Harvey Nichols' catalogue." After all the journeying and excitements of the past three days, I felt a powerful urge to go back to bed.

She handed it to me. "Don't just stare into space," she said affectionately. "You open it."

Obediently, I did. I pulled out a letter, which I put on one side, and a big sheaf of thick white paper. Its typed title was upside down, so I turned it and smoothed it on the table in front of us, and we sat and gazed at the Last Will and Testament of Cedric Algernon Vane Delmayne.

"Better read the letter first," said Zinnia at last, reaching for it and getting a pair of red-framed glasses out of her dressing-gown pocket.

"Well, what does it say?"

She smiled. "Briefly, when Leslie Brown tried to get probate for Cedric's will at Somerset House, the probate authorities discovered that a later will made by Cedric had been deposited there quite recently, by the extremely respectable London solicitor who wrote this letter," and she tapped it.

"I told Cedric to get a good lawyer!" I remembered.

"And he did. And you realise what this means. The will Leslie made Cedric sign is superseded. Leslie can't have known about this later one. This will, here, is the real McCoy."

My hand hesitated over the sheaf of pages. I thought affectionately of Cedric sitting in lonely splendour at the vast dining-table at Riverpark, bemused by a column of figures.

"You know," I said, "dear old Cedric had a positive genius for not getting things quite right. I wonder what he's done this time."

"Well, let's have a look!"

There were a good many pages, perfectly typed on thick lawyers' paper, with a generous sprinkling of Whereases and Hereinbefores.

"It's just a blur," I said. "I'm so frightfully tired I can't understand a word. Do please translate into English."

Zinnia put on her glasses again and leafed over the pages with a puzzled expression.

"'Whereas', let's see – Cedric 'by the Deed executed on the tenth day of March nineteen hundred and seventy is the sole beneficial owner of', et cetera . . . Good God!"

"What is it?"

"Well, it's rather nice, really. He's left Riverpark, together with its contents except as hereinbelow stated, to the National Society for the Prevention of Cruelty to Children, to be used as a Children's Home, together with all that Demesne . . . blah blah blah . . . Well, the drift of this bit is that the Children's Home is to be endowed by all his stocks and shares and securities, together with

all that farmland on the Riverpark Estate comprising . . .
blah blah blah . . . and including the farmland attached
to," she looked at me, "the Old Hall at Riverlaw."

"Oh . . . Poor Cedric, he had such a wretched childhood
himself. But the farm – how dreadful! What'll Vane do?
Go on."

" 'And whereas' . . . Oh Lord, this lawyers' language!
. . . 'all freeholds in the village of Riverlaw, comprising'
. . . et cetera . . . The upshot of this page," she tapped it
with an immaculately-polished fingernail, "is that he's left
every house to its tenant."

"Good old Cedric! Oh, that's marvellous! So does that
mean that the Old Hall belongs to Aunt Emily, or to Vane,
or who?"

She frowned. "The Old Hall hasn't been mentioned yet.
And come to think of it, Lizzie, if he's left the land to
the orphanage, how are our darlings going to live? They're
pretty old, and their only income is from the farm, you
know. Mother never saved a ha'penny; the solicitors sent
money every year for the upkeep of Ivy and her child, so
that took a big slice. Oh, Lord, trust dear old Cedric to
mess things up as usual!" She turned a page. "There's an
incomprehensible legal paragraph here – I think the drift
of it is that Cedric had made a sworn statement that he
had never fathered a child. And there's something about
the entail being determined – that means ended. Blah blah
. . . hereinbefore mentioned . . ."

"Well, go on!"

"His cars to Vane – that's nice – his gold half-hunter
watch and chain to Albert Nibbs. I rather regret I never
had any time for Cedric, there was something rather decent
about him, wasn't there? Other jewellery, pictures and
personal chattels to be divided between cousins Venetia,
Zinnia and Louisa – sweet of him, considering how foul
we always were to him. I think I'll bag the tiger from the
hall before it frightens the orphans – I always adored it.
I suppose he wouldn't leave anything to Mother anyway,

because she's so old; probably thought she'd be bound to die before he did. He must have made this will just after Aunt Letitia died – yes, look at the date. Oh, look – bequests of one thousand pounds free of tax to every servant in his employ for more than one year, ten thousand pounds for more than ten years. Very nice. Nothing to you, sorry, darling. I'm quite surprised, I always suspected he fancied you. At least – good *heavens*!"

"What is it?"

"My dear Lizzie, Cedric has left the Old Hall to you."

RIVERLAW

42

And that wasn't the last surprise I had that autumn.

It must have been a wonderful moment when Cedric's London solicitor, a titled and pinstriped gentleman of the utmost discretion and respectability, confronted Leslie with Cedric's will and revealed that, far from leaving himself in the hands of Leslie's crooked lawyer friend, Cedric had been getting a little legal advice on his own.

The interview was in the nick of time, because Leslie had just put down a deposit on a luxurious villa in the Bahamas with the first instalment of the purchase-price of the entire estate, which he had received in cash from an ambitious and fairly innocent scrap-metal dealer who was understandably indignant when the sale fell through. Later, he sued Leslie for the return of the money, and got it, because Leslie had not, of course, been granted probate and had had no right to put the estate up for sale at all.

In Riverlaw it was generally concluded that Leslie had been salting away some of the profits from Riverpark for years. After the case he was never seen again. Never in Northumberland, that is.

But some years after Cedric's death, Dr Bond's great-nephew, who was having a little flutter in the casino in Monte Carlo, noticed at the next table a slight, grey, cadaverous figure who was losing heavily. It was Leslie, looking very gloomy indeed. In the course of conversation he revealed that he had just been turned out of his lodgings for non-payment of rent, and at the end of the evening he asked Dr Bond's great-nephew for the price of a drink.

Meanwhile, Cedric's genius for not getting things quite right was causing a good deal of anxiety to the Riverlaw Delmaynes and myself. I was deeply happy to be the owner of the house I loved more than any other in the world; but it was in a parlous state of repair. I did have some capital – I had years ago invested the proceeds of my parents' house – but I was in no position to pay a colossal repair bill.

On examination, the Old Hall was not irretrievable. It urgently needed a new roof, certainly, and in the wing beyond the stable arch the dour smell of rot led to the discovery of malevolent fungoid growths in the back of long-unused cupboards. In the old maids' bedrooms a finger drawn along a beam would release a cascade of powdered wood on to one's head. But the main rooms on the garden side needed little more than redecorating, and although most people would have thrown up their hands at the old-fashioned kitchen and bathroom, we liked them as they were.

Cedric, I am quite sure, had known I would ask my cousins and aunt to go on living in the house, and I assured them of this. But separating the house from the farmland had pulled the rug, financially speaking, from under their feet. Apart from the orchard – which was old and not very productive – and the kitchen garden, the chickens and the pigs, they seemed to have almost nothing to live on. Venetia and Charles – who had retired – drove over to see them almost every week, laden with home-made jams and cakes and pies, and enormous bunches of flowers. Full-time Gertie retired, and was replaced by a part-time skivvy called Carole.

There were, of course, potential sources of income. Vane started a chicken-farm in some of the less tumbledown farm buildings, and he began to grow flowers and vegetables for market, and kept horses at livery for the local pony club. But there were three mouths to feed, all now over sixty-five, and Aunt Emily was over ninety and needed a lot of looking after.

Wizened and lame, shrunken and hunched, half-blind, and unable, now, to smell or taste, Aunt Emily was nevertheless still in full possession of her other faculties and still ruled the Old Hall as she had always done. She seldom came downstairs these days, but sat by the schoolroom fire, swathed in her rose-red cashmere cardigan and a shawl secured with knobbly fingers by means of a large marcasite brooch depicting a hound chasing a fox. If she wanted attention she would bang with her stick on the floor. When I was there, she and I spent a good deal of time playing Patience with giant cards that she could see. She usually won.

After the discovery of Cedric's will, Zinnia and I got the solicitor to write to Ivy's family in Ontario and send them a copy of it. For a time I was very apprehensive in case they challenged the will and carried out their threat of demolition. But nothing happened, and eventually I realised that the will had effectively spiked their guns. I never heard from them again.

But one omission niggled at my conscience.

Eventually I unpacked the old sweet-tin that I had removed from the train-room rafters shortly before my visit to Ontario. I went down to the schoolroom, sat down beside Aunt Emily as she stared into the fire with the timeless patience of the very old, and took out the letter I had meant to give to Theodore's son.

"What have you got there?" she said in her old cracked voice.

"A letter addressed to you. Written a long time ago. Afraid you didn't look at it at the time."

"Well, you'd better read it to me now."

"Are you sure you want that? It's about Theodore."

There was a long silence.

Then she said, so quietly that I could scarcely hear, "The greatest disappointment in my whole life, that boy.

411

I thought he was a hero. I couldn't bear it when he proved to be rotten. Well, it's all a very long time ago. Read it, read it, if you want to."

I opened the faded envelope with its brown stamp marked three halfpence, and unfolded the cheap ruled paper with its careful lines of pencilled writing.

The room was very still. In the orchard beyond the garden a distant blackbird exulted, and the leaves of the great pear-tree outside the window stirred a little among its lichened and dying branches. If I strain my eyes, I thought, I might see Theodore's old tweed jacket with the poacher's pockets, and the brown hair flapping over his forehead, and his rosy-cheeked grin between the leaves.

Dear Madam (I read),

I hope you will excuse the liberty I take in writing you at this time, but I have just learned from Major Johnson of the great sorrow you are called on to bear, by the loss of your dear boy.

On behalf of the men of the Durham Light Infantry, and on my own behalf, I beg to offer you my deep sympathy in your heavy loss, and trust you will find strength to take you through these dark times. I know that any words of mine are so futile, and can do little to ease the pain at your heart at this time, but it may comfort you a little to know how much the men trusted and loved your boy. It is no exaggeration to say that there was no officer or man in the Regiment who was more highly thought of than he.

If I may I will tell you one incident among many others which earned the great esteem in which your son was held by the Regiment. It was away up on a lonely Ridge in Flanders in the autumn of '16. We were lying in shell holes all day and night with no cover and very little food, and the Germans were putting over a very heavy barrage. We dared not show ourselves and had just to lie there in the sleet and rain. The men were losing heart, and it was then your boy, by sheer force of example, and by sharing what little food he had with the men, and wrapping the weakest and coldest of them in his own greatcoat, telling them jokes, creeping from one to the other all day long, talking to them and so kept up their spirits till relieved. His conduct during all that awful time made a deep impression on his men, so quietly and surely he found a way to their hearts. They would have done anything for him I am perfectly sure, and we had no officer we trusted more than he.

I hope you will forgive my intrusion in your grief, dear Madam,

I am, yours Respectfully,

John Fergus, Corporal, D.L.I.

Aunt Emily never said anything about Corporal Fergus's letter. But I detected in her a kind of serenity that she had never had before, and a mellowness I had not seen since those far-distant days when she had surveyed her children with Uncle Vane at her side.

I was glad I had not given the letter, as I had intended, to Theodore's son who had turned out not to be his son at all. It was an extraordinary turn of fate that the five Delmayne children of Riverlaw had no descendants apart from Anne Dawson in her convent, except the children of Zinnia's son Zadok Carroun, who was not Rednall's son. I kept the Corporal's letter to give to them when I knew them better and could tell them more about their Uncle Theodore.

But before I had carried the letter to Canada and back I had made a copy of it. This copy I now put in a sealed envelope with an explanatory note, and addressed it to Kitchener's grandson Dean, to be opened on his eighteenth birthday. I sent it to be deposited in the Royal Bank of Canada in Toronto, and posted a brief note about its existence to Kitchener and Bernice. I had grave doubts as to the kind of upbringing Ivy's family might give young Dean; but he was, after all, Uncle Vane's great-grandson.

413

None of the Delmaynes, in the years I had known Riverlaw, had proved to be quite what they seemed. And perhaps young Dean, despite the duplicity of his great-grandmother and the greed of his grandparents, might one day be moved by Theodore's heroism to make of his own life something wonderful.

And two more things were to happen, that autumn of 1970, which solved the last mysteries of Riverlaw, and in the end changed all our lives.

In October the Zeds, as Louie called them – Zadok and Zoe – descended on Riverlaw. Zadok brought his two tall, lively sons, Jim and George – Karen and Dru would have to visit later, in the school holidays. Zoe's dark, quiet, bright-eyed daughter Mary-Anne came with her, leaving Brad, Charles and David to hold the fort in the business, and come later when Charles's baby girl was big enough to travel. Zinnia, of course, came from London to be with us, and was desolated to have to go to Leeds for two days in the middle of their stay, to sit on a Royal Commission. She could hardly take her eyes off them, and the boys were clearly thrilled to have such an elegant and able grandmother.

"Say, may we call you Grandma?" said eager George from the sofa as we sat round a log fire in the drawing-room on the first evening.

"Call me anything you like, darling boy," and Zinnia put her arm round him. "You're just like your father was at that age — " and suddenly she turned away and tugged a lace handkerchief out of her sleeve.

Tactful Jim, from the far side of the room, leaned forward to distract us from her happy tears. "What was Grandma like when she was young, Cousin Lizzie?"

"Perfectly beautiful. Quite like Mary-Anne here," and my shy granddaughter beamed. "Rather wicked, though. I was always a bit afraid she was going to burn her boats."

"I guess this family has a tendency to boat-burning," put in Zadok drily.

"It's a curious thing, though," said Zinnia, who had already recovered her aplomb, "that I wasn't ever happy and contented until I'd stopped burning boats and started looking after other people."

"Don't burn 'em, build 'em," whispered Mary-Anne.

And when Jim's brown eyes twinkled they could have been Theodore's.

I could have listened for ever to my daughter's good sense and our grandchildren's jokes and cross-talk and earnest idealism. They sat on the floor at Aunt Emily's feet, and exclaimed at the charm of the house and the scented loveliness of the garden. They even went to Rednall-the-house and crept awestruck up the drive to gaze, although they told me that because Zinnia had explained that she and Rednall had got a divorce a short time before her second marriage, they dared not go right up to the portico.

Moved by this delicacy, I took my courage in both hands and, in Zinnia's absence, telephoned Rednall.

"Why, Elizabeth!" His light voice sounded just the same. "Seems years since we met. I'm rather geriatric now, you know. Don't go out any more."

I explained that Zadok and two of his children, as well as my daughter and granddaughter, were in England.

"Send 'em along! I'd like to see what they're like. I live at the back of the house now, you know – easier to heat, and I really only need a couple of rooms. Tell 'em to come in under the stable clock, and it's the second door on the left. D'you think they'll like Bovril?"

"Isn't he just charming?" exclaimed Mary-Anne when they streamed back into the Old Hall next day after their visit to Rednall. "So courteous, although he looked so old and ill. He talked to each of us and let us look at the whole house. It is *incredible*. Gilded columns and ceiling paintings, just for starters. We even went upstairs and there are bathrooms out of the ark, literally. He consulted Uncle Doc about the repairs to the dome as if he'd known him for years, and asked him about the hotel business. Uncle Doc liked him so much he offered him a free suite on Park Avenue, any time he wanted – I think they really liked each other, you know? And he even boiled a kettle himself, imagine, and gave us this weird drink. He's a real nice old gentleman. But imagine living in just two little rooms, when he has hundreds! You could quarter an army in there. What an amazing place!"

One of the nicest things about this speech was the way Zoe caught my eye in the middle of it, binding me into a complicity of fond amusement at the way her daughter's shyness had been forgotten. For the first time for many years, I wished that Chuck was there to see.

At the end of the week we hugged and kissed the Zeds and the darling grandchildren goodbye and made them promise to come back soon and bring all the members of both families who had had to stay behind.

Zinnia was going back with them to London to see them off at Heathrow. Vane was exhibiting produce at the county show that day, so Louie and I waved the Heathrow party off in their big hired car, and hurried down to the pineapple gates to get a last glimpse of them, just as we had always done in the old days, as the car diminished and disappeared past the doctor's house at the top of Riverlaw.

We turned back to the house.

"I got a letter this morning," said Louie.

I looked at her. Fat, ugly, grey-haired, Louie yet had a kind of dignity; and I saw that her dark, still-alert eyes, sunk now in folds of fat, were sad.

"Who from?"

"A publisher."

I took her hand as we walked along, and smiled.

"Still writing?"

"I did give up for a long time, but I never quite stopped hoping. I did so long to see my name in print . . . But I'm giving up, Lizzie. I've got to be realistic. The amount I've spent in postage over the years, alone, would have kept me in furbelows." She wasn't smiling.

"Poor old Louie. You've been a real trier, haven't you?"

" 'Spose so," she said. "But what good has it done? I'm a failure, that's what. Sometimes I almost feel like doing away with myself. All those years, all those millions of words, and nothing to show for it."

I turned on her. "But you *have*! Dear Louie, you *have*! It was you who taught me to read, and it was your letters that cheered me up and kept me going all those years in Canada — "

She looked at me doubtfully.

" — You've kept Aunt Emily and Vane happy, and been so wonderful helping us all to enjoy our lives. Any fool can write a book, Louie, but you have a gift that's much more precious. Because we all love you for what you are, and for being so nice, and we couldn't do without you!"

She swung my hand, as we had so often swung hands, years ago.

"Do you honestly think so?"

"Dear Louie, I do indeed."

And her eyes shone.

One day, a fortnight after the Zeds and Zinnia had gone, the telephone rang. It was Zinnia.

"I've just had very sad news," she said. "Rednall's dead."

"I am so sorry. What a wonderful thing that the Zeds got to see him. I hadn't seen him for years, which is awful considering we're so near."

"I know, I hadn't either. I was afraid of meeting his mother, but she died a couple of years ago so I really have no excuse. I did write to him when you originally found Zadok and Zoe, and told him all about them – I thought he might be interested to know – but he never replied."

"When's the funeral?"

"Friday. I'm going to stay a night or two at Riverlaw."

"Of course. I think we should all go, don't you?"

"I was hoping you'd say that," said Zinnia.

"Is Madge still alive? I should have asked her son Rupert when I went to see him in Italy, but I didn't get round to it."

"Yes, but she married an Italian Count, years ago. Only poor old Rednall lived in the house, all alone. I feel rather bad about it because in spite of everything, I rather liked him. He was really nice about getting a divorce when I married again, wished me happy ever after."

"Zinnia," I said, "what's going to happen to his house?"

"Well, that's the amazing thing. A very grand solicitor rang to tell me. I thought it would go to Madge, but I suppose he thought leaving it to someone younger would save the estate from paying capital transfer tax twice. The whole estate has been left outright to – and I quote – 'My son, Zadok Carroun'."

"*His* son? Zinnia, are you *sure*?"

"That's what it says. And you know what that means. He was born in wedlock. I put Rednall as his father on the birth certificate. Zadok will be Sir Zadok now, and Karen will be Lady Carroun. And the solicitor told me the date of the will – it was three days after the Zeds visited him."

"Zinnia, I'm totally confused. Are you telling me that Zadok actually was Rednall's son?"

"No, I'm not and he wasn't. But Rednall's will means that nobody will ever know that except you and me, and probably his real father. It was pretty decent of old Rednall, wasn't it?"

"Jolly decent, considering. And the house – d'you think it would benefit from a bit of Yankee knowhow?"

Zinnia laughed. "Exactly what I was thinking, and I bet Rednall thought so too. Zadok has profits and backers just waiting till he finds a good project – he told me so – and he knows how to raise more. A lot of the land will have to be sold, I suppose, to pay death duties, and the repairs will cost a small fortune, but if the house is his for nothing . . . It'll make the most splendid country-house hotel in the north."

"We'll have to tell everyone we know so that they'll go and stay there."

"Absolutely. But, Lizzie – I say – you weren't thinking of telling anyone who his real father was, were you?"

"No, of course not. Would I do that?"

"No, you wouldn't. All these years – you've been a real brick, Lizzie, a true friend. I've always been a bit afraid the truth would come out when Rednall died, and I'm so glad it hasn't, for Zadok's sake. But Lizzie – do you actually know who the real father was?"

I paused. My memory moved back over the years to the darkened train-room, to the shaft of moonlight on twined bodies, to my heart full of jealous and agonised love.

I said, "The less said about that, the better."

There flashed through my mind a day in February, halfway through the second world war, when I was travelling north from London to spend a seven-day leave at Riverlaw. The railways were economising on heating as part of the war effort, and the train was horribly cold. It was also worn and dirty, the windows were so coated with grime that it was hard to see out, and the corridors were full of knobbly kitbags and bored soldiers and sailors, all staring at me. I couldn't find a seat. I had to edge my way along trying to look unconcerned at their comments. The stink of cheap cigarettes thickened the stale air, and someone spilt ash down the immaculate navy sleeve of my Wren uniform, leaving a small burn-mark on the gold braid. Someone else started singing the Cicely Courtneidge hit,

"I'm one of the oldest hens (pom pom) in the Wrens,
I'm one of the oldest tugboats in the Fleet –

sorry, darling, didn't mean you!" But, of course, he had done it to attract my attention, to take a rise. I felt nettled and ruffled. Dash it all, I was only thirty-seven, and looked young for my age. I straightened my tricorne, grasped my duffel-bag more firmly, and pushed my way to the end of the coach. Luckily, the door to the first-class section was open. I fell through it, and turned into the first carriage I came to, which was empty except for one officer in khaki. I sat down and heaved a sigh of relief.

"Let me put that in the rack for you," and my new travelling companion got up, seized the duffel-bag, and lifted it to the netting rack above my head. He looked at the label, and back at me. I looked at him.

"It's Lizzie, isn't it?"

"Lizzie McIver now, yes."

"I can't believe it. You haven't changed all that much."

"Nor have you," I said politely. But he had. He was fat, his brass buttons straining against the buttonholes, and his face had become rounder and flabbier and the skin ruddy and coarse-pored. His hair had receded above the low forehead, leaving a greasy dome. Still, it was the same Bertram.

"You're looking very good," he said, with a smile uncomfortably like a leer.

"I owe you half a sovereign."

"What?"

"Oh, never mind. We met on another train, ages ago. I spent it on a wedding-present for Zinnia Delmayne, anyway." I thought fondly of the ginger-jar, which she kept in her London bathroom still, full of delicious French soap.

"Oh, God, yes. Now I remember. I was petrified you'd split on me, but you never did, did you? A wedding-present for Zinnia, well I'm damned. Very appropriate, I must say!" and he began to laugh, his jowls shaking, his fat stomach quivering under the taut khaki cloth. He laughed and laughed until it turned into the dry bark of a smoker's cough; his face turned crimson and his eyes popped.

"I'll get you some water," I half-rose.

"No, no." The cough subsided, and he felt in a pocket. "Mind if I have a gasper?"

"It'll make you feel worse, but no, I don't mind."

"How is Zinnia?"

"She's married again, didn't you know? And she's tremendously successful in the Wrens. She has rows of gold braid round her sleeves, and she's always going to briefings with admirals."

"Bet the admirals enjoy that. Always knew she'd go far, though in which direction — " and he broke again into wheezing laughter. "Yes, I heard about her second marriage. What did Ma Delmayne say to that, eh?"

"We all realised he was a wonderful chap," I said coldly. I wasn't going to have Bertram gossiping, if I could help it.

"Hope he hasn't bitten off more'n he can chew, that's all! Ah, happy days, happy days!"

"Bertram," I said, "what was so funny about the half-sovereign?"

"Oh, that. Well, it was more what you did with it. Well, the *reason* why I gave you that half-sovereign — " he stuck a Gold Flake in his mouth and held the lighted match to it with a podgy, trembling hand. "Don't you remember?"

"It's a very long time ago."

"Oh, you must remember! I was absolutely petrified in case anyone found out, because of the timing. The night before Theodore's funeral – fearfully bad taste, I must admit. But Zinnia was a lovely creature and – well – *possessed* really, I think you'd call it. I honestly think she was temporarily mad with grief, up in that attic. It was frightful of me, but she wanted it, and I couldn't resist her."

I looked again at this fat, greasy, repulsive creature. He hadn't always been like that. He had been tall, broad-shouldered, with a bold, arrogant eye; a fine figure of a man, in the same regiment as Theodore and Peregrine . . .

"Bertram," I said. "May I look at your cufflinks?"

At York the train stopped for a few minutes, and Bertram leaped out and bought us tired egg sandwiches and orange squash in paper cups from a trolley on the platform.

"I'm getting out soon, at Durham," he said. "Going to a regimental funeral in the cathedral on the way home. Won't take long – there's another train in a couple of hours. A splendid old sergeant – he came to grief in Flanders in '16, but he's looked after the Records ever since and kept in touch with everything. Got the George Cross at the Front in '15, marvellous chap."

"What was his name?"

"Bonfire."

I stood up and started dragging my duffel-bag down from the rack.

"I'm coming with you," I said.

DURHAM

43

The train was late, as wartime trains usually were. We hurried up the narrow streets from the station and came out on the green with the castle on our right, ancient stone houses crouching at either side and the great cathedral standing guard above the river at the far end, as it had stood for almost a thousand years. As Bertram's heavy footsteps echoed against the buildings, I wondered about the centuries of people like us whose feet had echoed against these same walls, who had gazed at the sombre grey stone of the cathedral in the eternal human hope of peace, forgiveness, love. I thought back to the old church at Riverlaw, and a verse of the old hymn came unbidden into my head:

> Frail as summer flowers we flourish;
> Blows the wind and it is gone;
> But while mortals rise and perish,
> Love endures unchanging on.

Inside the great doors the air was shadowy and still. We tiptoed past massive pillars incised with the strong, clear lines of Norman craftsmen who knew they were building eternity. How many old soldiers had been mourned here? The preacher's words gradually became audible as we walked the huge length of the nave, under shafts of dusty light crisscrossing from the clerestory, towards the altar screen where the coffin, draped in a Union Jack, stood in the centre aisle.

". . . A man of selfless and exemplary courage, a hero of our time, whose own life was saved at the Front by a deed of the utmost bravery which many of you will remember with admiration and gratitude . . . in the mud and horror of Flanders, a band of heroes the like of whom can seldom have existed in the history of our great country . . . In Sergeant Bonfire, as in many other officers and men who held the line for England in the first world war, burnt a flame of courage which has been handed down like a torch through the centuries, a shining spirit of generosity which does not hesitate to endure and suffer and be willing to make the supreme sacrifice for the sake of their country, and to preserve, for their children and grandchildren and all who come after, the eternal values of civilisation."

And I had thought, long ago, that there were no heroes left.

"Well, he had to say that, didn't he?" muttered Bertram as we came out afterwards blinking into the sunlight, with the thin, pure notes of the Last Post still lingering in our ears. "But conscription is conscription, there's no getting away from it. Still, I suppose he's got to make the best of it. Excuse me a minute, must have a word with — " and he pointed vaguely, and was gone.

Peregrine was standing alone, looking at me.

We walked towards each other. I had the curious and quite illogical feeling that he and I were the only people in the world. We met at the edge of the grass, and he took both my hands and held me at arm's length to look at me.

"What are you doing here?"

"I was hoping to meet you."

"I was so disappointed not to be able to get leave for Zinnia's wedding. I knew you'd be there." He leant forward and kissed me lightly on the mouth, and fell in beside me with one hand still in mine. We walked slowly across the grass. "What was it like?"

"Wonderful. There was a bit of a scene with Aunt Emily, of course, when she realised that Al, the rich and successful businessman turned naval officer, was Albert Nibbs, the coachman's son from Riverpark. But when she actually met him, he was so obviously a marvellous chap that she was entirely charmed."

"I think, really, she must have realised years ago that in dealing with Zinnia she simply had to give in to *force majeure*," and Peregrine's face broke into his wonderful, twinkly smile. "How is darling Zinnia? I've always thought of her as my mad, bad, yet curiously vulnerable sister. Nothing sexual, you know, which is rather surprising considering what I've always felt about you. Forgive me," and he shot me a sideways look so mischievous and delightful that I was hard put to it not to throw my arms around him there and then on the cathedral green in front of the entire funeral congregation.

After a short internal struggle, "It's funny you should say that," I said. "All these years, I've always thought you and Zinnia were passionately in love, and couldn't get married because either she or Rednall didn't believe in divorce. I never dared to ask her about you because I thought I wouldn't be able to bear the answer."

Peregrine stopped dead. He turned and stared at me in amazement. "So *that* was why . . . Oh, Lizzie," he groaned, "all those years wasted! We were friends, that's all. She's good company, old Zinnia. I felt sorry for her, and I admired her pluck. When she was in Australia she was completely down and out, you know – actually starving – but she tried to keep up a good front. Hiring the Rolls in Halifax was her idea – I couldn't really afford it, but it was good for morale, and I hoped it might impress you. I wouldn't have intruded on your marriage, or hoped for anything, if she hadn't told me you were desperately unhappy."

"I was. I only married because you'd disappeared to Australia," I burst out, and held my breath. Now I had burnt my boats. He had never said he loved me. Friendship, lust . . . would he ever want me again?

"And I only married because I thought you were in love with Chuck."

He gazed into my eyes, fierce, intent as I had never seen him, and then he flung his arms round me and kissed me, and the world stopped turning, the sun danced, the great sky engulfed cathedral and castle in the blue of heaven.

Hand in hand, we walked in silence to the end of the green and set off down the rainwashed cobbles.

"Talking of Australia," Peregrine resumed as if nothing had happened, "did you know I've sold out my interests there to my brother-in-law? Sold 'em very cheap, as a matter of fact, but he loved the old homestead and I didn't, really. Too lonely, and far from the likes of you," and he smiled down at me again. "Come and have lunch. I'm not as rich as I was last time we met, but the best hotel in Durham can't break the bank. I'm paying for my father's keep in a comfortable but horrendously expensive nursing-home, as well as the wages of a farm-manager till he gets better – or till the war ends, more likely. I really should go back and farm it myself, but it's a bad time to leave the regiment."

I thought of the great, lion-shaped castle floating in the mist that I had seen with Chuck, so many years ago. I remembered the intensity of my longing to go there, just on the off-chance of glimpsing Peregrine. "Is your farm near the castle?"

"We have a lovely view of it from the drawing-room window. You'll like it. You have family connections up there already, you know."

"I have?"

"Your Aunt Emily came from Barland, a village five miles away. Her father kept a chemist's shop. My father told me once. He said she was the prettiest girl for miles around, but very ambitious, and definitely had an eye for the boys."

"Aunt Emily? A chemist's shop? That can't be true! And how on earth could she ever meet Uncle Vane?"

Fragments of the past jostled inside my head. Venetia and Charles had been separated for years because the Dawsons were in trade. I heard Hannah's rasping voice float out of some interstice of memory: "She married above her, that's the truth of it. Them's allus the wust." And somewhere, somehow, I had recognised, among the bottles and scents and comforting unguents of the Old Hall bathroom, that this was where her guard fell and her voice reverted to its native Northumbrian accent; this was where she belonged.

"The old schoolmistress at Barland was a kind old spinster, my father said, and when she retired she moved to a house some relation had left her somewhere near Riverlaw. She was very fond of your aunt, and perhaps she thought her talents were wasted in Barland, or she needed a change, or something. Anyway, she took her to Riverlaw to live with her for a year or two, and that was where she met your uncle."

"So she did marry above her station."

"Oh, certainly."

"We're lucky to have known Riverlaw, aren't we?"

He smiled. "Yes, we are. If it hadn't been for Riverlaw, for instance, you and I would never have met."

The Crown Hotel appeared across the road in front of us.

"That looks a good place. Mind the traffic." He put his arm round me and, while he held up the other hand in imperious command to stop a lorry that was lumbering round the bend towards us, we set off across the road.

Suddenly, he stopped dead, and his face changed. He looked stricken.

"I've been making an unwarranted assumption."

"What?"

"I've been assuming — " There was a squealing of brakes from both directions. "Lizzie, I thought just now — " Cap in hand, Peregrine went down on one spotless khaki knee in the middle of the road, while cars and lorries shuddered to a halt all around us. I could hear some of the drivers swearing, others laughing. But Peregrine was oblivious. He was gazing into my eyes with a look of utter desperation.

"Dearest Elizabeth," he said, "I love you. I've loved you all my life. Will you marry me?"

And as I pulled him up and threw my arms around him and we danced across the road, all the traffic in Durham hooted in celebration.

I will always remember the joy of our wartime wedding at Riverlaw.

All the Delmaynes were there in their best pre-rationing clothes, and Aunt Emily wore the blue hat with roses which, considering the uses it had been put to over so many years, still looked remarkably pretty. Zinnia and Al came from London, and Janet and the Reverend sent cables from Stewiacke, and literally dozens of Peregrine's friends arrived – I had not known he had so many, and getting to know them would be, I saw, a delightful life's work. Some of his Australian in-laws, cheery young men in bush hats who were fighting with the Australian forces in Europe, had managed to get leave, and I was made to swear we would go and visit them in New South Wales as soon as the war was over.

How Aunt Emily and Louie managed to feed us all in the midst of rationing, I don't know. There were rumours that Vane had been fattening a secret pig, strictly illegally and unknown to the authorities, in a camouflaged shed in a coppice in a remote corner of the farm. When asked, Vane put a finger to his lips and shook his head. It was a wonderful day, full of sunshine and affection and laughter.

And that night, in Venetia's old stone house by the Roman Wall, which she and Charles had lent to us, I gave myself to Peregrine and he to me; and we knew then that we were made for each other, and all the years of waiting and longing seemed like a moment in the eternal happiness of our love.

RIVERLAW

44

So it was beside Peregrine, my beloved husband, that I was sitting at the breakfast-table at Riverlaw one summer Saturday in 1970, soon after Rednall's funeral.

When Louie and Vane heard that I had inherited the Old Hall and would not turn them out, they at once invited me and Peregrine to live with them. But as the two of us had lived happily at Shoreburgh for many years – he as a working farmer, I as a farmer's wife for which I had had, heaven knew, plenty of practice – we decided to stay there, and to come to Riverlaw mainly at weekends. We had our own room there, and the journey by car didn't take long. We would take food and wine, and occasionally I would see Peregrine leafing casually through the mail on the hall table at Riverlaw, and slipping the bills into his pocket.

Once he turned and saw me watching.

"We owe them, don't we?" he said.

And it was never mentioned again.

So we had the best of both worlds: Peregrine's farm, in which he took great pride, and the magical castle view from our drawing-room window; and the dear Old Hall that had played a major part in our lives.

Peregrine had more than enough income for the two of us to live on, so I sold the shares I had bought with the proceeds of the sale of my parents' house, and he added a large sum from his Australian inheritance, so that between us we managed to pay for the repair of the Old Hall.

And even better than the satisfaction of doing this was

the knowledge that we were still needed there. When we visited, Peregrine would be an extra hand in the garden, and Louie welcomed my help with Aunt Emily, whose health in the past weeks had deteriorated so that she was now confined to the old four-poster.

Louie was upstairs with her now, and the rest of us were munching our toast or scanning the newspaper headlines, when a shadow crossed the window.

It was the postman. He saw us, and leaned over the sill, waving two envelopes.

"A bill for Mr Vane, and a letter from the bank for Mrs Emily Delmayne," and he left them on the sill and walked away with a cheerful wave.

"Oh Lord," said Vane. "I can't face it." He scraped back his chair and reached for them. "Hello, this is from the Midland. Mother's never banked there. Must be an advertisement," and he made to tear the whole thing across.

I stretched out a hand and stopped him. "Better not do that. Maybe she's got some investments or something."

" 'Fraid not." He made a face, and slit open the envelope with the butter-knife. "Anyway, if it's anything worrying, it's me who should take the worry off her hands." He unfolded the letter. " 'Dear Mrs Delmayne, we are very sorry to inform you . . .' Oh, dear. Henry's dead."

Peregrine looked up from the paper. "Henry Grey?"

"Right. I'd forgotten who it was for a moment. Haven't seen him since . . . oh, the early 'twenties, I should think. 'By the terms of his . . . dated the first of July nineteen-fifty . . .' Good God."

He put down the letter and stared at it.

"What's the matter?"

"I don't believe this."

"Believe what?"

"I mean, do you *remember* Henry?"

"Rather a good chap," said Peregrine quietly.

"You could have fooled me."

"Here, let's have a look," and Peregrine took the letter

and smoothed it out in front of his plate. He read it in silence; and towards the end of the page his face began to break into an incredulous smile. "Henry bequeathed all his property to his estate manager, except that by the terms of his will his gallantry medals and personal effects are bequeathed to 'my beloved mother, Mrs Emily Delmayne.'"

"Good God. He must have gone off his head," said Vane.

"No," I said. "I don't think so."

I flew up the stairs to Aunt Emily's room.

Louie was tenderly wiping her mother's mouth. She looked at me sadly. She put the cup, spoon and cloth she had been using beside the water-glass on the bedside table.

I took Aunt Emily's papery hand.

"It's me, Auntie. It's Lizzie."

"Dearest Lizzie," came the cracked whisper.

"We've just had a letter about Henry."

The glazed eyes moved. "Henry Grey?"

"Yes."

"He was a good boy."

"Yes. And very brave. He wants you to have his gallantry medals. He loves you. He was a hero, you know."

"Yes. Wouldn't have done for any of you to marry him, though," came the slow whisper. "I never thought of it till it was nearly too late. I told them again and again that they were like brother and sisters."

"He did well in life, Auntie. And he never forgot Riverlaw."

The wrinkled mouth creaked into a rictus-like smile. Gently, she squeezed my hand. Hers seemed so light, it could have blown away.

Blows the wind, and it is gone.

"Who was Henry's father, Auntie?"

"Eh?" The sound was faint as a leaf alighting on a stream.

"Who was Henry Grey's father?"

I thought she was never going to answer. The eyes had a far-away look, the lips trembled into a smile. Then she whispered, "A lovely man. The best man in the world."

"What was his name?"

She looked from a great distance into another, happier age. "I never saw him again. Miss Hole brought me away from him. You must love his son, Lizzie, all your life. Promise me."

"I promise." I wasn't going to be the one to tell her Henry was dead. If there was a heaven, she would meet him soon enough.

"*It's love that matters most.*"

Her head lolled gently to one side, and her eyes closed. Outside, a dove cooed.

Louie, who had crossed to the open window and leaned out, closed it and came back to the bed with something in her hand.

It was a single Juranville rose. Its scent filled the room.

She put it in the water-glass, and moved it to one side of the bedside table so that it would be the first thing Aunt Emily saw, if she woke again.

45

Riverlaw in autumn.

Log fires in the drawing-room and schoolroom, the bittersweet smell of burning applewood mingling with shreds of bonfire-smoke from the kitchen garden, and the slow perfume of the last roses drifting along the front of the house. Bare branches above the lawn, and sepia and sienna leaves, floppy with damp, around every twig in the herbaceous beds. Mournful cooing from the dovecot, and elegiac twittering from the orchard.

One moist, misty, weekday morning Louie and I set off down the drive, gravel crunching under our feet, to lay a posy of late chrysanthemums on Aunt Emily's grave.

The stone pineapples on the gate-piers through which, once, so many carriages and dog-carts had rumbled, were blotched with lichen. Beyond, mist eddied and filled the village. Once past the gravel, I could almost touch the silence.

Autumn of year, autumn of love, I thought. Time telescopes. Worlds meet, lives cross, and somehow from out of our random days there grows a grand design.

I peered over our old cricket-ground and through the thick, whitish veil, and it was as if I were peering into another era, almost another life . . .

Ghostly cricketers peopled the grass. Boys in baggy trousers and tweed jackets with pleated pockets, girls in long skirts, high-necked blouses and high-laced boots, called inaudibly and ran, hair flying, into the mist. On the road the shade of little Mrs Hothersall hurried silently, hunched over her bucket, from the well. At every cottage door hovered the wraith of an aproned woman, smiling at remembered hollyhocks and pansies. The Gorgon leaned from her door, offering a ghostly toffee-apple. Outside another stood the jaunty shadows of the butcher and his son in their striped aprons and crisp boaters. A strapping, bare-armed woman, with fair, curly hair beneath a checked turban, floated down a dahlia-lined path to where old Fred's ghost bent over his spade. On a front step stood the transparent shade of Dr Bond, watchchain swelling over waistcoat, gold half-hunter glinting faintly below the brass coachlamps with which a later occupant had gentrified the plain doorway.

As we opened the churchyard gate, a young soldier beyond it, peaked cap in translucent hand, brushed the dark hair from his forehead, and laughed silently. A ghostly wedding-party jostled past us down the path to the darkness of the arched stone porch; an ethereal bride in glimmering white silk, and two blue bridesmaids – one fat, one slim – with blue muslin mittens and their flowered hair in earphones. Then came an elegant, dark girl carrying a baby, alone. And finally another shadowy bride, with a little retinue of morning-coated and long-skirted guests; and bringing up the rear, faint, fading, barely perceptible in the swirling mist, a weedy round-shouldered boy with flat feet beside a tanned, handsome young naval officer, a pair of white-whiskered old gentlemen, and a stately woman in ghostly rose silk wearing a cartwheel hat laden with roses.

I put out a longing hand to catch her sleeve . . . and they were gone.

Louie turned to me, her look unfathomable.

We crossed the wet grass in silence and stopped at the line of headstones. The Admiral, Aunt Letitia, Giles, Cedric, Theodore, Uncle Vane, and then the newest; each with their solemn Roman lettering, the dates, the brief inscription that said so little and meant so much.

"Us next," said Louie softly.

She stooped to arrange the chrysanthemums on Aunt Emily's grave, and straightened.

"Ancestor-worship," she said. "I suppose people have been putting flowers on graves since the beginning of time. Useless, really. I suppose truly well-adjusted people can just slough off the past and march boldly forward into the future. But it's a symbol, isn't it?"

"A sort of thank-you, do you think?"

"You're right. Where would we be without our families to praise or blame, or fly to in trouble? Or to love?" And she turned her back on me and walked slowly down the path.

I turned back towards the headstones, hoping against hope . . . but all I saw was other graves, their lettering worn, their crosses and coats of arms and mourning cherubs crumbling. I walked back into the mist. *Vane Delmayne, 1820–1896 . . . Vane Delmayne, 1784–1852 . . . Theodore Delmayne, 1761–1799 . . . Vane Delmayne, 1725–1784 . . . Theodore Delmayne, 1698–1730 . . . Louisa Delmayne, Charlotte Delmayne, John Delmayne . . . beloved wife, beloved husband, the Affection of all who Knew him, in Esteem and Love, his sorrowing Family . . .*

When Louie and Vane die, I remembered, there will never again be Delmaynes in Riverlaw.

These Delmaynes, I thought. Imperfect, like all of us. Weak, snobbish – wicked, even. But they loved each other, and they taught me how to enjoy life, and how to love.

Continuity of place, knowing where one's roots lay – that was important, that was good. But what really mattered in the grand design of life was the continuity of love. In an uncertain and dangerous world, that was the one vital thing that must be handed on to future generations.

A car purred down the village towards the Old Hall. High in one of the invisible elm-trees on the green, a blackbird began to sing. I strolled back to Louie.

"The thing is," I said slowly, "I believe they would be

439

happy with the way things have turned out. The house repaired . . ."

"And Riverpark full of laughing children – and who would have thought that Nibbs's son would be their trustee?" she grinned and mopped at her eyes.

"And who'd have ever suspected that Zinnia's son would be master of Rednall-the-house, supervising that army of workmen?"

"And that he'd ask your daughter and Brad to be partners again and manage the Rednall Hotel?"

"Isn't it amazing? And Janet coming over from Nova Scotia next Easter for a holiday with us . . . And Wilbur bringing his bride on honeymoon . . . And all the young Zeds coming here in turn next summer . . . I never imagined that life could be so good to me."

Footsteps were approaching from the village green.

"Venetia and Charles are coming to lunch. We'd better get back," Louie said.

As we turned to the gate:

"Lizzie . . ."

"Mm?"

"Did you see them?"

"Yes."

"Did you realise . . . we were with them?"

"It's not frightening," I surprised myself.

"No. Do you think it perhaps means that they loved us as much as we loved them? And perhaps," she continued earnestly, "if love is as strong as that . . . if we were so much a part of their lives, they will always be a part of ours?"

And she smiled, as Peregrine's dear figure loomed out of the Riverlaw fog, with Venetia and Zinnia beside him.